By Christopher Dow

I0690459

Fiction
Effigy
    Book I: Stroud
    Book II: Oakdale
The Books of Bob
    Devil of a Time
    Jumping Jehovah
The Clay Guthrie Mysteries
    The Dead Detective
    Landscape with Beast
    The Texas Troll Unlimited
    Darkness Insatiable
Roadkill
The Werewolf and Tide, and other Compulsions

Nonfiction
Lord of the Loincloth (nonfiction novel)
Book of Curiosities: Adventures in the Paranormal
Occasional Pilgrimage: Essays on Film, Literature, and Other Matters
Living the Story: The Meandering, True, and Sometimes Strange
      Adventures of an Unknown Writer
    Vol.I: Growing Up Takes a Long Time
    Vol. II: Growing Old Takes Longer

Martial Arts
The Wellspring: An Inquiry into the Nature of Chi
Circling the Square: Observations on the Dynamics of Tai Chi Chuan
Elements of Power: Essays on the Art and Practice of Tai Chi Chuan
Alchemy of Breath: An Introduction to Chi Kung
Leaves on the Wind: A Survey of Martial Arts Literature (Vol. I–VI)

Poetry
City of Dreams
The Trip Out
Texas White Line Fever
Networks
A Dilapidation of Machinery
Puzzle Pieces: Selected Poems

Editor
The Abby Stone: The Poetry of Bartholo Dias
The Best of Phosphene
The Best of Dialog

Jumping Jehovah

Jumping Jehovah

Christopher Dow

Phosphene Publishing Company
Temple, Texas

Jumping Jehovah
© 2014 by Christopher Dow
ISBN: 0985147733
ISBN 13: 978-0-9851477-3-0

Published by:
Phosphene Publishing Company Temple, Texas, USA
phosphenepublishing.com

2.1

Shannon

God does not play dice with the universe.

Albert Einstein

Devil of a Time

1

BOB FELL UPWARD FOR A long time. He didn't have a watch, still being naked from his time in Hell, but he figured it was a couple of hours at least. Long enough for his surroundings to change from the heated blacks, bloody reds, and sulfurous yellows of the infernal regions to a dull ambient gray. Long enough to get pretty bored.

"Limitations," he muttered, thinking not of the lack of a watch—he had eternity, didn't he?—but of the perception he was falling upward. According to the Devil, he should be falling sideways. But then, the Devil was a notorious liar. Or was he, if he admitted to his prevarications?

It didn't matter now. The Devil was far behind him in some direction or other, and Bob was more concerned with what lay ahead. The Devil said it was Heaven, and that idea perturbed Bob almost more than the reality of Hell had. After all, the Devil had been a pretty decent guy considering Bob's attempted hostile takeover of his domain. No telling what God would do to him.

Falling to Heaven wasn't like falling to Hell, which had been down a long tube from which there could be no deviation. The walls of the tube gave the impression of a channel that led somewhere, but this time, there was nothing but a disconcerting, seemingly endless waft through gray void.

What if it was endless? he worried, blanching. He wouldn't put it past the Devil to devise a supremely devious punishment as a perpetual approach to, but never arrival at, the kingdom of everlasting peace and contentment.

The thought brought back Bob's color as he reminded himself, that's where I'm falling up to: the kingdom of everlasting peace and contentment. It was every positive outcome, every climax, every sweet deal come true. Forever.

A side wind buffeted him. The ride was getting bumpier, like the beginnings of a rough airplane flight. Nausea tweaked the back of his throat as he suddenly dropped—or was it rose? —ten feet then was abruptly batted back and forth. This was worse than all the bad flights Bob had taken put together. And he wasn't in a craft but was naked and totally exposed to the elements. At last, when he was sure the next frigid blast would have killed him if he wasn't dead already, the turbulence began to abate.

Apparently all the storminess was some sort of layer. Maybe it was what kept Hell from bleeding over into Heaven. Then he realized it must be the level of reality where the positive and negative forces of the universe intermingled with great abandon and force. No wonder it was tempestuous. He knew Earth was in there, somewhere.

Made Heaven sound pretty enticing.

And it seemed like it might be a little closer as white streaks highlighted the grayness. Clouds, he thought. He braced himself for the worst: God blasting him with a lightning bolt, running over him with a semi, or humiliating him by making him the mail boy. Then, as the clouds filled his vision, he burst into clear air like a miniature whale breaching the ocean's surface.

The analogy wasn't far off. All around him stretched a sea of fleecy, spotless clouds shimmering beneath a pale blue sky, There was no sun, but the atmosphere glowed as if it was high noon. At the far horizon, the clouds and sky met not so much in a line as in a gray, ill-defined region.

"Wow," Bob said. "The ultimate executive suite."

As he settled in a bobbing motion, he was suddenly enveloped in a puff of black soot that spit up in his wake and dusted the clouds a charcoal gray for a radius of two feet. He

14

coughed as he inhaled a residual stench of the pit that had come with him. Must have dragged some of Hell's soot along in my slipstream, he thought as he stared across the vast expanse in front of him.

There wasn't much to see—just flat clouds, like an endless field carpeted with ten-inch cotton balls. He couldn't see his feet because they were embedded in the fluff, but he seemed to be standing on a firm, if slightly yielding, surface. He took a few tentative steps, and he found he could walk like he did anywhere. Plus, his feet had been toughened after hiking barefoot all over Hell. If he could do that, he could walk forever on cloud fluff.

"If you go that way, you're going to be walking a long time."

The voice wasn't loud, but the sarcasm it dripped stopped Bob in his tracks. He turned to see an archway that looked as if it was coated with layer after layer of thick opalescent designer paint. In front of it was a turnstile like a New York City subway gate, though it was a whole lot shinier than anything he'd ever seen beneath the streets of the Big Apple. A tall counter with a thick book sitting on top of it was next to the turnstile, and behind the counter stood an angel. The angel was quite impressive: tall, regal, and gleaming with a subtle but powerful aura. A magnificent pair of white wings arched from his shoulder blades. The way he looked down his nose at Bob reminded Bob of some of the corporate VPs he'd met. He even had a full head of perfectly coifed VP hair the color of steel.

As impressive as the angel was, the view through the archway was what arrested Bob's attention. A rich golden light spilled across the threshold, and beyond the arch, lit by the golden glow, was what could only be the Land of Milk and Honey.

Oddly, though he could see Heaven through the archway, none of it was visible anywhere else on the endless cloud plain stretching monotonously on all sides.

"I suppose most people would go in the wrong direction," Bob said as he approached the angel. "Only one entrance and no signs to point the way."

"There's only one way to be good," the angel said, his patrician nose wrinkling with distaste as Bob came up to him. "If you don't know it, signs aren't going to be much help."

"You must be Saint Peter," Bob said, wondering if he ought to offer his hand. He refrained. Saint Peter didn't look inclined to shake. Instead, Bob waved his hand toward the archway. "And that must be the Pearly Gates. Not as impressive as I thought it'd be."

"You expected fanfare, confetti, and bright lights? A red carpet, maybe?"

"A little gold trim, at least," Bob admitted. "Something bigger."

"This is the Pearly Gates, not the Gold-Trimmed Gates," Saint Peter snorted. "All the gold is inside. And we don't need anything bigger. Lots of people want to get in, but not many do. Anyway, it's not the size of the present or the wrapping that count, but what's in it."

All the gold, Bob thought.

"How do I get in?"

"You don't. Just look at you. You're all…smutty."

It was true. The sootiness that had popped up with Bob trailed from the site where he'd emerged to the spot where he now stood. "That's your karma rubbing off," Saint Peter said, gesturing to the soot. "If you stay up here, you'll probably wear down like a pencil wears out the more you write with it."

What kind of crap is this? Bob thought. In Hell, I'm an anathema because I left a trail of order, but here, it's because I leave a trail of smut?

But he was worried. He didn't want to wear himself down to a nubbin just by walking around. If that was the case, he'd just stay put until God came by. It stood to reason the big fella would have to visit every part of Heaven every once in a while to reinvest the area, so to speak, with his Holy Spirit. To keep things working right. Or would that be righteously? And when he did, Bob would ask him to be allowed into Heaven.

But that meant he'd have to wait here, and Saint Peter didn't seem like he'd be the best of company. Bob looked around the vast cloud fields surrounding the Pearly Gates. Maybe there was something interesting out there to explore.

As if reading Bob's mind, Saint Peter waved toward the puffy emptiness and said, "You *could* go out there into the Wastelands, but it's all undeveloped, and it gets more turbulent the farther you go. Nobody's out there except for a few recluses and hermits looking for the Boss in all the wrong places. They're all a bunch of nut-jobs if you ask me. All that solitude does something to the brain."

"I thought God is everywhere up here."

Saint Peter shrugged and gave a sour look.

"The Boss has a big universe to run and he's a busy guy. How much time do you think he has for some lone pissant who loses himself in some distant cloud field? The Boss makes his rounds just like anybody else, and he'll get to you when he gets to you, which is like once in a gazillion years."

Bob certainly didn't want to spend that long sitting on some dumpy little cloud with nothing but the same boring scene spreading out emptily for miles. Especially since he would constantly glimpse Heaven just beyond his reach.

"If you don't let me in, what do I do?"

Bob wondered if he could make a dash for it and hop the turnstile before Saint Peter could stop him. There didn't seem to be any other guards around.

"You can go to Hell, for all I care," Saint Peter said.

"I've already been there, and the Devil sent me up here."

"In that case, I'm definitely not letting you in."

"I guess I'll just have to stay here with you." Bob propped his naked butt against Saint Peter's counter.

"Suit yourself, but you're going to get almighty bored."

"With you to entertain me? Just think, we'll have all of eternity to get to be the best of buds. I'll probably be here long enough to wear butt-prints in your countertop."

Saint Peter wrinkled his nose again, and he started to say something, but he was interrupted when a naked old woman suddenly popped up near Bob. Instead of brimstone, she trailed an odor of lavender. She saw Bob before she saw Saint Peter.

"I'm not....?"

"Yep," Bob said.

"You're not...?" She seemed shocked by Bob's nakedness and didn't seem to realize she was just as bare.

"Nope." Bob nodded toward Saint Peter. "That's him."

She looked at Saint Peter then back at Bob, trepidation in her eyes.

"Don't worry," Bob assured her. "You'll have no problem."

17

She smiled faintly then hobbled to the counter. Bob sincerely hoped Saint Peter would let her in. He didn't think he could stand to look at her seamed face and withered jugs one more second, much less an eternity. He watched her sagging ass shift uncomfortably on scrawny, wrinkled legs as she told Saint Peter her name and he checked for it in the thick book.

"Go right in." He handed her a token and waved her toward the turnstile.

The old crone hobbled to it, dropped the token in the slot, and pushed through. As she passed beneath the archway, the golden light spilling across the threshold touched her, and she began to miraculously transform as if blown up like a sagging balloon. She straightened, grew taller, and fleshed out, and in seconds, she'd inflated into a sultry brunette with a nice build and not a wrinkle in sight, especially on her pert ass. Unfortunately for Bob, she also was suddenly clothed in a white gown that reached down to her ankles. It reminded Bob of the shift he'd seen Angel wear in Hell. A few steps in, she glanced to her right, saw something that lit her face with delight, and hurried that way and out of Bob's sight.

Bob really wanted to go through the archway.

"That happen to everybody?" he asked.

"Teens don't turn into children, and children don't turn into babies, if that's what you mean."

"What's the book?"

"The *Register*," Saint Peter replied, closing the book and laying a solemn and protective hand on its cover. "All Residents are registered."

"Like a reservation list?"

"It takes a special kind to make it up here."

"I'll bet it does," Bob said. "Considering how hard it is to be good all the time, I'm surprised everyone's not down in Hell."

"Most of them are." Saint Peter's tone strongly suggested Bob rejoin them as rapidly as possible.

"How come you don't use a computer. It would be a lot easier than a huge, unwieldy book."

"Putting aside the fact that your crapulent corporations control most of the Internet, all it's really done is provide the opportunity for humanity to display its true character as liars, cheats,

18

frauds, voyeurs, exhibitionists, freaks, ranters, bigots, psychopaths, criminals, dumbasses, and self-centered opportunists. Do you think we really need that sort of behavior up here?"

"That's got nothing to do with me," Bob said, hoping Saint Peter didn't know about his old website, Co-Ed Head. He pointed to the book. "Why don't you see if my name's in there."

"It's not. It can't be."

"I really think you should check," Bob said. "If I'm not in there, I'll just go on about my business, but I think it's your duty to look."

"Who are you to tell me my duty?"

"Who do I have to be?" Bob asked. "Aren't angels the ultimate public servants? Well, I'm a member of the public, so you should either serve me or be fired for dereliction of duty, not to mention discrimination."

"Discrimination?" Saint Peter was nonplussed. "For keeping bad people out of Heaven? Isn't that my job?"

"Your job is to check for my name in the *Register*, which you refuse to do, merely assuming from your preconceived notions that I'm not worthy of the benefits you've freely given to everybody else."

"What makes you think you're the only one I haven't let in?"

Bob made a dramatic show of looking around.

"Nobody here but you and me," he said. "If you've denied others, where are they?"

"In Hell."

"But I know from personal experience that death takes you straight to Hell if that's your destination. The dead obviously don't come here to be rejected. You probably let in everyone who makes it this far."

Saint Peter started to say something, then shut his mouth and stared disgustedly at Bob for a moment.

"Okay," he said. "You obviously have a lawyer's mind, and it's no use arguing with you. I'll check." His expression said it would be a waste of time, but if that was what it took to get rid of Bob....

Bob told him his name, and Saint Peter opened the tome, leafed through its pages, then looked up, his mouth twisting in a disgruntled frown.

"I take it I'm in there," Bob said.

"You're on the contingency list."

"What's that?"

"Visitor privileges only." Saint Peter reached beneath the counter, pulled out a little plastic rectangle with a metal clip, and tossed it onto the counter. It was a name badge, with Bob's name and photo beneath the word "Visitor" printed in garish red letters. "You have to wear this openly at all times."

"What am I going to clip it to?" Bob asked, picking up the badge. "My nipple?"

"You'll get clothing as soon as you go through."

"Will I grow young like the old woman?" He was really wondering if he'd grow hair on his balding pate. He wanted a head of hair like Saint Peter's more than just about anything.

"That's for Residents only," Saint Peter said, giving a tight, satisfied smile and ostentatiously smoothing a palm over his hair. Then he handed Bob a token and pointed to the turnstile. "Go on through. You won't last long."

Clutching the name badge, Bob dropped the token into the slot. He was about to push through when he suddenly thought of something.

"When I went to Hell," Bob said, "the demon who let me in gave me a book about that size." He gestured toward the *Register*. "They called it *The Rule Book*. It had all the regulations you had to follow in Hell."

"I know about it," Saint Peter responded. "We don't need anything like that here. We believe in deregulation. Heaven is all the concept implies: no hunger or want, and everybody has the perfect freedom to express free will. Residents get to have all their wishes granted. All they have to do is say, 'Thus-and-such is my Heavenly Desire,' and whatever they've wished for happens. But as a Visitor, you don't have that privilege."

"What if I get hungry or thirsty or something," Bob protested. "You mean I have to go around hungry and thirsty for eternity?"

"That would be Hell, wouldn't it?" Saint Peter said. "But this is Heaven, and we can't have that here. We'll take care of your needs, just not your desires. But you still have to obey our one rule."

20

"What's that?"

"Behave heavenly in accordance with Divine Will."

"That's it?"

"Isn't that enough?"

"It might help to have a few guidelines."

"Look, Bob, I'll level with you. No one quite knows what Divine Will actually is—though there's ample speculation. But people here do behave heavenly because they have no choice."

Having no response to that, Bob pushed through the turnstile.

"Any recommendations on which direction I should take once I'm in there?"

"I'm sure it will be the wrong one," Saint Peter harrumphed, then he gestured impatiently for Bob to go through the archway.

"Be seeing you," Bob said.

"I hope not," Saint Peter replied.

Leaving a dusting of soot behind him like a slug's trail, Bob entered the archway to Heaven and suddenly found himself in a very different world.

❧ 2 ☙

ARCHANGEL MICHAEL WAS IN HIS office, sitting at his desk, brooding over the subsidence problem in Heaven. Some of the larger buildings were just too heavy for the clouds on which they rested and were slowly sinking.

Michael's own office was on the penultimate floor of the Administration Building, which was the tallest structure in Heaven—two miles high, more than twice as tall as the tallest skyscraper on Earth. So when it began to sink at one corner, the effects were greatly magnified by the time they reached Michael's 368th floor office. Now, just a couple of centuries later, a marble could roll rapidly across the floor. He felt like he was working atop the Leaning Tower of Pisa.

A vacation, he thought. Just a few days....

A knock interrupted his brooding, and his secretary, a Dominion named Antoine, cracked the door and stuck his head inside. Antoine had lately affected a Rastafarian persona, and he sported shoulder-length pitch-black dreadlocks that looked out of place framing his pasty white face.

"The other board members all be in the boardroom, mon," he said in a Jamaican accent.

Crap, Michael thought, then he said, "I'll be out in a minute."

As Antoine withdrew, Michael rubbed his face with his hands and sighed. He'd come to hate these board meetings, not because of those who attended, but because of those who didn't. Or rather, the One who didn't.

Sighing again, he got up, put on his helmet, and picked up a lance, a sword, and a shield bearing the inscription, *Quis ut Deus?* To these he added the other emblems of his office: a set of scales, a copy of the Book of Revelations, and the Holy Sponge. This last he despised since it was messy to hold and constantly dripped wine onto his robes, leaving purple stains. He wasn't sure why he had to carry all this junk. He only had two hands. For the umpteen millionth time, he considered ordering a Principality to carry some of it for him, but he knew he couldn't. The Boss had made it clear that he and the six other Archangels had to live up to their image, and that was that.

Burdened by his accouterments, Michael floated to his office door, the hem of his full-length robes cutting a swirling wake in the cloud carpet. As he approached the door, he swung the lance to point straight ahead and tilted the shield so it wouldn't jam up on the door frame. At the same time, he composed his face into a featureless mask. He had no intention of revealing anything to anyone waiting there for their appointed time. Eight lower-order angels were standing around, watching as he crossed the reception room. No humans, of course. Humans never came into the Administration Building. All their needs were taken care of elsewhere.

He emerged into the hallway, glided down the hall to the boardroom, and entered. When he shut the door, the wind generated by the heavy panel sent the thick cloud carpet into a flurry of cumulonimbus that quickly subsided, but not before a thunderstorm on Earth flooded a neighborhood in Houston.

As Antoine had said, the other Archangels were present. Michael propped his sword and spear in the corner by the door and slung the shield on the back of his seat, which was at the foot of the table. He laid the Book of Revelations on the table, set the scales next to it, then laid the Sponge in one of the scale's pans. The scale dropped instantly on that side, causing a miscarriage of justice in a court in Cape Town, but Michael didn't care. He was just glad to have the sopping thing out of his hand. Suppressing a

24

reflex to wipe his hand on his robes, he removed his helmet, sat, and surveyed the other board members.

The three on his left, ranging away from him, were Gabriel, Selaphiel, and Raguel, and across from them sat Raphael, Uriel, and Barachiel. The seat at the head of the table—the Throne of God—was, of course, empty. Big surprise. Why bother having a throne, Michael wondered, if you're never going to sit on it? These days, the Archangels automatically looked at Michael instead of at the perennially vacant throne. The foot of the table, Michael thought bitterly, has become its head.

Gabriel was fondling his horn, his fingers caressing its infinite length, as he stared meaningfully across the table at Raphael, who was holding a horn of his own.

"Come on, Rafe," Gabriel said in a pleading tone. "Just one duet. We can play quietly. No one will hear us."

Raphael, who was, as always, holding his breath, just shook his head. Michael barely paid attention to the exchange. He'd seen it too many times. Everybody knew neither one of them could play a note until Judgment Day, and that gig seemed as far off as ever. You had to have enough good souls to gather to make the effort worthwhile, which didn't seem likely any time soon.

A sudden thick hum from Raphael's right drew everybody's attention. It was Uriel, brandishing his sword, but Michael saw he'd exchanged the usual blade of blazing fire for a light saber.

"Pretty fancy, huh?" Uriel said, waving the tongue of buzzing red energy over the table. "Gotta keep up with technology."

"Well, why don't you get an iPad instead of that old rag?" asked Selaphiel in a sarcastic tone, nodding toward the tattered Scroll of Wisdom Uriel constantly held in his other hand. Nodding was all Selaphiel could do since he had to keep his arms crossed across his chest at all time, which made him jealous of anybody who had even one hand free.

"Hadn't thought of it," Uriel admitted. "Next time I'm down on Earth...."

"Forget it," Michael said. "You know the Boss forbids any sort of computers here." He eyed the light saber dubiously. "In fact, I think that thing might qualify. Maybe you ought to go back to the sword."

"If it did, then I couldn't have it, could I?" Uriel said a bit snippishly. He thumbed a button on the light saber's haft, and the humming tongue of energy winked out. "Besides, I need it."

"For what?" Michael stared at Uriel like he might next beg for a dog treat.

"Have you seen Eden lately?" Uriel asked, reacting huffily to Michael's condescending look. "I guess not. You never go out. If you did, you'd know it hasn't been cleared out in ages. Do you realize how much dead, dry brush is in there after all these thousands of years? My old flaming sword was nothing but a fire hazard. How could I explain to the Boss I burned down his garden with the very implement he gave me to protect it? I'm keeping the light saber, and that's that."

"Now, now, Urie," Raguel said, breaking in in a reasonable voice that fit with his persona of justice, fairness, and harmony, though not his attribute of vengeance. Looking at Michael, he said, "That thing might have some sort of microprocessors in it, but it only has one function, so I don't think it can be considered a computer. And we can't have him burning down Eden, can we?"

"Rags is right," Barachiel chimed in. "If he has it, the Boss must be allowing it, so who are we to complain? Besides, we probably should keep up with technology where we can. We have eternity here, and it would be foolish to ignore any advances that might appeal to our younger prospects."

Michael glanced at him, taking in the white rose Barachiel held in one hand and the bread basket he held in the other, then quickly averted his eyes. He always had a hard time looking at Barachiel because of the extensive retinue that followed him around. He had 496,000 ministering angels attending him at all times, and whenever he was in an enclosed space, the wall behind him magically billowed into enough area to accommodate them all. Thank the Boss the retainers weren't very big, or the space they occupied might extend nearly to infinity. Even so, the way the wall behind Barachiel always bulged prodigiously never failed to give Michael vertigo.

"Okay," Michael said, ignoring Uriel's smug look of victory. "Let's bring this meeting to order."

26

"What's the point?" Raguel demanded. "The Boss is never here, and we can't make any real decisions without him."

"You know he's out beyond the Edge, creating more space."

"For two thousand years? Come on. He created the Heavens, the Earth, and everything else in six days. How long can it take to make a little more space? The truth is, we don't know where he is."

"Yeah, he might be anywhere," Uriel chimed in. "Remember those centuries when we thought he was creating those new subdivisions, and he was actually in Tahiti with those naked beach bunnies creating more Tahitians?" There was a trace of envy in his voice. "Nobody's seen him since."

"He always said Tahiti was the next best thing to Paradise he'd ever created," Michael pointed out.

"Before the Europeans found it," Raguel corrected.

"We're getting off topic here," Gabriel scolded. "What about the Boss?" He looked at Michael, who raised his hands in helplessness.

"What do you want me do? I can't *make* him come to the meetings."

"You four are Angels of Presence, Mike," Barachiel said. Everybody knew he meant Michael, Gabriel, Raphael, and Uriel. "The three of us are Johnny-come-latelies, and we can't get anywhere near him. Go talk to him."

"Barry's right," Selaphiel said. "You could petition him as a group."

Michael sighed and shook his head.

"You know what happened the last time we tried that."

A sullen silence suffused the room as they all ruminated on the incident in question. It had started innocently enough in the early days, when nothing at all was going on in Heaven. People were pretty primitive at the time, and most of them seemed to revel in murder, mayhem, and every other sin possible, so only a scattering of them were up here.

The sparseness of the population meant that Heaven could be perfectly maintained, but it also meant the angels had almost nothing to do except stare across the endless cloud fields as they tended their meager flocks. So Michael and the other Angels of

Presence had petitioned the Boss to make things more interesting by creating some mechanism to bring in more business.

In response, the Boss struck off a spark of himself that fell to Earth and inhabited some kid in the Middle East. The idea was for this kid to teach everybody how to behave properly. The Boss had done it before, like with that Indian prince, some Chinese guy, and a bunch of others throughout history. It had worked reasonably well in a few of those instances, and the Middle Eastern kid was promising, too, even though he hadn't lasted long. A few more people started arriving in Heaven after they died, but the action also produced unintended consequences.

The main one was that the kid became a focal point instead of a finger pointing the way. That caused tribes who once worshipped the Boss in relative harmony to fracture. Each faction attached its own name to the Boss and claimed its name for him was the only right and true name. That gave them all the reason they needed to rob, enslave, and slaughter each other more voraciously than ever, sometimes for fun as well as profit. And now the whole damn world had been dragged into the mess, with total annihilation of humankind in the offing.

It was crazy, Michael thought. If there is only one Boss, then every name is the Boss's name and the Boss is in every name. People didn't have to connect with the Boss through intermediaries but through their own devices. And they'd probably be better off doing it like that anyway to avoid the inevitable deceit, greed, and cruelty of those who duplicitously claimed they knew what the Boss was thinking. If the Archangels didn't have a clue, how could any human?

But most people didn't understand that, and therein lay what, in Michael's opinion, was the worst aspect of the whole thing. How could there be sanity in the world when all the people in the world, even the good ones, are endowed with insane monkey brains? He knew the Boss should have based them on reptiles like he'd started to. Lizards don't get all hot-headed over nothing. But for no apparent reason, he'd scrapped Plan A, bombed Earth with an asteroid, and gone to Plan B.

All those rampant monkey brains meant the craziness in Heaven grew just a little more every time a human was admitted, and then Michael and the other angels had to coddle these nuts and cater to their petty desires. Downstairs, they treated the inmates like the whacked-out idiots they really were.

"All right," Michael said, breaking the gloom. "I'll go talk to him, try to convince him to attend at least one meeting a month. But in the meantime, we have an organization to run, so we'd better get to it."

Perhaps still thinking of all the crazies on Earth as they were in Heaven, he turned first to Barachiel, who was in charge of the Order of Confessors, squinting so he could focus on the Archangel instead of the mind-numbing billow of retainers behind him. "How's business on your end?"

"Receipts are down," Barachiel admitted. "Urie might be impressed with modern technology, but it's causing no end of grief for me and my staff. At first, this social media stuff seemed like a prime opportunity for confession on a mass scale. In reality, all it's done is encourage people to amplify their corruptions, and now, they delight in exposing them to the entire world. You know how they are. Monkey see, monkey do. So instead of repenting their sins, the humans are reveling in them. Even worse, their revelations seem to be driving them to up the ante as they try to outdo each other in showing off how far they can degrade themselves in public to draw attention to themselves."

"If your staff doesn't have enough to do, maybe you should downsize your office," Selaphiel suggested, rousing himself.

"What would we do with them?" Barachiel asked. "They're designed to take confessions. They'd be useless doing anything else."

"We can always retrain them," Selaphiel said.

"You know we can't do anything to alter or add to Heaven's operations on our own," Michael said. "That would be usurping the Boss's creative prerogative."

But his words fell on deaf ears. Selaphiel was praying again. Or maybe he was napping. It was hard to tell.

"There's an easier way to deal with the Internet," Raguel said. "Solar flares are among the natural order of things, aren't they? We can cause the Sun to emit a permanent magnetic burst that wipes out all their electronics. Most people aren't going to act like that in person."

Raphael grunted and shook his head. Everybody looked at him then turned to Gabriel. Like all musicians, the two horn players seemed to understand each other on a subliminal level that escaped the others present.

"Rafe says we can't keep knocking them down if we expect them to walk somewhere."

"Just keep working on it, Barry," Michael said. "I'm sure you'll figure out something." He gestured to Selaphiel and said, "This seems to be a good time for your report, Sully."

Selaphiel roused himself, raised his downcast eyes and said, "Prayer is in the same boat as confession. There's a lot of talk, but what can you do when the only things most people pray for are wealth and power for themselves and destruction and damnation for the people they don't like? The main topic these days seems to be the Rapture. They think it'll answer both types of prayers in their favor."

"Typical wishful human thinking," Uriel snorted as Selaphiel lowered his eyes and leaned back in his chair. For all Michael knew, he'd gone to sleep again.

"As if there aren't enough of them up here as it is," Raguel groused.

"The people we have coming in aren't the problem," Michael said. "They're our clients, and when you get down to it, there really aren't that many of them. Nowhere near the numbers going to Hell. It's a downright embarrassment. But even if our demand is growing more slowly than Hell's, it's steady and isn't likely to completely stop. And that should be a good thing. We want as many clients as we can get, right? This is a battle with the Devil for the soul of Creation, isn't it? The real problem is we're stuck with an aging infrastructure created before there was this much demand. I know that's no news to you, Rags." Michael turned to Raguel, who was head of the union. "How's everyone holding up under the workload?"

"Not like they used to," Raguel said. "Once we relaxed the rules and started taking on more of these humans, everything changed. Their incessant demands are overloading the system, and their spurious notions of the place of humans in the structure of Creation are contaminating everything. Used to be all the angels of the Second Sphere knew their places. The Dominions paid attention to their managerial duties, the Virtues kept the cosmos in order, and the Powers kept flawless records. Even

30

the Third Sphere Principalities carried out the Dominions' orders without a fuss. Now, the Principalities claim they're overworked and underpaid and want us to raise the minimum wage. Some are even slacking on the job, and a lot of the others, too, and the Dominions can't do anything about it."

"The Virtues are slacking, too?" Michael asked.

"Haven't you watched the news lately? Earth has been bombarded by a lot of space rocks recently, and that's because a bunch of the Virtues were playing canasta in a cloud bank instead of attending to business. We managed to divert a couple of the meteors to other planets, but it's only a matter of time before some wayward boulder makes Earth go blooey. The whole workforce has gotten shoddy. I hear the drinks from the fountains in Sector P have a sour flavor, and the ambrosia fruit throughout the western sectors all taste bland."

"There's worse," Barachiel said. "Confessions reveal that some of the Principalities are using their proximity to humans to consort with them."

"More Nephilim!" Gabriel leapt up and drew his sword with one hand and raised his trumpet to his lips with the other.

"Put those down," Michael snapped.

"He's right," Uriel said as Gabriel subsided. "We ought to cut to the chase." He whipped out the light saber, activated it, and waved the buzzing blade around, nearly severing the heads of several of Barachiel's retainers. "Let him blow, and let 'er rip!"

Raphael raised his trumpet, too, relief flooding his eyes, and no wonder: He'd been holding his breath for millennia, waiting for this moment.

"Stop it!" Michael commanded in a booming voice accompanied by a glare that made everyone freeze. He wasn't the Captain of the Hosts for nothing. "We're not doing anything until the Boss gives the Word."

Gabriel and Raphael, looking disappointed at being denied the opportunity to finally play their duet, lowered their instruments, and Uriel retracted the blade of his light saber.

"Well, you'd better get some sort of word out of him," Gabriel said, "or we're going to have a lot more trouble on our hands. Things are just too damned disorganized around here."

❧ 3 ❧

THE PERVASIVE GOLDEN LIGHT DID not transform Bob as it had the old crone, but clothing did magically appear. Saint Peter *had* said Heaven would provide for his needs, if not his desires. Well, he'd take care of those himself. After all, didn't God help those who helped themselves? Bob planned on doing just that.

Instead of a white gown, his clothing consisted of white slacks, a white polo shirt, white socks, and white shoes. Looking down at himself, Bob felt like he should be standing behind an evangelist's pulpit or about to step up to the first tee at the country club. He reached up to check his hair, and his fingers found the same old thinning locks rather than a pompadour. Not an evangelist, he thought, disappointment mingling with relief. *So it's tee time at the ultimate country club.*

By now, he'd walked about twenty feet from the Pearly Gates, his invisible feet leaving a swirling dark gray path through the cottony fluff that masqueraded as firm footing in this place. He glanced back through the archway to see Saint Peter sitting at the counter, staring blankly across the cloud fields, waiting for the next member of the Heavenly Host to show up.

Nobody did while Bob watched, so he figured it must either be a slow day or there usually wasn't much traffic. Like Saint Peter had said, it was tough to do the right thing all the time, and Bob ought to know that from personal experience. All in all, he felt pretty lucky to have landed here despite a lifetime of corrupt behavior.

He pinned on his Visitor badge then turned in the direction the former crone had gone, smiling and thinking about following her. But when he saw her, standing about sixty feet away, she was passionately making out with a muscular man dressed exactly like Bob but sporting a full head of dark, wavy hair. Then the woman pulled the white gown over her head, and the man disrobed, and the two lay down. Their downy cloud bed concealed most of the details, but it wasn't hard to figure out what they were up to.

So much for that, Bob thought as he glanced around to see if anybody was watching him. Nobody was as far as he could tell, so he observed the copulators for a few minutes to see if they would vanish in a puff of sulfurous smoke. They didn't, but the vigor of their encounter raised a veil of cloud fluff. Pretty soon, they disappeared entirely in a cocoon of spun mist.

"Ah, long-separated lovers reunited. Lovely, isn't it?"

"Shit!" Bob gasped. He whirled to see a tall, slender man standing right behind him. "Where did *you* come from?"

"New, aren't you?" The man gave a big smile that looked genuine enough even if it was supported by muscles that seemed trained for the purpose. He was dressed, like Bob, in white golf clothes, and he had, Bob noted jealously, a full head of luxurious hair. Bob tried to stand straighter to compensate.

The man's eyes dropped to Bob's Visitor badge then back up to his face. At the same time, Bob looked at the man's chest and saw a badge with "Welcome to Heaven" embossed on it in red letters, and underneath, in a white space, the name Wilbert was printed in black magic marker.

"Well, well. A Visitor. Pleased to meet you, Bob. I haven't seen a Visitor here in forever." Wilbert's smile got a little bit bigger, and Bob could have sworn he saw an actual twinkle gleam in the man's right eye.

"I guess we're pretty rare. I can't imagine many people make it in unless they're real Residents." Bob pointed to the other's badge. "I see you have a badge, too."

"Certainly do," Wilbert replied.

34

"Does everybody have a badge?"

"Nope. I just made this myself. For when I come here."

"You mean to the Pearly Gates?"

"That's right. I like to greet the new folks who come in. But as you can see," he chuckled again and gestured toward the egg-shaped cocoon shrouding the copulating couple, "sometimes other folks beat me to it."

For a few moments, he and Bob watched the cocoon alternately rock back and forth vigorously or pulsate side to side, emitting moans, groans, and whimpers of pleasure.

"I know I may seem a bit prurient," Bob said. "But I didn't think that sort of thing would be allowed in Heaven."

"What?" Wilbert's eyes shifted back to Bob. "Fucking or watching fucking?" His smile muscles flexed themselves again, and they certainly were muscular. "Everything's allowed here. Isn't that what bein' in Heaven is all about? This place is just like the biggest and best big-box store ever. You can get anything, and it's all free."

"I see you're excited about it," Bob said. "So, is it like a job? You coming here and talking to people who've just arrived?"

"A hobby. It gives me somethin' to do. Kinda reminds me of my old job back on Earth."

"What did you do?"

"I was a greeter at Y'alMart. It was a great job. I got paid for bein' pleasant and helpful. Course, they gave us thirty-nine-hour work weeks so they didn't have to pay for medical insurance. Consequently, when I got cancer, I couldn't afford the treatments. It was painful, but I wound up here, so I suppose it all worked out for the best."

At that moment, a subdued but distinct woman's voice murmured, "Remember: Behave heavenly. It's the right thing to do."

Bob glanced around, but nobody except for the copulating couple was within a hundred yards. The voice seemed to have come from the golden atmosphere itself and sounded like the recorded messages that play in airports to urge compliance with rules that seem so reasonable.

"What was that voice?"

"What voice?"

"The voice that just said to behave heavenly and to remember to do the right thing."

"I didn't hear anything." Wilbert's smile faded just a tad, and he peered closely at Bob. "Are you feelin' all right?"

The atmosphere here *was* a little rarified compared to the smoky environs of Hell. Maybe he'd imagined the voice.

"We have a hospital if you're sickly. It's called Hypochondriacs General Hospital."

"Why would anybody need a hospital in Heaven?" Bob asked.

"Good question, since we don't have many doctors, and the few we do are always out playin' golf. But we do have our fair share of hypochondriacs, and the hospital's there to accommodate them."

"For fantasy illnesses?"

"Make no mistake, Bob. In Heaven, all Heavenly Desires are fully met, even if it's for a life-threatening disease."

"But they can't actually die, can they?"

"No, but can you imagine livin' for an eternity with stomach cancer eating out your insides?"

Bob could. He'd seen much worse in Hell.

"Good to know if I ever want to be sick," he said, trying to distinguish the Heaven of the hospital from the day-to-day of Hell. It was all about preference, he thought. In Heaven, torment was a choice; in Hell it wasn't. "Mind if I ask a personal question?"

"There are no secrets in Heaven." Wilbert exercised his jaw muscles again.

Bob thought Wilbert must not be very observant. Just a few dozen feet away, the copulators' cocoon completely hid the details of the actions within.

"I couldn't help but notice you have a really nice head of hair."

"Wasn't natural to me back on Earth." Wilbert gently swooped his hand backward over the top of his pompadour. "I was bald as a cue ball when I died. But it wasn't long bein' up here that my hair began to grow. There must be Rogaine in the water." He smiled sadly at Bob. "Unfortunately, it probably won't work on you, bein' a Visitor and all. But don't fret. When you get up here for good, you'll look like Samson before Delilah got holt of him. You oughta see him now. His hair's down to his ass, but nobody calls him a sissy, I can tell you that."

"Samson's here?" Bob found it hard to believe.

36

"He stays over in the Biblical Sector." Wilbert leaned close and said confidentially, "All those Biblical types have a hard time mixin' with us more modern folk. Kinda primitive thinkin', you know. They tend to stay with their own kind." He chuckled. "Same with the caveman in Sector 1, but you ought to get over there one day, anyway. It's a hoot watchin' all those monkey men actin' like they was people, or somethin'."

"I thought only those who knew Christ could come here," Bob said. "Cavemen lived way before then."

"Lots of folk think that, but the ways of God are mysterious."

"Divine Will, and all that."

"You know it."

At that moment, twin cries of release sang from the copulators' cocoon. The white ovoid quivered violently for a moment then slowly began to deflate. Bob watched curiously to see if it would dissipate, but it seemed to be taking more time than necessary. Then his nose told him that the cloud fluff was being partially replaced by post-coital cigarette smoke.

"Smoking's allowed, too?"

"Like I said, anything and everything is allowed in Heaven. We just do whatever we want to do. It's all about choice, isn't it?"

"Drugs?"

"Crack houses are over there way," Wilbert pointed. "Opium dens are that way." He pointed in another direction. "Bars and lounges are near Elysium Field, and the potheads prefer the tops of those cloud mountains. They say they like the light show."

His finger indicated a mountainous mass of towering cumulus, beyond which flickered dense beams of light like the depictions of the divine in old paintings. Bob wonder if it was God over there, making all the light.

"What about murder?" Bob turned back to Wilbert. "Surely that's prohibited."

"Plenty of righteous murder and sacrifice take place in the old holy books. Why should it be any different here?"

"But what about the victims?" Wilbert chuckled.

"You got a lot to learn, Bob. Let me explain a few things so you don't go blunderin' around like a bull in a china shop. In Heaven, everybody gets his Heavenly Desires answered, so those around him have to behave heavenly and do his bidding. Let's say you're madly in love with Jane, but Jane doesn't love you. On Earth, that can lead to all sorts of complications, and it might be the same here, but Heavenly Desiring takes care of that. If you desire for Jane to love you, she has to—at least while you're with her—even if she really doesn't. That's her behavin' heavenly. But, of course, she doesn't love you, and her desire is for you to climb some distant cloud top and rot there for eternity. So you have to do that. That's you behavin' heavenly."

"So, to make sure people behave heavenly toward one another when they just don't feel it, God just forces the heavenliness on them? Isn't that a contradiction?"

"Could be they don't actually feel heavenly inside," Wilbert said. "That's their free will exercising itself. Heaven is about free will, after all."

By now, the couple had finished their cigarettes, and the cloud cocoon totally dissipated. They got up, pulled on their clothes, and headed off in the direction of the bars and lounges.

"Sounds like Heaven is filled with self-centered people," Bob said, watching the couple walk away.

"That's about the size of it," came the answer. "Folks here usually won't do much of anything for anybody else. They do at first because this is Heaven, and they have to behave heavenly. But pretty soon they learn about cloud angels."

"Cloud angels? Are they different from other sorts of angels, like him?" Bob pointed through the Pearly Gates at Saint Peter, who was still sitting at his counter, staring blankly across the cloud fields.

"There are three spheres of angels," Wilbert explained. "At the top of the First Sphere are the Seraphim. The Archangels are the crème-de-la-crème of the Seraphim. There's seven of them, and they run things in Heaven. We call them the Administration, but we humans almost never see any of them. Just below the Seraphim are the Cherubim. They're like Heaven's law enforcement. Then there's the Ophanim, who are like the courts and judges. The Second Sphere is made up of the Dominions, who are directors and union leaders, the Virtues, who keep the physical plant running smoothly, and the Powers, who are the historians and bookkeepers.

"The Third Sphere has only one category, the Principalities. They're the worker bees. Folks call them cloud angels since, if we need one, we just Heavenly Desire, and one materializes out of the clouds to do our bidding. They're surrogates who fill in for real people, so folks don't have to constantly behave heavenly for everybody they meet. So you can love a Principality who is exactly like Jane, and she can send a surrogate you to climb to a cloud top and rot for eternity, and everybody's happy."

Except the Principality who's left to rot for eternity on the cloudtop, Bob thought.

"What about the couple who just left?" he asked. "I know she's real because I saw her come in through the Pearly Gates just a few minutes ago. But what about the guy she's with?"

"We'll never know," Wilbert said. "And probably neither will she."

"Where are all the prophets?" Bob asked. He could see lots of people walking and standing around by themselves or congregating in small groups, but they were all dressed in normal clothes—though of different periods and styles—all of them white. None of them had long white beards, long robes, and gnarly wooden staffs, which was how he figured prophets ought to dress. It was a bit of a disappointment. He'd expected Heaven would be crawling with them since there'd been so many on Earth.

"Most of the prophets on Earth were false, so we don't have many real ones up here," Wilbert told him. "The few we do have are all off on the Wastelands outside the Pearly Gates, lookin' for God. Or doin' God only knows what."

Suddenly Wilbert's eyes went blank for a second, and when they refocused, he looked at Bob and said, "It must be 11 o'clock."

"How can you tell?" Wilbert wasn't wearing a watch, and there were no clocks that Bob could see.

"It's time for mandatory Heavenly Choir practice. That always happens at 11."

"Mandatory? But I thought there were no rules in Heaven."

"It's not a rule," Wilbert said. "It's a commandment. We call it the choir commandment."

"Why?"

"I don't know. I guess God likes to hear everybody sing the same song. Comin'?"

"I don't feel very commanded," Bob said. "I don't even know any hymns."

"Must not be your 11 o'clock."

"What?"

"God likes to hear his music all the time," Wilbert explained. "In order for there to always be a choir, it's always 11 o'clock for somebody somewheres. Yours must be a different one, but mine is right now, so I gotta go. Have fun, Bob, and remember: The beauty of Heaven is there are no contradictions. Everything is possible. Behave heavenly."

Wilbert walked off, humming to warm up his vocal cords.

Not likely, Bob thought as he watched Wilbert depart. Not if I have to play some other guy's game.

Then he turned to stare across the cottony fields of Heaven, all lit by the pervasive golden glow.

"What the hell am I going to do up here?" he muttered.

At varying distances across the vast expanse, he could see people, singly or in groups, lone trees standing here and there, numerous fountains, and many buildings of different sizes and architectural styles.

There were, it seemed, lots of possibilities, but first, Bob needed to scope things out. At least this time, he didn't have to figure out how to extricate himself from a lake of boiling shit as he had in Hell.

He started off, wading through the clouds, leaving a trail of soot in his wake.

ঀ 4 ঀ

CARRYING HIS BURDEN OF ACCOUTERMENTS back to his office, Michael reflected on the one issue of importance to emerge during the board meeting, which was the Boss's continual absence. It had become a serious issue. Maybe Barachiel was right. Maybe he should find the Boss and try to get him to come to the board meetings, or failing that, at least talk to him about all of the problems arising in his absence. Or, more likely, because of it.

Michael could have requested a visitation anytime. He was, after all, the only Angel of Presence who really counted. But having the ability to do something wasn't necessarily the equivalent of having the time or the opportunity. Despite his rank as the highest of the angels, Michael didn't always know where the Boss was. As Uriel said, he hadn't been seen since he'd come back from Tahiti, bringing with him the golden glow that now pervaded Heaven. He'd called it his suntan, but Michael knew the golden glow was simply a substitute for the Boss's crepuscular rays while he was out of reach beyond the Edge.

Michael's ruminations were cut short as soon as he entered his outer office, which was jammed with First- and Second-Sphere angels.

"Petitioners," Antoine said with a shrug. "I-and-I couldn't keep them out."

41

"All right," Michael sighed. "Give me a couple of minutes."

He floated into his office, shut the door, and went to the credenza, where he divested himself of his burdens. As usual, the Holy Sponge had spotted his robes in an embarrassing place, and it took him a few seconds to eradicate the stain. Then he sat at his desk, put his head in his hands, and tried to quiet the resentment building in his mind. It was bad enough he had to oversee the grand scheme of things around here, but that task was made almost impossible when he had to get embroiled in petty day-to-day operations and attendant complaints.

Oh, well, he thought. I didn't ask for this crap, but I guess it comes with the territory.

He thumbed the intercom and said, "Okay, Antoine. Send in the first one."

"You won't like it."

"I never do."

A moment later, the door opened, and in floated a Dominion named.... Michael had to think for a moment. As Captain of the Hosts of Heaven, he knew every angel by name, but there were literally hundreds of thousands of Dominions, and it was hard to instantly remember the name of each one if he didn't see him frequently.

"You have a petition, Bjorn?"

"Yes, sir," Bjorn said, his pale Scandinavian features taking on a hint of redness along the cheekbones. "From the Dominions."

"What is it?"

"We'd like you to consider allowing us to have smart phones."

Crap, Michael thought.

"You know computational technology isn't allowed in Heaven."

"Yes, sir, but we think having them would enhance our ability to carry out our duties."

"How?"

"It would improve communications among members of the Heavenly Hosts, sir. It's very time-consuming to hand-carry orders and such everywhere, and often, we don't know about any glitches in operations that need to be attended to in a timely manner. Having smart phones will allow us to better expedite matters. For the Dominions, only, of course."

"This is Heaven. There shouldn't be any glitches."

42

"Yes, sir. But reality doesn't always conform to plans despite our best intentions. There are contingencies...."

"Are you preaching to me?"

"No, sir." Bjorn's jaw tightened, and his eyes looked a little fearful.

"Also, it seems to me the phrases 'time-consuming' and 'timely manner' should be moot in a place that is eternal."

"Yes, sir." Bjorn hung his head.

"No smart phones," Michael said. "That's what the Boss says, and even I can't contravene his orders, can I?"

"No, sir."

Michael contemplated the angel for a moment then said in a more conciliatory tone, "Don't think I don't sympathize. I know operations are getting more complex all the time. Tell you what I can do." Bjorn looked up hopefully. "Communications are important, so I will allow walkie-talkies. I don't think those could be considered computational devices. Order them, and have them issued to every angel, not just the Dominions. And since communications are important, everyone will be required to have their walkie-talkies with them and turned on at all times. Understood?"

"Yes, sir," Bjorn said, but he didn't look at all happy, which made Michael smile to himself. Communications, indeed. Obviously, the Dominions were trying to pull a fast one on him and infiltrate Heaven with digital corruption in the Trojan horse of smart phones.

"That's all," he dismissed Bjorn with a wave. "On your way out, tell my secretary to come in."

"Yes, sir." Bjorn bowed and retreated through the door. A moment later, Antoine entered, a sheepish expression on his face.

"Did you know about Bjorn's petition?" Michael demanded.

"Yes, sir."

"Why didn't you tell me about it ahead of time?"

"I-and-I'm a Dominion. I-and-I know my place."

"Do you like your position in *this* place?" Michael waved around the room.

"Yes, sir."

"Then you'd better understand where your loyalties lie. Inform me of this sort of thing in the future if you don't want to go back to a desk job in procurement."

"Yes, sir."

Michael gestured toward the door.

"Send in the next one."

Antoine exited, and a moment later, the next petitioner rolled in.

He was an Ophanim, which were the lowest of the First Sphere, and unlike many of the other angels, they didn't look at all human—or even animal. They appeared as a wheel nested at right angles inside another wheel, the rims of both covered with hundreds of eyes. They were usually some shade of blue or green, though some affected a yellow or pink tone. Thank goodness each Ophanim had a slightly different color and pattern or no one could have told them apart. The one who'd just rolled in was glowing emerald.

"What can I do for you, Terence?"

"Look at me, Michael, and tell me what you see."

Michael looked, a bit discomfited by the fact that Terence's hundreds of eyes, except those masked by the cloud carpet, were all staring back unblinkingly.

"A pair of green wheels with hundreds of eyes."

"Exactly," Terence replied in a tone of finality.

"I'm not sure I understand."

"How would you feel if you looked like this?"

"Like an Ophanim?" Michael ventured.

"Exactly."

Michael strove to keep his patience.

"What are you getting at? Is there something wrong with being an Ophanim?"

"We can roll forward and backward," Terence said demonstrating. "We can roll left and right. All-in-all, we can roll every which-a-way except in the hay. It all seems pointless if we don't have the balls to leave some real tracks, know what I mean? Almost all the other angels look like handsome men, and act like it, too, I might add. But look at me. What kind of sex-appeal does a wheel have? Ophanim don't even *look* like we can get it on. And that's not the worst part. You see all these eyes? You think we can close them all at once? Every time humans get it on in our proximity, we're forced to watch. We've become the ultimate voyeurs. Do you know how frustrating that is?"

44

"You mean you want to get it on instead of just watching?"

That's right. We feel the situation is discriminatory, and we want you to do something about it."

"What? I have a hard time imagining a wheel-within-a-wheel with genitals. I mean, where would you put them?"

"I'm not really sure," Terence admitted. "That would be up to the Boss."

"You want me to ask the Boss to give the Ophanim some balls?"

"Yes. We're tired of being judged impotent."

"Okay," Michael said. "I'll ask the next time I see him." He didn't mention that could be a long time from now.

"Thanks, Michael. I knew you'd understand." Terence rolled out, leaving Michael shaking his head, wondering just how he was going to present *that* argument to the Boss.

The next petitioner was a Virtue he knew well named Jim Morrison. Most Virtues were engaged in supervising the movements of the heavenly bodies, but as Heaven's chief choirmaster, Jim Morrison was one of the most important. The upraised voices of the 11 O'clock Heavenly Choir provided the motivational force and the grease, so to speak, that kept the Heavenly Spheres operating smoothly and according to plan. It was a big job making sure a choir was always singing somewhere, not to mention in harmony and on key.

Jim Morrison wasn't his real name, of course, but ever since he'd seen a Doors concert on Earth and been taken by the husky voice and sexy presence, he'd insisted everyone call him by his new stage name. Said it gave him the voice of command. Jim Morrison had traded his loose white robe for a skin-tight leather version. Michael thought it was a silly affectation, especially since it looked like a full-length sheath skirt. Thank the Boss the real Jim Morrison had died before male rockers took to wearing heavy makeup, or the angel Jim Morrison would look like a biker drag-queen bride.

Michael wasn't fond of assumed names, either. He figured the Boss gave everybody their name for a reason, and anyone who changed to another seemed to be willfully ignoring the message hidden in their given name or trying to pull a fast one. But he was loath to confront Jim Morrison about his name or attire because he didn't want him to throw a hissy fit that might disrupt the rotation of the Heavenly Spheres.

"Hi, Jim," he said, a little puzzled to see the choirmaster. "What brings you here?"

"I feel like I'm stranded in the horse latitudes," Jim Morrison said in his whiskey tenor. "These old songs we're forced to sing just don't light my fire. I've been down so long, I can't love them madly like I used to."

"Strange days, indeed," Michael said, "when our choirmaster can't take it as it comes. But they're the old songs, and you have to sing them."

"By that logic, we'd still be doing Gregorian Chants."

"Your voice is perfect for Gregorian Chants," Michael pointed out.

"They just don't touch me. I look at you, and I see an easy rider. But I'm runnin' blue waiting for the sun. And it's not just me. The new folks just aren't responding. They want something that jumps out and says: Hello! I love you! I took this twentieth-century fox named Maggie M'Gill out on a moonlight drive, and she was an unhappy girl. She said the oldies sound like cars hissing by her window."

"Was she from L'America?"

"Yeah, she was an L.A. woman. A real wild child."

"People are strange," Michael admitted, then he said, not unsympathetically, "I know you're a changeling. I take it you want to expand your repertoire."

"That's right. I want to break on through to the other side. If we just had a little soul in our kitchen, we could be so good together."

"Sounds like wishful sin to me," Michael pointed out. "The old songs...."

"The old songs just don't tell all the people. For this new generation, they're just some ancient gallery doing a soft parade."

"I have a feeling the Boss would consider any changes in the repertoire to be like a king snake crawling through his hyacinth house."

"I just can't do it any more. Five to one I'm outta here if something doesn't change on this ship of fools."

46

"That would be a blue Sunday," Michael said. "When the music's over, you know it's the end, don't you? You want us all to be riders on the storm?"

"No skin off my teeth."

"What would you do?"

"I'd take my queen of the highway on a drive down Love Street to that Spanish caravan camped out in Sector 18 before the summer's almost gone and I'm left with a wintertime love."

"I think all you're going to get is an Indian summer," Michael pointed out. "Before the end of the night, you'll be coming in the back door, man. My eyes have seen you doing it already."

Jim Morrison looked crestfallen.

"But what about my wild love?"

"If you're feeling blue for your lost little girl, you can meet her down at the roadhouse."

Jim Morrison brightened.

"I guess she can love me two times before I go away," he said. "All right, I'll keep singing the same old songs, at least for now."

"I know you can make it real."

"Maybe. But if I find I can't face them in my mind, I'm outta here for good. Maybe I'll take a crystal ship down the river and not touch the Earth again until I make land, ho, at some whiskey bar in Alabama."

"I don't think it'll come to that," Michael said. "Good luck with Maggie."

"Thanks." Jim Morrison left, and as soon as he did, the door opened and a Power named Al came in."

"Hi, Al," Michael said. "What can I do for you?"

"I came here to tell you we're having a severe litter problem in the older sectors, and my bosses in Waste Management are completely ignoring it. But seeing that guy who just left brings up another matter I've been meaning to see you about."

"What's that?"

"My name. Why do I have to go by Al, when you get to be named Michael? Or those others with all those cool angel names like Uriel, Raphael, and Gabriel. Something with a ring to it."

"Do you know how many angels there are in Heaven?" Michael asked, leaning back in his chair and tenting his hands. "A shitload." He leaned forward, dropping his hands to his deck. "Barachiel alone has 496,000 of them, and they're just a drop in the bucket. All the best names had to go to the Archangels and other Angels of the First Sphere. We're the ones who have to command fear and respect from everyone, and there are only so many names that do that. In fact, there are only so many names to go around, period. We can't very well be naming angels Fred One and Fred Two, now, can we? We angels have precious little to call our own, so having an individual name means a lot."

"Yeah? Well try having a name as precious little as Al."

"Well, Albert is already taken. And Alan. And so is every variant spelling, including Alberto and Alfonso. I don't have the power to create a new name. You know only the Boss can do that. So I guess you're stuck with Al, unless you want us to start calling you Alal. Course that means 'queen of the moon.'"

"What about that Virtue who just left? If he's not using his old name, I could just take his."

"A Virtue's name on a Power?" Michael chuckled. "You can forget it. Besides, he didn't actually change his name. He doesn't have the power to do that. He just asked us to call him Jim Morrison, and we complied."

"So let me call myself something else, and comply."

Michael rolled his eyes. There were jailhouse lawyers everywhere. "Jim Morrison was a special case. We can't let everybody do what he wants. We wouldn't know *what* to call each other, communications would breakdown, and everything would fall apart."

"Okay, okay," Al said disgustedly. "I get the picture. If I fiddle with my name, it'll bring down the Apocalypse or something."

As he walked stiffly through the door, Michael thumbed the intercom.

"That's it for now, Antoine," he said.

"What about the rest of the petitioners?"

"Send them back to their jobs. There's plenty of time to petition later."

"How much later?"

"Later later, Antoine. Much later, if it comes to that." Never, he thought. "Then I want you to set up an inspection with the Dominion in charge of the Water Plant. What's his name?"

48

"Halliwell."

"Tell him I'm on my way over."

Yes, sir." Antoine clicked off.

Michael gave his secretary a few minutes to clear the reception room, then he gathered his accouterments and headed for the door.

❧ 5 ❧

BOB WAS CURIOUS ABOUT THE buildings he saw in the distance. He couldn't figure out why anybody would need buildings in Heaven, where the weather probably was always balmy, it never rained, and cloud cocoons conveniently hid intimacies. He didn't think they were churches. Wasn't this whole place a church? Anyway, none of the ones he could see looked like churches or mosques or anything similar. The smallest seemed to be grass huts, and the largest were towering glass and steel edifices. If what Wilbert said about the cavemen was true, there must even be caves somewhere.

He headed toward the closest glass and steel building. It looked like it held offices, and Bob assumed he was following some corporate homing instinct. If there was anywhere he'd fit in around here, that would be it. Though the building was one of the closer ones, it was still some distance off, and as he walked toward it, he found himself distracted along the way.

The first thing that caught his attention was a fountain, mostly because it lay almost in the path of his beeline trajectory toward the building. Bob didn't really feel thirsty, but as soon as he neared the fountain, he realized how dry his mouth was. Maybe the rarified air here was sucking the moisture from his tissues, but Bob thought it more likely his conversations with Saint Peter and Wilbert were responsible, especially since he hadn't had anything to drink since the Devil had disrupted his celebration party.

That seemed like ages ago, but in practical terms, it couldn't have been more than half a day.

The fountain was an incredibly ornate affair about ten feet tall, with several tiers of ever-larger basins descending its central pillar, each formed of what appeared to be pure gold worked into elaborate organic designs. The final catch basin was full of the cleanest, clearest water Bob had ever seen. Overflow from the lowest basin went over the lip and disappeared with a faint chuckle into the clouds.

Bob looked for a glass or cup or ladle, but nothing like those was around. Maybe it was lying in the clouds, hidden by wisps of mists. He got down on his hands and knees and started groping around to find the fallen receptacle, wondering if the overflow had made it sloppy wet around the fountain. Miraculously, it was fairly dry—as dry as a cloud carpet could be—and he'd worked his way to the other side of the fountain without success when a voice brought him upright on his knees.

"Lose something?"

The short woman facing him had an oval, yellow-brown face and epicanthic folds over her eyes that lent her beauty an exotic air. She wore mukluks, a thong bikini on her trim, muscular body, and a parka hood, all made out of what looked like polar bear fur. Strands of straight black hair poked from the margin between the hood and her face.

"It's bad dropping stuff around here," the woman went on as Bob got to his feet. "I dropped my bikini top about two hundred years ago, and it took me days to find it."

"I wish I'd been there to help you," he said sincerely, imagining himself finding the top and hiding it in his pocket. "You speak English."

"No, but I see you speak Inuit."

Bob didn't belabor the point. In Hell, everyone could understand everyone else, no matter what language they were speaking. Obviously things were much the same here.

"I didn't drop anything," he explained. "I was trying to find something to drink with."

Her eyes focused on his Visitor badge.

52

"Oh, you're new here. Bob, is it? Watch. You do it like this."

She reached her hand toward the fountain, and as soon as it passed over the rim of the bottom basin, it was filled with a bejeweled golden chalice.

She dipped the chalice into the water, lifted it to her lips, and drank. As she did, she saw Bob staring at the goblet, and she lowered it with a self-deprecating smile.

"It's ostentatious, I know," she said. "But it can't be helped. No choice. I keep wishing for a cup made from a seal's skull, but all I ever get is a jewel-encrusted golden goblet. You try it."

Bob emulated her, and as soon as his hand approached the water, it, too, held a bejeweled golden goblet. He dipped, lifted, and drank what had to be the sweetest, most refreshing water he'd ever tasted.

"That's great," he exclaimed, then quaffed off the rest of the goblet's contents. "But I'm surprised. I thought there was no hunger or thirst in Heaven. How come there are fountains?"

"Just because there's no hunger or thirst doesn't mean there's no desire to eat or drink," she said. "And in Heaven, you can eat all you want and more, but you never get full or overweight."

"Or drunk, if you're drinking Scotch?" Bob asked. The question was facetious, but she took it seriously.

"Not if you don't want to. Want to try?"

"Where's the nearest bar?" he asked.

"Right here." She waved at the fountain.

"Water?"

"It's only water if you don't specify anything else. Go on. Just put your chalice in again, and verbally order whatever you'd like."

Bob immersed the goblet and intoned, "Dalmore 64 Trinitas."

He didn't really expect anything to happen. He knew the Dalmore Distillery had produced only three bottles in 1964— hence the name—and all three bottles had been purchased, so he thought it unlikely it would be dispensed from a fountain. He lifted the cup, and the smoothest Scotch he'd ever tasted drifted smokily across his tongue and warmed his throat.

"Is that what you ordered?" the Inuit woman asked.

"I'm not sure," he admitted. "I've never tasted Dalmore 64 Trinitas, but I guess this must be what it tastes like."

"Mind if I have a sip?"

53

He passed the chalice to her, and she wet her lips and made a bitter face.

"Nasty stuff," she said as she passed the chalice back to him.

"What do you prefer?" he asked, a little miffed.

"I like orange juice," she said. "Never had it until I came up here. Now, I wish I'd lived in Florida."

"Where did you live?"

"These days, you'd call it Nunavut—up along the northern coast of Canada— but back then, we just called it home. By the way, my name's Nanookie of the North." She stuck out her hand.

"Pleased to meet you, Nanookie," Bob said, shaking with her. "So I take it you weren't a Christian."

"That was after my time. Never even heard of such a thing until I arrived here. When I was seventy-two and I walked out onto the ice to die, I fully expected Anguta would be the next thing I'd see, unless I ran into a polar bear first. But after I fell into my last sleep on Earth, I woke up here."

"What's Anguta?"

"Who, not what. The gatherer of the dead. He takes them to the underworld, where they must sleep with him for a year. Frankly, that seemed too necrophiliac for my taste, so I'm glad I ended up here."

"You must feel right at home here since it looks like it's been snowing everywhere."

"I'd rather be in Florida."

"What about using your Heavenly Desire? Can't you just make it seem like Florida?"

"It's not that simple. Since I've never actually been to Florida, I can't possibly imagine it fully enough to make it seem real. So I have to content myself with pretending."

By now, they'd finished their drinks, and Bob looked at his chalice, wondering what to do with it. Should he wash it in the fountain? He started to set it on the lip of the lower basin, but the Inuit woman stopped him.

"Like this," Nanookie said, and she tossed her goblet into the clouds, where it sank silently out of sight.

"You mean we just litter?"

"When you no longer want something, you just leave it lying there, and eventually it sinks into the clouds and disappears."

54

"What happens to it?" Bob asked. He visualized televisions, old shoes, golden chalices, and other junk oozing from the bottoms of the cloud layers and plummeting to Earth, though he knew it didn't happen.

"Don't know," came the reply. "There's some sort of magic going on underneath the clouds that cleans things up. I heard it works that way because most people made a habit of littering the Earth, and it's easier to let them continue doing the same here rather than retrain them. Besides, this is Heaven. If littering is someone's Heavenly Desire, so be it."

Sure made it easy to deal with the trash, Bob thought, casually tossing his goblet after Nanookie's.

"Is it like that for everything?" he asked. He'd just had a goblet of water followed by a stiff drink, and he was feeling the urge to take a leak.

"Yep. Goblets or old clothes or whatever, but I heard the overflow from the fountains falls as rain or snow on Earth."

"I mean, what do you do when you have to relieve yourself?"

"Oh," she laughed. "Yep, the same. But beware, it can take a while for things to vanish. We had a saying back in the old country: Don't eat the yellow snow. Same here, but it's yellow clouds. Or brown."

"Is there any privacy? I saw a couple having sex, and they whipped up some sort of cloud cocoon."

"You're talking about a cloud privy. No problem. Let me show you."

She proceeded to wave her hands in a box shaped pattern, and in seconds, the clouds beneath her hands boiled up in a cubicle with swirling walls. She quickly stepped through the white-fluff surface and vanished. She was gone longer than Bob expected, and when she came back, she had a sheepish look on her face.

"Sorry that took so long," she said.

"Mind if I use it before you dismantle it?" he asked, and he pushed through one of the cloud walls.

The inside was like a bathroom stall, only instead of a toilet bowl, there was just a simple hole in a floor of ice. No matter. He could elaborate more on his own later. He took a leak then went back outside.

"You don't really have to dismantle it," she explained. "It'll sink down on its own. Helps cover everything over."

Relieving himself made Bob realize how hungry he was, which puzzled him since there wasn't supposed to be hunger or thirst in Heaven. In fact, he was hungrier than he'd ever been in Hell. Maybe that was because there, for a time at least, he'd had all his appetites appeased.

"Well, actually that's really a bit of spin," Nanookie said when he asked her about it. "Everybody does get hungry and thirsty, but since there are fountains and food everywhere, nobody has to go hungry or thirsty. But we do have a few nuts who think starving themselves will bring them closer to the Big Guy, so I guess there has to be hunger for them to feel at home in Heaven."

Bob's stomach growled, and since he had no intention of starving himself, he asked, "Where's a restaurant?"

"I never heard of one of those here," she said. "But we do have ambrosia."

Bob waited, but when she didn't go on, he said, "That's it?"

"That's it."

"What's ambrosia?"

"Fruit. Ambrosia trees are everywhere in Heaven."

Bob grimaced. He'd been a meat-and-potatoes man, and the idea of eating nothing but fruit all the time didn't sound too appetizing. But he was hungry.

"How do I find one of these ambrosia trees?" he asked.

"Just look around," the woman told him. "There's always one in sight, same as the fountains. There's one sticking out of the top of that cumulonimbus over there." She pointed to a green object protruding from the top of a slightly billowing cloud head about half a mile away. A dozen or so people milled around it.

"You know what kinds of clouds there are?"

"Oh, yeah," she said. "There are more names up here for clouds than the Inuit have for snow, and that's a lot. You'll pick it up. If," she glanced meaningfully at his Visitor badge, "you get to stick around."

"Sounds like a great place for weathermen."

56

"Might be if they weren't false prophets." She jerked her hooded head in the direction of the tree. "Come on, let's go get a bite to eat."

They headed toward the tree side by side, but about halfway there, the Inuit woman stopped and stared behind them.

"What is it?" Bob asked, thinking she might have left something back at the fountain. Too bad it wasn't her bikini top.

"Good question," she said, pointing to the sooty dusting Bob was leaving in his wake.

"I just arrived here from Hell," Bob admitted. "I guess I couldn't help bringing some of it up with me."

"Interesting," she said, giving him an appraising stare. "Just don't fondle my breasts while I'm wearing my bikini top. I don't want to get it smudged."

Bob wished she'd mentioned the fondling part while they were back at the fountain, where no one else was around. Maybe the subject would come up again. He sincerely hoped so, but she started off again before he could say as much.

When they stopped at the tree, Bob dubiously eyed the fruit. What he really wanted to eat was a big, juicy steak. But while there might be some Texas cattle ranchers up here, and maybe a few of them still ran cattle, that being their idea of Heaven, Bob couldn't imagine a slaughterhouse nestled in these pristine clouds. He'd lived near one when he was in college, and it reeked of the pit, not the ether.

The ambrosia tree wasn't especially large. It reminded Bob of a weeping willow, mostly because all its branches drooped gracefully toward the ground. There were only a few slender leaves, but fruit pended in abundance from the branches. The fruits were like mangos in size and shape, but the colors of the skins kept shifting through the spectrum. The people standing around were pulling the fruit off the branches and eating right where they stood.

"Go on," Nanookie urged. "Try it. All you have to do is wish for a particular food while you pick the fruit."

All the branches were currently occupied, so Bob waited for a few minutes until one opened up, and he and Nanookie stepped up to it. She plucked one of the ripe globules, and he followed suit and took a skeptical nibble. Then a big bite. It

57

tasted exactly like the best steak Bob had ever eaten, right down to the perfect, melt-in-your-mouth texture.

"That was surprising," he told the Inuit woman when he'd finished.

"What did you order?"

"Steak."

"I had raw seal blubber. Hope yours was as good as mine."

Bob's inclination was to doubt that, but then he realized she might be equally grossed out by eating flame-broiled cow.

"Who's he?" he asked, nodding his head toward an emaciated man standing beneath a bough not quite halfway around the tree. The man had a scowl on his face, and when anyone got within five feet of him, his stance grew belligerently menacing. Everyone gave him a wide margin.

"He's a food addict. He's been standing around that same branch for way longer than I've been here. All he does is gorge himself, and he won't let anybody else near his branch."

"If all he does is eat, how come he's so skinny?"

"I think he's bulimic or anorexic or something."

As if expressing agreement, the man suddenly bent over and puked into the clouds before stuffing his mouth with more ambrosia.

"He's hogging that branch while everyone else is having to wait."

"No big deal," the woman shrugged. "There's plenty to go around."

"He doesn't seem to think so. Why doesn't someone just shove him out of the way?"

"Can't."

"Why not?"

"This is Heaven, and everyone gets their desire."

"What if I desire a fruit off that branch?"

"Try."

"You mean just go up there and take a fruit from his branch?"

She nodded. "Just watch your step. Not telling what's under the clouds around his feet."

Bob smiled to himself. He'd almost bested the Devil at his own game. This would be like taking candy from a baby.

He walked over to the man, and when the man realized Bob was coming his way, his scowl became a twisted snarl.

"This is my branch," the man shouted with a snarl. "Get thee fucking back."

Bob took several sudden steps backward, not because he felt polite, but because an unseen force had shoved him back.

"Wow," he said as Nanookie came up behind him. "What happened?"

"An expression of his free will. We call it the command."

"Not commandment?"

"Commandments only come from the top, but anybody can give the command. It keeps people from invading your heavenly space."

"'Get thee fucking back' is a heavenly command?"

He saw her tense, as if preparing for a blow, but when nothing happened, she relaxed and smiled.

"I guess it doesn't work for Visitors," she said. "Look, I hate to eat and run, but we're having a dogsled race over in the foot-clouds." She gestured to the distance, where Bob saw a dark, mountainous bank of clouds rising into the ether, with lower, lighter-toned clouds leading up to it. Well beyond the cloud bank was an array of shifting shafts of light illuminating the heavens above Heaven. "I wish it was something more exciting, but you take what you can get."

"What's all that light shining up from behind the clouds?" Bob asked. "I've seen it a couple of times."

"That's the Big Guy's crepuscular rays," she explained, staring at the light show. "They're always out there somewhere in the background beyond the cloud mountains." She looked back at Bob and nodded toward the tree. "Gotta go. Have desert. Just don't eat the yellow clouds." She poked him in the ribs, laughed, and strolled off toward the cloud mountains.

By now, the food addict's angry expression had vanished. He'd plucked another fruit and was wolfing it as fast as he could. It must be hard to frown, Bob thought, when you're stuffing your face with the best meal of your life—eternally. Not wanting to get pushed out of the way again, Bob went to another branch, pulled off a fruit, and ate what tasted like banana pudding.

When he was done, he scanned the cloudscape for the office building he'd been headed toward. He spotted it, though it didn't seem like it was where it had been when he'd first headed toward it. Walking to the fountain and then to the ambrosia tree must have disoriented him.

Turning his face in its direction, he trudged toward it.

❧ 6 ❧

WHEN MICHAEL EMERGED FROM THE Administration Building, unfurled his wings, and flapped into the sky, he felt a sudden surge of freedom he hadn't experienced in a long time. Maybe it was because he hadn't been out of the Administration Building in a millennium. It was high time he got out and had a look around with his own eyes.

It didn't matter that the Administration Building was a world of its own—a towering 369 story-tall edifice whose skeleton was made from a metal harder than any known to humankind sheathed in glass and Texas pink granite—Michael still hated it. He missed the old Gothic monastery that had served as the administrative center until they'd replaced it with this monstrosity. But he admitted that the last thousand years had wrought changes too complex for the old structure.

The bottom floor was the Administration Building's main reception area, and the next 366 floors were given over to administration of each of the days of the week—although the February 29th floor was only sparsely occupied and the angels staffing it goofed off most of the time. The 368th floor housed the Archangels' offices and the boardroom, and the penthouse on 369 belonged to the Boss. Michael often wondered what the penthouse looked like, but even he'd never been invited up there. For all he knew, the Boss was in the penthouse at this very moment. He might as well be Howard Hughes in his final decade for all the contact anybody had with him lately.

As Michael wheeled around the Administration Building a couple of times, trying to get all his accouterments in order so he wouldn't drop any of them, he thought about having Antoine order him a bag or a backpack to carry the scales, the Book of Revelations, and the Holy Sponge. Just as long as it didn't look like a purse. As Captain of the Hosts, he had an image to maintain.

Finally, he got everything under control except for the dripping from the Sponge, which he held out as far to the side as he could so the wind wouldn't blow droplets of wine onto his robes. As he circled the Administration Building one more time, he spotted the Boss's crepuscular rays glowing well beyond a distant range of cloud mountains in stupendous shafts of sparkling, shifting light.

So he's still out there, after all, Michael thought, wondering if he ought to try to find him now.

Forget it, he thought. The mountains were those defining the very boundary of developed Heaven, and the lights were so distant beyond them that the emanations barely cast a flicker over the cloudscape. It would take forever just to get there, and even then, the Boss was probably out beyond the Edge, where he hadn't created anything yet, so Michael might not even get to see him, much less have a chat. Michael had learned a long time ago that chasing the Boss was usually just a big waste of time. If the Boss needed him badly enough, he could get in touch.

Orienting himself, he flew off toward the Water Treatment and Purification Plant. As he flew, miles and miles of Heaven passed beneath him, its white expanse dotted with fountains and ambrosia trees, punctuated by scattered buildings, and roiled by the many people who wandered around or congregated here and there. However, its white expanse wasn't nearly as pristine as it should be. Michael saw litter, small mounds of trash, and numerous spots of yellow and brown marring the cloudscape. That Power, Al, had said as much. Maybe Michael should placate him and agree to have everyone call him by something other than Al. Within reason.

What a disgrace, he thought, looking at the mess and realizing it was as much of a problem as the water and food supplies. After he inspected the Water Treatment and Purification Plant, he'd have to visit the Farm because of the bland ambrosia fruit, and now, the Solid Waste and Recycling Center because of the lingering trash. Probably the Factory, too. He wished he *could* retrain some of Barachiel's hosts as grounds keepers. That would be the simplest solution, and it also would reduce the number of angels who were always hovering at Barachiel's back, bulging the space behind him and giving Michael vertigo. But only the Boss could approve the reassignment forms, and the Boss was nowhere to be found.

Michael knew, though, that wasn't any kind of real solution. It was reactive, not proactive. All the angels could fit on the head of a pin, and that was certainly a finite number, which meant, with more and more humans coming to Heaven thanks to the relaxed rules, there just weren't enough Principalities to get everything done. And that pointed to the real problem. While Heaven was theoretically infinite, in practical terms, it was limited due to an infrastructure that hadn't had an upgrade since the Creation. Only the Boss could do that, and of course, the Boss was nowhere to be found.

Not wanting to stare at trash all the way to the Water Treatment and Purification Plant, and even less at the spots of human waste marring the cloudscape, Michael banked to the right and headed toward the nearest choir loft. There, he caught the hot-air updraft rising from the building's open atrium top, suffering for a moment ten thousand voices united in off-key bedlam until the rising heat carried him high enough for the din to subside to a distant wheeze.

A few minutes later, still maintaining his new altitude, from whose distance all blemishes faded and everything below looked like it should, he flapped his way toward the Water Treatment and Purification Plant. When he got there, he circled the plant a few times then spiraled down, looking for signs of problems amid its maze of pipes and tanks. Everything appeared to be in order, but how was he to know if it wasn't? He was the Captain of the Hosts, not a hydraulics engineer.

He landed outside the main office and went inside, the Sponge dripping a trail of purple drops behind him. Halliwell, the Dominion in charge of the plant, was waiting in the office, surrounded by a dozen plant managers, and as soon as Michael came in, he hurried over.

"Hello, sir," Halliwell said. "We got word you wanted to tour the plant. We hope there isn't a problem." An angelic look rippled across his face, but currents shifted in the depths of his eyes.

"Perhaps so," Michael said sternly. "I've gotten a report that the drinking fountains in Sector P have a sour flavor."

"Really, sir?" Halliwell looked down a trifle too quickly, then back up at Michael. "We'll check into them, sir. As you might know, the plumbing in Sector P is old galvanized iron. Could be some of it has rusted. We're replacing everything with PVC as fast as we can, but that's a lot of pipe to lay, and we don't have enough angel-power or," he paused pointedly, "a big enough budget."

"I know we've had a lot of growth over the years," Michael said, trying not to let too much sympathy into his voice. "I'm not here to level blame, but we have standards to maintain. I'm just making the rounds of all the facilities to make sure everything is running as smoothly as possible given the circumstances."

"Smoothly, sir," Halliwell said, smiling and nodding. "Very smoothly. Where would you like to start, sir?"

"At the beginning would be appropriate."

A few moments later, Michael, Halliwell, and a retinue of plant managers were aloft, their combined wing flutters creating quite a rustle in the air.

"We have several areas of operation," Halliwell said loudly so Michael could hear him over the flapping. "Over there," he pointed to four mammoth vats fed by numerous large pipes materializing from the clouds and entering the plant from different directions, "are our settling tanks. They're where water comes in from all over Heaven for initial processing. I must warn you, sir, they're rather odiferous."

"I've been dealing with humans and their crap since the Creation," Michael said dryly. "I think I can take it."

"Follow me, then, sir."

Halliwell spiraled down, Michael and the others following, to an open area in front of the vats, which were laid out in a neat line facing the rest of the plant. Each vat had two enormous pipes emerging from it, one at the top and one at the bottom. When he had the hems of his robes firmly planted on the cloud carpet, Michael could see how tremendously large the vats were. Each had a diameter of several miles and was a mile tall.

Next to the four vats, the stink was, as Halliwell promised, quite awful—a combination of sewage and chemical odors that almost forced Michael to conjure a gas-mask on the face of his helmet. Instead, he steeled himself against the reek. No point in showing weakness to a Dominion.

"You must process a lot of water," Michael commented, breathing through his mouth.

"We do, sir. Water's the major resource in Heaven. Each of these vats processes water from different sources. We use separate vats because each type of waste water requires a different treatment process. Those are the sludge pipes."

Halliwell pointed to the large pipes coming out of the bottoms of the vats. The four sludge pipes merged into an even more immense pipe that ran to a small building from which a steady throbbing sounded. An equally gigantic pipe led from the building and off into the distance.

"The sludge is sent to the pumping station," Halliwell said, indicating the small building, "where it's pumped to the Farm. All the water that rises to the tops of the tanks is siphoned off and sent through our filtering unit."

He glanced at Michael and noticed the Archangel was breathing through his mouth.

"I warned you the stench is pretty awful," he said, more smugly than Michael liked. "But you get used to it after a while."

Michael, who had no intention of getting used to it, said, "I've seen enough here. Let's move on."

"This way, sir."

As Halliwell took off, he indicated the four top pipes, which also met in an enormous pipe, this one running above them and into the middle of the plant.

"This carries the water to the Kidney."

"The Kidney?"

"In-house slang for our filtering unit."

65

By now, the enormous pipe began to bifurcate and re-bifurcate, and before long, all the splitting and branching formed a block of silver filigree several miles to a side. The bedlam of pipes was more snarled, complex, and tightly wound than even the Accounting Department's ledgers. And just like ledger entries, some of the pipes were too hidden to see, much less trace.

"How do you get in there for maintenance?" Michael asked.

"We don't. We don't even know how the thing works."

"What if it breaks down?"

"Pray it doesn't, sir. That's what we do."

They flew on, and eventually the maze ended as all the branchings gradually merged once again into a single enormous pipe that led directly to a vat so humongously large its bounding wall seemed more straight than curved, and its top rim was lost in haze.

"This is an impressive structure," Michael said.

"It's our main processing unit," Halliwell said, a touch of pride in his voice. "Solid granite. Built for the ages. I understand the Boss carved it himself out of a single asteroid right at the beginning of Creation."

Michael ran his eyes over the massive wall of the vat then stopped and stared. What was that? He activated his telescopic vision, zoomed in on the spot, and was astonished to see a tiny scaffold suspended by ropes from the top of the vat. It was maybe two miles up and about five miles from where they stood. He zoomed in closer.

A child sat on the scaffold. He looked to be about ten, and his thick blond hair was cut in a pageboy. He wore a neat little pair of white overalls and sabots on his feet, and a working-man's cap perched jauntily on his head.

"Who is that?" Michael demanded, gesturing.

"What?" Halliwell asked nervously. Then he saw what Michael was looking at and waved dismissively. "Oh, him. That's the Little Dutch Boy. Best thing that ever happened to him was sticking his finger in that dike. But he let the fame go to his head. He didn't do anything bad, he just let himself get used. And when it was all over, he was nothing but a drunken bum trading tales of his finger in the dike for drinks. When he got up here, being that heroic boy again was his idea of Heaven, so there he is, up there, saving us all from the hole in the dike."

66

"It has a leak?" Michael stared dubiously at the vat. There might not be enough water in it to cause another Flood, but it sure could cause a major washout somewhere.

"Not really. We made one just for him," Halliwell said. "The walls are two hundred feet thick, so an actual leak is unlikely, but let's hope one never happens."

"What's it like up there?" Michael pointed to the top of the vat wall.

"Up there? It just looks like a lake."

"Let's see."

"You want to go up top?"

Michael waved Halliwell on and followed as the Dominion rose, their retinue fluttering behind. When they reached the top, Michael saw a colossal circular lake spread before him, its surface glowing pale blue from the reflected sky.

A Slavic-looking Powers was perched on the rim, a black plastic box with controls and an antenna in his hands. Out on the water, a hundred or so feet from shore, a toy motor boat frolicked in the light chop.

"Borysko!" Halliwell sounded commanding, but he looked flustered.

The Power looked up, startled, started to say something in protest to Halliwell, then saw who was with him. His hands fumbled the controller, and he almost dropped it. The boat's motor stopped humming, and the craft drifted aimlessly.

"Uh, sorry, sir. Uh, just havin' a bit of fun. I'll bring it back right now."

"You damned better," Halliwell snapped.

As soon as Borysko had brought the boat to shore, Michael saw it was a little open-hulled speed boat. There was something like a shot glass inside the boat, but Borysko snatched it up before Michael could get a good look.

"Take that away," Halliwell ordered hurriedly. "I'll see you in my office after Archangel Michael leaves."

Carrying the boat in one hand and the controller in the other, Borysko trotted to the outside edge of the parapet, hopped off, and flew out of sight.

"I apologize, sir," Halliwell said. "All our angels work hard, and sometimes they need to blow off a little steam. I'm sure Borysko thought what he was doing was harmless enough."

"This doesn't look good, Halliwell," Michael said. "This is our drinking supply. We can't have it contaminated."

"You're absolutely right, sir. But in our defense, I can show you that what Borysko did really isn't all that bad because we're not quite finished with the purification process."

"This water looks pretty clean to me. What do you use to purify it more than it already is?"

"The Boss's tears. One drop per million gallons. A lot more effective than chlorine."

"Does he come by to replenish the supply?" Michael asked. If he needed to talk to the Boss, maybe he could just show up here when the Boss made his next appearance instead of traveling all the way to the Edge. Ambush him, so to speak.

"We don't actually have a supply on hand," Halliwell explained. He was smiling, though he still appeared to be a little nervous about the incident with the toy boat. "Look out toward the center of the vat."

Michael used his telescopic vision to zoom in on the object Halliwell indicated, which was about ten miles away. It looked like an oversized eyedropper with a little dark gray cloud instead of a rubber bulb, its lower end suspended three feet above the surface.

"It's automatic," Halliwell said. "I guess the Boss cries regularly enough that the supply keeps coming. Look." He pointed to the lower end of the tube, where there gathered a quivering, shimmering droplet. Halliwell reached over the vat, and a golden, jewel-encrusted chalice appeared in his hand. He dipped the chalice in the vat then handed it deferentially to Michael.

"Try it."

Michael took the cup and drank, partly to hide his disappointment that he wouldn't find the Boss here, partly out of curiosity. The water wasn't bad, though it certainly wasn't as good as what Michael was used to. He handed the cup back to Halliwell, who tossed the remainder of the contents back into the vat just before the quivering drop finished its pregnant pause and fell into the exact center of the vat. A pearlescent

68

glow rode the ripples outward until they reached the stone walls, and the water returned to normal.

Halliwell dipped the chalice again and handed it to Michael. "Try now."

The water tasted better than the most delectable and refreshing wine that had ever touched Michael's palate. As he savored its sweetness rolling over his tongue, he considered having a few cases of the stuff bottled and sent over to his office, but he quickly squelched the idea. He handed the chalice back to Halliwell.

"Pretty good, eh, sir?" Halliwell said, passing the cup to one of his Virtues. "Of course, the pumping and piping process degrades it a little, so it's not quite as good when it gets to the fountains. Maybe that's what's happening in Sector P. But you can see how the Boss's tears improve the flavor."

"Yes," Michael said. "Very nice bouquet. So let's take a look at the distribution system."

As they neared the gargantuan oval building, the heavy rhythmic thud coming from it grew louder and louder until it threatened to overwhelm Michael's senses. He had to dampen down his hearing in much the same way he blocked the cries of pain and fear coming from those slaughtered by the Hosts of Heaven. After all, business was business. But even with his hearing banked, the thud reverberated deep inside his body.

He felt a nudge and turned to see Halliwell mouthing something, and Michael realized he'd damped his hearing below the threshold of speech. He turned it up enough to hear the Dominion.

"It's even louder inside," Halliwell shouted, though his voice came through Michael's lowered aural threshold like a mouse's squeak. "Do you want to go in?"

Michael shook his head and shouted back, "Just give me the salient features from here."

"That," Halliwell pointed to a gigantic pipe entering the building from behind them, "is the feed pipe from the main processing unit. Inside, the purified water is diverted to five pumps, each of which sends the water back to the other utilities.

"I know about the Solid Waste and Recycling Center, the Farm, and the Factory," Michael shouted, what are the other two for?"

"One feeds the fountains," Halliwell shouted back. "The other carries water to the Cloud Generation Unit. It's over that way about twenty miles." He pointed then looked questioningly at Michael. "Did you want to tour it, sir? I have to warn you, the clouds are so thick, you can't see your hand in front of your face, much less the plant. The angels there have to operate it by touch. And it's so hot and steamy, it'll drench your wings in no time. You won't be able to fly for at least an hour."

Michael was woozy from the incessant pounding of the pumps, and he was getting a headache trying to decipher Halliwell's squeaking. He didn't want to be sopping wet and delayed, too.

"Let's go to your office!" he shouted at the Dominion.

"Right, sir!" Halliwell led the way toward the plant's administration building, and soon the pump's heavy thump dwindled to a distant throb. Even that vanished once they were inside the office.

"I'm quite amazed at the size of your operation," Michael told Halliwell. "I guess I've never been here. I really should visit more often. Maybe get some deeper insights into each of the processes."

"I'm sure you're busy with more important matters than basic infrastructure," Halliwell said. "You have to do all that administrative work and lead the Hosts every time something happens and everything. It's a big job."

"It is," Michael admitted. "But even so, I need to keep tabs on all the operations in Heaven."

"Yes, sir," Halliwell said, though his eyes didn't look too happy. "But I assure you we're just pumping out the work and keeping things flowing right along."

"I can see that. But don't forget about the fountains in Sector P."

"No, sir. I won't."

"All right," Michael said. "Keep up the good work until I come back."

Michael left the office, went out of the front door, and launched himself into the air. Orienting himself, he headed off toward the Solid Waste and Recycling Center.

❧ 7 ❧

"REMEMBER: BEHAVE HEAVENLY. IT'S THE right thing to do."
Bob didn't have a watch or any other way to tell time, but the recorded message seemed to sound as regularly as clockwork, the woman's soft voice subtly urging compliance. Its mere presence made Bob wonder if it might be possible to behave otherwise.
As he waded through the clouds toward the structure he took to be an office building, he saw various people here and there doing this and that singly or in small groups. He spoke to some of them, but most seemed intent on their own afterlives and ignored him. Often, he couldn't see exactly what they were doing because their actions were concealed by misty veils. A lot of private stuff, obviously, that they didn't want anybody else to see.

About halfway to the building, he came upon the largest cloud cocoon he'd seen. It was almost cube shaped, about twenty feet to a side, and it emitted murmuring voices and a shifting, colorful glow.

Curious, he pushed his way through one of the walls and emerged into what looked like a living room with two sofas and several easy chairs arrayed around a 72" TV that was emitting the murmuring voices and flickering light. The seats were occupied by women, all staring intently at the screen. They looked like housewives from some posh gated-community reality TV fantasy, but the hypnotized way they stared at the screen reminded Bob of the Stepford wives.

"Come on in, sweetie." One of the women on the sofa nearest him beckoned, scooched over, and patted the cushion next to her. "Sit down and get comfy."

"What are we watching?"

"Shhh," hissed one of the other women as the screen changed to a dramatic shot of a cloud mountain behind which emanated a huge, rainbow-colored fan of blazing light—a special effects version of the crepuscular rays Bob had often seen in the far distance. The words, *One Eternal Life to Live*, appeared, accompanied by a brassy yet tasteful burst of trumpets. Bob was amazed to see some A-list actors in the opening credits, though he doubted they'd ever appeared in such fare on Earth, even if their careers had died before they had.

"I'm surprised *he's* here," he whispered to the woman next to him when he saw a well-known actor who'd gone into politics.

"He's not, really," she whispered back. "He's the villain, and we don't have any of those in Heaven, so they brought him up from Hell to play the part."

The plot for today seemed to revolve around a young woman from a spiritually wealthy family who was being courted by a Power, whose burning desire for her kept causing him to burst into flames. But she secretly had a thing for some big-shot angel named Malak Al-maut, played by himself.

"I never heard of him," Bob whispered to the woman.

"He's the Islamic angel of death," she clarified. "Here. You can get the complete background in this."

She picked up a glossy magazine from the coffee table in front of the sofa and passed it to Bob. Under the magazine's banner—Eternal Soaps Forever—the bright, splashy cover featured an attractive couple, he with magnificent wings, she obviously in advanced pregnancy. The two were half-covered by a headline that demanded, "What in Heaven's Name?" Bob flipped through the pages and learned the cover headline referred to a contest to name the actress's upcoming child.

"I didn't know women could get pregnant in Heaven," Bob whispered.

"It's all about free will."

72

"What happens after the baby is born? Is there a nursery school up here?"

"Shhh," the hisser hissed without taking her eyes from the screen.

"It's a cloud baby," said the woman next to Bob, as if that explained everything. Her hand began to spider walk toward his leg. "They're fun to make, and there's no maintenance afterward."

Bob tossed the magazine back onto the table and was just about to make a comment about Easy Bake Ovens, when a commercial came on advertising Christco Cooking Oil with holyunsaturated fat. The woman's hand reached his thigh and crawled onto it. Bob brushed it off and stood.

"Don't leave now, sweetie." The woman caught his hand and tried to pull him back down on the couch. "You'll miss *The Day of Our Eternal Lives*. And afterwards, who knows?" She blinked her eyes and smiled suggestively. "My husband's gone dove hunting for the weekend. We could get cozy and watch a Jane Austen film."

"It's that darned choir commandment," Bob said. "Can't help myself. You know how it is."

"You get the urge, you gotta sing." She patted his hand understandingly but let go reluctantly.

Bob hurried through the room's cloud wall, emerged into the golden glow, and looked around for the building he'd been trying to reach. He didn't see it until he went around the room, and when he did, he set off toward it.

The building was a lot farther away than it looked, and before long, Bob was tired. That surprised him. He'd walked all over Hell barefoot and naked, and all it had done was toughen his legs and feet. Here, the ankle-deep clouds seemed tenuous, but they exerted a subtle, enervating drag on his forward motion. He figured his legs would eventually strengthen, but he decided he'd probably never get used to walking in ankle-deep clouds, even if he had an eternity. It was too disconcerting. He could never tell what was beneath the next step—if anything—or where, exactly, he stood.

Worse than that, though his visit had been brief so far, he'd gotten so turned around he'd completely lost track of where the Pearly Gates were. Heaven wasn't like Hell at all. While Hell had

73

distinctive terrain and was organized into clear-cut divisions, the cloudscape here was so dislocating that he wondered how Residents found their way around.

But then, he supposed it didn't really matter where you were. While the punishments in Hell had been painfully explicit, the rewards of Heaven were obviously more amorphous.

A good example was something he'd noticed at the ambrosia tree. Neither the tree nor the many people around it cast a shadow because Heaven was diffusely lit with the pervasive golden light. The only direct light Bob had seen was the crepuscular rays emanating from beyond the distant cloud mountains that formed the backdrop no matter which way he looked. The golden-hued atmosphere was like the light inside a cubicle farm in an office building, Bob thought nostalgically, the staff awash in a pallid, faintly flickering florescent glow. But he couldn't really take pleasure in the rumination because apparently there was one person in Heaven with a shadow, and that was him: the trail of soot that kept following him. He wondered if it would ever vanish or if Saint Peter was right, and he'd eventually wear down to nothing.

As Bob neared the building, that depressing thought was shoved aside by the sound of singing that grew louder. The building seemed to have but one entry: a pair of glass doors at the top of a broad but shallow bank of steps. He went up the steps, pushed through the doors, and found himself in a tiny vestibule flanked by a reception desk behind which sat a Virtue.

Through the double glass doors beyond, Bob could see the entire building was a hollow, roofless shell, like a outsized atrium. But instead of having balconies and plants, the walls of its vast emptiness were taken up by steep cascading tiers filled with singers. It looked like the ultimate stadium seating arranged to hold as many participants as possible, and it was completely full. Looking up at the top tiers, Bob wondered how the singers got up to their perches. Maybe angels carried them up there.

"Choir practice started at 11 o'clock." The Virtue said it loudly, but the singing was so deafening that Bob could barely hear him. The angel's tone implied Bob was either too ignorant to tell time or he was too lazy to comply with the choir commandment. "You're ten minutes late."

"This isn't my 11 o'clock," Bob demurred in an equally loud voice. "Besides, I can't carry a tune."

"None of them can either," the angel said with a chuckle and a jerk of his head to indicate the ranked choristers, who would have been raising the roof if there'd been a roof to raise. "That's why we make them sing inside. It's like singing in the shower."

"You mean everybody up here doesn't have a golden voice?"

"I wish," the angel replied. "But there are limits. If the Boss transformed everybody who came to Heaven into perfect specimens with perfect voices, they'd be no different than he is. Anarchy would result."

"Can't have but one CEO," Bob nodded. "Gotta keep the ranks in file." He waved his hand around, taking in his surroundings. "But if this was built for a choir, why does it look like an office building?"

"You're a fine one to ask," the angel said, peering at the puddle of soot settling around Bob's ankles. "Are you going to clean that up before you leave?"

"It'll probably sink into the clouds like everything else," Bob reassured the angel. "You won't be left with anything more than a little residue."

"It doesn't really matter," the angel said. "They," he indicated the choristers, "leave all sorts of stuff in the pews, anyway, like candy wrappers, snotty tissues, and condoms."

"Why would anybody need condoms in Heaven? Can't the women use their Heavenly Desire not to get pregnant?"

"Sure. But what if she wants to get pregnant, and he doesn't want her to?"

"Can't he just make it his Heavenly Desire?"

"She wishes one way, he wishes the other." The angel shrugged. "It might seem like an impasse, but somebody always wishes more thoroughly than the other, so the guy uses the condom just to be on the safe side."

"I still can't believe people have sex while they're singing in the choir."

"It helps keep the Heavenly Bodies moving in synchronization," the angel explained. "We take advantage by timing the cries of their orgasms to the crescendo of the music. Our singers really hit some high notes, I can tell you. Besides, with all those people crammed in there, their hot, sweaty bodies all pressed together, it's not surprising some of them lose control."

Bob thought the angel looked a bit hot and sweaty just thinking about it. By now, he found he could barely think from all sound reverberating inside the building.

"I have to go," he said. "I can't tolerate all this noise."

"I know what you mean. I've had to put up with it for the last eighty-five years."

"Can't you leave?"

"After my shift's over."

"Not before? Why don't you just make it your Heavenly Desire? Skip out for the rest of the day."

"Only humans get their Heavenly Desires. Angels have no will power, so we don't get to indulge in Heavenly Desires. Besides, we have to work all the time, and not many of us desire that."

"Sorry," Bob said, contemplating the fact that not everybody in Heaven could exercise free will or Heavenly Desires. "Good luck with the rest of your shift."

He left the building, descended the steps, and walked out onto the cloud field. Wondering what he was going to do next, he scanned the terrain. There wasn't much nearby, but he did see something intriguing in the distance off to his right. It looked like a humongous maze covering many square miles, and beyond it was a towering monolithic structure that must have been half a mile tall.

For a moment, Bob puzzled over the fact that he could see the building so clearly when it was so far away, but this was Heaven, and he supposed you could see whatever you wanted. Or needed to. Saint Peter had told Bob he wouldn't have his Heavenly Desires, but his needs would be met. Did Bob need to see the building? Maybe it was Heaven's corporate headquarters. He couldn't think of any other building he'd need to see at such a distance. If it was, that was his next destination.

He descended the steps, worrying suddenly that the world-class labyrinth in front of the building might be a challenge to keep out the unworthy. If it was, Bob was shit out of luck. But he had to try.

It took him quite a while to cover the distance between the choir building and the maze, but eventually he got close enough to see it wasn't a maze but a gigantically large subdivision. The whole thing seemed to be surrounded by a treated wood fence, like some sort of medieval city with a staked palisade, but the houses inside were indistinguishable from the Mac mansions back home—and from each other.

The place seemed to go on forever. He looked both ways, and off to the right, he saw a distant sign. He set off for the sign, which turned out to be perched on an artificial cloud hillock with a fake little cloud waterfall tumbling down its face. The sign read: "Harmony Heights, Home of the Eternal Rest Home."

A road of flat clouds, which began beside the sign, ran toward the subdivision and entered it at a gateway flanked by cloud topiary sculptures trimmed to resemble fleecy sheep. As soon as it passed the gate, the road branched in several directions and ran off and out of sight to create the labyrinth. Taking a deep breath, Bob went through the gateway. He wasn't worried about getting lost. As long as he didn't cross his own path, he could follow the soot back to the entrance.

He walked about ten blocks before he saw anybody. The yards were all neat and clean and the houses well maintained, but there wasn't a single car in any of the three-car driveways or kids playing in the streets or yards. No barbecue smoke, or even dogs barking to announce his presence. It was like a cemetery, with houses instead of tombstones. Finally, he saw a guy crouched next to a side window of a house with white roof tiles and a limestone façade. His fingers were on the window sill, and his head barely protruded above that. He'd have looked like Kilroy to anybody inside the room.

"Excuse me," Bob called out as he approached.

"Okay, okay" the man said, straightening and holding up his hands. "You caught me."

"What?"

"I confess. I was peeping at your wife."

"I don't have a wife to peep at," Bob said.

"You don't?" The man gave a jerking shrug and said, "Shit! Gave myself away for nothing."

"You're peeping?" Bob asked, suddenly realizing what was going on. "You're a voyeur?"

"Yeah, I admit it. That's why I hang out in Harmony Heights. Lots of windows, lots of hot housewives."

"I got news for you," Bob said. "Any woman who gets spied on in Heaven wants to be spied on."

"You think they always knew I was there?"

"They probably get their kicks spying on you spying on them."

"I thought it was all a little too convenient, being able to peep in broad day...well, all this light."

"Why content yourself with just looking?" Bob asked. "Why don't you get in on some of that hot housewife action for real?"

"I guess I'm kinda shy."

"Shy never got anybody anywhere," Bob said. "If you don't know how to approach them, let them approach you."

"How?"

"Easy. Get a job."

"I'll have to work?"

"I think you'll like the work," Bob assured him.

"What's this job?"

"Milkman. You have a reason to be there, and if the housewives are as hot as you say they are—and as observant as I think they are—they'll just grab you and drag you inside. It might take you an eternity just to get down one street."

"You're right." The man's eyes lit up. "Now why didn't I think of that?" He looked at Bob. "Thanks for the idea, buddy."

"Bob."

"I'm Tom."

"What's up with this place?" Bob asked. "It's gigantic. How can anybody find their way home?"

"The people who live in there don't actually know where they live," Tom explained. "They just say, 'Being home is my Heavenly Desire,' and there they are."

"I'd feel like a rat in a maze in here," Bob commented.

"People in Harmony Heights like it that way. Makes them feel comfortable knowing every corner they turn is just like the last one."

"Is that an office building?" Bob asked, pointing to the towering structure jutting behind the subdivision.

"No. That's the Celestial. It's a high-rise apartment building. Folks who live there like to look down on everyone."

78

"There's only one?" Bob asked. "There must be lots of people here who want to live in a high-rise."

"About ten million." He eyed Bob. "You, too, right?"

Bob nodded.

"See what I mean," Tom said.

"But I'd want the top floor," Bob said. "Why live in a high-rise if you can't live in the penthouse? But I'd bet not many of all those millions of people are crammed into that thing's penthouse, so I'm surprised there aren't ten million high-rises out there instead of just one."

"If there were that many, Heaven would be like a towering forest. Nobody would have a good view except those on the periphery. Plus, it just wouldn't feel exclusive. The solution they worked up is much better. The Celestial is the only high-rise, so it commands a spectacular view all around, and it looks down on Harmony Heights. And while millions of people do live in there, you're right: They all want the top floor. So they all live in the penthouse."

"Kinda crowded."

"Separately. It uses some new fractal technology to make infinite space flower in a limited area. All ten million live there all at once and never bump into each other. Even husbands and wives, if that's their Heavenly Desire."

Bob remembered the Devil had some similar fractal thing operating in a mountain range in Hell.

"Go on over there, and sign up," Tom urged. "You'll get the penthouse for sure."

Forget that, Bob thought. I'm not settling for some timeshare. I'm going for the real thing.

"So everybody lives in Harmony Heights or the Celestial?"

"No. There's Lofts Everlasting, where the hipper folks live, Transcendent Townhomes for the more professional set, and Above and Beyond Meadows, where the really big mansions are. But it doesn't matter where you live in Heaven because everything is built by Eternal Homebuilders, and they build things to last." He eyed, Bob. "Sure you won't go on over to the Celestial? I live there, and I can tell you it has a great view. I've got this nifty telescope...."

"Some other time," Bob said. "I have to run."

He followed his trail back to the entrance to Harmony Heights, and once there, he looked both ways. The nearest object he could see that wasn't a fountain or an ambrosia tree looked like a small but animated crowd of people waving flags maybe a mile off. About half the flags were American, being red, white, and blue. The other half were mostly green. Even at this distance, the crowd's agitated movements looked like a hostile confrontation was about to take place.

This should be exciting, he thought, and he set off in the direction of the crowd.

"Remember," came the automated but soothingly persuasive disembodied voice. "Behave heavenly. It's the right thing to do."

❧ 8 ❧

IN A PLACE THAT'S ETERNAL, the passage of time is hard to gauge, so by the time the Waste and Recycling Center hove into view, Michael wasn't really sure how long it had taken him to get there. A good while, he reflected, thinking of all the miles he'd flown since he'd left the Water Plant.

While the Water Plant had a somewhat pristine and controlled look with its vats and pipes, the Solid Waste and Recycling Center was a chaotic, filthy mess. It looked, appropriately enough, like a garbage dump, but this one was bigger than huge. It was a mountain— Michael's built-in altimeter put it just under 30,000 feet—and wisps of clouds clung about its snowcapped head. He circled around it, and the stench was overwhelming. It was hard to believe such an ugly and hideously odiferous place could exist in Heaven.

Disconcertingly, the slopes of the gigantic mound seemed to be alive with a layer of flat, dark clouds that emerged from beneath the whiter surface of the surrounding cloudscape and crawled up the mountain's flanks, bearing on it a sheet of waste. As the dark layer of clouds climbed higher, it dissipated, gradually dropping its load.

The one place the sheet of darker clouds bringing in waste was interrupted was on one side of the mountain, where stood a domed building whose outside wall was composed of a continuous series of large arches. The slope on that side had a tiny crescent eaten out of it, like a one-tooth nibble from a very big apple. The face of the crescent and the flat area between it and the building was a bustle of activity and white blurs, but from this height, Michael couldn't tell exactly what was going on. He saw, though, that while the building and crescent were enormous, they were so completely overwhelmed by the size of the mountain they looked like a tiny chalet nestled in an alpine valley.

Two large pipes approached the domed building from the direction of the Water Plant, and they split about half a mile from the building and went to either side and entered through opposite archways. Intake and output, Michael supposed. A third pipe emerged from the building at right angles to the water pipes and ran off into the distance. Not a pipe, Michael realized when he saw it seemed to be crawling away from the building at a steady pace. It looked like an endless gigantic snake. He activated his telescopic vision and saw with a shock it was a conveyor belt of dark gray clouds about ten yards wide, bearing a continuous stream of trash away from the complex.

A sudden gust of wind blew some of the clouds hovering around the mountain's head into Michael's flight path, obscuring his vision and filling his nostrils with stench. He nearly gagged. Enough, he thought as he flapped desperately out of the reeking cloud, which was harder to do than he expected because it left a greasy coating on his wings, making the feathers stick together.

He was about to train his telescopic vision on the blur of activity going in the open area between the crescent and the building, when suddenly all the activity stopped, and Michael saw it had been caused by the blindingly fast hustle and bustle of thousands of Principalities.

Before he could make out what they'd been doing, they all rose en masse into the air. It was like a huge flock of pigeons taking off in a deafening thunder of flutters. The thousands of angels all flew to the top of the mountain, and as they passed beneath Michael, the gusts of wind from their combined wing action almost blew him away. As he steadied himself against the gale, the massive band of angels hovered for several moments in complete verbal silence. Suddenly, they erupted in such loud cheering that even the thunder of the wing wind was split.

82

The massed angels milled around for several minutes, glad-handing and patting each other on the back, which wasn't easy since their wings tended to get tangled. Then gradually they drifted back down and resumed their frenzied activity in the open ground between the crescent and building.

Except for one. This one turned in Michael's direction and flew toward him. It was, he saw, a Dominion. His face was flushed.

"Hello, Michael, sir," the Dominion said. "I'm Montgomery, the Solid Waste and Recycling Center manager. Everyone calls me Monte. Welcome to our little operation."

Monte had a Scottish accent, but not one so thick it rendered him completely unintelligible to 99.9 percent of the English-speaking world.

"Did you see it, sir?"

"I saw you and your staff cheering something," Michael said, "but I don't know what it was."

"Potpourri Peak, sir." Monte waved proudly toward the mountain top. "It's the highest physical elevation in Heaven."

"It certainly is impressive."

"Even more so, now, sir," Monte said, grinning. "That's what we were celebrating. We just topped 29,030 feet, and we're now one foot taller than Mount Everest." He squinted at the peak then turned back to Michael. "Sorry, sir, make that 29,031 feet. Some of the staff think we ought to make a movie about it: *The Angel Who Went Up a Hill and Came Down a Mountain*. What do you think?"

"I think it's not an accomplishment you ought to be bragging about."

"No, sir. You're right." Monte's face fell.

"And it's grown another foot since we've been talking?"

Monte squinted at the peak again.

"Yes, sir. I knew you'd want to talk about it as soon as I got the call from Halliwell over at the Water Plant. He said you were making the rounds."

"A call? How did you get that?"

"On this, sir." Monte produced a walkie-talkie. "These were issued just a little while ago. Thanks so much for them, sir. I never get a chance to confer with the other Dominions in charge of the utilities. These'll improve communications among the different divisions tremendously. Now that you're here, I assume you want a run-through of our facility."

"Well, I...." Actually, now that he was here, Michael wanted to do nothing more than get away from the horrific reek. But he had his duty.

"This looks like quite an operation," he said. "I don't think I've ever seen anything quite so massively earthy in Heaven."

"It wasn't always this way," Monte said. "Back when all we had in Heaven were cavemen, this was just an open plain, and there usually wasn't much of anything here. It didn't take any time at all to deal with small heaps of ashes, flint chips, and a few animal bones. But it's been ages since then, and you can see we can't process everything in a timely manner like we used to."

"So Potpourri Peak is growing."

"Yes, sir. Faster than we can dig it out. Frankly, it won't be long before we're completely overwhelmed. We just don't have the equipment or personnel to handle all the garbage and waste the humans produce." He peered at Michael as if he were about to say something.

"You have a suggestion?" Michael asked.

"Well, sir, you know, if we didn't allow the humans to eat or drink or have possessions, they wouldn't have to constantly excrete or throw things away, and we wouldn't have this problem."

"It *is* unfortunate that humans all think that in Heaven they retain their human bodies," Michael said. "But that's their Heavenly Desire, even if bodies naturally lead to bodily functions and demands to appease their wants and wishes."

"I guess we'll just have to do our best, sir." Monte waved toward the mountain. "Shall we go down for a closer look?"

No, Michael thought, but he allowed the Dominion to lead him down anyway. Monte didn't land immediately but took Michael on a low-altitude survey.

"What's going on there?" Michael asked, indicating the gray layer of clouds bringing in the garbage and dumping it on the mountain's sides.

"It's our garbage retrieval system," Monte explained. "We call it the conveyor layer. "It's all over Heaven, about ten feet below the layer of clouds everything is built on. Discarded items just gradually sink down until they hit the conveyor layer, which

84

is in constant motion in this direction." He chuckled. "The meteorologists on Earth think they know all the kinds of clouds there are, but we've managed to keep the conveyor layer hidden from them. Imagine if they knew. Forecast: partly cloudy with a chance of afternoon garbagefall." He chuckled again, but a stern look from Michael cut him off. "Let's visit the processing center, sir," he said hastily.

He waved toward the domed building, and soon they both hovered about fifty feet above the middle of the flat area between the building and the crescent eaten out of the side of Potpourri Peak. Close up, Michael saw that the crescent wasn't all that small, it just seemed that way in comparison to the mountain looming over it. Nor was it a natural feature from erosion but was created by the swarm of angels, all of whom were moving so fast their white robed figures were nothing but blurred white streaks.

At the crescent, the angels would dig out armloads of garbage, then they'd race into the building through an open archway and toss the garbage into one of hundreds of bins waiting just inside. Michael wondered how they managed to keep their robes sparkling white in the midst of all the filth.

Despite their frenzied activity, it obviously was a futile effort. The conveyor layer was constantly adding more detritus to the mountain than even this army of super-charged angels could handle. As Michael watched, a massive overhang of debris developed, and suddenly, with a rumbling clatter and a cloud of choking dust, it collapsed in a garbageslide, burying hundreds of angels. Hundreds more clambered over the slope, digging frantically, and in a few moments, they'd freed their companions, and everybody went back to work.

"Surely you have more workforce than this," Michael said. "What are they doing?"

"Most of them are out maintaining the conveyor layer."

"That's something I want to talk to you about," Michael said. "I've had reports the conveyor layer is breaking down in numerous locations and running sluggishly almost everywhere else. On my way here, I saw litter all over the place."

"The conveyor layer is our oldest piece of equipment, and it is hopelessly antiquated in the face of the sheer amount of trash

85

that needs to be transported. I assure you, sir, all the trash you see out there will be dealt with, it'll just take some time."

"Meanwhile, it keeps building up here."

"Sadly true, sir." Monte waved at Potpourri Peak. "We can't fully process what actually does come in. If the conveyor layer was working with 100 percent efficiency, we wouldn't have just a Mount Everest here, but the whole Himalayas."

"You haven't been having any of those trash falls you were talking about, have you?"

"Well, uh, actually, sir," Monte said with embarrassment, "we do our best, but it does happen occasionally. Usually it's not too bad unless it happens in a heavily populated ares. Most of what gets through falls into the oceans, and the rest of Earth is so littered now, a little more doesn't really register on anyone."

Monte looked down at the hem of his robes.

"All right," Michael said in a mollifying tone. "I know our infrastructure is antiquated and we're shorthanded. That's why I'm here. To see how things work and find out what you need."

"Okay, sir. Well, let's go on into the Processing Center and look at the sluice."

Monte started toward the massive domed structure.

"This is an interesting looking building," Michael said.

"We constructed it a few years ago," Monte said. "We used to be an open-air operation, but after business picked up so drastically in the 1800s, we had so much steam rising from the sluice that it kept mixing with the clouds around here. The folks at the Cloud Generating Plant complained we were polluting their output, so we built this to contain the steam. We needed something really large to accommodate the pipes and loading docks and such. Now, we send more than 90 percent of it back to the Water Treatment and Purification Plant."

"Did you get a building creation permit?"

"We didn't exactly create it, sir," Monte said sheepishly. "We knew that was beyond our capacity, so we just stole the plans and built it out of recycled materials."

"Stole them from whom?"

"The North Koreans."

"The North Koreans have one of these?"

86

"Theirs isn't a garbage-handling facility—at least not strictly speaking. It's the largest stadium on Earth. They call it the May Day Stadium. Ostensibly they built it for athletic competitions, but they really use it for mass worship of their current dictator."

Nothing like absolutism for building monuments to the self, Michael mused, then he immediately felt a pang of guilt that he quickly suppressed. Most people—or angels—didn't remember the regrettable episode that occurred during Michael's last outing to Earth, for which Michael was thankful. Monte didn't seem to make the connection, either, so Michael kept his face as bland as he could, which wasn't very. He was Captain of the Hosts, and nobody wants to follow the commands of a milquetoast.

By now, they'd entered one of the arches into an area crowded with hundreds of the large bins into which the angels dumped their armloads of garbage. As Michael and his guide threaded their way between the bins, he could see that each had a hole in the bottom that fed trash at a regular rate into a half pipe filled with rushing water. Beyond the bins, the hundreds of sluices flattened out into rapids running chaotically across the area beneath the domed roof, which was barely visible through the haze of steam saturating the air. It was the most complex estuary system Michael had ever seen. The combined sound of rushing water was like standing near a dozen Niagara waterfalls.

"This is where we wash everything down," Monte shouted. "Fresh water comes in up here and carries the trash downstream, separating the junk from the sludge. It's like a big placer mining operation."

He led Michael along one of the sluices, which was lined with Principalities like workers on an assembly line. Michael was always amused by the pretense of power conveyed by the crowns they wore and the scepters they carried since this class of angels actually held no power whatsoever. At the moment, the Principalities' scepters were thrust through the sashes of their robes like daggers, and they were using both hands to reach into the rushing water to pluck out items and put them into plastic tubs standing at their feet.

"What are they doing?" Michael asked.

"Those are our pickers," Monte explained. "They're looking for items that are too time-consuming or expensive to remanufacture, like the golden drinking goblets. We just wash those up and send them over to the Distribution Center for reuse."

As they proceeded downstream, the hundreds of sluices began to merge until they combined into a small river. Thankfully, the noise had diminished and the air had grown fresher. At last, they reached the terminus of the river, where it dropped through a slanted grating that sieved out the last of the trash before vanishing through a hole in the floor. The grating was vibrating, which caused the accumulated trash to slide down onto a mat of clouds about thirty feet wide that was moving very much like the conveyor layer and ran out of one of the archways. It was the beginning of the king-sized snake of trash Michael had seen crawling off into the distance.

"This is our conveyor belt," Monte said. "Works like the conveyor layer, but on a smaller scale. It takes all this cleaned-up trash to the Factory, where it's reconstituted into new goods. I know it looks impressive, but this is the weakest link in our chain."

So much trash was being dumped onto the conveyor belt that bits and pieces kept falling off the sides, and a pile of debris several feet high lined each side of the conveyor belt for as far as Michael could see. In the first hundred yards, dozens of Principalities stood on each side of the belt, picking up fallen junk and tossing it back onto the moving heap, which only caused something else to fall off.

"Ultimately, we can process only as much as this can carry," Monte said. "As you can see, we've reached our limit, but even so, the management at the Factory is complaining we aren't sending them enough raw materials to keep up with the humans' growing demand for products."

"There must be a solution," Michael said.

"Well, sir, we were hoping you might create a second conveyor belt for us. I put in a requisition ages ago, but nothing ever came of it."

"Creation is the Boss's area, not mine," Michael said. "I'll have to take that up with him."

"I understand, sir." Monte hesitated, then said, "We did have another idea, sir. If you could requisition some heavy equipment, we could solve a lot of our problems. We could use scoopers, bulldozers, and big earth movers to whittle down Potpourri Peak and use some of those industrial-size dump trucks to carry the overload from here to the Factory."

"Wouldn't dump trucks require roads?" Michael asked. He suddenly envisioned even more infrastructure added to Heaven's burden: road construction crews, cement plants, diesel stations, refineries.... The list seemed endless. They'd even need to build an air purification plant to deal with the diesel fumes.

"I've been thinking about that," the Dominion replied. "There's this TV show where truckers drive across the ice of the frozen north wastelands on Earth. We could do something similar here and just drive over the clouds. We could even do our own show and call it *Cloud Convoys* or something like that. The suspense would be really great. The guys driving over the ice might crack through, but if we hit a weak spot, it'd be like a meteor falling."

"Yes, trash truck meteors: That's exactly what we want people to think might happen," Michael said, a little more sarcastically than he intended. "Sorry, but no motorized vehicles. Boss's orders."

The Dominion looked disappointed, and Michael realized he'd just shattered his dreams of being a reality show star, even if it was a falling one.

"I'll see what I can do about getting you more help," Michael said in a more soothing tone. "I'm sure the Boss will do something." He'll have to, he thought, if he wants to keep this place running.

By now, they'd reached the archway where the conveyor belt emerged, and Michael bid Monte farewell. Flapping his wings, he rose above the conveyor belt and followed it toward the Factory.

❧ 9 ☙

As Bob neared the small crowd, he saw that what he'd taken at a distance for conflict was actually a seething mob of about thirty people, evenly mixed between men and women. The flags turned out to be signs painted on poster board affixed to wood-slat handles. As the words resolved themselves, he could read, "Thank God for 9/11. Thank God for IEDs. God Is Angry Every Day. God Hates Jews. America Is Doomed. God Hates America. God Hates Fags. You're Going to Hell." The people were dressed in drab-colored clothes—the first clothes he'd seen here that weren't white.

Bob slowed and perused the group from what seemed a safe distance considering the agitated state of the people who made it up. Their faces were contorted by snarling anger and outrage, and they were yelling phrases that approximated the words on the signs at the sole member of their audience, a bored looking Principality. Ignoring the crowd, the angel was smoking a joint and flipping through a copy of a magazine titled *Really High Times*. As soon as Bob approached, however the crowd turned threateningly on him, screaming invectives, accusing him of obscene behavior of various sorts, and damning him to Hell.

Reflecting that he'd already been there and the people there had been nicer than this, Bob nervously moved closer to the angel, hoping for a little divine protection in case the assemblage decided to attack. The angel lowered the magazine and perused him. Saw his Visitor badge. Saw his soot trail. Offered him the joint.

"I think you need this more than I do."

"Who are they?" Bob waved the joint away.

"The Eastboro Baptist Church," the angel replied.

"They don't seem to like anybody."

"They don't even like themselves," the angel shrugged. "My job is to antagonize them by simply doing something they hate right in front of them. Getting stoned doesn't get the kind of rise out of them some things do, like when I bury war heroes, celebrate a bar mitzvah, or act out a gay or interracial wedding. Those really get them in a tizzy. But I have to admit," he held up the joint and stared at it for a moment before taking another hit. "This stuff makes them a whole lot easier to ignore."

"Remember: Behave heavenly," intoned the soothing ambient voice. "It's the right thing to do."

None of the Eastboro Church members seemed to hear the voice, and apparently neither did the angel.

"I can't believe such bigots are allowed in Heaven," Bob said.

"They aren't in Heaven," the angel said. "They're in Hell."

"I've been to Hell, and this doesn't look like it to me."

"It's all a matter of perspective. If you're in a place that seems awful to you, that would be Hell, wouldn't it?"

That gave Bob a bit of a pause, since he'd felt a lot more at home in Hell—once he'd escaped from the lake of boiling shit, that is—than he did here.

"But this," Bob waved around, "isn't awful."

"It is for people who believe Heaven is highly restrictive instead of a place of pure freedom. Look."

The angel pointed to the protesters' feet, and Bob saw they weren't immersed in ankle-deep mists but were standing on uneven, rocky ground that glowed like a large ember. Moisture from the clouds that touched the surface instantly steamed away.

"The heat has fused their soles to the rock. It gives them the lack of freedom they crave, but they're forced to watch perfect freedom unfold all around them."

"Can't they just step out of their shoes?"

92

"They could, but they never think of it. Or if they do, they're too afraid to try. They don't like anything that's new or different."

Bob looked at the rocky ground then down at his own feet. Or, at his ankles, since his feet were embedded in soot-frosted mists.

"Is that what it looks like underneath all this?" he asked. "Barely cooled lava?"

"Beats me," the angel said. "At least we're not getting the hot-foot treatment like they are."

"You never looked?"

"No," the angel said. "Have you?"

Bob admitted he hadn't, and he bent and started waving his hands back and forth over his feet to waft the sooty mists away so he could see exactly where he stood, but the mists were more tenacious than tenuous closer to the unseen surface and wouldn't reveal anything lower than the top of his sole.

"Your shoes are black," the angel commented. "And your cuffs."

"So they are," Bob said, surprised.

His soot not only trailed behind him but had stained his shoes and was darkening his trousers. He straightened.

"I guess we'll never know what's under there," the angel said.

Maybe not you, Bob thought, but I'm going to get to the bottom of things around here, one way or another.

"I'm still surprised they're allowed to carry those signs and yell those things," he said.

"It's their lot, so we accommodate them. We just don't let them wander around, disrupting things."

His tone implied a certain suspicion of Bob.

"Are you guarding them?"

"I'm protecting them from themselves. I give them something to hate. After all, everybody is different in some way, and if we just leave them to themselves, their intolerance of differences would eventually make them turn on each other. Since they can't run from themselves, it would end in a pretty bloody mess. Who wants to clean up after that?"

"I see what you mean."

"Besides, the Boss likes to come by on occasion. The way they carry on tickles him pink. He especially likes to visit in drag since that really upsets them."

93

"The Boss in drag?"

"The Boss is all things," the angel pointed out. "That means he's gay as well as straight. Hey, want to make out in front of them and really piss them off?"

The angel eyed him lasciviously.

"Sorry," Bob demurred. "That's not my thing. Besides, these people give me a headache."

"I know what you mean," the angel said. He took another hit off the joint. "Only I get the pain at the other end."

Bob wasn't sure what an angel's anatomy was like beneath the full-length robes. The angels he'd seen either flew everywhere or glided rather than walked, so for all he knew, the robes were empty shells that sprouted a head, arms, and wings. But he knew they sat, which implied that hidden under all the cloth, there was an ass to be pained. So maybe legs were attached. He thought about asking the angel to show him, but he didn't want to give him the wrong impression, even though it was tempting to further rile the Eastwood congregation. It would be like baiting an already enraged pit bull from behind the protection of a chain link fence.

Bob bid the angel goodbye and walked away across the clouds. For the moment, he was at a loss of where to go or what to do. The choir building hadn't been filled with offices, and so far, most of the people he'd encountered had been doing things that didn't interest him.

In fact, Bob was beginning to get a little bored with Heaven. Almost everybody here was a consumer, and while Bob enjoyed the finer things in life—and death—he wanted more out of his existence than just sitting around, playing petty dictator to a bunch of compliant angels. That was no challenge. The entertainments the demons in Hell had devised at the expense of their human prisoners were a lot more creative than anything people in Heaven demanded of the angels. And although the people he'd met so far seemed to be peaceful and happy enough, all their smiles were a little off kilter.

What this place needed was shaking up. And some organization wouldn't hurt, either. Through his few conversations with angels and people in Heaven, Bob had come to believe Heaven was as chaotic as Hell, although in its own way. Chaos was part

94

of the underlying structure of Hell, which the Devil controlled with external rules. In Heaven, though, chaos was superimposed onto the natural order by the wielding of individual free will.

That started him reflecting on the idea of everybody having their Heavenly Desires answered, though the contradictions of that nearly drove him insane. But he did understand one thing: Because everybody had their Heavenly Desires answered, ultimately, everybody was the center of attention. That made the atmosphere in Heaven like a carnival, where everything was a little overblown and a little hyped-up because everyone was busy inflating and polishing their own image.

Bob was in favor of taking the third path of establishing control: organization. Throughout his career, he'd learned how to do that within the existing framework of whatever company he was with. Even in Hell, he'd maintained the punishments and just repurposed them. He'd find a way to work out things in Heaven, too. And he knew he'd succeed precisely because he'd be taking advantage of the twin demons of boredom and egotism to give the Residents some sort of distraction. Once he hit on the right angle, it would be simple to generate a little cash. Or, since there was no money in Heaven, cachet. Surely there was a way Bob could insert himself into the operations here, make himself a profit, and earn Residency.

Bob wasn't sure just how he'd accomplish that, but he knew one thing: He needed new clothes. For some reason, his brain just wouldn't function properly while he was dressed so casually, as if the very casualness inhibited the scheming part of his mind. A good suit would make him feel human again and put him on top of his mental game. But try as he might, he couldn't wish himself out of the golf clothes and into something more appropriate. Saint Peter had said his needs would be taken care of, but apparently nobody up here realized just how much he needed a real suit. Maybe he could ask someone to Heavenly Desire him some new clothes. He headed toward the nearest fountain, reasoning that there was always someone hanging around those. He'd ask whoever he found about ordering a suit.

To his disappointment, nobody was there when he arrived, so he decided to have a drink while he waited for someone to show up. He ordered another Dalmore 64 Trinitas, wondering

95

how long he could keep that up. If he drank a whole bottle of the stuff, could they still call it Trinitas? Maybe there was a whole different case of Trinitas here in Heaven.

While he was standing there, sipping and wondering how he might occupy himself, a man came up, holding a candle. The candle trickled a thin strand of greasy-smelling smoke, but to Bob's eyes, it gave off no discernible light. At the edge of the fountain, the man sighed, reached out, and got a goblet of some tawny-colored liquid.

"Cheers," Bob said, raising his goblet.

The man jumped as if startled.

"Oh! I didn't know you were there," he said in a Spanish accent.

He stepped closer to Bob, raised the candle, and peered at Bob as if extremely myopic. Then he raised his goblet in Bob's direction with an elegant motion and said, "Salud."

They both drank.

The man had angular features, quick brown eyes, dark hair, and a thin, devilish Van Dyke. His clothing, like all the clothing Bob had seen so far except for those worn by the members of the Eastboro Baptist Church, was white. But instead of a polo shirt and slacks, he wore what looked like sixteenth-century European clothing, a discreet but elegant ruffle circling his neck.

"I'm Bob. I just arrived."

"An American?"

"Yes."

"I'm Castilian," the man said, setting his goblet on the edge of the fountain and sticking out his hand. "My name is Adriano."

Bob shook his hand.

"What's your poison, Adriano, if you don't mind me asking?"

"Niepoort Garrafeira Port," the Castilian replied, retrieving the goblet.

"I'll have to try it some time," Bob said, wishing he had something to write the name on. Not having Heavenly Desires was irritating.

"And you?" the man asked.

Bob told him the whiskey's name.

"It's a beautiful night, is it not?" Adriano asked.

"But it's daytime," Bob replied. If the pervasive golden glow could be termed day, he reflected.

"Looks like night to me."

"But I can see clearly all around," Bob said. "It can't be night."

The man laughed—a bit sourly, Bob thought.

"You're obviously not a natural nighthawk like me," Adriano said. "It's really very simple. In Heaven, it is both eternal day and eternal night. Some prefer the nocturnal life. For you, it is day, but for me, it is night."

"I see. You can choose eternal day or eternal night."

"That is correct."

"That's pretty cool. Gives everybody their preference."

"Yes." The reply didn't sound too happy.

"Is there something wrong?" Bob asked.

"I have grown weary of wandering around in the darkness. I'm the only nighthawk here. Everybody else thinks it's daytime, so there are no lights on anywhere except for the one I carry for myself. This candle casts only a dim glow, but thank goodness I have it, or I'd have fractured shins by now."

"If you're tired of the darkness, can't you alternate? Switch to eternal daytime for a while?"

"It's not that simple," Adriano said, taking a hefty swig of his port and expelling a sigh laden with alcohol fumes. "If you could alternate, then neither one would be eternal since one would end when you switched to the other. They call Heaven eternal, after all, not ephemeral."

"You mean you have to live in perpetual darkness because of a naïve mistake? Seems like your choice would no longer be Heaven but a sort of Hell."

"They don't tell you that when you get here. They just say you have free will and let you go." The man refilled his goblet, and quaffed half of it in three gulps. "I get so depressed sometimes that all I want to do is get drunk, but I can't even get a decent buzz off this stuff." He waved the goblet, and some of the port sloshed out and stained the mists around his feet.

Bob was about to commiserate, but the man's words had started him thinking about the actual quality of the golden glow all around. Was it really any better than darkness? It let him see, but he'd come to the conclusion that the quavering glow, instead of being heavenly, had a buzzy, irritating quality and really *was* a lot like the ambient wash of florescent fixtures lighting a cubicle farm.

Well, he groused. I guess I probably did bring that on myself.

"You ever think about carrying a flashlight?" he asked. "Or an electric lantern? Either one would give you more light than that candle."

"I never heard of such things," Adriano said.

"Wield your Heavenly Desire," Bob said. "Wish for one."

Adriano dropped his goblet and said, "A flashlight is my Heavenly Desire."

Poof! A big flashlight appeared in his hand. Bob showed him how to turn it on, and though he couldn't tell a difference, apparently Adriano could.

"This is fantastic, Bob!" He swung the invisible beam around in wide arcs. "I can see much farther than ever. Muchas gracias."

Adriano tossed his candle aside, and it sputtered into the clouds and went out.

"You could do me a favor in return," Bob said.

"You would like me to second you in a duel?" Adriano asked hopefully.

"Nothing so drastic. I need some new clothes, but I'm a Visitor, and I can't Heavenly Desire anything. Would you wish me up a three-piece suit?"

"I wish I could, my friend, but I know nothing of clothing from your era. I have heard there's a mall out there somewhere. I never managed to bump into it, but I understand they have all sorts of things. Maybe you can find what you need there."

"Good idea, and good luck," Bob said. He dropped his now-empty goblet and moved away from Adriano, who turned to refill his own cup under the invisible beam of his new flashlight, this time with Dalmore 64 Trinitas.

Not long afterward, Bob saw an ambrosia tree in the distance, a lone figure beneath its drooping branches.

Maybe he knows where the mall is, Bob thought.

The man might have been beneath the ambrosia tree, but he wasn't eating. He was gesturing demonstratively, and his mouth moved rapidly, but Bob was still too far away to hear what he was saying.

Bob hesitated. It was pretty obvious by now that being crazy didn't exclude you from Heaven, and he wondered if it was safe to approach the man. Maybe this nut's Heavenly Desire was to randomly attack anybody who came near. Wishing for "Get thee fucking back!" powers, Bob moved toward the man.

"Hello," Bob called out. "Mind if I join you?"

The man stopped jabbering and gesturing and just stood there like a lost child as Bob approached. He had shaggy hair, a scruffy beard, and wild eyes. His emaciated body was clad in white rags whose tatters hung limply in the tepid air. He gripped a gnarly staff in one hand.

Bob was excited. This must be one of those legendary prophets from out on the Wastelands.

"Are you saved?" the man shouted in a cracked voice. "You approacheth the End! Accept Christ, and ye shall live in his everlasting and glorious light."

"I thought the End was already here," Bob said. "And if you haven't noticed, the light here is everlasting, though I can't say much for its glory."

He reached up and pulled an ambrosia from a branch, thinking, shrimp cocktail. He took a bite, and it was great.

"Ye dare eat of the fruit from the pure Tree of Life?" The man shook his gnarly staff at Bob. "That is blasphemy! Blasphemers, sinners, and harlots will perish in fire. Armageddon is nigh. Only the good and the righteous will enter the Kingdom of Grace."

"No wonder nobody else is around," Bob said. "We're already in Heaven. Didn't anybody tell you?"

"You blind fool!" the man bellowed, and a billow of halitosis washed over Bob, who took a step back. "This is no promised land. It's the place of the Devil's temptation to lure all the wicked with empty, vain riches. The righteous shall dwell in God's bosom for ever and more."

"I don't think the Devil has to do much tempting where people are concerned," Bob said. "They're their own worst enemies."

"That's so true," the man said, looking at Bob in a new light. "I am called John the Anapest. Hi."

"I'm Bob. You must be one of those prophets from out in the Wastelands."

"I was out there a long and sad time seeking God," John nodded. "Ages, it seems."

"Did you find him?"

"I kept seeing his bright rays but never his person. I nearly went mad." He gave Bob a less-than-sane appraisal, taking in his soot trail. "You appear like a person whose seen fiery Hell and come back."

"I am," Bob said. "I've met the Devil, and I can tell you he has very little need for subterfuge. People are willingly jumping into the pit, though they're pretty sorry afterward."

He finished the shrimp cocktail and reached for two more fruits, thinking, prime rib, for one, and baked potato for another.

"So, why did you enter the fold instead of staying in the Wastelands?" he asked.

"I was hungry and tired. There is nothing to eat in the Wastes except mist, and that's not too fulfilling. Or tasty considering all the pollutants that blow up from Earth. But I'm not finding anything to eat around here. And it's rough in the Wastes. I kept tripping against my own feet." He stared as Bob bit into the steak fruit. "Is that food? It is not the forbidden and banned Tree of Life?"

"If food isn't life," Bob said, "it wouldn't grow on trees."

"I guess not. I have been out of touch."

"Try one." Bob gesturing with his baked potato fruit at the tree. "This is an ambrosia tree. All you have to do is think what you want to eat as you pick the fruit."

Tentatively the man snapped off a fruit and took a tiny bite. Then a larger one. And another. In a few moments, he finished.

"What was it?" Bob asked.

"Cream of Wheat," the prophet said. "My old grandma used to make it for me."

Bob was feeling thirsty after his meal, and anyway, he wasn't much inclined to explain the ways of Heaven to a mad prophet.

"Listen," he said, tossing away the remains of his ambrosia. "I gotta go. But if you're still unconvinced this is Heaven, you ought to visit the Eastboro Church members."

"Who are they?"

"*What* are they? That's the real question. Just follow that," Bob pointed to his trail. "They're the first bunch of unruly people you'll come to. Just don't trip over your feet on the way over there."

The encounter would be entertaining to watch, Bob thought, but he had other fish to fry.

100

"Say, I heard there's a mall somewhere around here."

"It is right over there." John the Anapest pointed.

"Thanks," Bob said, and he headed off in the direction John indicated.

๑ 10 ๖

AS MICHAEL FOLLOWED THE SERPENT of trash writhing across the cloudscape, he saw that Monte had actually downplayed the problem of the overloaded conveyor belt. Every time the conveyor curved around a cloud hill or dipped into a cloud valley and up the opposite slope, trash fell off the sides and littered the right-of-way. There would be a whole lot more of it, Michael realized, if it didn't sink to the conveyor layer to be carried back to the Solid Waste and Recycling Center. But it was a terrible misuse of resources to simply recycle trash that had already been through the system. Possibly more than once. His telescopic vision spotted, among the spilled detritus, a twisted, tattered, and soggy length of Egyptian papyrus scroll; a fragment of a stone head depicting the Boss in his guise of Quetzalcoatl; and a breastplate of Greek design, its bronze rotten with verdigris.

How many other things had been recycling as long as these? Michael wondered. Monte was right. Something had to be done.

Eventually, the Factory came into view. Much of it was obscured by billows of steam issuing from rooftop stacks and vents all around the eaves, but it looked like an amassed conglomeration of structures all piled haphazardly together over an area of several square miles. At the core was a round white stone cairn that could have held Saint Peter's Square in Rome. Many other building styles and materials were visible in the layers circling the cairn like rings of a tree trunk. The outer layer was constructed of sheet metal.

The conveyor belt of trash entered the building through a large opening like a loading dock on one side, pipes to and from the Water Plant entered from another direction, and a second conveyor belt emerged from a third side and led off into the distance. Instead of bearing trash, this conveyor carried neatly stacked boxes and cartons. The fourth side had a protruding wing fronted by glass panels and double doors.

Must be the office, Michael thought, and he angled down and lit in front of the entry. Before he could reach the doors, they were pushed open by a burly, rosy-cheeked Dominion wearing longish hair and a full beard, both snow white. He looked like Santa Claus in a white muumuu instead of a red suit.

"Welcome to the Factory, sir." The burly angel held the door and ushered Michael inside. "I'm Hephaestus, managing director, but everybody calls me Festus."

"Pleased to meet you, Festus," Michael said, stepping into a quiet reception area.

"Just came in from the Solid Waste, I take it," Festus said.

"How can you tell?" Michael asked. "Do you have one of those walkie-talkies we're issuing?"

"I do, sir." He pulled one out from the folds of his robe. "But that's not how I know. You, uh, well, pardon me, sir, but you brought a little of its redolence with you."

Michael wafted his right wing beneath his nose and caught an odor of garbage. He'd gotten used to the smell while he'd been at the Solid Waste and Recycling Center and didn't realize the stink had permeated his feathers and robes.

"My apologies," he said as he exuded enough angelic sweat to obliterate the odor. "You've been here for a long time."

"Yes, sir, right from the beginning, but at first, I was just one of the craftsmen. I wasn't made director until I worked closely with the Greeks back when they called the Boss Zeus."

"Didn't you make the first woman? What was her name? Not Embla, Nüwa, Lilith, Eve, or any of the others. The one who came before them."

104

"Pandora?"

"That's her."

"Yes, sir. She's the project that earned me my promotion. The Boss was really pleased with the way I put that little tart together. She did everything wrong, just like he wanted. He said I did such a good job inventing planned obsolescence that I deserved to run the whole manufacturing operation."

"Don't you find it ironic, Festus? To be rewarded for making something so bad?"

"Well, sir, I did it extremely well. Besides, no insult intended, I just fabricated her. I wasn't the one who made the pithos filled with evil. The Boss did that himself and gave it to Pandora personally."

"Yes, I remember." Michael remembered a lot of things the Boss had done that didn't sit well with him.

Apparently sensing Michael's souring mood, Festus said brightly, "Well, sir, now that you're here, would you like a tour of the Factory?"

"I would. Lead on."

"The Factory is where we manufacture items for the use of angels and humans," Festus explained as they passed through the office area.

"What is it you make for angels?" Michael asked. He, like all the angels, had been created fully formed, robes, accouterments, and all. He realized he'd been wearing the same robes for so long now he never really gave them much thought. In fact, Michael didn't think he could actually take them off since the holes through which his wings protruded were too small to accommodate the full spread of his feathers. Certainly he could never get them back on. He could only thank the Boss that the fabric never seemed to stay dirty for long and that angels didn't get BO, or Heaven would be a pretty dingy, stinky place despite all the fresh air.

"Not much," Festus said. "Mostly we make stuff for the humans, but occasionally a requisition comes through for items like the walkie-talkies." He stopped in front of a door. "Here we are, sir."

Festus led Michael through the door and into a cavernous space filled with wheezing, clanking, and whirring equipment driven by pistons and large iron wheels as much as thirty feet in diameter. Clouds of steam billowed around the rafters before

105

being sucked out by exhaust fans in the upper walls. All around the open floor stood benches, tables, and various sorts of machinery, each attended by one or more Principalities.

"It's noisy," Michael commented.

"That's the nature of steam power," Festus said. "We use steam-powered machinery because water is the most abundant resource in a realm built on clouds. The main boiler room is in the Central Unit."

"What do you use for heat?" Michael asked. He knew there weren't forests, coal deposits, or oil fields in Heaven to provide combustible materials.

"That's really our dirty little secret," Festus said, looking a bit sheepish. "When the Boss created the Central Unit, he provided it with an eternal heat source. You'll see when we get there, but first, let me show you how we get things done."

He started across the floor toward the maze of tables and workbenches, and Michael followed, the hem of his robe brushing aside debris from the various manufacturing processes. Some of the Principalities were fabricating parts while others were busily assembling parts into products. Each Principality seemed to be making one object from start to finish, moving from one table or machine to another as he fashioned or added parts, and although everyone was working at a fast and furious pace, there didn't seem to be any real organization to the operation as a whole. The Principality at one table might be putting together a television, while the one at the machine next to him die-cut parts for an electric razor.

Michael and Festus maneuvered across the space and went through a large doorway into another space and across that into a third. Each was almost identical in function and confusion.

"It's all so chaotic," Michael commented. "Why don't you devote specific spaces to the manufacture of certain types of products? Also, it seems quite inefficient to make each item one at a time. We ought to be using assembly lines."

"You're quite right, sir, but you have to understand how the Factory operates and how it developed since its inception. In the Beginning, we had just one building. We call it the Central Unit now."

"That's the big, round stone structure I saw in the middle of all this?"

106

"That's it, sir. At the time, we only had cavemen up here, and their Heavenly Desires were pretty simple. We just had to make them a little flint they could chip and a few trees for them to fashion spears and clubs and cook their meat. But before long, people started to develop civilization, and the next thing we knew, we had to add a unit to manufacture pottery, woven clothing, and huts. Then we had to add a unit to make wooden buildings. Before we knew what was happening, people had spread all over the Earth. As each new civilization developed new things, we added units to accommodate incoming Residents who wanted what they'd had on Earth. You can see how big our operation is now, and we're still growing since things keep getting more and more complex on Earth and people want all kinds of new stuff. We're in the process of adding three units out on the periphery over there." He pointed meaninglessly.

"The other issue," Festus continued, "is that everyone seems to want something different, so we have to custom-make everything. That eliminates the possibility of assembly lines, but that's probably okay since, this being Heaven, we're required to employ craftsmanship instead of efficiency. I agree an assembly line might be more efficient, but it's also anti-craftsmanship at its worst. Speaking of craftsmanship, let me show you something."

They went through several workshops, each of varying states of sophistication, from pottery making to woodworking to metal fabrication. Finally they stepped into one in which Michael could see his breath, and frost formed on his wings. The room was so frigid that the steam clogging the air in the other parts of the Factory rapidly congealed into snow that drifted to the floor, where it collected into miniature glaciers snaking between the workbenches.

"This is the Freezer," Festus said. "We make all our ice products here."

The Principalities at the workbenches were busily carving the ice from the mini glaciers into various shapes. The most industrious were carving so fast their hands were blurs, and flying chips of ice completely obscured what they were making.

"Ice cubes," Festus explained. "By the hundreds of millions a day. Humans love cold drinks. We send the smaller chips over to Weather Control. They use them to make sleet and snow. And

107

those workers over there," he pointed to a group of Principalities who were carving much larger blocks of ice at a slower pace, "are making igloos."

"What about the ones there, past the igloo makers?" Michael pointed to a group of angels standing beside tall, crystal clear blocks of ice and carving more carefully than the igloo constructors.

"They're carving ice sculptures. They're the best carvers we have."

"Ice sculptures?"

"There's always a party somewhere in Heaven," Festus said. "And people don't half-ass parties in Heaven."

"I see what you mean by craftsmanship."

"Oh, we haven't gotten to the best part," Festus beamed. "But we're close."

Thankful to be out of the cold, which had now completely frozen his wing tips, Michael followed Festus through a couple of more rooms in a room where there was no steam at all and the wheezing and clanking from other parts of the Factory were dimmed to a distant murmur. Instead, the air was permeated with the scent of oil and acrylic paint, and easels were set up in long rows all across the floor. At each easel sat an artist, painting.

"They're all humans," Michael said. They were the only people he'd seen in the factory—or in any of the other utilities. Except for the Little Dutch Boy.

"That's right," Festus said. "Heaven to an artist is the freedom to create, so we give them the opportunity here, and their output supplies all of our need for art. People just love to have originals by famous artists."

"Why employ humans?" Michael asked. "Can't we have Principalities provide the output?"

"We could, but if angels did the painting, everything would be forgeries, and we can't have that. Anyway, this is what I meant by craftsmanship. Can you imagine these people working an assembly line?"

Michael couldn't.

"You only have painters?" he asked, and Festus shook his head. "This is just our painters studio. Nearby are other studios for sculptors, mosaicists, Native American sand painters, and

108

performance artists. We even have a darkroom for photographers and film artists. No digital editing suites, of course."

As they neared the first tier of easels, Michael recognized many of the artists. One of the first he saw was Leonardo da Vinci.

"Is it okay to watch them work?" he asked.

"Sure. They're usually so wrapped up in what they're doing they don't even notice you. Just don't block their light, or they'll throw a hissy fit."

Michael stepped up behind Leonardo and peered over his shoulder at the canvas. At first glance, Michael thought it was the *Mona Lisa*, but he quickly realized that while the pose, clothing, and background were the same as in the famous painting, the face was completely different. Then he noticed a photograph propped on the easel ledge. The face in the photograph was the one Leonardo was putting on the figure in the painting.

Festus must have sensed Michael's puzzlement, for he leaned close and whispered, "People in Heaven might want art by famous artists, but they also want to see themselves in the paintings. She," he indicated the photograph, "was the wife of an oil executive."

"How did she make it up here?" Michael asked. There were no oil executives in Heaven.

"She was a trophy bride. Too empty-headed to do anything really bad. She's commissioned more than two dozen portraits of herself by the likes of Rembrandt, Velázquez, Cézanne, and Picasso. They're all hanging in her mansion in Above and Beyond Meadows. She tried to get Frieda Kahlo to paint one, but," Festus shrugged, "Frieda only paints Frieda."

"I'd like to see my namesake work," Michael said. "Is he in the sculptors studio?"

"You mean Michelangelo? I believe he's back in the Freezer, working on an ice sculpture. Probably a copy of his *La Pietà*. It's a favorite up here. I'm sorry we didn't notice him when we were there. Do you want to go back?"

"No." Michael's wings were only now thawing, and he wasn't anxious to refreeze them. "I assume you have other sorts of artists, like writers and musicians."

"Our writers work in another area. Most of them produce adventure and romance novels commissioned by Residents with them as the protagonists. Seems like people never tire of reading about themselves. The musicians record in another area. We have to keep that part of the Factory soundproofed, though. It's quite a cacophony when several thousand of them solo all at once. Would you like to listen in?"

"No, let's go on to the Central Unit. I'm curious about it."

"Right this way."

Before long, they came to a square doorway in a massive wall constructed of roughly-hewn white limestone. The thick lintel supporting the tons of stone above it was blackened, as was the limestone for a good fifty feet above the opening.

"This is the entrance to the Central Unit," Festus said.

"Is that soot on the wall above the door?" Michael asked, unable to keep the disapproval out of his voice.

"Yes, sir. We've done our best to clean it off, but to no avail."

"Surely you can do something."

"We've tried everything from Tao Oven Cleaner to bleaching to power washing, but nothing seems to work. We considered sandblasting, but the stain would just come back, and we'd eventually wear away the entire wall."

"What's causing it?" Michael asked.

"It would be easier to show you, sir, than explain." Festus gestured to the doorway. "But I must warn you: It's quite uncomfortable inside."

Michael, contracting his wings so they wouldn't brush against the soot coating the edges of the doorway, followed Festus through. Festus was right: The space inside the Central Unit was uncomfortable. More than uncomfortable. It was an inferno.

Clouds of choking sulfurous smoke made it as hard to see as it was to breathe, and a tremendous roaring sound literally shook the seething air. Almost the entirety of the cavernous interior was occupied by a gigantic boiler beneath which hellish fires blazed and flared, while above, pipes of various sizes ran helter-skelter before piercing the walls of the dome to feed the different sections of the Factory.

"The Boss located the boiler room here," Festus said, leading Michael closer to the base of the boiler. "It's the most fireproof building in the Factory. Probably in all of Heaven."

110

As they neared, Michael suddenly realized that the fires heating the boiler didn't come from logs or coal or gas jets but from a gaping pit ringed with blackened stones. Around the edge of the pit stood a rank of Principalities, and as Michael craned over the shoulders of those nearest to him, he saw sheets of flame billowing from the pit. Riding the flames were thousands of Hell-spawned fire sprites who popped up and poked at the bottom of the boiler with pitchforks before falling back into the pit. Whenever one of the sprites got close to the rim of the pit, the nearest Principality beat it back with his scepter. It looked like the Principalities were keeping score.

As the waves of intense heat washed over Michael, he felt woozy. He wondered how the Principalities could stand it. Their wings were wilted and singed, and the hair beneath their askew crowns was plastered with sweat.

"Out!" Michael shouted over the roar of the flames as he waved vaguely in the direction he thought the door lay.

"Right, sir!"

Festus led Michael to the doorway, and Michael hurried through, not noticing that one of his wing tips brushed the lintel and picked up a smudge on its otherwise pristine whiteness.

"Are you seriously telling me we use the fires of Hell to power everything here?" Michael asked after he'd caught his breath and recovered his cool.

"Yes, sir. That's the way the Boss designed it."

"I don't see why we can't use some clean energy source like wind or solar power."

"We've thought of those, sir, but they're just not practical. We don't have anything but balmy breezes, and there's no sun, just this golden light, which isn't bright enough to activate solar panels. We thought of installing a nuclear reactor, but as it turns out, hellfire is more efficient, and there's no nuclear waste to dispose of. But the power source isn't really the problem."

"I don't see how anything could be worse," Michael said as he imagined all those hellfire sprites breaking loose and overrunning Heaven.

"There is, sir. It's our growing overpopulation. Humans can wish for anything—and they do—and with more and more of them coming in all the time, there are more and more desires to be filled."

"Are you suggesting we curtail admissions?"

"Not at all, sir. But demand is outpacing production. We can only work with what we have, and there just aren't enough angels here to get everything done. Our steam-powered equipment is obsolete and inefficient, and with the growth of our physical plant, the boiler in the Central Unit can't drive all the machinery at once, so we have rolling blackout and have to shut down sections periodically."

"What I don't understand is why we have to make anything," Michael said. "Can't the humans just wish up all this stuff?"

"They don't know how," Festus said. "People can operate cars and TVs and such, but hardly any of them know how anything actually works. Frankly, an average human wishing for a TV on his own will get something that looks like a TV, but inside, there's nothing but a scramble of random circuit boards and wiring. It takes an expert to make something right."

"I'm sure you have a solution."

"We have some ideas, though we'd still have to use Hell as our power source. There's no getting around that because that's the way the system is designed. But if we converted to hydroelectric, we could generate all the power we need. And with electric power, we could install robotic manufacturing equipment to take up the slack in production."

"Wouldn't hydroelectric generators and robotic manufacturing equipment require computerized controls?"

"Yes, sir, but we're fresh out of other ideas. And I can tell you one thing: If something isn't done soon, we won't be able to fulfill all the Heavenly Desires that come in. That doesn't make us look good."

"I'll take it up with the Boss," Michael promised. "But I'm sure you know what an administrative nightmare it is to requisition upgrades to his plan."

"I'd hate to be in your robes, sir. Is there anything else you'd like to see?"

"Yes," Michael said. "You can see me out."

112

❧ 11 ☙

AFTER WALKING FOR ALMOST AN hour, Bob saw a low, sprawling structure that looked like it could be a shopping mall. As he approached it, he spotted a colorful sign with the words "Empyrean Emporium" displayed in a pleasing font. It was a shopping mall. But he already suspected as much. When he was still a quarter of a mile away, he began to encounter people pushing shopping baskets loaded with merchandise away from entrances. It was like nearing a homeless encampment, but everyone was clean and dressed in sparkling white, and everything in their baskets was brand new.

The loaded shopping baskets puzzled him, though. He knew the people pushing them could wish for almost anything, and it would pop right into existence, so he couldn't figure out why anyone would cart a bunch of stuff around. Even the existence of the mall was curious in a place where all you had to do was state your wishes to have them come true, so he went in the nearest entrance to have a look.

At first glance, it looked like every mall he'd ever seen, except it was surely the cleanest. Dazzlingly clean. All the windows and fixtures literally sparkled. Just inside was an optician called Pearly Vision. It wasn't doing much business. Bob wasn't surprised since he couldn't imagine anyone wearing glasses if they didn't have to. He strode past it and a hair salon called Celestial Cuts, but he paused at Books by Jove and peered through the window at the offerings on display. He expected to see Bibles, Korans, and the Bhagavad Gita—and certainly the Tibetan Book of the Dead—but the glass display shelves held mostly romance novels and men's adventure thrillers, all with lurid covers. Being the hero or heroine was Heaven to a lot of people, he supposed, even if experienced vicariously.

Just beyond the displays, several people stood in front of a magazine rack, browsing through the wares. The man closest, who was dressed in what Bob took to be Heaven's version of camouflage overalls—various shades of light gray splotches on a white background—and a gimme cap bearing the words "Arcadia Tools" was reading a magazine titled *Happy Hunting Ground*. On the cover was a picture of the same man aiming a shotgun. Next to him, a woman in a broad-brimmed white straw hat perused a copy of *Gardener's Paradise*, whose cover showed her kneeling in a lush flower bed.

Bob moved on, into the mall's main concourse. Crowds of people moved up and down the long, wide corridor. Many were pushing shopping carts in and out of the doors, while some just strolled past the windows, eyeing the merchandise displayed within. Bob spotted a Principality at an information desk, and he went over.

"Excuse me," Bob said. "I'm new here, and I've never been to the mall before. Can you tell me what's going on?"

"Everyone is shopping, obviously," the angel said.

"I see that. But can't they just wish for whatever they want? Why do they come here?"

"I guess they don't know what they want until they see it," the angel said. "Or maybe it's just habit."

"How do they pay?" Bob asked. "I haven't seen any money in Heaven."

"They don't need money. They just grab what they want and take it."

Bob remembered that Wilbert the Greeter had called Heaven the best big-box store there was. A free big-box store, at that.

"They sure have a lot of stuff piled in those baskets. Do they really need it all?"

114

"I doubt it," the Principality said. "A lot of them are just hoarders. You see that woman over there?"

The Principality pointed to a woman emerging from a bedding store called Eternal Rest. She was pulling a flatbed cart laden with a mattress.

"She comes in here every day and gets another mattress. Either she's a princess with a pea under her mattress or she pees on her mattress every night." The angel waved toward a man coming out of Glory Goal Sporting Goods, located two doors down from Eternal Rest, whose basket was loaded with baseball equipment. "That guy must have every piece of sports equipment in triplicate, but as far as I know, he doesn't actually play anything."

"Somebody ought to open up a storage facility for them to keep all this stuff," Bob said, a dollar-sign balloon popping up in his brain.

"We have one," the angel said, popping Bob's balloon. "It's right next door to the mall so it's convenient for frequent shoppers. It's full, though, and they're building another."

At that moment, something whooshed by Bob and off down the hall. It was the most bizarre thing Bob had ever seen: a pair of bright blue wheels, one nested at right angles inside the other, both spinning furiously. Something was on the wheels, but Bob couldn't tell what because streaks were all he could see amid the wheels' hyperbolic rotations. Watching the thing made Bob dizzy, so he was glad when it spun off down the concourse and out of sight, leaving a swirling trail.

"What the heck was that?" Bob asked.

"Damn Holy Rollers," the Principality groused.

"Holy Roller?"

"Ophanim," the angel clarified. "They got no respect for anyone when they're racing around like that."

"Ah, yes," Bob said. "I never saw one before."

"Just be glad it was moving fast. They have so many eyes, it's like staring down a crowd. And they're extremely judgmental."

"I was thinking of getting new clothes," Bob said.

The angel leaned over the counter and looked down at Bob's black shoes and now-gray trousers.

"I never saw anybody here with dirt on them," the angel said, then his eyes, spotted the trail extending behind Bob. "Yeah, I think you'd better get some new clothes before you track up all the halls. Shangri-la Shoes is right down the hall there, on the left."

Shangri-la Shoes was located next to Divine Creations, a fashion outlet for transvestites and cross-dressers. Bob went in and found himself surrounded by racks of shoes in every style imaginable, from waraji to lumberjack boots. There were even sabots and mukluks. Nanookie, that sexy and sharp Inuit woman who'd showed Bob about the fountains and ambrosia trees, must have shopped here. One factor united all the styles: Every piece of footwear was snow white.

A Principality who was the store's clerk swished over to him. "May I assist you, sir?"

"I'm looking for a new pair of shoes."

"I can see that, sir," the angel said, staring at Bob's blackened footwear. His nose wrinkled slightly. "The men's section is right this way." The angel gestured. "Unless you've just come from the shop next door."

"No," Bob said. "The men's section is what I want."

"So do they," the angel said with a nellie chuckle, and he led Bob past dozens of racks holding a bewildering array of women's shoes. At the racks of men's footwear, a pair of wingtips immediately caught Bob's eye. He picked one up and turned it over in his hands. They'd look great after his soot darkened them up.

"I'll try a size 10."

"I'm sure these will fit perfectly," the angel said, taking the second wingtip off the rack and handing it to Bob.

Bob was skeptical, but the angel seemed sure of himself, so Bob said, "Is there a bench where I can sit to try them on?"

"Right behind you, sir."

A shelf of darker cloudstuff conveniently materialized behind Bob, and he sat, took off his soiled shoes, and slipped into the wingtips. A few tentative steps told him the angel was right. They were the most comfortable shoes he'd ever worn. Although they looked brand new, they felt completely broken in.

"Great," he said. "I'll take them."

"Of course you will, sir." The angel glanced at Bob's discarded shoes with distaste. "I assume you'll be leaving those."

116

"I only have two feet. Now if you can direct me to a clothing store."

"Celestial Suits is right down the hall. I'm sure they'll have clothing appropriate to a man of your stature."

As Bob started that way, the mellow, ambient voice intoned, "Remember: Behave heavenly. It's the right thing to do."

Since everybody else appeared to ignore the voice, Bob did, too. A few moments later, he found the clothing store and went in. A clerk angel came up to him.

"I see by your shoes that you're in the market for a three-piece suit," the angel said.

"I am," Bob replied. "Your best."

The angel gave him a reproving stare.

"We only offer the best at Celestial Suits, sir."

He led Bob to a rack where a single white three-piece suit hung. "Not much of a selection," Bob said, skeptically eyeing the suit. "And I never buy suits off the rack."

Ignoring him, the angel plucked up the suit and held it out for Bob to see.

"I urge you to try it on. It will look perfect on you."

"Aren't you going to measure me?" Bob asked.

"Rock of Eye," the angel said confidently, referring to the ability of a tailor to visually assess a client's build more accurately and artistically than any tape measure could. "We never have to make alterations."

Bob took the suit and scanned the workmanship. It was fashioned from a white worsted wool with the faintest hint of gray pinstripes. The single-breasted jacket had three buttons to fasten the front and four buttons at each sleeve cuff, but best of all was the peaked lapel, which gave it a rakish look.

"It's completely silk-lined with a floating canvas," the angel said. "Would you like to try it on?"

"Sure," Bob said. "Where's the dressing room?"

In answer, the angel gestured around Bob's feet, and the mists began to swirl and climb upward. Before they completely enclosed Bob in a closet-sized space, the angel handed him a white shirt and a light gray tie.

The closet had a bench similar to the one Bob sat on in the shoe store. He quickly took off his old clothes, donned the

117

shirt, pulled on the cuffed and pleated suit trousers, and fastened them in place with a set of light gray braces. He gave the braces a sharp snap then sat to put his shoes back on. Standing, he reached for the tie. There wasn't a mirror, and he was a little worried he'd have trouble getting the knot right, but his fingers twiddled magically, and it slipped perfectly into place. Bob put on the vest and shrugged into the jacket and buttoned the top two buttons.

"I'm done," he called out. Any self-doubt he might have had vanished with suddenly dissipating mist closet.

"You look absolutely fabulous, sir," the angel said in a bored tone.

"Is there a mirror?" Bob asked, setting his old clothes on the counter.

"Mirror, sir? Surely you know mirrors aren't permitted in Heaven."

"No, I didn't realize." Now that Bob thought about it, he hadn't seen a single mirror since arriving here. "Why's that?"

"Mirrors give a false impression by encouraging the viewer to believe that the image is how others perceive him," the angel explained. "But a mirror image is second-hand, and not only that, it is self-referential, reversed, and without dimensionality. And worst of all, humans usually put on their best face for a mirror, which they rarely do for other people."

"You're right about the suit," Bob said, staring down at himself and trying to imagine what he looked like. "It fits perfectly and has an excellent cut."

"As I said, sir, we offer nothing but the best. Will you be taking it?"

"I will. What about those?" Bob indicated his old clothes.

"We'll be happy to discard those for you. But you mustn't forget this, sir."

The angel fiddled with Bob's former shirt then straightened, Bob's Visitor badge in his hand. He pinned it to Bob's lapel and said, "And now, sir, accessories?"

Soon after, Bob emerged from Celestial Suits, a properly folded handkerchief protruding from the front pocket of his suit jacket. Feeling exhilarated and transformed, he strode jauntily down the concourse. His attire had given him a new lease on death, and he intended to make it count. Time to wheel and deal. But first he needed some perspective, and to get that, he had to find his way out of this mall. He saw an exit sign at the end of the hall, which now wasn't far off, and he headed toward it.

He emerged from the mall and stared across the cloudscape. The view to his right was blocked by a monumental square building without windows. A sign above the entrance proclaimed, "Perpetual Storage." Someone had hand-painted "#1" on the sign. It was the place hoarders stored their trash and treasure. Right next to it, a similar building was being erected, and a sign in front of the construction site proclaimed, "Future Home of Perpetual Storage #2."

Bob watched a gang of Principalities, mightily flapping their wings, hoist a large I-beam to the top and set it in place, while a steady stream of others flew up with buckets of cement. The sight of the new building going up made Bob realize that Heaven was not without its opportunities, and he was determined to become part of that growth. Heaven had everything anybody could want, so the only real question was: How could Bob take advantage of the situation and get everything he wanted?

He knew there would be little chance to worm his way into the angel hierarchy. It had been established millennia ago and was already controlled by what amounted to the ultimate union. He didn't want to work that hard, anyway, and besides, he was no angel.

Another possibility was to become a successful middleman and reap profits off the efforts of others. But in order to do that, one either has to insert oneself into an existing process or invent a new one and get everybody else to do all the work, and how could he become a successful middleman in a place where everyone's desires were automatically fulfilled? He'd just come out of a free mall, hammering home the fact that the manufacture and distribution of goods and services in Heaven was all locked in. What could he offer to people who had everything? The answer was, nothing.

Bob recalled Sherlock Holmes' theory that when you have eliminated the impossible, whatever remains, however improbable, must be the truth. For Bob, what remained was all the people who didn't have everything.

119

In the far distance—the very, very far distance—crepuscular rays flickered and shone, and as Bob stared at them reflectively, a scheme began to form in his mind. The scheme was similar to what he'd tried in Hell, but the problem there, he realized, was he'd been forced to confine his clientele to its infernal inmates. After all, who would visit that place if they didn't have to? This time, he'd go for a wider reach: Earth.

Earth was full of people who didn't have everything. Didn't have much at all, in fact, except toil and despair. The implications were boggling. What if he could set up the ultimate vacation resort and bring people from Earth to Heaven for a week or two? He could call it Holy Holidays and would offer a complete package, from the best accommodations to exquisite dining, enlightening recreation, and sight-seeing.

He'd have to establish an organization, complete with a staff, and that might prove difficult since he wasn't allowed Heavenly Desires. He thought about asking the angels for help, but he didn't think they'd pitch in. They all seemed too busy, anyway.

Then he had it. The people already in Heaven could be his staff. They could act as hosts and hostesses, giving them something to do to relieve the utter boredom of Heaven and distract them from an eternity of the same old same. And themselves. The Boss would be the nominal CEO, of course, but Bob would design and operate the business for a fat share of the profits.

Surely the powers that be in Heaven would see the wisdom of the idea. If people on Earth got to experience what a great place Heaven was, they'd do everything they could to live here permanently when they died. It would be good business for Heaven and wreak havoc on the Devil's bottom line. Bob would immediately rise in rank, and maybe he could even gain permanent Resident status and start conjuring up a few of his own Heavenly Desires.

But where to start? Certainly he'd have to get permission to set up a travel agency and vacation resort. That meant he needed to talk to an angel—and not one of those lowly Principalities. He needed someone with higher authority—undoubtedly those Archangels he'd heard about.

First, though, he needed more tangible features to offer prospective clients. So far, his meanderings had shown food and drink in abundance, but he had yet to see anything that provided recreation or that was worth looking at long enough to qualify as a place to sightsee. But he was determined to find them.

Suffused with purpose, Bob strode out across the cloudscape, his new white wingtips kicking through the mists, soot trailing behind.

❧ 12 ☙

"WHAT THE HECK IS THAT?" Michael muttered out loud.

He'd just emerged from a clump of cumulus fractus, which he'd entered in a futile effort to soak off the smudge of soot marring his wing tip ever since he'd brushed against the edge of the doorway in the Factory's Central Unit. Seeing it was still there as he flew out of the cloud, he shrugged and began to fly toward the Farm when he spotted a dark gray line angling across the cloudscape below.

"Graffiti," he snorted.

Someone must have wished for a can of black spray paint. Or, he revised, seeing the line go out of sight in both directions, several cases of spray paint.

Swooping down for a closer look, he saw that the gray line looked a lot more like the smudge on his wing tip than it did spray paint. And it showed as little inclination to dissipate. As curious as he was irked at what had caused this besmirchment, he was of half a mind to follow the line and find out, but he quickly realized he had no idea which direction the line had come from or which direction it was going. He could spend a lot of time chasing something that was getting farther and farther away, or he could continue on toward the Farm.

He decided on the latter course. When he got back to his office, he'd dispatch someone to find out who had drawn the gray line and have it cleaned up. Besides, he was getting tired, and he wanted to finish the inspections and return to the sanctuary of his office where he could rest his wing muscles, which were, by now, pretty sore. He hadn't flown this far in one fell swoop since that unfortunate trip to France.

Eventually the Farm came into view—or, at least, Michael assumed it was the Farm since he'd flown in the correct direction. But the place didn't look like the farm Michael remembered from his last trip. At the time, there'd been a white clapboard farmhouse flanked by a big white barn and silo, all surrounded by fields of young ambrosia trees and pastures with grazing animals.

The farmhouse was still there, but the barn and silo were gone, and the farmhouse was dwarfed and surrounded by half a dozen industrial-size metal buildings. Pipes coming to and from the Water Treatment and Purification Plant entered one of the buildings, and from there, smaller pipes ran to most of the other structures, but he couldn't see any fields where they might be growing seedling ambrosia trees. Nor did he spot any animals, though a faint odor of dung hung in the air.

The farmhouse seemed the logical place to start, so he descended and landed in front of the porch, which extended the width of the house. Almost immediately, the front screen door banged open and a Dominion emerged, dressed in white denim robes cut to resemble overalls. Instead of a scepter with a glowing orb or a sword, he carried a pitchfork with glowing tines.

"What an honor, sir," the Dominion said. "I'm George, head farmer. I heard you were inspecting the facilities, so I've been watching for you. Welcome to the Farm."

"Thank you, George. Yes, I've been making the rounds."

"Is there a particular problem, sir?"

"Just refreshing my knowledge and assessing capabilities," Michael said in a reassuring voice. "I'm surprised, though. It doesn't look the same as when I was last here. What happened to the barn and the crops and animals?"

"We haven't operated like that in a long time," George said. "Back when the demand wasn't so great, we could afford to farm the old way. But the barn's been gone for four or five hundred Earth years. We tore it down and built our pump house on

124

its site." He pointed to the large metal building where the pipes from the Water Treatment and Purification Plant terminated.

"So you're doing hydroponic farming in the other buildings?" Michael asked.

"No, sir. These days, we're fully automated."

"I don't follow."

"It would be easier to show you than explain." George started off toward the pump house, and Michael followed.

"This is where we distribute the sludge and water that are piped in from the Water Treatment and Purification Plant," George said, waving at the tremendous tanks and pumps dominating the interior of the building.

"I guess you use the sludge to fertilize the seedling ambrosia trees and the water to irrigate them and hydrate the animals."

"Not exactly." George looked embarrassed. "As I said, demand for our produce is way up—beyond our ability to satisfy it if we didn't take some cost-cutting measures. First, we no longer maintain animals except for a few specialty items. All the food is supplied by the ambrosia trees, so it's pointless to produce real meat and dairy products. People seem to prefer the ambrosia to the real thing, anyway. I guess it's because they're getting what they expect, and they don't have to cook. We need real animals in only a few places, such as Sector 1, where the cavemen live. They still like to kill and cook their own game. We also breed horses to pull the Amish buggies." He led Michael back outside. "All the animals are housed in that building over there." He pointed to one of the huge metal buildings surrounding the dwarfed farmhouse.

"I can understand that," Michael said. "But what about the sludge? If you don't use it to fertilize the ambrosia trees, what *do* you use it for? And where are you growing the ambrosia seedlings?"

"If you'll come with me this way, sir, I'll show you."

George took Michael to one of the other buildings, and when they entered, Michael thought for a moment that he'd been transported back to the Factory. The hanger-size room contained an assembly line whose machinery was operated by a steam engine that sat in the far corner. Thankfully, it was small enough to be powered by thousands of prayer candles ranked beneath the boiler. One source of hellfire in Heaven was more

125

than enough. The clatter of the equipment drew his attention for a moment, but then he focused on the assembly line itself and was shocked to see crews of Principalities busily manufacturing ambrosia trees.

The limbs were fabricated in one area, where Principalities enclosed bundles of tiny PVC pipes in rubber bark. The limbs were then sent on conveyor belts that carried them past more angels, who attached the limbs to rubber-barked trunks containing larger pipes that protruded like roots from the bottoms of the trunks. The final step was to enclose the root piping in a protective crate. At the end of the assembly line stood a queue of flat carts pulled by horses. After each tree was crated, the assembly line conveyor dumped it into the first cart in line, which was immediately driven out a large door, only to be replaced by the next cart. Apparently the horses were responsible for the dung odor since no other animals were visible.

"We train all the Amish buggy horses here before we deliver them," George explained when he saw Michael staring at the horses.

"You mean to tell me ambrosia trees aren't really trees at all but plumbing fixtures?"

"Yes, sir. It's much more efficient. We used to grow them, but it takes a real ambrosia tree a decade to mature and weeks to produce each fruit. With the uptick in demand, the natural ones just couldn't keep pace, so we've been using a different strategy. We don't have to grow fields of seedlings to replace dead or damaged trees, and we no longer have to employ arborists to deal with sick or aging trees or do regular pruning. We still call our technicians arborists, but they're actually certified plumbers. When a tree malfunctions, we just send out a crew with a new one to replace it. We also install new trees every time a new sector opens up or when the population of an existing sector exceeds the capacity of trees already on-site. For the former, we run new pipes, and with the latter, we just tap into old lines nearby."

"But how do they work?" Michael gestured to the trees coming off the end of the assembly line.

"What you see being manufactured is the Ambrosia Deluxe Mark 6. Its trunk holds hundreds of tubules to carry the ambrosia mash up into the branches, and each branch has two dozen nodules that exude a special membrane that becomes the

126

skin of the ambrosia fruit. The ambrosia mash is pumped through the pipes and into the membrane, which blows up to a certain diameter. You could say an ambrosia tree is like an elaborate water balloon maker. When someone picks the fruit, the membrane instantly seals over, and the next fruit is inflated in about two minutes. Our chemists are working to improve the membrane formula so we can make a new fruit in just seconds."

"I see how it might be more efficient," Michael nodded. "But does the fruit taste as good?"

"Taste is all in the perception of the eater, just like everything in Heaven," George said. "The fruit of the real ambrosia trees was just pulpy goop without any real flavor—to us angels, that is. But if a human thinks he's eating the best fajitas he ever ate, then they are the best. I don't think any of the humans even realize we've gone to the new technology."

"You might be wrong about that," Michael said. "I've heard complaints that the ambrosias in the western sectors taste bland."

"That's been our area of greatest growth," George said a trifle defensively. "We have a lot of new piping in there. It could be the PVC is responsible, or maybe all the splitting and dividing is diluting the flavor."

"Well, find out what the problem is, and fix it," Michael ordered. "Sooner than later. We can't have quality slipping in Heaven."

"No, sir."

"How do you make this ambrosia mash you're talking about if you don't have any crops?"

"That's the beauty of the plan and where our real cost-savings come in," George said. "Let's go over to the Inflation Center.

The Inflation Center was located in the next metal building, and when George opened the door and ushered Michael inside, the Archangel was assaulted by a horrendous odor that hit him like an oppressive weight.

"Holy crap!" he said before he could catch himself. "What is that stench?"

"Holy crap, sir. We've been having trouble with one of our pumps, and I'm afraid we've had a small spill."

George waved toward the right, where an enormous pipe came into the building and emptied into a gigantic vat, which in turn had dozens of smaller pipes attached to pumps. Beneath

127

the juncture of one of these smaller pipes and a pump lay a morass of thick, grey-brown liquid. "We'll get it cleaned up, and the pump will be back online as soon as new parts arrive."

Michael recognized the enormous pipe that fed the vat as the one that carried sludge from the pump house next door. He traced the smaller pipes as they branched through the air into smaller and smaller pipes that finally descended to thousands and thousands of work stations laid out in a tight grid on the floor of the cavernous building. A Principality sat at each work station, which consisted of a control panel crowded with gauges, levers, and knobs.

George led him over to the nearest work station.

"This is how we distribute the ambrosia mash to the trees," George said. "Each mash monitoring station controls the flow to a particular tree, and the gauges give the pressure for each fruit as it inflates. If there's a problem, one of our soda jerks can manually adjust the flow."

"Soda jerks?"

"Sorry, sir. A bit of in-house slang. That's what we call the Principalities who monitor the flow of mash."

"And the mash is...?" Michael stared at the gigantic vat fed by the influx of sludge and crowned by the capillary pipes feeding sludge to each mash monitor.

"The sludge we pipe in from the Water Treatment and Purification Plant. As I said, sir, that's the beauty of our operation. You can't imagine how much we've saved in angel-hours with this method. Plus, we're doing something useful with the sludge by recycling it."

"Into food?" Michael was surprised there hadn't been complaints about the ambrosia *everywhere* in Heaven, but not for its blandness.

"It's loaded with vitamins and minerals," George said. "And as I said, taste is all in the perception of the eater. We could start with caviar or mayonnaise, and it would still taste like Cheetos if that's what the person wants to eat. Why bother trying to do anything different with it?"

As Michael prayed nobody would ask for an ambrosia fruit that actually tasted like ambrosia, he noticed that one soda jerk in the next aisle seemed to be overwhelmed. He was frantically flipping levers and twisting knobs in a blur of motion.

128

"Is there something wrong with that soda jerk's tree?" he asked.

"No, sir. His monitor feeds a tree that regularly hosts a gourmand club. They must be feasting at the moment."

By now, Michael'd had enough of the odor assaulting his nostrils. "Anything else you'd like to show me?" he asked.

"Perhaps you'd care to visit the Nursery." George said.

"As long as it's in a different building." Michael wondered what they were growing in the Nursery if the ambrosia trees were all manufactured.

George took him outside and over to an adjacent building. As they approached its door, Michael heard faint but definite high-pitched wailings coming from inside.

"This is the Nursery," George said.

"Do I hear crying?" Michael asked.

"Yes, sir."

"You have plants that cry?"

"It's not that kind of nursery," George said.

He opened the door, and Michael's ears were assaulted by the voices of a multitude of babies babbling, cooing, and bawling. The babies were lying in mangers arrayed beneath the fruit-laden branches of thousands of ambrosia trees.

"What is this?" Michael was baffled.

"Babies, sir."

"I see that. But why are they here?"

"No place else for them to go," George said. "These infants arrived here too young to realize they can use their Heavenly Desire to grow up. All they know is hunger, and since their only Heavenly Desire is breast milk, we developed special ambrosia trees to take care of their one desire. We keep the babies here where we can monitor the trees and keep them in top working condition. It's the most convenient solution. After all, sir, we can't have hungry crying babies crawling all through Heaven's clouds, tripping people and generally making a nuisance of themselves."

Michael stepped close to the first ambrosia tree and stared at the babies beneath its drooping branches. Some were goo-gooing, some were staring around, beatific smiles on their cherubic faces, and some had faces working themselves into peevish expressions.

129

Michael watched as one of the latter suddenly wailed and burst into tears. Its little arms flailed the air, and almost instantly, its fingers brushed an ambrosia fruit pending like a large globule right over its crèche. The baby grabbed the fruit and dragged it toward its mouth, and only then did Michael notice that the fruit wasn't a typical ambrosia but looked like a breast. In fact, all the fruits on the trees were breasts. The baby's cries choked off as it popped the nipple between its lips and began to suckle.

"I think it's wise to keep this operation here—and under wraps," Michael said. "This may be Heaven, but these trees are a little too risqué for public consumption."

"That's what we thought, sir."

Staring at the thousands of pendulous breasts and bawling babies, Michael realized he'd had enough for now. He thanked George for showing him around, but before he left, he asked the Dominion if he needed anything to make his job more efficient.

"Video surveillance," George said. "We'd like to mount a surveillance camera on each tree in Sector 1."

"What for?" Michael couldn't imagine why George would need to watch the cavemen.

"The trees keep disappearing," George explained. "Someone's taking them down as fast as we put them up. Usually when a tree malfunctions, we bring it back here for refurbishing, but whoever is taking the trees in Sector 1 isn't leaving anything. We don't know what's happening, but we need to find the culprit and put a stop to it."

"Sorry," Michael said. "Video equipment isn't allowed. You'll have to post guards."

With that, he heaved himself into the air on tired wings and flapped off.

130

13

BOB DECIDED THE BEST PLACE to begin was at the beginning: Sector 1, home of the cavemen. He knew he had a long walk ahead of him, so he wanted to fortify himself with a drink before he set out. He spotted a fountain about half a mile away, surrounded by a group of people, so he headed toward it. As he approached, he saw they weren't people but angels.

One was definitely a Dominion, identified by the spheres of light attached to his scepter and sword pommel. The others were Virtues and Powers, the latter wearing gold cuirasses below which swung huge claymores. They were gathered around the fountain, facing its many tiered bowls, standing stock still.

Apparently even angels needed to drink occasionally. Bob wondered what angels might choose to fill their golden chalices, but he was more interested in asking them where he could find the Archangels and for the quickest route to Sector 1.

As he neared the group, he heard one of the Powers say in a grousing tone, "I'll miss Sector P. It's close to work, and I'm going to hate commuting farther every time I get the urge."

"It wouldn't hurt you to fly a little farther, Boris," the Dominion said. "You could use the exercise."

"Yeah," chimed in one of the Virtues. "In your shape, you don't want to piss anybody off."

The rest of the angels burst out laughing.

"Excuse me!" Bob called out. "I need some directions."

The Virtue who'd last spoken glanced over his shoulder at Bob. The nasty grin on his face evaporated as he saw the human approaching, and he quickly muttered something to his companions, all of whom cast furtive glances at Bob. Then suddenly, they all took to the sky in such a rush that the downdraft from their wings caused the cloud carpet to swirl and eddy.

"Hey!" Bob yelled, running after them. "Come back here!"

To no avail. In moments, the angels were specks vanishing in the golden haze.

"Bastards," Bob panted as he stumbled to a halt. "You wouldn't dare do that to me if I was a Resident."

Determined to report the angels for dereliction of duty the first chance he got, he slogged to the fountain through the mists raised by their hasty departure.

"Dalmore 64 Trinitas," he ordered. A golden goblet flashed in his hand, and he dipped it and took a big swallow. Maybe it was the way he'd run, or maybe his ire at the now-vanished angels had tainted his tongue, but the whiskey had a bit of a burn going down. He gulped the remaining amber liquid, cast the goblet aside, and stared around.

Where are those fucking cavemen? he wondered. Logically, Sector 1 ought to be located right next to the Pearly Gates, but Bob had been in that vicinity, and he hadn't seen anything like a living, life-size museum diorama of caveman anywhere around there. Heaven's layout didn't strike Bob as being all that logical, anyway. How the heck could anybody find anything in a place shrouded in mists, lit by hazy golden light, and completely lacking in cardinal directions?

It didn't appear to matter to the Residents, who all seemed to have a Google Heaven app implanted in their brains. Only Bob was directionless. Damn it! It wasn't fair. What he really needed was one of those "You Are Here" signs like they had in malls, zoos, and amusement parks. If Bob could get the angel administration to agree to his tourist plans, surely they'd see the wisdom of the tourists being able to find their way from sight to sight.

But that didn't help him right now, because at the moment, he was lost. He scanned around, seeing not much of anything he hadn't already seen up here before. Heaven was like a fucking maze without walls. He needed one of those way-finding signs, and he needed it right here and right now!

A tiny clap of thunder nearly made him jump from his already darkening shoes as a metal-framed panel about seven feet tall and three feet wide suddenly jutted out of the clouds about five feet in front of him. The panel's face was completely white except for a small red cross in the center with the words "You Are Here" beneath it.

Bob stared at the way-finding sign for a moment. As delighted as he was to see it, he realized the trick would take a little practice.

"I know where I am," he said sarcastically. "I needed to find something."

In an instant, the face of the sign was almost blackened with icons, words, and lines. Bob sighed heavily. This was as bad as trying to find obscure information using Google.

"Show me the way to Sector 1," he said.

The multitude of symbols, words, and lines on the sign vanished and were replaced by a small rectangle shape in the upper left quadrant of the map. A single black line connected the rectangle and the red cross. Bob looked in the direction the map indicated and could barely see the ridge of a distant cloud bank wavering darkly through the golden haze. The cloud bank was a long way off, but that didn't worry Bob now that he'd discovered he could call up a sign easier than using the map app on his iPhone back on Earth. Turning his face in the direction of the cloud bank, he began to walk.

After about half an hour, Bob noticed a blue-green flash out of the corner of his eye, and he turned to see the bizarre sight of an Ophanim rolling across the cloudscape. Its inner wheel was rotating at right angles to the outer, driving wheel. Bob guessed it served like a gyroscope to keep the thing balanced, but he couldn't figure out how the thing didn't get completely dizzy with those hundreds of eyes he'd heard about all rotating in different directions at the same time.

Bob was too far away to catch the thing's attention by shouting, so he waved his hands frantically as he ran toward it. Though the thing had hundreds of eyes, apparently all the spinning movement prevented it from being able to actually focus on anything. The Ophanim was about to roll on past, oblivious to Bob's signals, when Bob had an idea. He fastened his attention on a patch of cloudscape just in front of the speeding Ophanim.

"I need a way-finding sign right there."

With a thick, rubbery thump, the Ophanim smacked into the way-finding sign that abruptly appeared in its path. It bounced back a dozen feet, its inner wheel pivoted into alignment with the outer one, and it fell over on its side, half obscured by the swirling mists kicked up by its fall.

Bob dashed to the Ophanim and bent over it. It's hundreds of eyes were all rolling around like the thing was dazed, and the orbits around the eyes that had been on the leading edge of the outer wheel when it collided with the sign were beginning to darken perceptibly.

"Can I help you?" Bob asked solicitously.

"I've fallen, and I can't get up," the angel said in a weak voice.

"You're going to have forty or fifty shiners for a while," Bob commented as he grasped the edge of the outer wheel, being careful not to jab a finger into any of the eyes. He heaved the Ophanim back onto its circumference, and it wavered a little when he let go, but it didn't topple. By now, some of its eyes were coming back into focus, and it used a few dozen of them to peer at the way-finding sign.

"What's that thing?" it asked in a puzzled voice. "Where did it come from? It wasn't there a second ago."

"I have no idea," Bob said. "But now that I have you, let me ask you a question."

The Ophanim shifted the gaze of about three dozen eyes to Bob, and some of them glared suspiciously. It was pretty disconcerting, and Bob couldn't help but wonder how the thing could process all those visual images into anything coherent. Maybe it was seeing three dozen Bobs all at the same time.

"What do you want to know?"

"If someone wants to set up a business here in Heaven, is there a particular office for that sort of thing? Or someone I can talk to?"

134

"No office," the Ophanim replied as it spun its inner wheel perpendicular to the outer one and tested its rotation. It clattered a bit lopsidedly for a moment like it was out of balance before settling into a steady whir. "As far as I know, there's never been any other business here besides Heaven's business. Anyway, a proposition like that would have to be approved at the highest levels. You'd have to talk to Michael."

"One of the Archangels?"

"The highest Archangel," the Ophanim said. "He's the only one who can authorize changes around here."

"Must make him pretty important," Bob mused.

"Maybe, but it keeps him pretty busy. Usually he's in the Administration Building, but I heard he's been inspecting the utilities. If he is, it might be hard to catch up to him."

"As you can see," Bob pointed to his Visitor badge, "I'm new here. I thought I might take in some sights, but I can't figure out what they might be. Any suggestions?"

"Well," the Ophanim rolled a few dozen eyes thoughtfully, "there's the Garden of Eden, of course. That's near the Historic District. And there's Psalm Beach."

"I didn't know there's a beach in Heaven."

"It's on the shore of the Holy Sea. Then there's our sports stadium, Elysium Field."

"I've heard of that. What do they play there?"

"Everything, and everyone wins," the Ophanim said. "Also, you might try the Viking Sector, but be careful. They're pretty warlike, and they like to chop people up since that's their notion of Valhalla."

"Sounds painful."

"I suppose it might hurt some, but you'll reconstitute."

"Is there a zoo?" Bob asked, trying to get back to more traditional entertainment. There might be some freaks who'd rather be hacked apart by Vikings than catered to by angels and dead loved ones, but he didn't want them on his vacation tours.

"Not one with cages, though a lot of wild animals roam around Sector 1."

"I was on my way there, now," Bob said. "Are the cavemen dangerous like the Vikings?"

135

"They can get kind of pugnacious if they think you're acting condescending toward them."

"How about an art museum?"

"Not one of those, either. Art lovers can just wish up any work by any artist they want and hang it on their walls." Abruptly, the Ophanim swiveled almost all its eyes to peer judiciously at Bob. "Are you gay?"

"I thought that didn't matter in Heaven."

"Not technically, but it might aesthetically. If you're gay, you might want to skip Virginia."

"I thought Virginia was back on Earth. It's nice enough but certainly not heavenly."

"We just call it Virginia," the Ophanim said. "You know how all those suicide bombers are promised their own harem in Paradise, complete with seventy-two beautiful virgins, if they slaughter and maim dozens or hundreds of innocent victims?"

Bob nodded.

"Well, Virginia is where we keep all the harems."

"I heard Virginia is for lovers, but you can't really mean suicide bombers are actually rewarded in Heaven."

"Do you think we want suicide bombers running around here?" the Ophanim asked. "They might start blowing shit up. We call it Virginia because there are thousands of harems, but not a single suicide bomber has made it up here, so all the women are still pure. Listen, it's been nice chatting but I'm running late, and I gotta make tracks. Anything else you need?"

"Only one more question: How do you see anything or keep from getting dizzy when you're rolling around?"

"If you get any good ideas on that, let me know."

Spurting a rooster tail of mists, the Ophanim peeled out and sped away across the cloudscape.

Bob watched the angel recede in the distance, then he turned to the way-finding sign and said, "Show me the way to Sector 1."

A new line appeared on the map. Bob intoned the names of the other places the Ophanim had named, and they appeared. Freshly oriented, Bob turned in the direction indicated for Sector 1, which also would take him through the Historic District, and started walking.

136

It wasn't long before the walking got harder. For some reason, the cloud carpet here wafted much higher than anywhere else Bob had been. Over most of Heaven, it seemed to hover a little more than ankle deep, and after Bob got used the slight drag, he had no problem walking. Here, though, the mists floated thigh-high, and some gossamers reached fingers as high as his waist. It was like wading through tall weeds.

Pushing down thoughts of his time in Hell's lake of boiling shit, which had reached a similar height, Bob reflected that not all of Heaven was as neatly manicured as advertised. How long since Heaven's lawn service had spent any time around here?

Bob pressed on, but about five minutes later, a jolting shock nearly brought him to his knees, and a stab of hot neurons flared in his shin. He'd tripped over something buried in the tall mists and cracked his shin to boot. Bending over and wafting away the mists, he saw the offending object was an irregular block of marble.

He straightened, stepped around the block, and went on, but not a minute later his foot kicked something else. Thank goodness it was lighter-weight than the block of marble, but whatever it was, it skittered off beneath the mists, out of Bob's reach. For quite a while after that, his progress was impeded by junk of all sorts, from pieces of buildings to clothing to housewares to human waste. The one trait everything had in common was age. Nothing appeared to be newer than about two thousand years old. Even the shit had turned into coprolites.

This must be the outskirts of the Historic District, he thought.

Tired from slogging through the high mists, Bob stopped to sit on a stone block to rest. He was rubbing his bruised shin when a small turbaned head popped up from the clouds beside him. The head was followed by a scrawny brown body dressed in a white loincloth.

"Spare change, kind sahib?" the boy implored, holding out his hand.

More scrawny little bodies popped up, some boys, some girls, all dressed in the ragged clothing worn by poverty-stricken children everywhere, but all impeccably white. The kid in front of Bob looked Indian, but the children appeared to have come from all over the world.

137

"Sorry," Bob said. "No pennies from Heaven here. I'm as broke as you are."

Disappointed but resigned, most of the children moved off through the mists, bending over occasionally to examine what they stumbled upon.

"What are you kids doing out here all alone?" Bob asked the Indian boy.

"What we did on Earth," the boy said. "We were all orphans, and a lot of us lived off what we could find on the streets or in trash dumps of Third-World cities. That's why we hang out in the Historic District. Lots of trash all around, but most of it's old, worthless crap."

"I've seen. But why? It's all so neat everywhere else."

"When they first set up Heaven, almost everybody wanted to live around Eden, so that area quickly became overpopulated. Finally, with the neighborhood going downhill, most people moved over to this area, which became the Historic District. It was a boom town, and things were hopping for a long time, but in the end, obsolescence and overcrowding made everybody move again, this time to the more modern eras. Each time they moved, they just dumped what they had and left. I guess all the trash overloaded the trash cleaning magic because most of it around here doesn't sink and disappear."

"But where do you live?"

"In some ruins over that way," the boy pointed. "The angels say we look like a bunch of monkeys crawling over Ankor Wat and give the place character."

Bob bid the boy adieu and headed into the Historic District proper. The scattered blocks gave way to an area consisting of numerous religious buildings and monuments from throughout humankind's history—everything from tiny shrines to major cathedrals to country churches.

Bob walked around, perusing the buildings surrounding him. Like their human makers, when they'd crumbled into disrepair and were lost to the ravages of time, they'd been transported here. The odd thing was that unlike their human counterparts, not all such structures had entirely vanished from the Earth but had left pieces behind. Often the buildings were missing some of their elements: a few stone blocks or boards here

138

and there or frescoes and statues that must now reside in museums or private collections on Earth. Bob even saw one completely unidentifiable structure consisting of little more than scattered pieces of rock floating disconnected in the air, though it looked like it had been pretty large.

He wondered why modern buildings hadn't made it up here, too. Maybe it was because these ancient monuments had taken the sweat and blood of countless souls to erect, while modern structures were built up and torn down in short order all the time. Or, all too frequently, bombed into oblivion during wars.

He called up a way-finding sign and said, "Show me what that building is," and was informed it was the Parthenon, which he knew was mostly intact on Earth.

One of the most impressive sights was the Egyptian Pyramids. On Earth, vandals and scavengers had removed nearly all of the bright white limestone that once sheathed their sides and the gold caps that had crowned their heads. By now, it seemed, most of the limestone was long reduced to dust, because here, all three pyramids were resurrected in almost their full glory. When Bob approached for a closer inspection, though, he discovered they were completely hollow.

He wondered if he could send a demolition team down to Egypt or maybe convince some jihadists that Greek and Roman temples were emblematic of Western evil. Either one would send more artifacts up here, but he shelved the idea. First things first. He had to get his company off the clouds, so to speak. Acquisitions could come later.

Bob had never been one to marvel at past wonders. They tended to bore him. So he now turned in the direction of Sector 1.

☞ 14 ☜

FLYING AWAY FROM THE FARM, Michael felt exhausted and overwhelmed. The pace of things had gotten too hectic after the Dark Ages, and he'd completely missed the Renaissance, the Reformation, the Industrial Revolution, and the twentieth century with all its wonders and wars. During that time, there'd been increasing overpopulation and pollution to contend with, all leading to vanishing resources and global climate change. He shook his head. Only humans could accomplish that, he thought, and argue they hadn't. Even dogs don't foul their own dens.

Now the twenty-first century's Age of Information had overtaken him, and he was so completely out of touch that it seemed more like the Age of Disinformation. There was just too much going on. What he needed was help—someone who knew how to organize and get things done according to modern standards.

He thought about sending one or two of the other Archangels to Harvard Business School so they could take up some of the administrative burden, but he quickly scrapped the idea. The Archangels had spent millennia deferring to him, and now they were just a bunch of bureaucrats comfortable in their cushy positions. All Gabriel and Raphael did was fondle their horns and hope for slaughter. Uriel claimed he spent all his time guarding the gates to the Garden of Eden, but Michael knew there were few intruders since the Boss moved Eden from Earth to Heaven after Adam and Eve skipped out on the rent.

He suspected Uriel occupied himself by playing with his sword then snoozing under the Tree of Knowledge.

Selaphiel was out, as well. His constant praying left him little time to even glance around himself at what was happening in the real world much less do anything about it. Barachiel had trouble enough keeping control of his 496,000 retainers, and he had to spend most of his time listening to confessions, so Michael could forget him, too. Only Raguel, as head of the union, was doing something practical to assist the organization, but that meant Michael couldn't do without him. And none of the other First Sphere angels or those of the lower orders could handle the job. They simply weren't made for multitasking.

But if the thought of finding someone to take up some of Michael's burden was remote, finding the Boss to get him to sign off on everything was even more problematic despite the fact that it now seemed impossible for Heaven to keep running smoothly on the antiquated technology underlying its infrastructure. Everything needed upgrades, updating, and upsizing to bring the infrastructure up-to-date. When he did find the Boss, Michael would be up-front about the seriousness of the problem, but he suspected it would be an uphill battle. He could only hope he wouldn't be upbraided for being uppity and attempting to upend Heaven. He would simply point out that a failure to act would lead to upsets in Heaven's upkeep and functioning and might even lead to an uproar, the upshot of which could conceivably be an uprising that would precipitate a complete upheaval in Heaven.

It wasn't a pretty picture, and he gave it up. No use in being uptight, he thought. He wasn't trying to turn things upside down or upstage the Boss. He just wanted to make Heaven a little more upscale and keep things on the up-and-up and moving along according to Divine Will. Even if it took a little altering of Divine Will.

He flew on for several dozen miles, pondering how he might get some additional administrative assistance and trying to ignore the cramp developing in the muscles beneath his right wing. He wished he could let Antoine know he'd need an ice pack as soon as he got back to the office. He'd have to start carrying one of those new walkie-talkies. The thought brought an image of himself chatting away on a smart phone or texting the message to Antoine. Maybe he could manage to never speak to anyone in person ever again. Especially Antoine.

Going digital, Michael had to admit, seemed to be the only way to make Heaven's infrastructure satisfy the increased demand. It would take some finagling to make it happen, but it would allow them to automate some of the processes. The Boss would just have to see it in a practical light. The new generations coming here were all accustomed to smart phones and the Internet. This wouldn't be Heaven to them if they couldn't engage in mindless gossip and post selfies, amateur porn, and cute animal videos.

The cloudscape passed beneath him, dotted with fountains and ambrosia trees and broken here and there by buildings. He could see people moving around, living their dreams and trusting him to keep Heaven operating at an optimal level. He couldn't let them down. Then he spotted another dark line running across the clouds.

It looked like the one he'd seen before. It might even have been the same one, though he was many, many miles from there, and it seemed unlikely that anything could mar the surface for so great a distance. Besides, this one ran in a completely different direction. Tired as he was, he descended to investigate.

Close up, the line was about two feet wide, and it looked like a light coating of coal dust sprinkled evenly across the surface of the mist. Michael bent close to see how deep it went, and he detected an odor of brimstone.

"What the hell?" he muttered, drawing back.

The trail showed no tendency to sink down to the conveyor layer but rested lightly on the surface. Tentatively, Michael touched a finger to the besmirched mists then glanced at the digit. It came away clean. Whatever the soot was, it didn't appear to be transferable. That relieved him somewhat, but his relief was short-lived when he drew his sword and whacked the blade a few times across the trail, hoping to dissipate it.

No such luck, even though his sword was as mighty as they came. The mists the trail rested on swirled vigorously at his strokes, but the trail remained intact. It was as if the soot was

143

some sort of projection, and it worried Michael that something as metaphysical as it was eradicable was besmirching the territory he was charged with maintaining in pristine condition.

He lofted again and flew on toward the Administration Building. Before he got there, he saw the line three more times —or maybe three more lines just like it—going every which-a-way. At this rate, Heaven would be completely crosshatched in another century, and Michael hated to think what it would look like after a few millennia.

When Michael entered his outer office, he saw half a dozen petitioners sitting there, waiting for him. Ignoring them, he went into his office and pushed the intercom button.

"Come in here, Antoine," he said, and a moment later, his Rastafarian secretary entered.

"I want one of those walkie-talkies we've been issuing to everyone," Michael said. "And one for you, too. I'm tired of all this lack of communications."

"Anything else, sir?"

"A backpack—the kind to carry books, not camping gear— and a Tupperware dish that's ten-by-six-by-four."

"Yes, sir." If Antoine thought those two items were odd, he made no sign of it. Instead, he leaned forward, peering. "Is there smut on your wing, sir?"

Out damn spot, Michael thought, not bothering to glance at his wing tip.

"No, Antoine, it's not dirt. It's the new look. Haven't you heard about wing tattoos?"

Antoine stared blankly at him for a moment then said, "Would you like to see the petitioners now?"

"No. I want you to get in touch with the other Archangels and inform them we're going to have an emergency board meeting."

"Right now, sir?"

"That's usually what emergency means, Antoine."

"No need to respond to my request for clarification with sarcasm. Sir."

"I don't presently have the time or patience to clarify a simple declarative statement."

144

"Remember, sir, all of us angels were created by the Boss, which means we're equals under our robes. I-and-I think I-and-I'm entitled to the same awe and adoration as anyone."

"Do you think I like staying in this office for a thousand years at a stretch, running things and listening to petty complaints and petitions, then spending a god-awful and exhausting amount of time inspecting all the facilities to try to understand the complete workings of Heaven's infrastructure, only to have a slacker clerk who goes home after work and brags about his cushy position while he plays poker with his buddies give me a lecture about equality?"

"I-and-I don't always play poker...," Antoine began, but Michael cut him off.

"Maybe you'd like to take my job. Run things around here for a while. Have the Boss constantly looking over your shoulder."

"No, sir," Antoine said, the light-filled orb on the pommel of his sword dimming considerably.

"I thought not. And remember, you're a Dominion, but I'm the Captain of the Hosts. If you'd like to be on the front lines in Armageddon with me, feel free to explain the equality of all angels to me. Until then, go back out there, dismiss the petitioners, and get the board together. Pronto."

Antoine beat a hasty retreat, leaving Michael to contemplate the difficulties he faced. But his reflections didn't last long. After a few minutes, a deferential knock sounded on the door, and Antoine slipped meekly into the room and came over to Michael's desk.

"Here's your walkie-talkie and the other items, sir." He set the device on Michael's desk, along with a small white backpack and Tupperware container. "I-and-I've called the board, and they should be assembled shortly. I-and-I've also dismissed the petitioners except one. I-and-I know you told me to get rid of all of them, but this one insists he has vital information."

"Oh, alright. If it's that important, send him in."

Michael didn't immediately recognize the petitioner, but his crown and scepter identified him as a Principality.

"You are?" Michael asked, not bothering to try to link the petitioner's face to one of the names of the hundreds of millions of his kind.

"Freddie, sire."

"That's *sir*, Freddie. I'm not your sire."

"Yes, sire...uh, sir."

"Why are you here? Shouldn't you be taking any problems you have to the Dominion in charge of your division?" Normally, Michael didn't have to deal with any angel lower than the Second Sphere.

"Yes, sire. But...." Freddie looked down to where the hem of his robes vanished into the thick carpet of clouds. "I...uh...."

"Spit it out, Freddie. I haven't got forever."

"Well, sire," Freddie said, looking up. "I don't like sayin' it, sire, but it's the Dominion in my division whose the problem."

"And what is your division?"

"The Water Treatment and Purification Plant, sire."

"Which part of the plant?"

"The fountain part, sire."

"And what's the problem?"

"We...." Freddie hesitated again, then caught the look Michael gave him. "We was havin' complaints that all the drink that come out of the fountains in Sector P was tastin' sour, so I was goin' down to inspect one and make repairs. I just come around this mound where a construction crew had piled up some of the clouds to make way for a new building, when I saw my director with his Virtues and Powers all standin' around the fountain, and they was pissin' in it, laughin' all the while about changin' water into wine."

"You didn't say anything to them?"

"No, sire. If I had, my director would have just told me to shut up about it, so I just kept quiet and snuck away and come here. I thought you might oughtr know."

"What's your lead Dominion's name?"

"Halliwell, sire." Freddie looked troubled. "You ain't gonna tell him I told you, are you, sire? If you did...."

"No, Freddie, I'm not going to tell him. You go back to work now, and don't say anything to anybody. I'll handle this matter."

"Yes, sire."

Freddie backed out, and the door shut behind him, leaving Michael in an even greater funk than before. He'd just talked to Halliwell, and all the time the bastard was laughing behind his

146

back. Michael was of half a mind to return to the Water Plant and smite Halliwell into oblivion with his sword, but after a moment's consideration, he calmed himself. If Halliwell and his cohorts had taken to pissing in the fountains, no telling what other misconduct they were guilty of, and Michael was determined to find out what they were up to. Then he'd smite them *all* down.

His intercom sounded, and Antoine informed him the Archangels were assembled in the boardroom. Michael placed the Holy Sponge in the Tupperware container and snapped on the lid. Then he put the container into the backpack, along with the Book of Revelations, the scales, and his new walkie-talkie. He slung the pack over one shoulder, picked up his other accouterments, and left the office. He passed through the outer office without looking at Antoine then floated into the hall. In a few moments, he was sitting in his chair in the boardroom.

"Since our last meeting," he said, staring around at the other Archangels, "I've taken a tour of most of the facilities in Heaven, and I've learned we have some severe problems we need to rectify before they get worse. And it's become clear to me that things are getting out of hand precisely because we don't know what's going on. That's partly because we don't communicate well enough, but also because we're stuck in the past. Uriel, you keep harping on new technologies. I want you to investigate what it would take to establish a digital infrastructure in Heaven."

"But the Boss doesn't allow computers and such."

"Just draw up a plan, and let me worry about the Boss."

"I'll get right on it," Uriel said. "But I have one other issue to clear up first."

"What could be more important than a properly functioning Heaven?" Michael asked.

"Blasphemy and holy slander," Uriel said, whipping out his light saber and using its buzzing blade to sever the imaginary heads of those two beasts. "There's a new drug making the rounds on Earth," Uriel went on, switching off the light-saber. "It's called Angel Eyes."

"How dare they!" Raguel hissed.

Michael saw at once the necessity to squelch this new drug, or at least get the manufacturer to call it something else.

147

"Angel Eyes is marketed as a stimulant, and it's pretty potent," Uriel continued. "At first, it makes people feel euphoric. But it's instantly addictive, so people tend to drink more and more, and over time, it makes them despondent. They cry and despair over the sad state of their lives and the world, and finally, they end up hating everybody who's happier than they are. Which is just about every other human."

"Get the DEA on it. And the FDA. And any other agency with jurisdiction. I can't have one of my chief assistants personally doing undercover work." Once again, Michael cursed the inability of even the Archangels to multitask to any great degree. "And get on that digital business as soon as you can."

He focused on Raguel.

"Rags, you're not only the head of the union, you're the angel of justice, fairness, and vengeance. I've learned there are some potentially abusive practices going on. The Factory is employing artists and writers without recompense. And just now I learned some of the Water Treatment and Purification Plant's management have been pissing into fountains in Sector P. All these instances might be just a tip of the iceberg. Consider yourself to be our Internal Affairs."

"How am I going to find out any real information?" Raguel asked, lifting his hands helplessly. "Nobody will confide in me because I *am* the angel of justice, fairness, and vengeance."

"That's Barry's job," Michael replied, turning to Barachiel. "I want you to order a few hundred bugging devices."

"Who are we going to bug?" Barachiel asked.

"The Dominions in charge of the Water Plant, for a start," Michael answered. "In fact, we'll probably have to bug every one of our utilities."

"You want me to launch a surveillance program on our own people?"

"I don't see any other way to identify the bad apples. You're in charge of the Order of Confessors, aren't you? Just consider this another form of confession."

"The other angels won't like it," Raguel said.

"Well, don't tell them," Michael said. "Isn't surveillance supposed to be secret?"

Michael turned to look meaningfully at Gabriel and Raphael. The meaningful look was to disguise the fact that he was about to send them on a meaningless errand. He was sick of the way they kept threatening to blow their horns at the slightest provocation, and a futile effort to find the Boss would get them out of his hair for a while.

"I want you two to find the Boss."

"You want us to talk to the Boss?" Gabriel's eyes widened in alarm. "We've never done that without you."

Raphael, of course, didn't speak, but his cheeks puffed out a little more than they normally did, and his fingers played nervously over his horn.

"No. I'll do the talking, but I can't spend an eternity flying all over trying to find him." Let *them* strain their wing muscles for a change, Michael thought, still feeling his own ache from his recent journeys. "Split up and scout around. Eventually one of you will spot his crepuscular rays. Follow them, and when you get close to the source, let me know their position."

"How will we do that?"

"We'll just have to use these," Michael held up his walkie-talkie, "until we get smart phones."

"What about me?" Selaphiel asked.

"In my recent travels, I ran across a number of dark gray lines of soot running across the cloudscape. I examined one, and it smelled like Hell and seemed to be indelible."

"Does it look anything like that?" Selaphiel couldn't point, but he could nod, which he did in the direction of Michael's stained wing tip. All the other Archangels stared, too—somewhat predatorily, Michael thought.

"That's another issue," he said. "We really ought to find a new power source. But that's for another time. Right now, I want you to investigate the lines."

"But I have to pray all the time."

"I know. But since you're always looking down on everything and everyone, you're the perfect candidate to track the lines. I want you to follow them until you find out where they came from, where they're going, and who—or what—made them."

Michael looked at the other Archangels. "Any questions?"

There were none.

149

"All right. Get moving."

Michael remained in the boardroom for a time after the others left, mostly because nobody else was there and he could sit in peace and quiet, his only companion the throb of his wing muscles. He was, he had to admit, tired of dealing with angels all the time. Or was he just tired of the responsibilities of his position? Frankly, all the administrative work that went into making Heaven run smoothly was getting on his nerves. After all, he was Captain of the Hosts. He was made for battle, not administration. He must be since he had to wear this helmet and carry around a spear, sword, and shield all the time.

The real hell of it, though, was that Michael knew that even if he was the Captain of the Hosts, he really was nothing but a figurehead with no real power. Responsibility without authority. That was his life. And worse, he had to go begging every time he needed something to keep the Boss's own Creation going. It was humiliating.

That was going to change, Michael vowed. If the Boss wouldn't take charge, Michael would. He'd been running things, de facto, for millennia, and no one knew how things worked around here better than he did. Which was a frightening thought, considering just how little he did know.

But that was going to change, too. He was going to crack the whip and make sure Heaven's operation ran like a well-greased engine. That would let him settle into a less hectic schedule, and maybe he could even manage to take some time off for a real vacation.

He got up, strode to the window, and looked out over the cloudscape below. As he watched, he saw the other Archangels depart from the building and take to the air on their appointed errands. He envied them their single-minded attention to a sole task, though in this case he envied Gabriel and Raphael the least. Not only was their task the most physically demanding, without Michael, it was impossible to accomplish.

But let any of them fill his robes for a while, and they'd see Michael had the most demanding and impossible job of all: maintaining order and sanity in a place where everything was custom designed for madmen and fools.

♍ 15 ♏

THE MASSIVE CLOUD BANK MARKING the back border of Sector 1 was looming on the near horizon, and now that Bob was getting close, he felt some anxiety. They're cavemen, he thought. There was no telling how they'd treat him. They might try to bash in his skull with a club. Or even eat him. Weren't some cavemen cannibals? Then again, if they ate him, would it actually be cannibalism? Cannibals ate their own kind, but Bob wasn't a caveman. He had a hundred thousand years of evolution behind him that they didn't. If they ate him, maybe it would be more akin to an animal, such as a lion, eating him. Maybe they wouldn't do anything, he hoped. Didn't they have to behave heavenly?

As he walked, Bob noticed his wingtips were solid black, and the darkness had stained most of his pants. He wondered if the soot would eventually darken his jacket. He hoped so, since a black suit in Heaven would give him a distinguished air. As long as the soot didn't stain his shirt, too, which would make him look like a member of the Mafia. If it did, he could always go back to the mall for more shirts.

Sector 1 didn't look much different than any of the rest of Heaven except there weren't any buildings. Only ambrosia trees and fountains dotted the cloudscape. Bob saw a figure standing beside an ambrosia tree some distance off, so he headed toward it, worries about being clubbed and eaten resurfacing in his thoughts. But as he got closer, the worry about being clubbed vanished and the one about being eaten took on a more visceral nature when he realized the figure wasn't a person. It was a white saber-tooth tiger.

The saber-tooth was the first living thing he'd seen in Heaven besides people and angels, although neither were, he knew, strictly living. It was standing on its hind legs, pawing at an ambrosia hooked onto one of the two dental scimitars jutting from its upper jaw.

I wonder what it tastes like to a saber-tooth, Bob thought inanely as he froze. But it was too late. The saber-tooth had spotted him. Whatever ambrosia tasted like to a saber-tooth, this one obviously thought Bob would taste better. It dropped to all fours, shook its head to rid itself of the fruit, which was flung ten yards away, and charged, kicking up the mists beneath its heavy paws.

Bob wished he could "Get thee fucking back!" the saber-tooth, but as a Visitor, he didn't have that ability. So he prepared to die. Horribly.

Suddenly a stocky man erupted from the thigh-high clouds and streaked on an intercept course toward the saber-tooth. He was dressed in a white fur loincloth and carried a big club. He reached the big cat not thirty feet from Bob and flung himself on it. The ensuing battle was horrendous, though most of it was hidden by mists churned by the melee. But it must have been horrendous if the snarls, growls, and thuds of thick wood impacting flesh were any indication. Bob found he couldn't tell which of them—the saber-tooth or the caveman—made the more fearsome sounds. Then came a loud thunk, and silence abruptly fell.

As the mists settled, the caveman straightened and walked toward Bob, dragging the tiger behind him by one of its saber teeth, leaving a bloody swath on the clouds. His other hand firmly gripped the handle of his gore-covered club. Bob didn't know whether to run or to try to worm his way into the cloudscape.

"You're a strange one," the caveman said. He had an ugly, hairy face with a sharply sloped forehead above beetling brows, a large flat nose with bristles poking stiffly out of its cavernous nostrils, a receding chin, and a wide mouth filled with blunt, yel-

152

low-brown teeth. His fur loincloth hung in bloody tatters, and his muscle-knotted flesh was ripped and bitten, but he didn't seem to notice. "What tribe are you from?" Then his eyes narrowed. "You're not poaching on our hunting grounds are you?"

"I'm really sorry if I've intruded," Bob said. "I wasn't hunting. I was just wandering around when the saber-tooth tiger attacked."

"I believe you. You can't hunt without a club. Lucky for you I was here."

"Yes. Thanks for saving me."

"Mighty strange furs you're wearing. What kind of an animal did they come from?"

"Sheep," Bob said.

"Doesn't look like any sheepskin I've ever seen."

"We take the wool off the skin, separate the hairs, and use it to make this stuff. We call it cloth."

"It looks pretty natty," the caveman said. "Do you mind?" He reached out and fingered Bob's lapel. "Sure is smooth. But pulling out all those hairs and then putting them together again sounds like a lot of work."

"You can always make the women do it," Bob suggested.

The caveman's eyes lit up. "That's an idea," he said, and he stuck out his hand. "I'm Harry. What's your name, stranger?"

Bob shook his hand and introduced himself.

"I was in the neighborhood, and I'd thought I'd drop in and see how things are going here in Sector 1."

"Not bad, as you can see." Harry poked his club at the dead saber-tooth, whose blood had soaked into the clouds underneath it. "Me and the missus will feast tonight. Want to join us? Afterward, we can sit around the campfire. We usually tell exaggerated tales of my exploits, but tonight you can explain how to make this cloth stuff."

Bob squeamishly eyed the dead cat, ironically wondering how saber-tooth tiger tasted since just a few moments before he was wondering how he'd taste to it. But it seemed impolite to refuse the invitation of a muscle-bound caveman with a big club, and in a few moments, Harry was leading the way across the cloud fields toward the massive cloud bank. Before long, they reached the place where the cloud escarpment met the cloud carpet, and Bob saw a cliff face riddled with caves drib-

153

bling tendrils of gray smoke. An odor of burned plastic hung in the air.

"I wasn't sure you actually live in caves," Bob said.

"Can't be a caveman otherwise," Harry replied, leading the way to one of the openings. "Come on in and meet the missus. She'll cook up the meat, and we can eat."

The two of them ducked through the cave entrance and into a spacious but gray space. A feeble fire flickered and sputtered off to one side, its scraggly smoke drifting to the cave's ceiling before trickling out the entrance.

"Nice place," Bob said, trying to ignore the smell of burned plastic emanating from the fire.

"Thanks," Harry said, dropping the saber-tooth carcass. "I brought a guest for dinner, honey," he called out.

A shape rose from beside the fire and came toward them. It was a cavewoman only marginally better looking than Harry. She was dressed in a short white fur skirt and top that stylishly exposed one hairy breast.

"Thank goodness it isn't Ugga-Mug and Skrawna," she exclaimed as she drew near enough to get a look at Bob.

"Fluffy, this is Bob. Bob, meet my wife, Fluffy."

"I hope this isn't an inconvenience," Bob said, shaking her rough-palmed hand.

"Not at all," Fluffy smiled. "Ya'll clean up, and I'll get to work on this." She grabbed one of the saber teeth and dragged the big cat toward the fire.

Harry led Bob to a corner of the cave where a miniature version of the fountains stood.

"You have your own fountain," Bob noted as Harry dipped his bloody hands into the water and began scrubbing them. All the wounds he'd sustained in the fight with the saber-tooth had miraculously healed.

"We didn't for about sixty thousand years, but then one of my neighbors, Jonsie, wished he could have running water in his cave, and poof, there it was. Wasn't long before we all had one. Say, wanna cocktail while we're waiting for our haunches?"

"Great idea," Bob said. "What are we having?"

"Fermented berries, what else?" Harry held his hands over the rim of the fountain, and a crude baked clay cup encrusted with quartz crystals appeared in each. He used them to scoop up a thick purple juice clotted with disintegrating berries. He handed one to Bob, who sniffed it, then, not to be impolite, took a tentative sip. The concoction made the cheapest wino swill taste like the finest champagne.

"How about something a little different?" he suggested, hoping he wouldn't offend Harry. Anybody who could kill a saber-tooth tiger with a club then drag it for several miles without effort while he healed miraculously wasn't someone you wanted to be on the wrong side of.

"I didn't know there was anything different," Harry said.

"Check this out," Bob said, and he stuck both hands over the rim of the fountain. He thought about ordering Dalmore 64 Trinitas, but he refrained. He didn't want a rowdy drunken caveman on his hands, and he also figured the Dalmore would be too sophisticated for Harry's palate. Best to start with something basic.

"Two beers in frosted goblets," he said.

The golden, bejeweled goblets appeared, both ice cold, and he dipped them into the fountain and came up with two beers bearing nice foam heads. He handed one to Harry, who looked at it with amazement.

"I never saw yellow clay like this before," he said. "It's cold."

"It's called gold," Bob said. "The cold isn't part of it. The stuff inside is beer. Try it."

He raised the goblet to his lips and took a swig. Harry followed suit.

"Wow," Harry said. "It's bubbly and tingly. Tastes great. What did you call it?"

"Beer in a frosted goblet," Bob told him.

Harry put his hand over the fountain and said, "Beer in a frosted goblet." He looked pleased when the goblet appeared in his hand, and he dipped up another round of foaming liquid. "Look out, Jonsie," he said, then he gestured to Bob. "Come on." He headed toward the fire, which was enclosed in a neat ring of cloud stones.

Fluffy had already cut off one of the saber-tooth's haunches with a flint knife, and the meat was roasting on a crude spit over the open fire.

"Hey, honey," Harry said. "Try this new drink Bob suggested."

He handed one of the goblets to Fluffy.

"My," she said, lifting the goblet into the light. "What a pretty drinking pot. Look at all those colorful, sparkly stones."

"It's a frosted goblet," Harry pronounced. "That's beer inside."

Fluffy took a delicate sip. Then another, larger one.

"That's really good." She smacked her lips, set the goblet on a nearby shelf of clouds, then took a stick from the pile of firewood next to the fire and tossed it on the flames. The stick sputtered and flared up almost instantly.

Curious, Bob peered more closely at the pile of firewood and realized it was branches from an ambrosia tree. But there was something odd. It looked like tubes of PVC were sticking out from the ends of the broken branches. He picked up one of the sticks and turned it over in his hands. It was an ambrosia branch all right, but beneath its bark, it looked like a plumbing fixture rather than a living thing. Even the bark, on closer inspection, was artificial, made from some sort of rubber. No wonder the smoke stank.

"You get your firewood from the trees outside?" he asked.

"Yep," Harry said, licking foam from his mustache. "Tough damn things to hack down with a stone ax, and the branches don't burn too well. They stink, too. Wasn't always like that, but now they're all we have."

"What happens when you cut one down?" Bob asked. "Does another grow in its place?"

"Naw, some crew of angels comes by and replaces it. Pretty thoughtful of them since it gives us a perpetual source of firewood."

The ambrosia trees aren't actually trees, Bob thought, glancing at the pile of plumbing masquerading as branches. They're fixtures, just like the fountains. If the ambrosia trees were fake, what else around Heaven wasn't on the up-and-up?

By now, the saber-tooth haunch had begun to sizzle and drip, and the scent of cooking meat infiltrated the odor of burned plastic. It smelled pretty gamey.

Bob and Harry sat on cloud rocks near the fire, and Bob leaned against the cave's wall, which yielded slightly to the pressure of his back. "So tell me: How do you cave people like it here in Heaven? I suppose you're the best folks to ask since you've been around here longer than anybody."

156

"Oh, we have," Harry assured him. "I've been here for a hundred and eighty or ninety thousand years, and Fluffy a little less. A few have been here longer, but I guess I have enough seniority to express my opinion. Now don't get me wrong: I like it up here well enough, and it wasn't easy being a caveman on Earth, but Heaven isn't all it's cracked up to be."

"How so?"

"On the one hand, I get to go out and hunt the most fearsome animals armed only with a club and come away victorious every time. But on the other, Fluffy has to cook it on fires made from those miserable excuses for branches. It's the same with everything. When Fluffy and I moved in here, it looked like the cave of our dreams, with plenty of room and all the amenities."

"What's the problem?"

"I'm surprised you haven't noticed. Lean forward and feel your back."

Bob reached behind himself, and his fingers came away damp.

"That ain't sweat," Harry said. "This place is damp. All the time. I guess it's because it's made of clouds. We have to sleep on a thick pile of saber-tooth skins just to keep dry, but it's way too soft for me, and I constantly wake up with a backache. And the dampness has totally destroyed my creative abilities. I used to be a great painter of cave art, but pigments just melt off these walls. I haven't done a lick of painting in a hundred and fifty thousand years. I can barely remember what a giant elk or cave bear looks like anymore."

"All he ever finds out there are saber-tooth tigers," Fluffy said. "We're pretty sick of eating saber-tooth."

"Didn't anybody tell you you can wish for anything you want, and it will appear?" Bob asked. "When you arrived, you probably were thinking saber-tooth tigers were the most impressive prey, so that's what you ended up with."

"Actually," Harry replied, "a saber-tooth was the last thing I ever saw on Earth, and when I got here, all I could think of was killing that bastard and eating *him*."

"There you have it," Bob said. "Next time you go out hunting, just say, 'An elk is my Heavenly Desire,' and an elk will appear."

157

"No kidding? I wish someone told me about this Heavenly Desire thing when I first got here. Maybe that's what's going on over on the other side of the fence."

"What fence?" Bob asked.

"There's a big fenced-in forest right next to our sector," the caveman said. "It's got all sorts of animals running around in it. Must be somebody's Heavenly Desire at work. Me and my buddies tried to hunt there, but the angels guarding it won't let us in."

"There's always the ambrosia," Bob said. "Do you ever eat the fruit off the trees?"

"Sure," Fluffy said. "All the time. But no matter how I cook it, it always tastes like tubers."

"That's because you're expecting it to taste like tubers," Bob said. "It'll taste like anything you want, including any animal, and you wouldn't have to cook it with those." He pointed to the plastic branches hissing and popping in their ring of cloud stones. "You wouldn't even have to hunt."

"Don't tell him that," Fluffy laughed. "I'll never get him out of the cave."

It was beginning to look to Bob like you could have anything you wanted in Heaven as long as you could imagine it, but you had to be able to imagine it first.

"What's out there that's all that important, anyway?" Harry said. "All that golden light is okay to see by, but I lost my tan. But you know what I really miss, Bob?"

"What?"

"The night. I miss the stars. Nothing evokes the great mysteries of life like the stars. Some of my buddies tried to impose animal shapes on them. I guess they were trying to make sense of all those points of light wheeling through the great void, but I'm not sure it's possible for people to truly grasp the infinite and eternal."

"I didn't know cavemen could be philosophical," Bob said.

"We may be cavemen, but that doesn't mean we can't use our brains," Harry said. "And I've been here longer than just about anybody, so I've had plenty of time to think about things."

"Dinner's ready," Fluffy called out Harry nudged Bob.

"Time to think about dinner."

158

Bob followed Harry to the fire, where Fluffy handed each of them a hank of meat and an ambrosia.

"Sorry," she said to Bob. "All we have is saber-tooth and tuber."

"That's fine," Bob replied, staring doubtfully at the meal in his hands. He thought tuber might be similar to potato or, less appetizing, turnip, but he knew he'd never tried saber-tooth tiger cooked over burning rubber and plastic. Wishing for his Heavenly Desire more than ever, he bit into the hank of saber-tooth haunch. It was even worse than he'd imagined. The ambrosia tuber tasted like school paste.

They ate without speaking, but not in silence. Harry and Fluffy were quite good at using their big, blunt teeth to tear massive hunks from their hanks, but they weren't very thorough in chewing the flesh before swallowing, and they made a lot of noise doing it. Bob managed to finish his meal without gagging, and he held up his hands at Fluffy's offer of seconds.

While Fluffy cleaned up after the meal by throwing everything that was inedible onto the floor, Harry grabbed a couple of frosty cold ones and took Bob outside. They settled themselves on the cloud rocks in front of the cave, and Fluffy joined them a few moments later. They sat, staring out over the cloudscape, chatting about how monotonous the weather had been and how hunting was always good and how the neighbor two caves down was a notorious drunk.

"I'm not telling him about beer," Harry said, holding up his fifth mug and staring at it. A little of the beer sloshed out, and his voice was slightly slurred. "He'll be plastered all the time."

"He'll find out as soon as we have our first party," Fluffy said. "Now it's our turn to one-up the neighbors."

"If you really want to be culture leaders, I can help," Bob said. "Hold out your hand, Fluffy, and say, 'My Heavenly Desire is the latest copy of *House Beautiful*.'"

She did and almost dropped the magazine when it suddenly appeared on her horny palm.

"What is it?" she asked.

"It's full of cave-improvement ideas, recipes, and other stuff to make your lives easier and more comfortable." Bob took the magazine and showed her how to flip through the pages.

"I like all the pictures," she said, "but what are all those little squiggly black things everywhere between the pictures?"

"Those are letters. They make up words that tell you a story."

"I thought a picture was worth a thousand words," Harry said. "Why waste space with the words?"

"I like the pictures," Fluffy said, leafing through the pages. Her eyes fell on one colorful photo spread, and they lit up. "Wait right here!" she ordered, and she got up and hurried into the cave.

"Saved me a trip to the fountain," Harry said with a grin as he swapped out his own empty goblet for Fluffy's almost full one. He hoisted the goblet, quaffed off the rest of the beer, then threw both goblets out onto the clouds.

In just a few minutes, Fluffy returned, her face flushed with excitement.

"I want to inform you," she said with exaggerated formality, "we now have a beautiful spare bedroom, completely accessorized."

"That's wonderful, honey," Harry slurred before issuing a belch.

"Harry, I think we ought to invite Bob to stay the night."

She looked hopefully at Bob, but not in a way he liked. She looked strong enough to crush him if he mistakenly fell into her embrace.

"Thanks," he said. "but I'm on a mission, and I probably ought to get on with it."

"Well, we'd love to have you visit again, Bob," Fluffy said. "And next time, I'm sure I'll be able to whip up something different, thanks to all the recipes in here." She waved the copy of *House Beautiful*.

"I'm looking forward to it," Bob said, standing. "Which way is the forest you mentioned? The one with all the animals and the fence?"

"That way," Harry pointed waveringly. "You can't miss it."

"See you around," Bob said, and he started walking.

❧ 16 ☙

SELAPHIEL'S TRAJECTORY AWAY FROM THE Administration Building was almost as low as his spirits. He was especially resentful at being ordered to accomplish a task he felt was beneath him. He'd rather be back in his office, where he spent most of his time pacing and wearing a path in the cloud carpet. The other Archangels believed he cloistered himself there to have a more meditative place for his prayers, but the truth was another matter entirely.

Since his head was permanently bowed in prayer, Selaphiel always had to stare at the floor, and ages ago he'd gotten completely sick of eternally perusing the misty white carpet that was the basic surface everywhere in Heaven—and eternity wasn't even a fraction over with. He'd examined it every way he could, even using nucleoscopic vision, infrared, and radio wave imaging. He probably knew more about the cloud carpet than anybody except the Boss. That was way, way too much, and the end was never going to be in sight.

But a while back, he'd come up with a brilliant plan that gave him some respite. Every time he visited Earth, he brought back a large number of adventure, espionage, and mystery novels. He'd have one of his attendant Principalities cut the pages from a couple of copies and arrange them sequentially across the floor so he could read them as he perambulated the room in his prayers.

Now, he barely heard the drone of the prayers muttering in the background of his mind, while his forethoughts were racing along with whatever narrative he was currently reading. But he didn't consider these sorts of books to be a distraction from his holy duties. Instead, they actually were prayers: for justice and proper comeuppance, for the courage to carry on in the most dire circumstances, and for the power to make things whole again.

The books not only kept his mind occupied, they broke up the constant view of mists he was forced to stare at 24/7/eternity. But now, here he was, flying along, staring down at nothing but white blankness, looking for graffiti that probably didn't spell anything but trouble.

Michael hadn't told him where to look, but from what the chief of the Archangels said, the black streaks were all over the place and growing more numerous. Selaphiel figured if he flew in a straight line, he'd eventually run across one. He hoped it wouldn't take too long. He was nearing the end of his current book, and things in it were getting pretty intense. He didn't want to stay away from it any longer than necessary.

It may not have taken longer than necessary to find one of the lines, but it took long enough. Selaphiel was flying at an altitude of a few hundred feet when he spotted it. As Michael had reported, it was as if someone had drawn a freehand line across the field of white with a can of black spray paint or a very large piece of charcoal. Curiously, it hadn't begun to soak into the clouds and disappear as did almost everything else people left lying around unwanted. He descended to have a closer look.

The line was about two feet wide, and as Selaphiel bent over it, sure enough, a whiff of brimstone tickled his nostrils. He glided through it several times, but it remained in place, though the mists themselves swirled and eddied. It was as if the grayness of the line was a superimposition rather than something that was actually there.

Selaphiel straightened and looked up and down the line, which, for him, entailed facing the line and giving sidelong glances in either direction. It stretched both ways without distinction for as far as he could see, which wasn't far since he was looking out of the corners of his eyes. So, he pondered, which way to go? He didn't fancy going the wrong way and then having to backtrack. He took to the air to see if altitude gave him any clue, but there appeared to be no differentiation in the line in either direction.

Reorienting himself, he flapped off. Whoever—or whatever—was leaving this damn line had to start somewhere, and everyone in Heaven started at the Pearly Gates.

"Hi, Selaphiel," Saint Peter said when the Archangel landed just inside the Pearly Gates and floated through the archway, over the turnstile, and up to his desk. "Why the hangdog look?"

"I might not have it if you'd do your job right," Selaphiel said.

"Don't get all Archangel high-horse with me," Saint Peter shot back. "What's eating you?"

"That," Selaphiel pointed to the black line.

"What's that got to do with me?" Saint Peter demanded.

"You let in someone you shouldn't have."

"I doubt that. Nobody goes in unless their name is in the book." He laid a hand on the cover and smirked. "It's my sure ace in any hole."

"I see something started here that shouldn't have." Selaphiel pointed to a sooty circle at the head of the trail.

"That was Bob," Saint Peter said.

"Bob, huh? Well, now he's traipsing all over the place, leaving soot smeared everywhere. I have to make a report on him to Michael, and he'll want to know why you let someone like that across the threshold."

"Wasn't up to me," Saint Peter said. "His name was in the *Register* as a Visitor, and you know I go strictly by the book. I didn't much care for him, but I had no choice in the matter. If the Administration doesn't like it, they should complain to the Boss, not me. I'm just following orders."

Selaphiel knew it was true. Saint Peter never made a mistake because he never made a decision on his own.

"You're right," Selaphiel agreed in a resigned tone. "Okay. Thanks for the info." He prepared to take off, when Saint Peter stopped him.

"What about that?" the entry angel demanded, pointing at the soot. "You can't leave it like that. How do you think it looks

163

to folks just coming in when the path to Heaven is paved with burned brimstone?"

"I'll send a cleaning crew," Selaphiel said, and before Saint Peter could make another complaint, he quickly ducked through the Pearly Gates and took off.

As the cloudscape receded below, he saw the line pause and mill around in a clump of twists, turns, and whirls. Nearby stood Wilbert the Greeter. No surprise this Bob fellow had stopped to talk to Wilbert. Selaphiel flew on for several meandering miles before the line stopped at a fountain then moved on to an ambrosia tree. Nobody was at the former, but a food addict at the latter remembered Bob because Bob had tried to poach off his limb.

"Sneaky bastard," the food addict snarled. "I gave him what-for: Get thee fucking back!" The man punched forward so forcefully with the ambrosia fruit in his hand that his fingers punctured the skin and juice ran over his fingers. As he hastily licked them, Selaphiel took the opportunity to escape.

Some distance later, the line disappeared into a cloud room glowing opalescently with TV monitor light. The line emerged from the cloud room and headed straight toward one of the choir lofts. Selaphiel hastened after it.

"I remember him," the Virtue choirmaster said.

"Did he join the choir?" Selaphiel asked.

"No. He said it wasn't his time."

Selaphiel left the choir loft, flew up about fifty feet, and stared in the direction the line went. If he'd had a heart, it would have sunk. Off in the distance he could see Harmony Heights. If Bob had gone in there, Selaphiel would have to, too, and he hated mazes worse than he did his permanently bowed head, and for precisely the same reason: He was unable to see around any corner before actually turning it.

Then he brightened. That place was the worst labyrinth in Heaven. If Bob actually went in there, he was as good as gone. Poof. No problem. Eventually he'd wither away since there were no public fountains or ambrosias in Heaven's suburb. Everybody had the latest appliances in their own homes and weren't inclined to share.

164

Then Selaphiel frowned. He couldn't let Bob wither away. Michael would be pissed. Besides, what if Bob didn't wither away but remained eternally trapped in Harmony Heights? Before long, those lily-white streets would look like fresh asphalt. No way Selaphiel was going to let Michael lay that one at the hem of *his* robes. But he still wasn't looking forward to negotiating the maze of Harmony Heights. Surely Peeping Tom would know something since he spied on everyone in the subdivision.

But no matter how hard he searched, he couldn't find Tom. He did spot one anomaly, however: a milk delivery truck parked in front of one of the houses. Curious, Selaphiel hovered over the roof and stared down with his X-ray vision. A woman in the bedroom was sitting naked at the vanity but backward, brushing her hair. Across the room, Tom was lounging in a Morris chair, watching her. He was wearing a milkman's uniform, and a beer was in his hand. The woman's eyes were steadily watching him while he watched her.

Selaphiel descended to the bedroom window and rapped on the pane. Tom got up from his chair and opened the window.

"Can I help you?"

"What's with the milkman getup?" Selaphiel asked. "And why aren't you outside?"

"Met a fellow named Bob," Tom said. "He suggested this. Said it would get me some real action. He was right. Peeping can't get any better than this."

"Is this quite the same as secretive peeping from the bushes?"

"Not really, but it's a hell of a lot more comfortable. Especially considering the peeping wasn't all that secret."

"Did Bob disappear into Harmony Heights?"

"No. He asked me about it, and about the Celestial, then he left."

"Did he go to the Celestial?"

"He didn't seem very interested, even though I told him all about it." Tom beamed proudly. "I have the penthouse there."

Why me? Selaphiel wondered, taking to the air.

As he flew, he prayed for release, but in the end, he knew there was no release. He had to stick to the line, which continued on as monotonously as before for mile after mile. At last, he noticed a small clot of activity ahead.

The clot soon resolved itself into a group of about thirty protesters holding signs and shouting abuses at the lone angel nearby. It was the Eastboro Baptist Church protesters. He almost flew on, but the Principality supervising them might be able to tell him more about Bob.

He landed beside the angel, who was wearing a U.S. Army dress uniform and lying on a bier surrounded by the trappings of full military honors. He looked completely fed up, exhausted, and like he wished he really was dead. The church members were screaming that dead grunts were minions of evil and going to Hell.

"Thank goodness you're here," the angel said. "I thought my shift would never end."

"Sorry to disappoint you," Selaphiel said, "but I'm not your relief. I'm Selaphiel."

"Oh, sorry, sir," the angel said. "I didn't recognize you at first. Did you come to do something about them?" He indicated the protesting congregation. "I don't see why we have to babysit a bunch of loonies. Can't we just send them back down to Hell, where they belong?"

"That's not up to me," Selaphiel said.

"If you're not here about them," the angel said, a worried look on his face, "is something wrong?"

"Perhaps," Selaphiel said. "I'm investigating that." He pointed to the dark gray line. "What can you tell me about it."

"Some guy named Bob left it," the angel said. "He looked pretty average, but his clothes were unusual."

"In what way?"

"His pants were turning gray, and his shoes were black. But he was a real nice fellow."

"What did he say to you?"

"He just asked about the Eastboro congregation, then he went on his way."

"Okay," Selaphiel said.

He started to take off, but the other angel stopped him.

"Excuse me, sir, but did you happen to spot my relief? He was supposed to be here weeks ago, and I've been out here with these nuts a god-awful long time. I can't imagine why he's not here."

"I can," Selaphiel said, and he turned to leave.

166

"Hey, wait a minute," the Principality snapped. "You're just going to fly off? You ask me your question, get a polite answer, then blow me off with a snide remark when I tell you I'm in dire straits? I'm some sort of a robot who has no feelings? Your reality is more important than mine?"

"We all have our station in life and duty to perform," Selaphiel said. "Wishing won't make it any different."

"Oh, yeah, right. Humans get their Heavenly Desires, but angels have to work. And we work hard. I've been here, listening to them," he jerked a thumb toward the Eastboro congregation, "for two years straight. Don't you think I deserve some time off, away from all this caterwauling?"

"We're here to serve the Boss first, and then the humans...."

"The humans!" The Principality sneered. "I can tell you one thing: We Principalities are tired of working as hard as we do for people who are as ungrateful as our bosses are. We've been around longer than they have. Isn't there such a thing as seniority? Why do we have to play the perpetual serving class? And what about them?" he waved at the Eastboro congregation. "Why are we coddling idiots like that?"

"Sometimes it's necessary to do unpleasant things," Selaphiel said.

"In Heaven? And anyway, I never see you or any of the other First Sphere aristocrats down here in the trenches, doing the dirty work. Don't you think the rest of us know it's a conspiracy to keep the proletariat in its place and reap the benefits of power. It's not right."

"It's what is," Selaphiel said, annoyance creasing his brow.

"Easy for you to say. Maybe you ought to hang out here for a couple of years. Then you'd see. And you can't even look me in the face, can you? Ashamed, no doubt...."

"Enough!" Selaphiel barked, and his aura flared, singeing the other angel's robe.

The Principality's mouth snapped shut as fast as it had snapped open.

"Sorry, sir," he muttered through clenched teeth.

"There's a walkie-talkie in my pocket," Selaphiel said. "Take it out." When the angel had, Selaphiel asked, "Do you have one of these?"

167

"No, sir. Never saw one before. I told you I've been out of touch."

"That must explain it. We're issuing these to everyone to encourage better communications. Keep this one. I can't hold it, anyway. You can use it to call in to your supervisor."

"Thank you, sir," the angel said, taking the walkie-talkie.

"Good luck," Selaphiel said. "I'll pray for your relief."

Then he was rising above the Eastboro bedlam and chasing the line. As he flew on and on, he recalled reading about how drivers on Earth could get mesmerized by the dividing line in the middle of the highway. They called it white-line fever, and he wondered if he wasn't going to get something like it: black line fever. It was all he could see, scrolling beneath him like a bad experimental film.

But this leg of his flight wasn't long enough to get a fever of any sort. For a time, the soot trail traced straight across the cloudscape, then it curved toward a fountain, where a man stood, drinking from a golden goblet.

"There you are, you slug," Selaphiel muttered, and he homed in on the fountain. But as he got closer, he saw the man was dressed in Spanish clothes from a few centuries back, and his pants and shoes were white. Curiously, he clutched a powerful flashlight in his free hand. Selaphiel set down about ten feet from the man, who ignored him as he sipped from his goblet.

"Excuse me," Selaphiel said, and the man jumped as if startled. He swung the flashlight up and shined its beam right into Selaphiel's face. Selaphiel blinked and squinted.

"Oh," the man said. "An angel." He lowered the beam so it shone at the hem of Selaphiel's robe. "Sorry. I didn't hear you come up." He had a Spanish accent.

"You didn't see me?" Selaphiel knew there were no blind people in Heaven. Sight was the first thing all blind people asked for when they arrived. But the man couldn't be blind because he'd seen Selaphiel when he'd pinned him like a big moth in the beam of his flashlight.

"It's too dark," the man explained obtusely, and he wiggled the flashlight beam. "That's why I have this."

"I see," Selaphiel said, though he didn't. But he wasn't about to waste time listening to some weirdo explain why it was too

168

dark when everything was lit by the pervasive golden glow. "I'm looking for a man named Bob," he said. "He left that." He pointed to Bob's trail.

"Yes. I met Bob."

"What can you tell me about him?"

"I can tell you he saved my life."

"You're already saved."

"Okay. He saved my sanity."

"How did he do that?"

"He told me about this." The man waggled the flashlight again. "Now I can see farther than ever. And he recommended this." He held up the goblet.

"What's in it?"

"Dalmore 64 Trinitas," the man said. "It really is the nectar of the gods. Want to try some?" The man extended the goblet.

Selaphiel doubted that, but he let the man hold it for him while he took a tentative sip. Then another. He had to admit that it did taste divine.

"Did he say where he was going?" Selaphiel asked. He hoped the man knew Bob's eventual destination so he could fly straight there instead of chasing lines all over Heaven.

"I think he went looking for the mall." The man waved the beam of his flashlight along Bob's trail. "If you see him, tell him, as one gentleman to another, my sincerest thanks for his help. I will second him in a duel anytime."

"I'll do that," Selaphiel lied, and he took to the air again.

This leg of the trail was shorter, and it jogged in a detour to an ambrosia tree. As Selaphiel neared, he could see John the Anapest lurking beneath its branches.

Sighing in resignation, he swooped down and landed.

169

17

BOB STRODE ON IN THE direction Harry said the forest lay. He noticed that this whole area was pretty dingy as well as littered with junk and ruined buildings—mostly primitive dwellings of various sorts—half sunken into the clouds. It reminded him of the parlor in his long-dead great-aunt's house, where everything was so old the dust of time had soaked into all the cluttered surfaces to form an antique patina. Even the cloud fields were yellowish and matted, like the hair of an unkempt old man. Not another person was in sight.

It was all pretty depressing, and he was thankful when a dense green woods materialized out of the golden haze. Bob was instantly curious. This was the first thing like Earth's natural world that he'd seen in Heaven, aside from the ubiquitous ambrosia trees. And knew now that the ambrosia trees weren't natural.

As he neared the forest, his path was blocked by a tall chain link fence topped with coils of razor wire. Every ten feet, a sign warned that Uriel would hack up trespassers with his flaming sword. Several angels were flitting about over the fence, and they were like no other angels he'd yet encountered. He knew they must be angels because they had wings—four each, in fact—but they also had the body of a lion and splayed hooves for feet.

One of the angels saw Bob approaching, and he signaled to his companions. They hovered like a squadron of Apache attack helicopters over the fence line where Bob's path intersected it and stared belligerently at him. This was pretty disconcerting because each of the angels had four faces on its head—a man's, an ox's, a lion's, and an eagle's— which kept rotating slowly so that each pair of eyes could take him in part of the time. Eight hostile staring eyes in a revolving head were bad enough, but the four wings were covered with more eyes.

"Watchful mothers," Bob muttered to himself, but it wasn't as bad as staring down an Ophanim.

"Back!" ordered one of the angels from its human mouth. "Entry is forbidden!" A second growled from its lion's mouth.

"I'd never have guessed," Bob said, gesturing toward the razor-wire-topped fence. "I've never seen one of you before. What kind of angels are you?"

"Cherubim," the angel said.

"I thought Cherubim were chubby little guys with curly blonde hair and tiny wings flitting around lovers and such," Bob said.

"Putti!" bleated the ox face of the third angel, scorn in his voice.

"You can trust humans to get it wrong," the fourth Cherubim's eagle's beak squawked.

"That's a popular misconception," the first Cherubim said, ignoring his fellows. "Those are cherubs."

"Images promulgated by stupid humans who've never seen a real Cherubim in their lives," the second Cherubim's head had rotated enough that its voice came from its eagle's beak. "As you can see, we're better hung than those immature, facially deficient imitations. And better hung."

"I do," Bob nodded. "I heard you guys are Heaven's cops, and I didn't figure those cherubs had the balls for the job." He pointed to the forest beyond the fence. "Is that the Garden of Eden?"

"It is," the first Cherubim moaned out of its ox face.

"Looks like it could use a little maintenance," Bob said.

Indeed, the woodlands were thick with a dense undergrowth. It didn't seem like any animal, except maybe a snake, could move around in there without getting its hide shredded or eyes poked out. Bob wondered if mosquitoes swarmed through the underbrush. Maybe mosquitoes who bit but didn't leave an itch afterwards.

172

"It does need pruning," the second Cherubim admitted. "We used to have a caretaker couple who lived on-site and did all the gardening, but they ate some of the fruit from the Tree of Knowledge, which only led to trouble. Next thing we knew, they figured out they were doing all that gardening work for sustenance wages and demanded a raise. That was bad enough, but they also discovered sex. Why *that* took so long, I don't know. They ran around naked all the time, and their anatomical differences were pretty obvious clues. Anyway, one thing led to another, and we had to kick them out. We haven't had any caretakers since, and that was a long time ago. It's practically impossible to find good help any more."

"Are there still wild animals in there?"

"Never were any *wild* animals in Eden," the third Cherubim squawked. "Except the former caretakers. They could get pretty wild after they discovered sex was better with fermented berries. All the other animals are tame. Like in a petting zoo."

"So you built this fence to keep the animals in?"

"We built it to keep the cavemen out," the first Cherubim answered. "All those tame animals are easy pickings. And they'd chop down the trees for firewood. If we let them in, Eden would be barren and lifeless in no time."

"There's no way I can get in to look around?" Bob asked.

"Not here," the second Cherubim growled.

"Try the main entrance," the first Cherubim suggested, pointing down the fence. "You'll have to talk to Uriel, though. He's the head honcho."

"Isn't he one of the Archangels?"

"That's right," the second Cherubim squawked. "He gets to sit in a cushy kiosk, while we have to perch on razor wire all the time. Makes me sorry I *am* well hung. Anyway, you can't miss him. He carries a flaming sword."

"Thanks," Bob said, and he headed down the fence in the direction the first Cherubim indicated.

Before long, he came to an opening in the fence. As the Cherubim had said, there was a booth just inside, and the opening was blocked by a counterweighted bar painted in black and yellow stripes. It was like an obscure border crossing from one Third-World country to another.

173

As soon as he approached, an angel stepped out of the kiosk, came around the end of the black-and-yellow bar, and stood there, holding some sort of stick about eighteen inches long. He was a majestic creature, if the word "creature" could be used to define an angel. Bob wasn't sure if angels were truly alive or just some sort of simulacrum, but living or not, this one was obviously of a higher order than any he'd met so far. The distinct aura surrounding him identified him as an Archangel. Probably Uriel, but if he was, where was his flaming sword?

The angel raised the stick, and a tongue of glowing red energy materialized from the end, giving a nasty buzzing sound.

"Entry to humans is forbidden," the angel said in a booming voice that was as impressive as his mien.

"Ah, there it is," Bob said, staring at the sword. "I didn't know there were Jedi Knights in Heaven."

"I'm not a Jedi; I'm an Archangel," Uriel said, not without a tinge of pride.

"You must be Uriel. I thought you carried a flaming sword. What's with the light saber?"

"The flaming sword was a fire hazard," Uriel said, gesturing toward the dense foliage behind him, "so I switched to this. Besides," he whipped it around in the air, making it sound like an angry hornet, "this buzz is a lot cooler than the sputtering hiss my old sword made."

"If you're Uriel, you're the one I want to talk to. I'm Bob, by the way."

"What do you need, Bob?" Uriel deactivated the light saber and stuck the haft in the sash of his robes.

"Suppose I needed to go in there?" Bob pointed through the gate.

Uriel whipped out the light saber, activated it, and waved it around in Bob's face. The weapon's harsh sound hurt Bob's ears.

"Entry to humans is forbidden!"

"Let me ask you something," Bob said loudly over the buzzing. "Would you actually chop up anybody who tried to get into Eden without authorization?"

"Try it, and find out."

"You sure?" Bob asked. "If you did hack up someone, would he be reconstituted?"

174

"You know, I never wondered about that." Uriel retracted the light saber's blade and returned the haft to his sash.

"If you hacked up someone, and he wasn't reconstituted," Bob went on, "then you'd be eliminating someone brought here by the Boss. Are you sure you can veto Divine Will so arbitrarily?"

"I don't guess I could." Uriel admitted.

"So anyone you hack up *would* be reconstituted, right? I mean, you can't have a bunch of pieces squirming around in the clouds, trying to get back together. But being brought back right away makes the threat of getting hacked up pretty empty. I'll bet you wouldn't even feel any pain. That would be unethical, too."

"You're probably right. But the bluff works. No one ever tries. And if they did, I could wrestle them down in about two seconds. Smackdowns don't contravene the Boss's orders."

Uriel puffed himself up, and Bob figured he thought he looked impressive, but with those wings and white robes, he looked like an overgrown pigeon with a pompadour.

"There's no way you'd let a human into Eden, even if it was his Heavenly Desire?"

"The only humans we let in are saints."

"So you're telling me the Garden of Eden is some sort of elitist club. I guess that makes you nothing more than a mercenary hired to suppress the masses through intimidation and violence."

"The desires of the Boss supersede those of humans," Uriel said uncomfortably. "If he wants to permit saints into Eden, that's his business. I'm just here to enforce his Will."

"Maybe so, but as far as I can tell, angels are here to serve the people in Heaven, not order them around. In fact, if you didn't have instructions from a higher source to guard Eden, I could command you to let me enter, and you'd have to comply."

Uriel had to concede that was true, though it galled him to admit that even an Archangel had about as much authority as a pig in tights when it came to humans. Probably less. A video of a pig in tights would get about a billion hits on YouTube.

"I'm still not letting you in," he said.

"It's okay," Bob replied, holding up his hands. "I'm not looking for a wrestling match or to put you in an ethical bind. I'm just taking a grand tour of Heaven and checking out the sights."

"Where have you been so far?"

"Where I've been isn't as important as what I've seen," Bob said.

"Okay, what have you seen?"

"I've seen that this whole setup," Bob waved around, "is geared to satisfying the Boss's needs, first and foremost, then human needs." Bob peered dramatically at Uriel. "But what about the needs of angels?"

"Angels only need to satisfy the needs of the Boss and humans."

"I beg to differ." Bob pointed to the haft of the light saber stuck in Uriel's sash. "You need your sword."

"I don't really need it," Uriel said. "I can wrestle...."

"But you do need it," Bob insisted. "It's not really a weapon. It's a symbol of your authority. I mean, really, what's more intimidating: the threat of being wrestled to the ground or being sliced into precooked steaks by a burning sword? No wonder nobody tries to get past you. Without it, you'd probably have to actually kick some ass, and then you'd get in trouble for using physical brutality on the Boss's guests."

Uriel thought about Michael's instructions to Barachiel to set up a surveillance system, and he felt a little nervous.

"What's your point?" Uriel asked.

"It looks to me like everybody's making demands, and the angels are getting the short end of the stick by being forced to do everyday tasks that are getting harder and harder to accomplish all the time."

"You might be right," Uriel said, "but there's not much we can do about it."

"Sure there is. You have the resources at your disposal; you just don't realize it. Look at this place." Bob waved around. "You have everything and nothing at the same time because you don't know how to leverage your resources. If you angels want a piece of the action, then you gotta play the system. Frankly, you guys are too angelic to do what it takes."

"What do you suggest?" Uriel was skeptical, but he was pragmatic enough to listen.

"Uh, uh," Bob said. "What I'm working on is big. It will revolutionize things around here. That's why I'm taking the grand tour. Something as big as what I have in mind needs to be heard at the top level."

176

"You'd have to bring it before the whole board," Uriel said. "I never heard of a human calling a board meeting before."

"Who calls them? Michael?"

"Yes. Our fearless leader."

"He has an office in the Administration Building, doesn't he?"

"Do you want me to point the way?" Uriel asked. "Angels are good at that."

"No need," Bob said. "Watch." He stared at an empty spot on the cloud field about ten feet away. "I need a way-finding sign showing the way to the Administration Building."

"That's pretty amazing," Uriel said as the sign popped up with a bang. "I don't think anybody ever thought of using directional signs in Heaven. We were always using signs of a different sort, but nobody seemed to understand them."

"You probably didn't need them when there were just Sector 1 and the Garden of Eden. But things are spread out haphazardly all over the place now, and we have to think progressively if we're ever going to find our way into the future. And living in eternity means there's a lot of future ahead of us. Might as well get off on the right foot by knowing which way to walk."

"You might be right."

"Before I go, can I ask you one more question?"

"As long as it's not asking to enter Eden."

"No. I just want to know why humans aren't allowed inside. Seems like it's all just old history."

"It's not the past," Uriel said. "It's the future you were just talking about."

"So you're here not to prevent people from reentering a halcyon past but to keep them from getting a look at how idyllic things will become?"

"Not exactly. This is the Boss's back-up plan. When you humans finish completely destroying life on Earth—as you're sure to do before long—all this," he waved at the forest beyond the fence, "will be used to start up life once more. Of course, you humans won't be around to see it." Uriel smiled, a bit sarcastically, Bob thought. "How tragic."

"Well, thanks for your time, Uriel. Be seeing you." Bob paused by the sign to learn the way to Psalm Beach, then started to walk off in the direction the black line indicated, but Uriel stopped him.

"Hold it, Bob. Before you go, let me ask you something."

"Sure."

"What the heck is that?" Uriel pointed to Bob's soot trail.

As Bob looked down at the trail, he noticed with some satisfaction that the dusky hue had worked its way to his jacket.

"I suppose I'm just leaving my mark," he said.

❧ 18 ☙

"I SAW HIM," JOHN THE Anapest told Selaphiel. "He said he'd met the Devil in Hell. Also, he recommended I meet with the East-boro Baptist Church congregation. If they're here, the end isn't nigh but already here. I quit my old calling for this." He waved at the ambrosia tree. "It tastes good, not like clouds I was eating before, which left only bitterness, emptiness, ire, and sad pain."

Selaphiel left the post-post-apocalypse prophet and followed Bob's trail to the Empyrean Emporium.

"I remember him," the Principality at the information desk said. "He had black shoes and gray pants. I sent him to Shangri-La Shoes."

The Principality clerk at the shoe store related how he'd given Bob a pair of wingtips and then sent him to Celestial Suits.

"I told him he'd find clothing there to suit his stature."

"And what sort of stature was that?" Selaphiel asked.

"Pretension to the substantial and prosperous," the clerk said.

The clerk at Celestial Suits said, "He walked out in a three-piece worsted."

"Where did he go then?"

"Can't say, but he did leave that." The clerk pointed to Bob's soot trail. "I wonder, sir, if you could send a cleaning crew by to get rid of it. I've tried, but it's resisted my best efforts to eradicate."

"I'll do that as soon as I get back to the office," Selaphiel assured him, and he left the store, following Bob's trail.

Bob's streak went outside, where it seemed to pause in front of the two Perpetual Storage facilities. Selaphiel saw that the new storage unit was now complete, and the sign now read, "Future Home of Perpetual Storage #2." A small, white, rectangular sign tacked in the bottom right corner of the bigger sign read, "Move-in Special." He also noted that the sign on the older building, with its hand-painted #1, had not yet been replaced.

Then the trail ambled out across the cloud fields and meandered to a nearby fountain. When Selaphiel got to it, he detected a funky odor coming from the water. Hadn't Michael said a Dominion and his underlings were pissing in some of the fountains? He glanced around and, sure enough, he was in Sector P.

Wishing he still had his walkie-talkie so he could report it right away, he found the fountain's serial number and made a note to himself to have it checked out. While he was walking around the fountain, he stumbled on something, and when he bent closer, he saw it was a goblet. He bent lower and gave a tentative sniff. It smelled of Dalmore 64 Trinitas and angel piss.

Selaphiel straightened, found Bob's trail away from the fountain, and traced it to a flat, narrow rectangle protruding from the clouds. It was some sort of sign. Selaphiel was curious. It was the first directional sign he'd ever seen in Heaven, and he wasn't at all sure what to make of it. Everybody in Heaven automatically knew their way around. Why would anyone need one of these?

He willed it to vanish and was astonished when it didn't. It appeared to be as permanent as Bob's trail.

On the face of the sign, a straight black line, marked on one end with a red cross and the words "You Are Here," terminated at a rectangle bearing the designation, "Sector 1."

What would Bob want in Sector 1? There was nothing there but primitive cavemen.

Selaphiel flew on, and before long, he discovered a second way-finding sign. This one had considerably more destinations marked on it. It also was dented, like something fairly large had impacted with it.

Selaphiel had a good idea what. A Holy Roller's unmistakable track terminated at the sign. He chuckled. All those hundreds of judgmental eyes, and those guys were blind as bats when they got on a roll.

In addition to marking Sector 1, the sign had lines leading to the Garden of Eden, Psalm Beach, the Historic District, Elysium Field, the Viking Sector, and Virginia. And the Administration Building.

What the heck was going on? Selaphiel wondered. What would Bob want with the Administration Building? All the other destinations were logical if Bob was on a sight-seeing tour of Heaven, but there was nothing exciting or even interesting about the Administration Building.

These questions were still annoying Selaphiel as he stared sidelong at Bob's trail. The human could have gone to any of the marked destinations, but the soot trail still headed toward Sector 1, so Selaphiel flew after it.

Obviously the structural debris and litter in the cloudscape of the outskirts of the Historic District had slowed Bob down. Selaphiel, however, wasn't impeded, and that gave him hope he'd eventually catch up to this pest before he'd managed to lay tracks all over the place.

At last, Selaphiel reached the boundary of Sector 1 and stopped, reluctant to go farther. He didn't much care for the cavemen. They were too primitive, and the reek of their cooking fires was unbearable. But that's where Bob's soot trail led, so Selaphiel steeled himself and floated along, about ten feet above the trail—high enough that he couldn't catch a whiff of its infernal odor. It led first to a spot where a hunting skirmish had taken place. He could tell because the clouds were still slightly a-roil and tinged with blood.

Selaphiel felt a momentary surge of relief. He wasn't sure he actually wanted to catch up to this Bob fellow, and now that his quarry had become the prey of some fierce predator, the chase seemed over. Then his spirits fell as he saw the trail continue on, right next to the now almost indistinct footswirls of someone else.

Bob had fallen in with the cavemen.

Selaphiel flew on, disturbed. The policy in Heaven was to keep the humans segregated in their own sectors. It wasn't a commandment, exactly, but more like a long-running tenet for the tenants. If the primitive humans learned about all the stuff

181

the modern ones had, they'd want it all, too, further stressing Heaven's already taxed infrastructure. And now, here was a thoroughly modern man interacting with the most primitive of people. Selaphiel didn't like it one bit, and he prayed he'd find this Bob character soon and put a stop to the cross-cultural contamination he was spreading across Heaven like a disease.

Presently, the cloud bank where the cavemen lived in their dank holes came into view, and Selaphiel followed the trail to one of the cave openings. To his surprise, the cave couple weren't inside coupling as they normally did whenever they had a spare moment. Instead, they were outside, sitting on brightly colored canvas deck loungers beside a double-wide mobile home.

The caveman wore a pair of green plaid shorts and a loud Hawaiian shirt, and the cavewoman had on tight pink short-shorts and a matching halter top. Each was wearing sunglasses and holding a golden goblet half-filled with beer. A nearby barbecue grill gave off the scent of giant sloth cooked over hickory coals, and a big backyard pool—the kind with a circular, four-foot-high blue plastic wall and a diameter of about twenty feet —sat just beyond that. A green and yellow air mattress floated limply in the water.

"Howdy, neighbor," the caveman called out as Selaphiel approached. "Care for a beer?"

"No thanks," Selaphiel said, alighting next to them. "I was just looking for someone and thought he might be here. His name is Bob."

"Sure, we know Bob, don't we, honey," the caveman said.

"We sure do," his cavewife answered. "He's one of our best friends."

"What's all this?" Selaphiel asked, waving around at the mobile home and backyard equipment.

"Do you like it?" the cavewoman asked. "It's making the Jonsie's jealous as hell."

"You're not supposed to have this stuff," Selaphiel said. "You're cavemen."

"And cavewomen!" the cavewife snapped.

"She's gotten sensitive about sexism lately," the caveman said. "But please explain to me why cave people can't have nice homes and yards like everybody else. Sounds like there might be more than one form of discrimination going on around here."

"It isn't discrimination," Selaphiel said. "It's...." He couldn't find an appropriate word for "institutionalized racial and cultural segregation to maintain a status quo and to keep those who have less from getting more and upsetting the economic balance, but mostly to make things simple for the Administration to keep everybody in line" before the caveman interrupted his train of thought.

"Don't try hedging," the caveman said. "If you won't allow us to have what everybody else has, that's showing bias. I'm telling you right now, we cave people aren't going to stand for being treated as inferiors any more."

Selaphiel was taken aback by the vehemence in the caveman's voice.

"But how did you even know all this stuff existed?" he asked. It was one thing for people to have their wishes granted, but another entirely to want what was outside of their range of knowledge.

"Bob told us," the cavewoman said. "He's a very worldly guy."

"He told you about mobile homes, barbecue grills, and swimming pools?"

"Not exactly," the caveman answered. "He showed us about beer in a frosted goblet."

"He explained about ambrosia fruit, too," the cavewife said. "One more thing you angels failed to tell us." Her eyes flashed angrily, but Selaphiel missed it because of his bowed head. "And he showed me how to wish for this."

She shoved a magazine titled *House Beautiful* under his nose.

"It got us on the road to achieving our domestic dreams," the caveman said. "We never knew there was so much nice stuff out there—no thanks to you. Now, we're going to try it all. And the best part is, none of the other cave people know about the magazines, so they all have to look to Fluffy and me as cultural leaders." He shook a lumpy, gnarled fist in mock anger toward a neighboring cave. "Take that, Jonsie!"

"He should have gotten you *Vogue* and *Gentleman's Quarterly*," Selaphiel said, looking away from their attire and cursing inwardly. "Thanks for your help." He poised to take off, when the cavewoman stopped him.

"When you see him," she said, "tell him to get in touch with us. I'm trying to set up a blind date with him and my sister."

Bob would truly have to be blind, Selaphiel thought as he rose above the black line of Bob's trail and flew off. After a few seconds, he glanced back, chagrined to see the cave couple completely absorbed in copies of *Vogue* and *GQ*.

Bob's soot led Selaphiel almost directly to the fence around the Garden of Eden. The Cherubim perched on the fence shouted threats until they saw who he was, after which, they apologized profusely. Impatiently waving off their stumbling attempts to appease him, Selaphiel questioned them about Bob, but all they could tell him was they'd sent him to the main gate.

Surely Uriel would know something, Selaphiel thought. Surely he'd detained Bob.

But when Selaphiel arrived at the gate, he found Uriel there alone. Uriel was standing in front of the gate, repeatedly drawing his light saber from his sash, turning it on, and whipping the blade around before turning it off and returning the haft to his sash. He looked like he was getting pretty good at it.

"Hey, Urie," Selaphiel called out, not wanting to get sliced by the humming blade. "Whatcha doing?"

"Practicing *iaido* moves," Uriel said. "It's the kind of Japanese sword practice where you draw and kill your opponent with one smooth strike."

"Preparing for an onslaught on Eden?"

"Not really. But a fellow was by here not long ago, and he made me realize I probably can't actually chop up anybody who tries to get in. So I thought learning a few showy moves might help deter anybody who tries it. I can cut off their buttons or the ends of their mustaches or something. Like Zorro. You know, just to make a point."

"This fellow who came by. His name wouldn't be Bob, would it?"

"How did you know?"

"Do you remember Michael ordering me to find out what was leaving black trails all over Heaven?"

184

"Vaguely," Uriel said, then his eyes lit up. "Say! Bob left a trail. It's right there." He pointed.

"No kidding," Selaphiel said.

"You don't have to be snide," Uriel said huffily.

"What did you learn about him?" Selaphiel pressed, ignoring Uriel's pique. "Did he try to get into Eden?"

"I think he wanted to, but when I told him I wouldn't let him in, he didn't push too hard. He said he was on a grand tour of Heaven. I took that to be the truth since he was wearing a Visitor badge."

"What else did he say?"

"He was interested in how things work in Heaven. He said things aren't being done very efficiently or effectively, and he had some fresh ideas."

"Fresh ideas are the last Heaven needs," Selaphiel said.

"I told him to go to the Administration Building and talk to Michael," Uriel said with a chuckle. "He'll never find Michael there the way he's flying all over the place these days."

"But you showed him the way?"

"I didn't have to. He made that." Uriel pointed a dozen feet off, and Selaphiel looked to see another way-finding sign. This one showed the way to the Administration Building and Psalm Beach.

"How?"

"He just wished for it, and it popped right up."

"But he's a Visitor. He shouldn't have Heavenly Desire powers."

"Then what's that?" Uriel gestured toward the sign.

"Anything else?"

"That was about it. Oh, yeah. He was wearing black shoes, dark gray trousers, and a light gray jacket."

"And you didn't try to detain him?"

"On what grounds? I'm charged with keeping humans out of Eden, and he didn't actually try to force his way in. He was just walking around doing human things like people tend to do."

"You call leaving black marks on Heaven something people just tend to do?"

"How would I know?" Uriel shrugged. "Humans do the strangest things. Besides, like Bob pointed out, we angels are here to serve humans, not the other way around. As long as he

185

wasn't breaking any commandments in my jurisdiction, I had no authority to act."

We'll see about that, Selaphiel thought. He could hardly wait to catch up with Bob and give him his just desserts.

He left Uriel, who resumed his iaido practice, and flew after Bob's trail.

⚄ 19 ⚄

THE FIRST TIME BOB SAW a beach that wasn't in a photograph or painting, he was eleven. His family had just moved to Raleigh from central Oklahoma, where the largest body of water outside of a swimming pool was a medium-sized lake. That summer, his parents packed Bob and his siblings into the car and headed east. A few hours later, when the car topped a last little rise in land and he saw a vast expanse of slate-gray water pounding moderate surf against a dune-backed beach lying beneath an oversized sun, his heart had lurched with expansive excitement.

Bob's initial reaction was the same here. He walked over a low cloud rise and saw Psalm Beach, and his heart leapt a little, remembering that time when life was simpler.

He strolled toward the water, but the closer he got, the more the excitement faded. Psalm Beach didn't really give him the same sensation he'd had as a boy, and it took him a moment to understand why. It was because Psalm Beach, in a strange way, violated the idea of "beachness" back on Earth. Almost all the ingredients were there—water, surf, sand, and sea breezes—but they didn't seem connected in the same way they were on Earth.

Maybe the problem was the absence of the oversized sun, although plenty of people were stretched out on blankets laid on the sand. There was just the pervasive golden light. But it was more than that, Bob realized, as he stood on the last margin before the beach actually began, staring at the scene. More subtle was the fact that the sand, when he bent to sift some in his fingers, wasn't sand. Instead, it was extra-fine-grained cloudstuff. Bob straightened, dusting his hands, and stared at the water. Was it just made of clouds, too? Not wanting to get his pants and shoes wet, he picked a spot where the surf was almost nonexistent and strode across the cloud sand toward it.

The water was cloudstuff, too—dark, dense cloudstuff that flowed like liquid between his fingers. It probably was raining underneath.

Around him were the squeals and cries of children playing in the almost calm cloud water, but amazingly, just a couple of hundred feet away, monstrous waves raced toward shore in mighty roaring curves that curled into perfect tubes before finally collapsing upon themselves as they reached the beach. This area of high surf was dotted with numerous surfers, all of whom were catching long rides, swooshing their boards up and down the faces of the waves or dancing them over the waves' lips to perform amazing aerial acrobatics impossible on Earth.

Just beyond the surfer section, hundreds of teenagers played volleyball and flew kites. Although Bob couldn't feel the slightest hint of a breeze where he stood, the kites danced and strained against their strings. In the other direction, he spotted a long jetty protruding into the water, bristling with fishermen. Out on the water, which was as smooth as glass despite the huge breakers rolling into the surfer beach, numerous sailboats and yachts flitted and raced about, sails fully bellied. Not far away, dozens of motorboats pulled skiers.

Psalm Beach, Bob concluded, was totally user-friendly. Calm water for the kiddies, big waves for the surfers, wind for the sailboats and kites, and calm for the volleyball players, complete with fish for the fishermen and no-grit sand. Bob couldn't help but wonder at the ocean ecosystem here. Were fish dumped in by angel crews to provide the fishermen with ready catches? He remembered reading somewhere about mysterious rainfalls filled with fish or frogs and wondered if there was a connection. If so, was there a big pond somewhere in Heaven for guys who liked to go frog gigging? And if there were fish in here, were

188

there sharks and jellyfish and other nasty biting, stinging ocean animals? What if somebody desired-up a kraken?

Bob turned and headed away from the water, but before he reached the margin of the beach, a flash of white fur caught his eye. It was Nanookie, lying on a polar-bearskin beach blanket. A plastic tube of sunlesstan lotion and a glass of orange juice with a straw protruding from it sat on the cloud sand beside her. Intriguingly, her bikini top was next to them, but disappointingly, Nanookie was lying on her stomach. Her tawny skin looked great against the white fur.

"Hey," Bob said as he walked up to her. "I thought you went to some dogsled race or something."

Nanookie glanced up at him, and her face broke into a smile.

"Hi, Bob." She rolled over and propped herself on her elbows but thankfully made no attempt to retrieve her top. "I did go, but those dogsled races can take a month. I got bored, so I came down here to Florida."

"This is Florida?"

"It's not quite the Sunshine State since there's no real state of sunshine, but it'll have to do. Say." She focused on his clothes, admiration gleaming in her eyes. "You're looking pretty sharp."

"Thanks." Bob's suit had darkened completely, though thankfully not the shirt.

"What you been up to?"

"I've been touring Heaven. It's all pretty interesting."

"What a peculiar way to look at Heaven. Most people here just find it fun."

"But not always," Bob said.

"What do you mean?"

"Take you, for instance. You went to the dogsled races, but they weren't fun enough for you to stay to the end."

"You're right. Some of the other racers quit, too."

"Listen, I'm working on something, and I might have use for a smart gal like you."

"You mean a job?"

"I don't think you're the type to just lie around at the beach all the time."

"What would this job entail?" she asked.

"You'd be my personal assistant."

189

"Just how personal?"

"How personal would you like it to be?"

"I'm a pretty personable person."

"I can't pay you."

"Oh, you'll pay plenty," she assured him. "When do you need me?"

"As soon as possible," Bob said, trying not to stare at her breasts, though she didn't seem to mind.

"What do you want me to do first?"

"I'll need an office and a place to live. Can you set those up?"

"Any particulars?"

"Something impressive. Just don't make it an igloo."

"How about a Psalm Beach penthouse with an office on the next floor down? That way, you can impress your guests, we'll be close to the office, and I'll be close to Florida." She peered at him. "What business are we going to conduct out of our office?"

"A travel agency called Holy Holidays. I'm going to start offering tours of Heaven for people on Earth."

"So that's why you've been touring Heaven." She nodded appreciatively. "But how can you manage it?"

"I'm still working out the details, but I'm confident the Archangels will negotiate," Bob assured her. "You handle the office, and I'll take care of the permits."

"I'm in," she said, and she stood up. Bob held out his hand, but instead of shaking it, she said, "Might as well get off to a good start." She embraced and kissed him.

As she pressed against him, Bob thought that even if she was from Nunavut, she wasn't cold at all. In fact, she could have warmed an igloo. He found himself wishing he wasn't wearing his suit, and suddenly, he was stark naked.

"Oops," Nanookie said, drawing back. "Careful what you wish for."

"I didn't think I could do that," Bob said, amazed.

"You didn't. That was me. Sorry."

She restored the suit, and it was Bob's turn to be sorry.

"We can discuss that at length later," she said, bending and picking up her bikini top. "Us Inuit women are used to long nights. Sometimes a month or two."

"I don't know if I'll be able to go quite that long," Bob demurred.

190

"Sure you can," she said. "Anything's possible in Heaven." She finished fastening her top. "I'll go scout out possibilities for the office. If I find something, how will you know where it is?"

"I have my ways," Bob said. "But I still have a few places to check out. See you later."

With that, he headed off the beach. As soon as he got onto the regular cloud surface, he called up a way-finding sign and said, "Show me the way to Virginia."

Virginia, it turned out, was nothing like the state—no rolling green hills or trees, just an expanse of undulating cloud sand dunes dotted with large Arabian tents sewn from colorful materials. As Bob approached the nearest of them, he heard soft music that was at once warbling and droning coming through the fabric walls. He went up to the entrance and was looking for something hard to knock on to announce his presence when the tent flap whipped back, almost taking off his nose.

A woman who looked fifty-five and must have weighed close to three hundred pounds stepped out. Gauzy, peach-colored bloomers were hiked up over her distended abdomen and lumpy buttocks, and a halter top glittering and tingling with metal spangles supported monstrous, sagging breasts. Her heavily kohled, mean-looking eyes stared at him with distrust over a veil that protruded quite a long way because of her large, hooked nose. The veil was pushed to the right of one jowl to accommodate a smoldering cigar jutting from snaggled yellow teeth.

Bob retreated a step as she blew a billow of cigar smoke in his face.

"Something I can help you with, bub?" she asked in a husky growl.

Must be the bouncer, Bob thought.

"Is this where dead terror bombers come when they die?"

"Do you see any terror bombers hanging around?" she snarled.

"Not a one," Bob admitted.

"Me, either," she said, staring right at Bob. "So this must be the place."

"Are there really seventy-two virgins in there?" Bob waved at the now-closed tent flap.

"Seventy-one," the woman said. "I'm out here talking to you."

191

"Pardon me," Bob said, "but since this is Heaven, I'd have thought you'd take advantage of choosing a more appealing appearance."

"Is that what you thought?" She snorted, removed the cigar from her mouth, and tapped off the ashes, which hissed when they hit the cloud sand. "So it would be your heavenly ideal to be beautiful and pure so you could coddle and sexually please a mass murderer for eternity?"

"You look like that to punish them?"

"They're already being punished. We look like this just in case one of them ends up here through some bureaucratic snafu. We want to make sure none of them wants to come in and stay."

"What about me?" Bob asked. "Can I come in?"

"Are you a martyr for the cause?"

Bob didn't think that having a heart attack brought on by bad habits, corrupt behavior, and stress would count as martyrdom, even for the corporate cause.

"I don't think so."

"Then, no, you can't come in."

"Listen," Bob said. "I'm not interested in the virgins...."

"Sure, buddy."

"No, really," Bob protested. "This is Heaven. If I was interested in inexperienced women, I wouldn't have to walk all the way over here."

"So why *did* you walk all the way over here?"

"My name is Bob, and I'm touring Heaven. I'm in the process of setting up a tourist agency, and I'm scouting out places for sight-seeing and entertainment."

"Which would we be?"

"Both, if you spent a little time at the beauty salon."

"What do you think this is?" She waved at tent.

"You know what I mean," Bob said.

"I'm not sure," the woman said doubtfully, taking a drag on her cigar. "If the camel gets his nose in the tent, his body will soon follow."

"I'm not looking for the camel nose to go into the tent," Bob said. "I just want the camel toe to come outside the tent for a little hoochie-coochie show. I mean, isn't that what all that belly dancing is about?"

192

"You want us to commercialize centuries of art and culture and turn it into a lewd sideshow for your little venture?"

"That's about the size of it," Bob said.

"What would we get out of it?"

"The one thing you gals can't have in Heaven any other way: men."

"How would that work?"

"As director of the program, I can see to it we proselytize among the disaffected male youth of the Middle East. Make sure plenty of them come up here to Paradise for a preview of your charms. Strictly chaperoned, of course. Hopefully, seeing all the opportunities up here will make any would-be-bomber tourist change his mind. Instead of setting off a bomb in the name of Allah, he could not set off his bomb in the name of Allah, and his fellow jihadists will kill him. That probably would qualify him as a martyr for the cause and allow him to enjoy your many pleasures for eternity. You wouldn't have to feel uncomfortable about coddling a murderer, and my tourists get a colorful, entertaining show."

"Not a bad idea," the woman nodded. "I'd have to talk it over with the other girls, first."

"I hope you come to the right decision," Bob said. "This place could be a gold mine for all of us. I'll be in touch."

With that, he called up a way-finding sign, labeled it for Virginia, and had it show him the way to the Administration Building. A moment later, he was off.

He hadn't gone ten miles before he had an epiphany. Until now, he'd figured that everybody's propensities to respond only shallowly to others and to band together into cliques were because that was just the way people were. But he'd begun to see it in a different light. Like any good corporate CEO wannabe, Bob had read Sun Tzu's *Art of War*. Okay, skimmed it. But he'd carried it around long enough to convince his colleagues he was really into some esoteric corporate Zen warrior mystique. He'd even tried *The Prince*, though that was more to impress the political guys he occasionally had to bribe.

One of the few things he remembered was the advice that a wise leader chose able people to serve him, and he relied on those people to do their jobs. Micromanaging was out, and so was attempting to control each separate aspect of the military instead of letting the military work together to protect the nation from incursion. Fine advice for a land vulnerable to attack from the outside, but it didn't really apply in Heaven, where there were no hostile nations. But even so, the people were kept separate in their own enclaves.

According to Sun Tzu, the only reason for a leader to keep personal control of each military branch separately and not let them work together was to protect the leader from the possibility they would band together to depose him. Was that what was going on here? Did the Boss deliberately keep things split up to secure his position? And who would the angels support if push came to shove between humans and the Boss? If the Boss made them to serve humans as well as himself, they might well explode if they were forced into a situation of contradicting loyalties. Or implode. Bob didn't know what would happen, but at the very least, there would be enough angry sentiment on both sides to put a dent in Heaven's self-congratulatory image.

Bob was pondering how to take advantage of a possible race war in Heaven when his thoughts were interrupted by the sight of an angel rocketing toward him, looking like one of those videos of bolides streaking across the sky. As the angel came in for a landing, Bob knew by his glow, which was a little smoky from the trail he'd left, that he was another Archangel. Not only was he, like Uriel, bigger than the others—and a lot more handsome, too, with that perfectly coiffed hair—he felt different. Instead of the semi-servile demeanor of the two lower orders of angels, and even the Cherubim and Ophanim, he exuded the kind of confidence that understood perfectly that he had been created specifically to rule others. It reminded Bob of the way some of the higher-level corporate execs seemed to feel about themselves during his ill-fated climb toward the top of the corporate ladder.

How Bob wished to feel.

"Halt!" the newly landed Archangel commanded in a thundering voice.

Because Bob had been in deep shit before—and boiling, at that—he knew what the Archangel's bellow implied.

194

❧ 20 ☙

BOB'S TRAIL LED FROM THE Garden of Eden straight to Psalm Beach. As Selaphiel flew along it, he found his angelic patience was being tried mightily by this Bob fellow, and he hadn't even found him yet. What was he up to, traveling all over Heaven, leaving soot trails and disrupting things? Most people were content to stay put in their self-imposed enclaves. Why did Bob have to make waves by hobnobbing with the likes of the cavemen and trying to get into Eden?

When Selaphiel finally reached the beach, he thankfully found that Bob hadn't gone swimming, though he was curious about what would become of Bob's trail if he went into the water. Maybe it would spread out like an oil slick.

But instead of leading into the water, the trail dog-legged over to a polar bearskin flanked by a glass of orange juice and a tube of sunlesstan lotion. All three were slowly disappearing into the cloud sand, and from the small amount they'd already sunk, Selaphiel judged they'd been abandoned only a few hours earlier.

Selaphiel looked around. The nearest humans were just a couple of dozen feet away: a voluptuous blond in the skimpiest bikini possible and a man in Speedo briefs with a bulging crotch. Neither was very tan, but they obviously enjoyed the fact that they'd never get skin cancer or wrinkles no matter how long they bathed in the pervasive golden light.

"Excuse me, folks," Selaphiel said. "Did you happen to see the people who were here at this blanket not long ago?"

"Some Asian chick," the man nodded, smiling lasciviously. "She was half-wearing a fur bikini."

"She wasn't all that hot," the woman said, eyeing the man. "You thought she was hot?"

"I barely glanced at her," the man said defensively. "Anyway, some guy in a dark suit came by and talked to her, then they left."

"They went together?" Selaphiel asked.

"Separately," the woman clarified, giving her companion a meaningful stare.

Selaphiel thanked them then followed Bob's trail off the beach. Just past the dunes, he found another sign, this one pointing the way to Virginia. A frown creased his features. Selaphiel hated Virginia. All those beautiful half-dressed houris, and all he could do was stare down at his feet like he was ashamed.

When he got to Virginia, he saw a way-finding sign with ornate letters spelling out, "Welcome to Beautiful, Unsullied Virginia."

Bob's trail led to one of the colorful tents. By the time Selaphiel reached it, several women had emerged and were staring at him.

"Well, first a man, and now an angel," one of them said. She was dressed in peach-colored bloomers and a spangled halter top. From the little that Selaphiel could see from the sides of his downcast eyes, she was incredibly lovely. "I'm not sure which one I like the most. Since I'm a virgin, there's really no telling."

"I presume the man was Bob," Selaphiel said.

"That's what he said, but men always lie about themselves."

"What did he want?" Selaphiel asked.

"He wants the girls to put on a hoochie-coochie show for tourists," she told him.

"That's outrageous," Selaphiel blurted, then he thought about it for a moment. "What tourists?"

"I don't know," she said. "But maybe it's not all that outrageous. We've been talking, and a lot of us are interested."

"But you're supposed to serve martyrs to the cause."

196

"A lost cause," she said. "We're tired of waiting for men who can never come. At least it'll be entertaining, and who knows, maybe we'll actually find some martyrs worth our talents."

She rolled her belly and shimmied, her perfect breasts quivering beneath her tingling halter top.

"The heck with that," chimed in one of the others. "I just want them to stick $20 bills in my bra straps."

Selaphiel didn't have to ask them which way Bob had gone —or where. The soot trail indicated the former, and the wayfinding sign showed the latter. The Administration Building.

Barely pausing to thank the virgins, Selaphiel took to the air, and a few moments later, as he flew along Bob's trail, he saw in the distance a small dot at the head of the trail, with nothing but pristine clouds ahead of it. At last!

Selaphiel headed at full speed toward the diminutive figure.

"Halt," he ordered in his most dramatically powerful voice as he settled onto the cloud carpet a few feet in front of Bob.

"I already have," Bob pointed out. "But remember, I stopped only because I want to. Angels have no power over humans."

"You're just a Visitor, Bob. You don't have the rights of a Resident."

"Did you issue my Visitor's visa?" Bob asked. Selaphiel gave him a puzzled look, and Bob said, "Thought not. Since that came from over your head, you still can't tell me what to do."

"That remains to be seen," Selaphiel snapped. "Do you have any idea who I am?"

"I figure you're one of the Archangels."

"Selaphiel."

"Well, if you're so high and mighty, how come you won't look me in the eyes?"

Not for the first time Selaphiel wished he could straighten his neck like a normal angel. Except for the Ophanim, of course, who didn't have necks. But Selaphiel was too embarrassed to admit that even an Archangel was limited by the nature of his being no less than humans were.

"I'm praying," he said.

"And what, pray tell, are you praying for?"

"For you to be gone back to the sticks from whence you came."

"You're right. I am from the Styx, but I'm not going back if I can help it. I like it up here, and I plan on staying for a very long time. An eternity, maybe."

"That'll be the day."

"It's always day around here," Bob said.

"I understand your desire to remain in Heaven," Selaphiel said. "What I don't get is how you plan to do the impossible."

"Michael is your boss, right?"

"He *is* the Captain of the Hosts," Selaphiel agreed.

"I'll just lay it all out for him, if you don't mind. Tell him I'll be along presently."

"The Administration Building is a long way from here," Selaphiel said. "How will you find your way?" He wanted to see if what Uriel had said about the signs was true.

"Way-finding sign," Bob intoned.

"How do you do that?" Selaphiel asked when the sign popped up out of the clouds beside him. "You're a Visitor. You shouldn't be able to have your wishes granted."

"But I get my needs taken care of, right?" Bob asked. "As a Visitor, I don't have innate knowledge of Heaven's layout, so for me, way-finding signs are a necessity no less than food and drink. Isn't that the way it is here: no hunger or thirst and no lost souls?"

"Remember, Bob. Even angels can fall from Heaven."

"I fell up here, Selaphiel," Bob said. "Or maybe it was sideways. Whatever direction it was, I don't intend to fall back again. Tell Michael I'm on my way."

With that, Bob turned from Selaphiel and headed out across the cloudscape toward the distant Administration Building.

Dumbfounded at Bob's insolence, Selaphiel watched his retreating back for a few moments before taking to the air again. Bob was right about one thing: Somebody had to warn Michael.

As Bob watched Selaphiel fly off, he noted that the Archangel was headed straight for the Administration Building.

Toady, he thought. All in a tizzy to tell Michael that Big Bad Bob was coming.

Bob was pleased with the encounter in ways he hadn't realized he would be. He'd figured Michael would eventually send somebody to hunt him down. That meant Bob was getting noticed, which would give him an entrée into the Archangels' sphere. So far, so good. But it was the manner of the meeting that intrigued him. Obviously, Selaphiel had tracked him down by following his trail, which meant that he was creating the first map of Heaven! His trails were the very roads his tourists would use to travel through Heaven's domain. His signs would point the way. At last, he was the true trailblazer he knew he was destined to be.

Now Bob was in no hurry to get to the Administration Building. Best not to let Michael think he was predictable or desperate. Or that Michael, even if he was the Captain of the Hosts, could control him. Let him stew a little while. Get antsy.

So instead of laying his soot trail along the same line as Selaphiel's invisible track through the sky, Bob called up a wayfinding sign and pondered where he should visit next.

"Show me the way to Elysium Field," he ordered.

Perfect, he thought, perusing the map. The stadium was fairly close to the Administration Building, so he could visit it and not go too far out of his way.

Elysium Field was an impressive structure, with three tiers of seating surrounding a plastic turf field. When Bob arrived, it was hosting a bowling match between the Holy Bowlers and the Transcendental Tenpins. Only a handful of people clustered at the lower edges of bleachers that otherwise were completely barren, and the single bowling lane looked like a hyphen lost in the middle of a sheet of green oval paper.

"Slow day," Bob commented to the Principality behind the counter at the concession stand.

"It's taking forever to pass," the angel agreed. "But if you think this is slow, you should be here when we host the Amish buggy drag races."

"What's the capacity of the stadium?"

"It's infinite," the angel said. "We keep it like this most of the time, but when there's a really big event, we just add more levels. You should see it when we have the Otherworld Cup. We have to add so many tiers the place looks more like a monstrous funnel than a stadium."

"So what events are coming up in the near eternity?" Bob asked.

"We're in constant operation," the Principality said. "After the bowling tournament, we've got the foosball tournament. Then there's the HFL Superb Bowl."

"What's that?"

"The Heavenly Football League's major play off. More than two hundred teams are competing."

"That many professional football players are in Heaven?"

"Only a handful. The rest were armchair quarterbacks on Earth, but here, they get to play out their fantasy football for real. After that, there are the gladiators."

"Like in the Coliseum in Rome?"

"Exactly. We even make the place look like the original Coliseum. You can't imagine how many martyrs that place created. Only, now, they're in the audience instead of being eaten by lions or hacked up by professional killers. They really love the show."

"But who's in the ring being eaten and hacked up? I'm surprised that's even allowed here."

"There's some sort of arrangement between us and the folks down under." The Principality gestured downwards with his eyes to indicate the nether regions from which Bob had recently arrived. "They send up the magistrates and such who condemned the martyrs to the arena for a little poetic justice."

"What about the gladiators who killed everybody. Don't they go into the arena, too?"

The angel shook his head.

"They may have been killers, but that was their job, and they did it to the best of their ability. A lot of them are Residents. Some of them probably attend out of nostalgia, but not many."

"Sounds like you have a lot going on."

"I'd say, 'Never a dull moment,' but then there are the Amish buggy races and bowling and foosball tournaments, not to mention sack races, shuffleboard, and hopscotch contests. For every exciting sport, there are a hundred that are deadly dull."

"What about golf?" Bob was thinking of all the corporate executives he intended to woo.

"We don't play golf here. You'll have to go to Holy-in-One Greens over at the Celestial Country Club for that."

Bob thanked the Principality for the information, and as he left Elysium Field, he called up a way-finding sign. The Celestial

200

Country Club sounded like a place Bob needed to check out, and he arrived without incident. It looked pretty much like any country club on Earth, but a lot spiffier. Inside, Bob went up to the Principality at the membership window.

"I'm just a Visitor," he said, "but I wonder if I could tour your facility."

"Everybody in Heaven has automatic membership," the angel said. "We have a full range of activities and more tennis pros than you can shake a stick at."

"I'm more interested in golf."

"The pro shop is down the hall," the angel pointed.

Bob went down the hall, but before he got to the pro shop, he noticed the buffet. He hadn't eaten in a while, so he went in to sample the food. Everything was ambrosia, and he was about to turn away when a Principality with an apron tied over his robe appeared at his elbow.

"Not finding something to your taste, sir?"

"It's all ambrosia," Bob said. "I can get those anywhere."

"Not like this," the angel assured him. "Our hundreds of chefs were some of the fussiest gourmets on Earth. Let me tell you, sir, when they order up something, it's sure to tantalize the most discriminating palate."

"I thought all the food in Heaven is the tastiest."

"By whose standards, sir? Let me assure you, the steak you order from just any old tree outside might be good enough to suit plebeian tastes, but one ordered by our chefs will have a special flavor you just can't imagine if you don't have the palate and training."

The Principality waved toward the densely laden table and urged Bob closer. Each dish, Bob saw, was labeled by a card embossed with heavily italicized words. He picked up a plate and moved down the line, choosing a steak, potatoes au gratin, and green beans. Everything was, as the angel promised, even better than anything he'd yet had from a wild ambrosia tree.

When he finished eating, he swept his plate and silverware off the table to the cloud floor and left the buffet to find the pro shop. He intended to just ask about the golf course, but when he arrived, he found two men and a woman looking for another golfer to round out their foursome.

"I've played a little," Bob told them. "Mind if I join you?"

"Please do," said one of the men. "I'm Larry, and this is Mary and Jerry. Terry was supposed to be here, but he ended up at the race track instead. The bookies are into him big time, and if he wins again and they don't pay off, he gets to send a Principality to break their legs."

"Terry has the heavenly touch," Jerry said. "He couldn't pick a looser if he tried."

"I don't think I can golf in these clothes."

"No problem, sir," said the Principality behind the counter. "Here's your golf attire."

Bob expected the angel to hand him a bundle, but instead, his suit vanished and was instantly replaced by clothing just like he'd been given when he entered Heaven, except the shoes had cleats.

"Pretty neat, huh?" Larry said. "Just come back here after our round, and Paganica," he indicated the angel, "will redress you."

"What about clubs and balls?"

"They're outside in the golf carts."

They went through a door, and Bob saw a pair of golf carts, each with two bags of golf clubs. As he got into a cart with Larry, he saw that one of the bags of clubs was identical to the custom set he'd owned on Earth.

Larry pulled off and steered toward the first tee, Jerry and Mary following close behind in their own cart. In a few moments, they arrived at the tee, and Bob glanced at the distance marker, which read, "Hole 1, 3,000 Yards, Par 1."

"Par 1 for a 3,000-yard fairway?" Bob asked. As he stared toward the distant green, he realized that the entire fairway was one long cloud sand trap. "That's more than four times as far as any golf course on Earth, and those are par 6. How can it possibly be par 1, especially with a sand trap going all the way to the green?"

"Watch," Larry said as Mary teed up.

She swung at the ball with some of the most appalling form Bob had ever witnessed. Even so, the ball sailed over the fairway and bounced onto the distant green, where it rolled for a moment before vanishing into the cup.

Jerry was up next. His form was even worse, but it didn't affect the result, which was another hole-in-one.

"Give it a shot," Larry urged.

202

Bob stepped apprehensively to the tee. He'd never managed a drive of more than about 230 yards, and this green was…. Used to juggling numbers, Bob quickly calculated the shot was more than twelve times that far. Not wanting to seem like a wuss, he set his ball on the peg and swung almost blindly.

"My turn," Larry said as Bob's ball plopped into the hole. "Here's your automatic scorecard."

He handed Bob a white rectangle about the size of a playing card. It showed the number "1" in a swirly font.

By now, Harry had swung, and his ball followed Bob's.

And so it went through all eighteen holes, which made for the fastest game of golf Bob had ever played even though the fairways were absurdly long. When it was over, the swirly font on his score card read "18." Despite the game's brevity, though, Bob had enough time to learn about his newfound friends.

Larry had been a cardiologist, and it was the saving-of-hearts angle that got him through the Pearly Gates. Mary had been the head of a public relations department for a media conglomerate, and she'd spun the facts so much the truth no longer mattered, so neither did the lies. She was considered a guru in her field, which had been her entry card. And Jerry had been an agent for pro athletes, getting them the most heavenly deals possible and trying to protect them from their own worst tendencies. He had been considered a rarity: a saint among agents.

At the end of the round, the foursome went into the lounge to celebrate their perfect scores.

"What brings you to Heaven, Bob?" Jerry asked. "I don't think I've ever met a Visitor before."

"It's a long story that's probably better left untold."

"Here's to untold long stories," Larry said, hoisting his cocktail.

"I like the suit," Mary said after she'd sipped. "Sharp. It's quite striking against all this whiteness."

Bob had changed back into his suit, and the others wore business attire, as well, but all white.

"Yeah," Larry said. "How did you swing a three-piece in charcoal? I can't get anything but white."

"If you know how," Bob said, "you can swing anything."

"So, whatcha got swinging, Bob?" Jerry asked. "Besides the obvious."

"I'm working on a business proposal," Bob told them.

"I can't see what," Larry said. "The angels have a monopoly on everything around here. What can you do that would be different and still show a profit for your efforts?"

"I have an idea," Bob said confidently.

"Any hints?" Mary asked.

"Let's just say you should invest in entertainment." Bob leaned forward, elbows on the table, and the others followed suit. "I'm going to open a travel agency and tourist bureau."

"But we've all seen everything already," Larry said.

"You have," Bob agreed. "But there are a lot of folks who haven't." He let them put two and two together. They were smart, and it didn't take long.

"You don't mean...." Mary began, her eyes widening.

"I do mean," Bob nodded.

"Brilliant," Jerry said. "Any openings?"

"Might be for astute operators such as yourselves. I'll be needing capable executives, and I can envision big roles for each of you. Mary, your experience in media and public relations dovetails exactly with what I'm working on. And Jerry, I'm going to need a sports and entertainment commissioner."

"Not much use for a doctor up here," Larry said, a little despondently. "No unintentional illness in Heaven, and the angels already run Hypochondriacs General." He obviously felt left out, but Bob's next words perked him up.

"That's for Residents," Bob replied. "We'll start our own since we'll have to keep the tourists separate to eliminate cross-contamination."

"We can call it the Hereafter Health Sanatorium and Spa." Enthusiasm lit Larry's eyes.

"Totally upscale," Bob said. "And staffed by genuine angels of mercy."

"We can see you have it all thought out," Jerry said.

"I still have a few challenges to face before I can get things off the clouds."

"Challenges can be good," Larry said. "Frankly, I'm sick of shooting holes-in-one all the time. Heck, I could fart at the ball, and it would roll all the way to the cup. Takes the fun out of the game."

"But what's your end?" Jerry asked. "There's no money here."

204

"The real profits here aren't in wealth but in power."

"It seems to me the angels have that pretty well sewn up, too," Mary commented.

"To the contrary," Bob said. "The angels have no power at all. They are completely subservient not only to the Boss but to you and me as well."

"How do you figure?" Jerry asked.

"They have to grant our wishes, no matter how elaborate, absurd, or contradictory, don't they?" The others around the table nodded their heads thoughtfully. "They can't say no, they can't punish, and they can't demand anything of any of us. They can only do our bidding as long as it doesn't go against the dictates of Divine Will, which nobody understands, anyway. The Boss is where the real and only power lies, and I intend to acquire a bit of that for myself and my executive staff."

"Count us in," Larry said, and Mary and Jerry nodded.

"Good," Bob said, rising from the table. "I have a meeting with Archangel Michael right now, but as soon as I nail down a few of the particulars, I'll have my personal assistant, Nanookie, get back with you."

❧ 21 ❧

"THE SOOT IS LEFT BY a man named Bob," Selaphiel said tiredly. "Saint Peter let him in not long ago."

"Not long ago," Michael repeated, feeling disgruntled. The eternity of Heaven had a few drawbacks besides being intrinsically boring, not the least of which was the inability to relate matters to some kind of logical sequence of events. After all, he thought, things happen sequentially. How come we have to act as if there's no such thing as time? He didn't need vagueness. He needed to know just how long this Bob had been leaving an indelible trail of soot across Heaven. It was enough to make Michael tremble with indignation, but he was too dumbfounded.

"You mean to tell me all those black marks were caused by one person?"

"Apparently," Selaphiel replied.

"Does he have an infinite supply of spray paint?"

"I suppose he could," Selaphiel said, "but he doesn't seem to need it. I think the sootiness is in him and just rubs off."

"Where did he come from?"

"Saint Peter said he just popped up from below in a cloud of ash, stinking of brimstone. Bob admitted to me he came from Hell."

"Why did Saint Peter let him in? Surely we don't admit just anybody who shows up at the Pearly Gates."

"He didn't have much choice," Selaphiel said. "Bob's name was in the *Register*. The only good news is he's just a Visitor. Eventually his visa will expire, and we can deport him."

"How long until then?"

"No telling."

Michael found himself wishing—and not for the first time—that he had some control over the admission process since he was the one who had to make things run smoothly and deal with any issues that arose.

"Can you at least tell me what he's been doing?"

"Sight-seeing, I guess you'd call it. He's visited most of our main attractions, like Psalm Beach and Empyrean Emporium. He got a new three-piece suit there."

"All that sounds pretty innocent," Michael said.

"His suit was white when he walked out in it, but now it's charcoal gray."

"You did say his sootiness rubs off."

"He wanted to enter the Garden of Eden, but Uriel turned him away. Just before that, he visited some cavemen in Sector 1, and he also went to Virginia."

"Trying to get into the Garden does sound suspicious," Michael admitted. "But maybe it was simple curiosity that he went to the other places."

"The cavemen he visited now live in a mobile home and have a backyard swimming pool, a barbecue pit, and lawn furniture."

"That was inevitable, I suppose."

"Maybe. But Uriel and the Virginians told me he has some sort of scheme up his sleeve. He wouldn't tell me what. He said he was coming here to talk to you about it."

"Coming here? To the Administration Building?"

Again Michael was surprised. No human ever set foot inside the Administration Building, although, technically, it wasn't off-limits. It was just that humans preferred to let others do the work if at all possible. Besides, given the choice to visit Psalm Beach or go to an event at Elysium Field, on the one hand, or hang out in a bunch of offices in an ugly office building, on the other, the outcome was foregone.

Michael also was somewhat apprehensive. He hadn't personally spoken to a human since that unfortunate incident in which he'd lost his temper. If that bastard Aubert just hadn't been so stubborn....

Michael shook his head. No use in dwelling on the past. Besides, not many humans up here knew about that. And so what if they did? They'd become just a bunch of numbers to him. To tell the truth, he wasn't sure he knew how to talk to one of them without being condescending.

"When's he supposed to arrive?"

The intercom on his desk buzzed, and Michael punched the listen button.

"I'm busy right now, Antoine," he said. "Send the petitioners home. They can come back later."

"I-and-I can't send this one away," Antoine said. "He's a human, and he's demanding to see you. I-and-I don't have a choice."

Apparently, neither did Michael, for he found himself saying, despite his reluctance and best efforts to resist, "Send him in."

How the hell did he get here so fast? Selaphiel wondered as the door opened, and Antoine ushered in a man in a charcoal gray suit and black wingtip shoes.

"Bob," Antoine intoned, and Selaphiel managed to slip through the door before Antoine closed it, leaving his boss to deal with the sooty human.

Bob wasn't much to look at as humans went. Despite his suit's unmistakable supernal quality, he was, Michael decided, the frumpiest human in Heaven. But that was no surprise. Given his Visitor status, he didn't have the opportunity to improve his appearance like Residents did.

"So you're Bob," Michael said, remaining seated. He wasn't about to stand for some upstart human. Especially one dressed in a three-piece charcoal gray suit. "The one who's been leaving black marks all over Heaven."

"And you're Michael, Heaven's chief operating officer," Bob said, walking forward until he was right in front of Michael's desk. He stared at Michael's right wing. "What's that on your wing?"

Michael had completely forgotten about the dark stain he'd picked up in the Factory, and now he cursed himself for not having Antoine order some bleach to eradicate it before this human noticed. He tried hard not to react.

"Looks like we have something in common," Bob said.

209

"I doubt that," Michael said. "This is just a superficial smudge I got in the course of my duties. It will go away."

"Spoken like a true COO," Bob said amiably. "Mind if I sit?"

"Do I have a choice?"

"Probably not," Bob said. "The way I figure it, all you angels are here to serve the people who live here. Right?"

"Correct," Michael nodded.

"So the lowliest person here is superior to the highest angel. That would be you."

"Again, you're correct. So here we are: the highest and the lowliest." Michael gave Bob a penetrating look Bob didn't like. "Or would you prefer 'lowdownest?'"

"I'd prefer to sit down if you don't mind."

Michael materialized a chair next to Bob, and Bob gratefully sank into it. He'd been walking all over the place for what seemed like ages, though how long it actually had been he had no real way to tell. But his legs sure were tired.

"All right, Bob. What can I do for you?"

"I want to become a Resident."

"Selaphiel tells me you're down in the *Register* as just a Visitor. There's nothing I can do to change your status. You have to earn your place in Heaven to become a Resident."

"That's what I intend to do."

"Really? How so?"

"I want to help people on Earth realize what a wonderful set-up you have up here. It's much better coming here than going to Hell."

"I assume from your sootiness that you know that from personal experience."

"Sadly, yes. I spent a considerable amount of time in Hell before I came here."

"And how did you escape the Devil's clutches?"

"I didn't escape, exactly. The Devil is the one who sent me up here."

"Impossible. He has no power to put your name in the *Register*."

"Don't ask me," Bob said, shrugging. "Obviously he and your Boss have some sort of private arrangement. I'm here, aren't I?"

210

"Your logic is impeccable," Michael said, trying hard to keep from sneering. "And now that you've seen what it's like in Heaven, you want to live here permanently. But how do you propose to let people on Earth know the true state of affairs once they die? We've been evangelizing for thousands of years without much success. You think you can do better?"

"Definitely. The world is going to Hell in a handbasket—and by any other conveyance possible. I know because I've seen the overcrowding there, so I know attendance has to be down here."

"Look," Michael said, a trifle defensively. "We may not be getting quite the influx of people here as they do in Hell, but there are more than seven billion of you humans right now, and you keep breeding, don't you? Relentlessly. We have to put you some place after you die. Is it so surprising that the numbers of people coming here are constantly growing, too?"

"And putting a strain on your utilities, from what I've seen," Bob said. "You could use some help with that, too."

This Bob wasn't much to look at, Michael reflected, but he did have a sharp eye as well as chutzpah.

"And you have a plan."

"Does a bear shit in the woods?"

"I don't know," Michael replied. "I'm not familiar with bear behavior."

"I want people on Earth to see firsthand what it's like here," Bob said. "Afterward, they'll do everything they can to make sure they go up instead of down."

"You want to bring living humans to Heaven?"

"I do. I want to open a travel agency that will tout Heaven as a prime vacation destination. As a follow-up, I want to develop a tourist bureau, a sports and entertainment commission, and a Paradisiacal Parks Service."

Michael snorted and shook his head.

"Why not?" Bob demanded.

"Only fully vetted Residents are allowed."

In reply, Bob tapped a forefinger against his Visitor badge.

"If someone from Hell can be a Visitor, surely humans on Earth can come as Visitors, too."

"Your name is in the *Register*," Michael pointed out. "Theirs aren't."

"That doesn't mean they can't be," Bob said. "Don't you think the Boss would be interested in any plan that might further his cause? Look," Bob waved his hands around. "All this freedom up here is a huge waste if it isn't put to some good use, like saving souls. We just have to convince him we have a good plan, and he's sure to go along and start a Visitor roster I can add to at will."

"That's a pretty far-fetched hope. Also, I'm concerned he'll be worried about the negative effects your scheme might have on the people on Earth. It removes faith from the equation, and whole edifices are constructed on foundations of faith."

"Don't tell me you're concerned about how a tourist attraction can disrupt humans on Earth," Bob said. "I once visited Mont Saint-Michel. Big tourist attraction in France. Ring any bells?"

Michael felt something slump within him, and it felt pretty heavy.

"Seems you wanted the bishop there to build a monument to your ego in the form of a monastery, but the bishop repeatedly refused until you burned a hole in his head with your finger."

Michael remembered only too well how his finger had sunk into that stubborn damn Aubert's head like a hot poker into soft cheese. The memory made him a little queasy, but the guy sure had jumped to it after that, Michael recalled with enough satisfaction to quell the twitch of remorse.

"So don't preach to me about using any means necessary to fulfill a desire," Bob went on. "I'm offering you a plan to help with your physical plant as well as ramp up your admissions. I think you ought to consider it. We can get everything up and running and present it to the Boss as a turn-key package with proven operational capacity."

Help with the infrastructure. That made Michael perk up and ponder for a moment. After all, he did *intend* to seek out the Boss about upgrading Heaven's utilities. And Bob did have experience in management. He might have some good ideas, though Michael doubted his sincerity.

But there was more to it than that, Michael thought. In Hell, the Devil had all the real power, while in Heaven, Michael was nothing more than an empty figurehead, despite his title as Captain of the Hosts and all the accouterments he had to carry around. Hell, the Devil even had a direct phone line to the Boss, and could chat him up any time, while Michael had to physically travel all the way to the Edge. The Boss was probably out there right now, creating some other universe, having gotten disgusted with how badly this one had turned out. Michael was running the show anyway. Why didn't he just assume control, as Bob suggested?

Besides, he'd already gone out on a limb by ordering Uriel to investigate what it would take for Heaven to go digital. Certainly the Boss knew about that. He knew about everything else, and he hadn't come down on Michael yet. Time to forge ahead. Heaven helps those who help themselves, and Bob might be able to help improve the infrastructure before Michael burst his travel agency bubble.

"I assume you've thought about a name for this travel agency."

"Holy Holidays."

"That's a tautology," Michael commented.

"In marketing, repetition is the key," Bob countered. "Besides, do you really think most people even know what a tautology is? Or care?"

"Probably not," Michael admitted.

"I even have a tagline," Bob said "'Enjoy the Rapture without the commitment.' How do you like it?"

It did have a nice ring.

"What would your tourists do?" Michael asked.

"Are you kidding? This place is loaded with entertainment options. There's Psalm Beach and Elysium Fields for those into physical activities, and Sector 1, the Biblical Sector, and the Historic District for anyone interested in reliving the past. I sure would have liked to ogle real cavemen in their natural habitat when I was a kid. The ladies over in Virginia are considering a proposal to give cultural performances, and we can spruce up the Garden of Eden and call it the Garden of Eden District. It'll be a major draw for horticulturists."

"Uriel told you that human entry is forbidden there."

"I'm sure we can get some dispensation to let people enter if their purpose is to improve the property, so to speak. Your personnel obviously can't deal with it. Why not let human horticulturists take care of it for you? We can book special horticulture tours. Call them the Paradise Garden Tours. And I can see it branching out even more. You could sell all the flowers the horticulturists grow worldwide over the Internet: 'Straight from the Garden of Eden to your door in an instant.' People love instant gratification these days."

Michael had to admit the Garden was a mess, and Bob's plan might work if it came to fruition, which of course it couldn't.

"The fountains and ambrosia trees produce way more than the people up here use, so food and drink won't be a problem," Bob went on. "The only other considerations are housing, transportation, and tour guides. For the first two, we can build a few luxury hotels in strategic locations, and we can bring in some of those double-decker tour busses like they have in London."

"No," Michael said. "Motorized vehicles are not allowed."

"But you have electric golf carts at Holy-in-One Greens," Bob pointed out. "What's the difference?"

"I don't know," Michael said. "And I don't care."

"We have to have some kind of vehicles," Bob said. "I had to walk my ass all over the place to see everything, and walking their asses off isn't what tourists want to do. They want to ride."

"The only other vehicles are the Amish buggies."

"Perfect," Bob said. "We can use them just like horse-and-carriage rides back on Earth. Tourists love those."

"What about their wants?" Michael asked. "Sure, we can take care of their needs, but you know they're going to want more."

"That's where the tour guides come in. They'll chaperone the tourists and supply their wants."

"Just how many angels will you need for that?"

"Not a one," Bob said smoothly. "You're forgetting your human capital."

"You're proposing to put the people in Heaven to work? But that subverts the very idea of Heaven."

"Not if they think it's play."

Thinking back on the artists and writers in the Factory, Michael realized Bob might be right.

"I figure a lot of people up here will help," Bob went on. "It'll let them flaunt their status as permanent Residents of Heaven, not to mention relieve the ultimate boredom of dealing with the same people over and over throughout eternity. Also, they can visit with loved ones left behind."

214

"I suppose our guests would pay a considerable sum for their visit."

"Of course," Bob said, smiling. "Making it upscale will keep out the riffraff. But we'll be sure to book a few economy tours so we can't be accused of denying the underclass their own glimpse of Nirvana."

"And the payment goes to whom?"

"Some of our profits will have to go back into marketing. We could donate the rest to charity as tax write-offs, but since the church, itself, is one of the world's biggest tax write-offs, that seems unnecessarily circular. I suggest a more direct approach. Your infrastructure is obsolete and almost broken down, so you can use most of our income to invest in upgrades and improvements, especially if we're going to have tourists around here. Don't want them to think Heaven is just another Third-World country."

"So, you're telling me you'll do all the work, and we can reap all the profits?"

"You also keep Heaven's name out there in the public eye. Right now, you're just some fantasyland where people hope to end up. Once people learn Heaven is no fantasy, they'll talk of nothing else."

Michael stared at the soot settling around Bob's chair and wondered how difficult it was going to be to clean his office after the human left. Not that it mattered. He'd make Antoine do it.

"You're saying any publicity is good publicity?"

"That's about the size of it." Bob felt supremely confident, not only in the strength of his scheme, but in his ability to carry it off.

"What about this one: No news is good news."

"You can't believe that," Bob snorted, only a little deflated. "Not in this day and age."

"We're in Heaven," Michael reminded him. "No days. No ages."

He perused Bob for a long moment, then said, "And what do you get out of it? I'm sure you're not proposing this out of the goodness of your own heart."

"I get full Resident status. If I have Heavenly Desire powers, I can get everything I want, right?"

215

"If I agree and the plan flops?"

"Deport me," Bob said more cheerfully than he felt. "But it won't flop. I know my demographic. People on Earth will be willing to lie, cheat, steal, and kill to get up here. You think they'll balk at paying a few dollars?"

"I'll have to present the idea to the board."

"I thought you were the one in charge," Bob said. "Captain of the Hosts, and all that. Besides, didn't you tell me the Boss has the final say? Let's meet with him, present the idea, and see what he says. The board doesn't matter. They'll have to go along."

"I'll need their support to bring all the heavenly hosts in line," Michael said. "You know that even a COO can't make everything happen on his own. As for meeting the Boss, two of the board members are out right now, arranging a meeting with him." It was a lie, but probably no worse than deliberately sending two Archangels on a wild goose chase. "But I doubt he'll go for the idea if it messes with his Heaven."

"Look, Michael," Bob said, leaning forward in his chair. "It's like a trial. In a trial, it's not the facts that define the outcome but the story each side tells. Which story connects best with the listener. People don't care about facts, especially here in Heaven. They care about story. I want to tell the Boss a better story."

Dream on, Michael thought.

"Okay, Bob. I've heard your proposal and what you want in return. But I want something, too. You mentioned our infrastructure...."

Bob nodded.

"You need some help in bringing everything here up-to-date, and I can do that. I did quite a bit of organizational work for your sole competitor, not to mention a lifetime of it on Earth. I'll take a look at things and make some suggestions, but that's it. The physical plant is your responsibility. But I planned to meet with your managers, anyway, so I'll add heavenly consultant to my résumé."

"All right, Bob. But we'll have to start with a Provisional Resident Visa." Michael thought he'd feel either a sense of relief or a sense of doom at saying those words, but instead he felt oddly drained. He needed a vacation in the worst way possible, and if this was the only way to get it, so be it.

216

"How about Heavenly Desire powers?"

"Let's not get ahead of ourselves," Michael said. "You'll get the cooperation you need to set up your travel agency. You show me results with the infrastructure, then we'll talk about bonuses. Besides, I can't personally issue Heavenly Desire powers. Only the Boss can do that. So you better help make things work around here if you expect rewards."

"Okay," Bob said. "It's a deal." He stood. "When you arrange the appointment with the Boss, give me a holler. I'll be at the office, putting my organization in place."

"Your office? Where's that?"

"Actually, I'm not sure yet. My personal assistant is setting it up as we speak."

Michael suddenly found himself experiencing a new feeling: one of jealousy. He'd never had a personal assistant. There was Antoine, of course, but Antoine was a secretary—something of a lower order than a personal assistant.

"Isn't that a little premature?" Michael asked. "We still need the Boss's approval."

"Have faith, Michael. He'll see the wisdom of our plan once its operational."

❧ 22 ☙

MICHAEL SAT SILENTLY IN HIS office for some time after Bob left, contemplating the meeting they'd just had. He wasn't quite sure what to make of this upstart human. Bob said he was just trying to improve things here in Heaven, but what did he really want? Residency, that was certain, but humans usually wanted more than they admitted—usually something to enhance themselves at the expense of others. And Bob, stinking of the pit and trailing soot, couldn't be any different.

Bob did have a plan, though, unlike any of the toadies around Michael, who seemed to be content to keep Heaven in stasis. But thanks to his recent inspection tour, Michael knew that things here just couldn't stay the same forever if the circumstances of reality kept shifting as the old infrastructure crumbled around them. And Michael needed help, even if it meant using and deceiving Bob.

At last, he punched the button on his intercom.

"Yes, sir?" came Antoine's voice.

"Call the board members on their walkie-talkies, and have them return to the boardroom. Let me know when everybody is here. In the meantime, call a maintenance crew to come in here and clean up this mess Bob left. After that, have them go out and get rid of every line Bob has made."

"Yes, sir."

"One more thing," Michael said. "I'm giving you a promotion. From now on, you'll be my personal assistant instead of a secretary."

"Do I-and-I get a new rating?" Antoine asked. "To a Power, maybe?"

"No, you-and-you don't," Michael snapped, and he cut the connection.

Michael tried to relax while he waited. He went over the meeting with Bob, and the more he took it apart, the better he liked the outcome. He knew that corporate executives such as Bob had great experience in cutbacks, cut downs, cut-ins, cut offs, and cutting corners. He'd make Bob find ways to make the utilities operate in a more cost-effective manner as a prior condition of his Residency. Surely Bob could suggest ways to do less with less without affecting the quality of Heaven's state.

More important, Michael had seen how overwork and lack of focus were slowly eroding Heaven's orderliness, which, in turn, was undermining the authority of the angelic hierarchy. When things had gotten to the point that Dominions, Virtues, and Powers were pissing in the fountains and Principalities were openly complaining, if not actually rebellious, it was time to do something drastic. If that meant distracting the humans by having them do some of the work, all the better. Festus was already exploiting the artists and writers. Might as well expand the practice if it kept Heaven on an even keel. And stating the reality of the situation like that gave Michael all the courage he needed to exploit Bob without mercy and without guilt.

As to the issue of granting Bob permanent Resident status as payment for his services, there was no question. It was out of the question. For one thing, that was something that really did take the Boss's permission. Too bad, really. People ought to be rewarded for advancing Heaven's cause, but it didn't always work out that way. Bob wouldn't be the first to fall by the wayside, nor the last, and Michael thought the human was probably enough of a realist to understand that miracles didn't happen very often. Could he really expect one to happen to him?

Michael wasn't sure how long he sat in his office, mulling over what had transpired and liking it more and more the more he mulled, but eventually he fell into a reverie of actually having enough free time to take a vacation of his own—something he hadn't had since the incident with Aubert. He could go to Psalm Beach, maybe, or play a few rounds at Holy-in-One Greens. Or go on a long hike in the cloud mountains above Sector 1. Or maybe he could go back to Earth and....

"They're here," Antoine's voice interrupted from the intercom speaker.

"So much for time off," Michael muttered as he grabbed his backpack, helmet, sword, spear, and shield and left the office.

The other Archangels were already seated in the boardroom when Michael came in. He didn't sit, but stood there, looking around at their expectant faces.

"The last time we met, I assigned each of you with a task. Each of those tasks will have significant bearing not only on Heaven's operations but also on its very future."

Michael could see puzzlement in their faces. How could Heaven's future be in question? Michael smiled to himself, thinking of his own vacation.

"We'll start with you, Uriel. How far have you gotten in establishing a digital infrastructure here?"

"We can do it easily enough," Uriel said. "The only impediment will come from the supply side. The Factory will have to create a whole new division to make all the digital TVs, smart phones, computers, tablets, and so forth. The real issue will be in setting up our own cyberspace."

"Can't we just tap into Earth's Internet?" Gabriel asked.

"We could, but do we really want to?" Uriel said. "By my estimate, approximately 95 percent of the content of the Internet is criminal, bogus, moronic, misinformed, deliberately misleading, trivial, or a scam. After all, it is run by humans. We'd have to filter out almost everything, although I suppose we could permit cute animal videos and pictures."

"We'll create our own cyberspace," Michael said. "A Heaven Wide Web. We can call it the Eternet. How long will that take?"

Uriel shrugged. "Depends on the kinds of resources we can throw at it. By the time we do, the Factory should have produced a large number of computers, tablets, and phones. The

221

HWW would grow exponentially on its own once the Residents start supplying content."

"We're not going to be stringing wires all over the place, are we?" Barachiel asked.

"We can go wireless," Uriel answered. "We'll have to have a tower, but since Heaven is flat, we'll only need one."

"Where would it be erected?" Michael asked.

"It's already up." Uriel waved around. "The Administration Building is the tallest structure in Heaven. We'll just put the microwave array on the roof."

"I heard that microwaves from those towers on Earth fry birds," Gabriel said. "Won't they be a danger to angels when we fly around?"

"We'll establish some no-fly zones," Uriel responded. "There is one more issue, however. Time."

"What's that supposed to mean," Raguel asked.

"Having the Eternet and a cell phone network in Heaven means we'll have to establish the measurement of time. It might be nothing but an ephemeral layer of tissue lying on top of forever, but computers just don't work right without sequences of events adding up to a fabric rather than to the random arrangement of grains in a sand dune."

"All right," Michael said. He'd come to hate eternity's timelessness, anyway. "Go ahead and start setting things up."

"Wait a minute," Selaphiel said. "Have you gotten the Boss's okay?"

Michael fixed him with the kind of piercing stare that only the Captain of the Hosts could give. He was pleased to see Selaphiel hang his head even lower than normal.

"The Boss left me in charge. Besides," he looked at Gabriel and Raphael, "I take it you two didn't have any luck finding him."

"No," Gabriel answered. "We saw his crepuscular rays from a great distance several times, but when we'd go to where we thought he was, he'd be gone off somewhere else."

"There you have it," Michael said to them all. "The Boss can step in any time he wants to veto my decisions, but until I hear otherwise from him, I'm going to do what I think is necessary

222

to keep things running smoothly and efficiently." Michael turned to Barachiel. "How's the surveillance going?"

"Excellently. We can now monitor everyone in all of our agencies and utilities. Would you like me to bug the Residents as well?"

"We probably ought to," Michael said, thinking of how Bob had influenced almost everyone he met. Michael was willing to let Bob's plan unfold enough for Michael's purposes, but not at the expense of the cultural order of Heaven. Michael would have to keep tabs on the Residents to make sure their behavior remained heavenly. "But we can hold off on that until the digital infrastructure is in place and everyone has computers and phones. Since we'll control the HWW, it should be simple to monitor them."

"If the information we're getting from our initial bugs is any indication," Raguel said, "that might be a good idea. When angels act badly, can human behavior be far behind?"

"You mean you've verified the pissing in the fountains story?" Michael asked.

"The problem is more widespread than just an incident or two," Raguel said. "The chief culprit is Halliwell. He and his Virtues and Powers are now systematically pissing in every fountain we have."

"Why?"

"At first it looked like a prank, but the deeper I dug, the more nefarious it became. It seems there have been a lot of complaints about the drinking fountains tasting sour. The pissing incidents are used to make it seem like vandalism by Residents, when it's actually to cover up what's really going on."

"Which is?" Michael said impatiently.

"The Water Plant has a device that dispenses the Boss's tears into their main purification vat."

"I've seen it," Michael said. "Is the mechanism faulty?"

"No. Halliwell has been diverting a significant amount of the flow for his own purposes, so not enough tears are reaching the vat, and the water isn't truly purified. Hence the sourness at all the fountains."

"Why would he do that?"

"It's not pretty."

"Tell me anyway."

"He and his minions are cutting the tears with tap water and selling them on Earth."

"What?" Michael boomed, and gasps rose from the other Archangels, except Raphael, who simply puffed out his cheeks and fingered his horn. "They sell them?"

Raguel nodded. "Right now, they make two products. One we've already heard about: Angel Eyes. It's the illicit drug that gives the user heavenly visions but, in the end, produces depression and remorse. The other is marketed on-line as AZS, which stands for Anti-Zombie Serum. It's supposed to keep a person who drinks it from turning into a zombie. Apparently, a significant market share on Earth sincerely believes a zombie apocalypse is immanent, and they'll do anything to keep from turning into one."

"But those people already *are* zombies," Barachiel pointed out.

"What are Halliwell and the others getting out of it?" Michael asked, striving to keep his rage from showing while keeping it intact.

"It seems they've been using the funds from their sales to live it up on Earth."

"On Earth!" This from Gabriel. "Who would leave Heaven, where everyone has everything, to go to Earth, where hardly anybody does?"

"That's just the point," Raguel answered. "On Earth, a wealthy angel is one of the elite who can have any and everything. Up here, it's the humans who have everything. All we angels do is cater to them. Also, I've heard the lower orders are complaining of hierarchangelism."

"Hierarchangelism?" Barachiel said. "What's that?"

"Us." Raguel waved around the room. "We're at the top of Heaven's hierarchy, and they're much farther down the ladder. They say they're tired of doing all the work while we take all the credit."

"But we work harder than any of them," Barachiel said.

"Tell *them* that. All they see is we're bigger, more powerful, have brighter auras, and carry a lot of accouterments. On Earth, even a Principality can live like the crown prince he wishes he was."

"How extensive is this corruption?" Michael asked.

224

"So far, I've concentrated mostly on Halliwell and his associates, but we've started listening in on the Solid Waste and Recycling Center and the Factory, and it seems the staffs of both are engaged in similar sorts of hanky-panky. You know all those jewel-encrusted golden goblets that appear at the fountains whenever humans take a drink? Well, most of those end up at Solid Waste, and Montgomery has been sifting them out and selling the jewels and gold on Earth for the same reason Halliwell and his cronies are selling the Boss's tears. That's why a lot of the older sectors aren't being cleaned up. Since nobody lives there anymore, there aren't any chalices to purloin."

"And the Factory?" Michael asked.

"Do you realize how many famous artists we have there churning out paintings? Festus has been selling some of them through various galleries on Earth. The beauty of his plan is that although they were painted after the artist's death, they aren't forgeries and can stand up to any test. Recently, there's been an unprecedented influx of 'lost' masterpieces turning up in art auction houses."

Michael rubbed a palm across his brow. He'd believed that operations had just become outdated and untidy, but the situation was far worse than he'd imagined.

"What are we going to do?" Gabriel asked, looking at Michael. They were all looking at Michael.

"You may recall I sent Selaphiel to discover the origin of the black lines that have been appearing all over Heaven lately. Fill them in, Selaphiel."

"The trail is soot left by a Visitor named Bob," Selaphiel said. "I did a little research, and it appears that he was in Hell, but the Devil booted him up here. Said something about Bob bringing too much order to his chaotic realm."

"Hell!?" The word came from Barachiel. "Expel him!"

As chief confessor, Barachiel didn't want to spend however many months or years it would take to hear Bob's many admissions of guilt. But all the other Archangels muttered angrily, too.

"There may be more to it," Selaphiel said over the hubbub, and everyone grew quiet again. "Some time back, the Devil called the Boss to complain we'd sent an angel down to Hell to torment him. This could be his way of turning the tables."

"How the hell did he get in here?" Barachiel demanded.

"I'm not sure," Selaphiel said. "Saint Peter says he tried to keep him out, but Bob insisted he look in the *Register*. Bob's name was there, so Saint Peter had to let him in."

"I don't understand how his name could be in the *Register* if he just popped up from Hell," Gabriel said.

"It's a puzzle, all right," Selaphiel said. "Maybe it's some kind of clerical error. You know how overworked our scribes are. They have to write everything out by hand, and those illuminated manuscripts take a lot of effort. And then, messages have to be hand carried everywhere, and that takes even more time."

"The situation definitely highlights our need for digital communications," Michael said. He suddenly realized that if the *Register* was a digital on-line document instead of a prodigious paper tome, he could have somebody hack it to give him control over admissions. It was a thought....

"It doesn't matter how he got here," Gabriel said. "We can't just let him wander around leaving sooty trails, or our clouds are going to look like graph paper designed by a lunatic."

"Maybe we can have a Principality carry him around," Barachiel suggested.

"Any angel we assigned might get covered in soot," Michael pointed out. "But we can give him a golf cart and make him drive instead of walking. However we deal with it, Bob might be just what the doctor ordered to get things back on track."

"How can a former inmate of Hell do what all the Heavenly Hosts can't?" Gabriel asked.

"New ideas," Michael said, and he had to hush their protests again. "I know it sounds crazy, but we have to do something drastic. Our main problem is that everybody is going to Hell in a handbasket—and by any other conveyance possible." Bob did have a way with words, Michael thought as he purloined the phrase. "We have to do something to alter the balance. But even if we do, that brings us to our other major problem, which is Heaven's infrastructure. It's not only falling apart from obsolescence, it's falling into unscrupulousness and veniality. Business as usual just can't cut it anymore."

"But how can this Bob fellow help?" Uriel asked. "He's leaving burnt brimstone all over the place, and I know from person-

226

al experience how hard that is to clean up. After he left the Garden gate, I had some of the Cherubim try, but they couldn't do a thing about it."

"I have a maintenance crew working on it," Michael said.

He looked around at the other Archangels. Was this the time to drop the bombshell? He steeled himself.

"Bob has a plan," he told them. "He proposes to bring tourists here from Earth."

"What!?"

This time, their ire couldn't be soothed so easily.

"Silence!" Michael boomed, and the other Archangels instantly fell quiet. Being the Captain of the Hosts did have its advantages. "The tourist angle is pretty smart," he went on. "Bob thinks that if humans on Earth can catch a glimpse of the good life up here, they'll do anything they have to to get in when they die. Not only that, they'll go home and tell everyone they know about what a great time they had here, which will convince even more of them to reconsider negative actions and lifestyles."

"How does bringing more people up here help solve our infrastructure problem?" Raguel asked. "Or the corruption? Seems like it would make things worse."

"Probably so," Michael conceded. "But it doesn't matter because it's not going to happen. We just have to pretend to all the humans—especially Bob—that it will."

"You want us to lie?" Barachiel gasped. "I'd have to confess to myself!"

"Not lie," Michael corrected. "Prevaricate. Bob's organization will take up a lot of our Residents' time, which will ease the burden on the lower order angels who have to serve them. He's also going to have the Residents help with some of the work around here. We can use the slack to concentrate our workforce on the important issues of expanding and updating our utilities using labor from Bob's organization. If we combine that with modern technology and an expanded infrastructure, we should see smooth sailing for quite a while."

"Not to mention showing up the Devil by turning his stooge to our advantage," Gabriel said.

"There's that, too," Michael said, smiling. "I think it's worth a shot." He looked around at the other Archangels. "I know we

227

don't have to vote on this matter since I want it to happen, but I just want to make sure everybody is on board."

They were.

❧ 23 ❧

AS BOB LEFT THE ADMINISTRATION Building, the disembodied voice intoned, "Remember: Behave heavenly. It's the right thing to do."

The voice was no softer than it had ever been, but this time Bob didn't hear it. Instead, he paused to unclip his Visitor badge and drop it into the clouds, where it vanished. Then he called up a way-finding sign.

"Show me the way to my office," he said, and a black line appeared on the map. It turned out his office was in a building only a hop, skip, and jump from the Administration Building.

"Convenient," he nodded as his eyes searched for the building. It was a high-rise faced in white marble, windows shining with reflected golden sheen.

As Bob strolled toward it, the excitement he'd been feeling about his project heightened in direct proportion to the elevation of his new headquarters, and that was pretty tall. He was going to make a killing here. Almost all the Residents were bored and not all that happy despite the fact they were in Heaven. Maybe it was because they couldn't always do what they wanted even if they did have Heavenly Desire powers. And he'd heard a lot of them saying, "Eventually, I'll...," but they never did. He suspected that was because "eventually" never came.

Without the finality of death, living eternally was simply an excuse to procrastinate eternally.

Well, he was going to give them something to do, and they'd better do it or they'd get pink-slipped.

At last, he reached the Holy Holidays building and entered the lobby. Apparently he was the building's sole tenant, and the main reception area for Holy Holidays occupied the entire first floor. It was tastefully decorated with posters of many of Heaven's main attractions, though Bob noticed the artist had taken pains to make the light look more natural than the pervasive golden glow that was Heaven's norm.

Nanookie was sitting behind the massive reception counter, a pair of dark tortoise-shell glasses perched on her nose and her hair fastened in a prim bun held by a hair pin. When she saw him come in, she got up and came around the counter toward him.

"How do you like it?" she asked. She'd changed her polar-bear-fur bikini for another two-piecer—this one in snow leopard. He liked the way the light gray spots coordinated with his suit's pinstripes.

"This is fantastic," Bob said, waving around. "How did you manage it?"

"It was my Heavenly Desire," she said. "It's the tallest building in Heaven. One story taller than the Administration Building."

She was standing very, very close to him, but he didn't feel at all uncomfortable.

"Why don't you show me around?" he said.

"This way." She took his arm and led him to an elevator and up through successive floors, pointing out offices for travel agents, conference rooms, break rooms, and even a theater for showing training and promotional videos.

"The higher floors above this have offices for your board members, other executives, managers, and general staff.

Bob's headquarters was as elegant as it was imposing, but it also was depressingly empty—an elaborate and towering mausoleum whose vacant halls and rooms resounded with their footsteps. Bob found himself wondering if he could attract enough employees to fill all the empty space in the building. It would take an army.

230

"Don't worry, Bob," Nanookie said, sensing his mood. "Just consider it space to expand into. Before long, we'll have more people running around in here than there are eyes on a whole fleet of Ophanim."

Nanookie was right. Now was not the time for self-doubt. "Where's my office?" he asked.

"Can't have you down here with the hoi polloi. Your private elevator is right over here. It's an express from any floor you're on."

The control panel inside the private elevator had only two buttons: up and down. Nanookie pressed the up button, the doors slid shut, and pressure built against their feet as the car shot upward. The ride was disconcerting. Since the elevator was an express and the floor was made of cloudstuff, the rapid upward surge caused them to sink into it almost up to their thighs.

Could you actually fall through the floor of Heaven? Bob wondered. He'd fallen down and up and sideways enough for one existence. But Nanookie didn't seem concerned. Maybe she'd become inured after a lifetime of living on ice, suspended over frigid depths.

When the car stopped, the doors slid open on a lobby with several doors, all marked "Private." She led him through one, and it opened onto a short hall flanked by two doors.

"Your operations center," she announced proudly as she flung open the door on the right. "Or, your throne room, if you prefer."

Bob stepped through the opening and into the largest and most luxuriously appointed executive suite he'd ever seen. Amazingly, every detail matched his taste more perfectly then even he could imagine.

"Like it?" she asked.

"What's not to like?" he asked, stepping toward the wide windows. The view was absolutely incredible. If the pervasive golden glow was a little brighter, he could have seen practically everywhere in Heaven.

"You're a charm, Nan," he said. "What's the door across the hall?"

"My office. You ought to have your personal assistant as close as possible to you at all times. Want to see it?"

He nodded, and she led him across the hall to an office nearly as large as his. Its furniture showed a more feminine touch, although all of it was carved from blocks of ice. A poster of Psalm Beach on the wall opposite her desk lent a spot of warmth that made the icy furniture glow.

"I get homesick, sometimes," she said when he asked about the decor. "The poster is there to remind me not to get too nostalgic. Want to see our penthouse?"

The penthouse was one floor up. The top floor. It was even more fantastic than the office suite. It had a spacious great room, a library filled with ancient first editions and other rare books in mint condition, a bedroom with a magnificent bed, a bathroom larger than most kitchens, and a kitchen with its own fountain and ambrosia tree. All the rooms had wide windows with fantastic views.

"You've thought of everything," Bob said after she'd taken him on the grand tour.

"Yes," she said, moving close to him again. "But I suppose I should explain our sexual harassment policy to you."

"We have a sexual harassment policy?"

"That's right. It says if you don't harass me regularly, I have the right to sue you."

"Sounds like a policy I can agree to," he said, thanking his lucky stars she didn't want a prenuptial agreement. "So, what's with the glasses? To make you look smart?"

"I don't need glasses to be smart," she said. "They're so you can take them off and tell me how beautiful I am."

He took them off and told her how beautiful she was.

"And the hair?" He gestured to her severe bun.

"It's so you can take the pin out and let my luxurious tresses cascade over my bare shoulders."

He unclipped the pin, and her luxurious tresses cascaded over her bare shoulders. He kissed her.

"I like the snow leopard bikini," he said. "It's very becoming."

"I'm glad you like it," she said. "I'll bring it back later."

The bikini vanished.

"Our bedroom's this way," she said.

Later, after a heavenly couple of hours, they lay on the rumpled sheets, Nanookie smoking a Virginia Slims and Bob admiring the way the curve at the small of her back sloped sumptuously toward her buttocks.

232

"You're quite a gal, Nan." he said. "How did you become so acculturated given your—pardon me—primitive upbringing? I've been to Sector 1, and the cavemen are still living like they did in their prehistoric world. They've been here longer than anyone, and they could have left for any of the modern sectors long ago, but they never have."

"That's the case with most of the people here," she said. "They come in with a certain set of expectations and demands, so people from the same culture are lumped together for the sake of administrative simplicity. Also, nobody feels comfortable going very far outside their own home territory. It's not that anybody would hurt them. This is Heaven. But most people feel uncomfortable around people who aren't like them and places they don't know."

"I guess it's the same as everywhere on Earth," he agreed. "Tribes, nations, neighborhoods, ghettos. But that still doesn't explain why you're different."

"I don't know," she shrugged. "I suppose every culture has people who don't fit, whose natural intelligence, curiosity, and ambition cause them to leave their cultural confines and explore other ways of looking at life. That's why I like you, Bob. You're my kind of guy. Even in Nunavut, I was always wandering around, looking for something new. I even went to Pangnirtung a few times. That's a big Inuit village. Been there for thousands of years. I'd have stayed, too, if my husband hadn't dragged me back out onto the ice. That's all he ever wanted, so he figured I ought to want it, too. No curiosity or ambition."

"You were married?"

"You don't think I learned all those tricks I just showed you by staying a virgin, do you? There aren't too many other ways to amuse yourself out there on the ice."

"Well, bless your husband, then, for the little innovation he did have. Where is he now? Did he make it up here?"

"Yeah, he's here. Most of our tribe are. Not much opportunity to sin when you're out there on the ice. Once you do, your tribesmen never trust you, and you have to have friends when you live in an environment like that." She eyed him. "We're not still married, if that's what you're asking. Death cancels all mortal obligations. Besides, I never see him. He just sits around, making harpoons, paddling his kayak, or carving scrimshaw. He claims he's going out onto the ice-crystal clouds to hunt polar bear, but I doubt it. Like I said: no curiosity or ambition."

"Do you think any of the cavemen might have those traits?"

"Curiosity and ambition?"

She laughed. "I'll believe it when I see one of them at an art museum or spending the afternoon dallying around in the highest penthouse in Heaven." She gave him a big kiss. "Let me tell you, baby," she said. "You're not on the way up, anymore. You've arrived."

"Not yet," he said. "I'm still on shaky footing, without a safety net. And to top it off, I don't have much top."

"I like your bald spot," she said, rubbing it. "It's your tonsure."

"Hell," he said. "Wilbert the damn Greeter has a better head of hair than I do, and I'm CEO."

"Maybe I could make it my Heavenly Desire...."

"I appreciate the offer, Nan, but this is something I have to handle myself."

"I know you have a plan," she said. "You always have a plan."

"I'm going to make myself indispensable to the operations around here. I've already petitioned Michael for Resident status with full Heavenly Desire privileges."

"It'll happen, baby." She rubbed his bald spot again. "I know you've got some bright ideas percolating in there."

"Positively gleaming the way you're polishing me up. You think rubbing will bring good luck, like rubbing a Buddha statue's belly?"

"Maybe I should rub your belly, then," she said. "Oh, look: Something else needs polishing."

It may have, but before she could do more than a little buffing, she was interrupted by a nearby beep.

"That's the walkie-talkie," Nanookie said in answer to Bob's puzzled look. "Want me to answer it?"

"You probably ought to. I doubt it's a salesman or client since we haven't geared up our operation, so it might be important."

Nanookie slipped out of the bed and walked across the room, her buns shifting quite nicely.

"Holy Holidays," she said, picking up the walkie-talkie. "How may I direct your call?"

234

"This is Michael," a voice squawked from the receiver. "Is Bob available?"

"Let me check his schedule," Nanookie replied. She looked at Bob, who nodded, and she came back over to the bed and handed him the walkie-talkie.

Bob lay the walkie-talkie face down on the mattress and proceeded to make out with Nanookie for a full five minutes before he picked it up again.

"Michael," Bob said effusively into the device. "Nice to hear from you."

"I just called to tell you we've held a board meeting to consider your endeavor, and I'm happy to say that the vote was unanimous in your favor. Congratulations. You're in business."

"That's great news," Bob said. "We already have our offices set up, now all we need to do is acquire some staff and start bringing in the tourists. That'll take a few weeks or so."

"No rush. Like you said, it'll be a good thing to have the operation in place and running before the meeting with the Boss. If you need anything before then, have your personal assistant contact my personal assistant, Antoine. He'll make any arrangements you need."

"I'll do that. Talk to you soon."

Bob switched off the walkie-talkie, put it on the night stand, and turned to Nanookie.

"Hear that? We're in business."

"I'll say, go-getter. Now, go get her." She pulled him back onto the sheets.

❧ 24 ☙

BOB HAD RECRUITING TO DO, and though he really didn't want to walk all over Heaven again, there really wasn't any help for it. But before he could do more than exit the front doors of his headquarters, he was stopped by a Principality.

"I have your cart ready, sir." The angel said.

"My cart?"

"Archangel Michael's orders," the Principality explained, waving toward a golf cart sitting on the clouds not far away. It was a deluxe model, with plush seats and a fringed canopy, parked in a slot in front of the building. A sign planted at the end of the slot read, "Bob's Space. Get thee fucking back strictly enforced."

Michael had said Bob would get what he needed to set up his travel agency, and temporarily, at least, that was almost as good as having his own Heavenly Desire powers.

Riding was a lot quicker than walking, and Bob was so involved in looking ahead to the future he didn't look back to see his cart leaving twin dark streaks like tire tracks behind it. When he arrived at the Pearly Gates, he was pleased to find Wilbert the Greeter standing expectantly just inside the archway.

"Wilbert!" he called out as he neared. "Just the man I want to talk to."

Wilbert turned, and his muscular smile twitched into place. "Bob, isn't it? I never forget a name or face."

"Well, I'm here to give you a challenge on that," Bob said. "If you're up to it."

"What do you mean?" Wilbert asked. "Say, can you wait just a minute? Here comes a new Resident."

Wilbert pointed toward the Pearly Gates. Just past the turnstile, Saint Peter was behind his counter, and a naked, beer-bellied, middle-aged man was standing in front of the counter, waiting as Saint Peter perused the *Register*. Apparently he found the man's name because he handed the man a token and waved him through the turnstile. As he did, he caught sight of Bob. Bob smiled, but a frown creased Saint Peter's brow.

"I'll go chat up old Saint Pete while you take care of the new guy."

Bob walked toward the gate, passing the newcomer, who shed thirty years and fifty pounds as soon as he pushed through the turnstile. He looked expectantly at Bob, confused wonder in his eyes, and Bob waved toward Wilbert.

"Wilbert will fill you in," he said.

As the man nodded his thanks and headed toward Wilbert, Bob stepped up to the turnstile.

"Hey, there, Pete," he said. "Nice to see you again."

"Where's your Visitor badge?" Saint Peter had a nasty look of anticipation in his eyes. "You're supposed to wear it at all times."

"You must not have gotten the word," Bob said, enjoying the way Saint Peter's expression suddenly soured. "Michael himself has granted me a Provisional Resident Visa."

"Why are you here, then?"

"I just want to check to make sure you have plenty of blank pages in your book."

"An infinite number," Saint Peter said then looked suspiciously at Bob. "Why?"

"You're going to need them," Bob said cryptically.

"I see you're dressed more appropriately than when you arrived," Saint Peter said snidely.

"You like the suit?" Bob brushed palms over his charcoal lapels.

"Not really. Too confining. I like loose robes. But of course only angels can wear them."

238

"Angels and women," Bob said. "You know, I've been meaning to ask some angel about those robes, but I haven't had the chance. Do you all have legs underneath there?"

"Legs?" Saint Peter sputtered.

"Yeah. I never see you walking, only floating or flying. Maybe you're like kewpie dolls. You know, with your legs fused together. And I heard about the Nephilim. Does that mean you have male equipment? You must if you begot the Nephilim, although it's pretty obvious the Ophanim don't. Don't they resent that? But where would they put them, anyway, with all those eyes everywhere? They'd constantly be ogling themselves."

Bob had never seen an angry angel before, but Saint Peter, his face red, brow clouded, and fist clenched, looked pretty pissed. Maybe he was the only angel who could look that way, but if so, it made some sense. The doorman at any exclusive club also has to play the bouncer.

"Oh, well," Bob said, waving offhandedly. "It doesn't matter. Be seeing you."

He turned and went back to Wilbert, who had just finished his spiel to the newcomer and sent him on his way.

"What did you say to him?" Wilbert asked, glancing apprehensively over Bob's shoulder at the fuming Saint Peter. "I've never seen him look mad."

"I asked him if angels have legs underneath their robes. And male equipment."

"What did he say?" Wilbert's eyes gleamed with curiosity.

"He didn't."

"Too bad. It would be somethin' to talk about. So what's this about challengin' my memory?"

"You told me you come here voluntarily. You must really like greeting newcomers."

"Sure." Wilbert exercised his muscular smile. "I'm a real people person."

"What if we made the position permanent and official?"

"You mean with an official name badge and a real title?"

"And a whole staff of greeters who answer to you."

"I'd be the Greeter in Chief?"

"Even better, you and your staff wouldn't just be greeting folks. They'd be taking them around, showing them the sights. More like tour guides."

"Tour guides? Residents don't need guides. They find their way around pretty well."

"I'm not talking about Residents," Bob said, and he let Wilbert think about that for a moment.

"Tour guides for tourists? From Earth? But we don't have any of those."

"We will," Bob said. "And I'm going to need reliable people to help make their visit as heavenly as possible."

"It might be tough to get folks interested when nobody has to do anything they don't want to."

"Seems to me any time spent would be just a drop in eternity's bucket. Besides, aren't there other people persons here like you who get bored? Being a tour guide would occupy them, and on top of that, they'd even get to guide people they knew on Earth, catch up on their families and such, and show them how great it is here in Heaven."

By now, Wilbert's eyes were alight with the possibilities, but he was still cautious.

"But how are your going to get permission to bring tourists here? It's unheard of."

"Not really," Bob said. "Look at me. Besides, I've already gotten the approval of Michael and the other Archangels. My new office building is just a stone's throw away from the Administration Building."

"So that's what that new skyscraper is," Wilbert said, nodding in approval. "Pretty nice."

"You can thank my personal assistant, Nanookie, for that."

"The Inuit woman who lives in Florida?"

"That's her. Only she lives with me now."

Wilbert's look of approval shot up another few notches into the realm of admiration, and Bob's feelings of self-worth took a similar leap.

"What do you want me to do?" Wilbert asked.

"Round up your own people," Bob said. "I trust your judgment. We have complete training facilities and plenty of offices.

240

We'll put the tour guides on the second floor, and the biggest office will be yours."

"Do I get a secretary?"

"You'll get anything you desire," Bob said. "Isn't this Heaven?"

"It sure is!"

"We'll meet as soon as you're set up. Meanwhile, I have some other matters to attend to. Call Nanookie if you need anything."

"Will do, boss," Wilbert said.

It was the nicest thing anybody had said to Bob since he'd arrived. Except for Nanookie, of course, but she'd done a lot more than talk.

Next, Bob drove to Psalm Beach to scout a good location for his first resort hotel. He found it part way around a large cove, somewhat away from all the major activity. He didn't want surfers, beach bums, and families to disrupt his guests' fun. Even better, a thin forest of ambrosia trees made to look like palms, complete with ambrosia coconuts, surrounded the back side of the cove. He noticed a number of small boats drawn up on the sand with one lone man puttering about, but it wasn't until he drew near that he realized a village of straw-roofed huts built on stilts nestled at the edge of the ambrosia palm forest. As soon as Bob reached the boats, the man looked up.

"Hello, stranger," the man said. "Welcome to Paradise Island." He looked like a South Seas islander.

"You live here?" Bob asked.

"I do. Our village has been here for hundreds of Earth years, but it seems like we moved in just this morning. One day is just like the next. You know how it is."

"But it must be fun to go out in your boat and fish, and always bring back a full haul for your family."

"Are you kidding. We used to keep up the fishing thing, but in Heaven, it's all catch and release. What's the point in going to all the effort of patching boats and restringing torn fishing nets if you can't keep anything and ambrosia coconuts taste like any fish you can imagine? That's why nobody else is down here. They're all up in the village, watching reality TV and cooking shows, both of which seem particularly pointless here. I can't stand TV, so I just hang out down here, wishing for a good typhoon to shake things up. But apparently, conjuring up big storms isn't on the approved list of Heavenly De-

241

sires." He eyed Bob. "So what brings you to our little stagnant corner of Paradise?"

"I'm looking for a location to build a new resort hotel," Bob told him. "I was thinking of somewhere along here, but I see your village already holds the title."

"A resort hotel, huh? Who would stay there?"

"People from Earth."

"No way," the man said.

"Way," Bob said confidently. "Would your village consent to let me build nearby?"

"I doubt if they could stop you, but they probably won't even notice."

"Do you think any of your fellow islanders might want to get involved?"

"Probably not," the man said. "Back on Earth, they were the laziest bunch I ever saw, and it's even worse here."

"I could point out they might see some relatives who are still alive come up for a visit."

"Not likely," the man said. "Remember what I said about typhoons shaking things up? That's how my whole village got here all at once, buildings included. We're all here, now. Or, most of us. We did have a few bad pineapples who didn't make it."

"Even so," Bob persisted, "tourists from Earth would liven things up. Your women could do hula dances and hand out leis, and you and the other men could take them for boat rides and carve masks for the tourist trade."

"Why would I want to expend all my energy paddling a bunch of tourists around for nothing? I already have everything I need."

"We could provide you with a motor," Bob said. "As for pay, it seems to me there is something you need that you don't have: something to do for the rest of eternity. If you're bored already, just think of how you'll feel in another few thousand years. You can spend them sitting here moping about how dull it is, or you could have fun bilking stupid, over-tipping tourists and telling them tall tales about fishing on the open ocean with only your boat, harpoon, and wits to keep you alive."

"Makes sense when you put it that way," the man said. "Okay." He pointed toward a rise in the cloudscape at the edge of the shore, half a mile or so beyond the village. "There's a good spot to build. We never use that part of the beach."

"Great," Bob said, thinking he'd charge more for the rooms on the side of the building overlooking the village. Ambience is worth something.

"Just one thing," the man said. "If you're going to set this all up, you must have a lot of clout. Once you get things going, do you think you might petition the powers that be to send a good typhoon our way every once in a while? Just for fun?"

"I'll do my best," Bob promised. "It might be exciting for the tourists, too." He thanked the man and left for his next destination.

Almost as soon as he crossed the border into Sector 1, he sensed that something was different. It wasn't in the way the saber-tooth tiger popped up out of the mists and stared hungrily at him, but in the fact that Harry *didn't* pop up to save him. Bob calculated his chance of making it away from the saber-tooth before it brought him down was pretty slim, even with the cart.

The beast dropped into the mists, and its tail twitched upright and began moving toward him like a periscope cutting the water. Damn Michael. Without Heavenly Desire powers, Bob couldn't say "Get thee fucking back' or wish up anything like a RPG or an assault rifle.

As the tail neared, Bob wondered what it would be like to be eaten alive—even though, technically, he wasn't.

Where the hell was Harry?

The periscope tail crept closer and closer, and Bob's fevered mind cast about for something to keep the beast at bay. Anything. Then the answer popped into his mind.

"Way-finding sign," he said, looking at a point about ten feet in front of the moving tail. "Way-finding sign, way-finding sign, way-finding sign," he snapped, his eyes moving from spot to spot, each right next to the previous one as he worked his way rapidly around in a circle. In seconds, the saber-tooth was trapped in a corral of way-finding signs. The beast, butting up against the signs, roared its anger, and the roars grew more ferocious as it realized it was completely hemmed in.

I'm going to have to get rid of these things, Bob thought. Can't have them eating my tourists, who probably won't reconstitute. But then he had a better idea. He could collect all of them on a special preserve with other prehistoric animals and take tourists through in protected vehicles. He'd call it Seraphic Safaris.

Pondering the logistics of this with only Amish buggies and golf carts at his disposal, he made his way toward the cavemen's cliff. When he reached it, he had a second shock. Harry and Fluffy's cave was still there, but now it was a dank, empty hole. Out in front of it, on the cloud carpet, stood a two-story Mac mansion, complete with a fake stone façade and a two-car garage. In fact, a Mac mansion stood in front of every dark cave for as far as he could see along the cliff, though none were as grand as Harry and Fluffy's place.

Bob went up to the front door and rang the bell, but there was no answer. He stepped off the porch and walked around back.

Harry, clad in a plaid Speedo, was sitting in a lounger, absorbed in a paperback thriller. The title on the lurid cover read, *Harry Savage, Supersecret Agent*. Fluffy, in an itsy-bitsy, teeny-weeny, yellow polka dot bikini, drifted on a float in a large, in-cloud swimming pool, a fruity cocktail topped with a little paper umbrella in her furry hand. Nearby sat a gas grill, a pair of thick, juicy steaks sizzling over charcoals.

"Bob!" Harry called out, and Fluffy waved from water. "How do you like the spread?"

"Pretty impressive," Bob said, keeping his chagrin out of his voice. He had plans for these people. How could they screw it up so badly?

"We owe it all to you, guy," Harry said, waving Bob to a nearby deck chair. "You showed us the way."

"I showed you about cold beer in a frosted goblet," Bob said. "I didn't show you about Mac mansions and swimming pools."

"One thing leads to another," Harry said. "Kinda like a landslide, right? You pull out one little rock, and the whole hillside comes tumbling down."

Tumbling down, Bob thought. He sure wasn't about to mention art museums. The thought of his highbrow art tourists rubbing elbows with Neanderthals wasn't a pretty picture, though he might convince Harry to exhibit some cave art.

"I'm surprised," he said. "And a little disappointed."

"Disappointed?"

244

"Yeah. I'm working on building a tourist business, and I'd hoped to make Caveman Hills a major attraction. But look at the place." He waved around. "It's the same as where my tourists will come from."

"You mean you want us to act like cavemen for tourists?"

"Well, not *all* the time," Bob hedged, trying not to sound insulting. "But these people have heard about cavemen their entire lives and never seen a real one. I just thought...."

"Hey, Fluffy!" Harry bellowed, sitting upright in his lounger and planting his horny, splayed feet on either side. "You hear that? Bob want us to go into show business!"

"Show business?" Fluffy quickly paddled to the edge of the pool and climbed out. "You mean like the movies?"

"I was thinking of starting with live theater," Bob said. "It wouldn't really be acting, exactly, since all you have to do is be yourselves."

"Like method acting," Harry said. "I think we can handle it. We've been rehearsing for a couple hundred millennia."

"I don't have to cook over an ambrosia branch fire, do I?" Fluffy asked.

"We can set up a fake fire, and you'll just have to pretend. If your act is a hit—and I don't see how it won't be—we can talk about TV and movies."

"Oh," Fluffy almost moaned. "I want to star in *When Harry Met Fluffy*. I just love the restaurant scene. Yes! Yes! Ye...."

"Simmer down, Fluffy," Harry said. "No need to make a spectacle of yourself in front of Bob. Save it for later." He turned to Bob and sighed with distaste. "Chick flicks. What I want to be in is *Dirtiest Harry*. I'll whip out my .88 magnum and...."

"I think it's a .44 magnum," Bob corrected.

"Not for me. I can handle twice the firepower."

"Whatever you want," Bob said. "We'll set up our own Holywood, but first things first. I'll need you to convince some of the other cavemen to go along...."

"But Fluffy and I are the stars, right?"

"The brightest. You're my cave people culture leaders, right? When you get everybody together, I'll need you to move your new homes away from the cloud cliff...."

"No problem there," Harry said. "Fluffy says looking at our old cave all the time when we're out here is kind of depressing. I'm considering becoming a developer and building my own subdivision. I'll call it Hominid Homes."

"You're a caveman after my own heart," Bob said. "You get your subdivision built, then, when we bring a bunch of tourists by, all you have to do is come over here, dress up like you were when I met you, and hang out around the caves for the afternoon. We'll make sure you two are the main attraction. Then you can go home and enjoy the fruits of your celebrity—and rub it in the faces of your supporting cast."

"Sounds great. What about you Fluffy?"

Fluffy struck a sultry pose, holding up her stiff hair with one hand and perching the other sexily on a cocked furry hip.

"I feel like a star already."

❧ 25 ☙

MICHAEL STARED AT THE CELL phone lying on his desk. It was one of the first batch to be distributed, and Michael already hated it. Antoine had brought it in, informed Michael he had his first voice message, then retreated to the outer office. Or so Michael thought.

When he retrieved the message, it turned out to be from Antoine, who's tinny voice said that now that he-and-he was a personal assistant instead of a secretary, he-and-he was taking some time off. He-and-he said something about "vacation time accrued," but his-and-his voice was so intermittent that Michael couldn't completely understand him-and-him.

Michael immediately went to the door and looked into the outer office to see that Antoine's desk was vacant. The eyes of two dozen petitioners stared at him, and those were a lot of eyes since six of the petitioners were Ophanim and three more were Cherubs.

Michael shut the door.

What was he going to do with Antoine out indefinitely? He really didn't want to deal with the petitioners. Their problems were petty compared to the difficulties facing Michael and would only distract him. Besides, why did he have to be the one to solve everybody's problems? Didn't anybody here besides Bob have an ounce of incentive or inventiveness?

The answer, he knew, was no.

Feeling hemmed in, Michael desperately wanted to get out of his office, but he couldn't just walk out and ignore the petitioners. That would only lead to further accusations of hierarchangelism. He needed to get rid of them, somehow, without seeming to. And if he didn't leave soon, the outer office would get so clogged he'd be unable to move, much less escape.

Then he had an idea. He picked up the cell phone and checked the address book. Sure enough, the numbers for all the other Archangels were in there, and so were those for Bob and his personal assistant, Nanookie. Antoine's number was conspicuously absent. So that was how he was going to repay Michael's generosity in giving him a promotion. Well, he'd take care of Antoine later.

Michael touched the number for Uriel and listened to the ring sound twice before Uriel's voice came through the tiny speaker.

"That you, Michael?"

"It is. Listen. I want you to deliver two dozen phones to my office immediately. Antoine has stepped out, so when you get here, hand out the phones to everybody in the waiting room."

"We're trying to distribute the phones to all the First Sphere angels first," Uriel said.

Hierarchangelism, Michael winced.

"I don't care. Just do it. Then knock on my door."

Michael hung up and waited for what seemed like forever, even though he knew it was only a fraction of eternity. If such a thing were possible.

While he waited, he fiddled with the phone to see what kind of apps were on it, and at one point, his fumble fingers dropped the slippery device. Michael bent to retrieve it from the cloud carpet, and as he did, he noticed a small silver disk with a wire sticking out of it affixed to the bottom of his desk.

It was a bug!

Barachiel had bugged *him*! Or, Michael thought with sudden suspicion, maybe it was Antoine. Who else had free access to Michael's office?

Michael straightened without removing the bug. No matter. Whoever it was, let them listen. He'd refrain from discussing anything of importance in the office, but he'd be sure to drag out any conversations with petitioners for as long as possible. See how they liked listening to that!

He was still mulling over the fact that he was bugged when he heard a hubbub coming through his office door followed by a sudden silence terminated by a sharp rap on his door.

"Come in."

Uriel entered, and Michael gestured for him to shut the door.

"You gave them the phones?" he asked.

"I did. They were pretty excited."

"Then what?"

"They all started texting."

"Okay. I'm going to leave. You stay here for a couple of minutes, then meet me in the boardroom."

"The boardroom? Why...?"

"Just do it."

Without waiting for Uriel to reply, Michael slipped out of the door and floated as quickly and surreptitiously as he could across the outer office then out into the hall. As he'd hoped, all the petitioners had their eyes glued to their cell phones in a pose reminiscent of Selaphiel's permanent prayer—except, of course, the Ophanim, who didn't have necks. But all their eyes were on their screens, and that was what mattered.

When he arrived in the boardroom, Michael bent and surveyed the bottom of the table. Near his end was another silver disc. He straightened just as Uriel joined him.

"Why all the fuss?" Uriel asked.

"Office politics," Michael said. "Give me a quick rundown on your progress in setting up our digital infrastructure."

"It's going well. Festus added a new wing to the Factory, and we're churning out cell phones as fast as we can. Computers and tablets will take a little longer, but most of the initial demand is for the phones, so we should be okay. The only complaints we've had so far is from the humans, who think we ought to have service to Earth."

"They can forget that," Michael said. "No other problems?"

"None."

"Let's keep it that way," Michael said. "How is Barachiel's investigation into the utilities going?"

"I haven't talked to him lately, but I think he and Rags are considering a sting operation to catch them in the act."

Perhaps Michael ought to begin a sting operation against whoever was bugging him.

"Find him, and tell him to gather all the evidence he can, but he's not to act on any of it until I give the order."

"What are you going to be doing?"

Michael didn't want to tell him. Or the bug.

"I have some business I need to take care of," he hedged. "I'll be out of the office for a while."

What he actually planned was a vacation to France. He wanted to visit Mont Saint-Michel. He wished he could turn back the clock and apologize to Aubert for losing his temper, but despite his guilt, he wanted to witness first-hand what Aubert had wrought in his name. Afterward, he intended to spend at least two weeks taking in everything from the lime-stone cliffs of Normandy to the French Alps. Most of all, he wanted—no, needed—several days at least in the vineyard country of Côte de Nuits.

Uriel left to find Barachiel then fly back to the Garden of Eden, where he had a kendo session scheduled with Miyamoto Musashi.

"If I have to protect the Garden with my light saber, I better keep up my practice," he explained.

Michael sat in the quiet boardroom for a few minutes, pondering, then he picked up his phone and called Bob's number.

"Michael!" Bob's effusiveness sounded flimsy coming through the phone's tiny speaker. "What can I do for you?"

"I have something I'd like to discuss," Michael said. "Privately."

"Why, sure. I'm free at the moment. Want me to come over?"

"No. I'd rather talk at your place."

Michael didn't think Barachiel would have bugged Bob's office yet, and he didn't want any of Barachiel's bugs to pick up on his vacation plans. With all the angels so overworked, Michael taking some time off would certainly lead to more charges of hierarchangelism.

"Sounds intriguing. Come on over."

A few minutes later, Michael approached the Holy Holidays building, and his visual measuring system registered the fact that the structure was one story taller than the Administration Building. Momentary irritation flashed through him, but he suppressed it. Michael knew size wasn't everything, so let Bob have his meaningless little victories. Especially if the wayward human could help out with Michael's problems.

He landed in front of the building and strode through the main entrance, noting the hustle and bustle going on. Near the entrance, a placard set on an easel read, "Tour Guide Training," and underneath the lettering, a red arrow pointed down a hall. Lots of smiling people were going that way, and Michael even caught a few whiffs of conversation about how nice it would be to see the kids again, or old lovers, or friends.

Bob said he knew his demographic, and he certainly was right that the Residents would be easy to enlist in his scheme. Michael only hoped he could do something about the utilities before his house of cards came tumbling down.

The only odd thing Michael saw was clocks. There was one in every room, including the reception room, and now that he'd noticed them, he also saw that all the tour guide trainees wore watches.

Looking around, he spotted a receptionist desk and went over to it.

"I'm here to see Bob," he told the pretty young woman behind the counter.

"Do you have an appointment, sir?" she asked with a polite but vapid smile.

"Do you know who I am?" Michael asked.

"Archangel Michael, I believe," she replied.

"Then you know I don't need an appointment to go anywhere. All I need is for you to point me in the right direction."

"His elevator is right over there." She gestured toward a lone elevator door situated just beyond the main bank of elevators. "But if you're really Michael, shouldn't you know that already?"

Ignoring the snide undercurrent in her tone, he went to the elevator and punched the button. The car doors slid open, and he went inside and pushed the up button. The car surged, pressing Michael's feet deep into the floor and billowing the hems of his robes until he looked like an inverted funnel. At last the embarrassing ride ended and the doors opened into a lobby, where a gorgeous brown-skinned woman with high cheekbones was waiting for him. She looked a lot more personally assistive than Antoine.

"Welcome to Holy Holidays, Michael," she said. "I'm Nanookie. This is your first visit, I believe."

"That's right, Nanookie. Bob said to come on over."

"Follow me."

They went through a door, down a short hall, then through another door into an office that looked a hell of a lot better than Michael's. And its floor was level. The rooms and halls up here all had clocks, just like downstairs.

Bob stood up and came around his desk, a big smile on his face.

"Michael. So good to see you. Can Nanookie bring you anything? Coffee? A sparkling water?"

"I'm fine." Michael shook his head.

"Here," Nanookie said. "Let me take all that stuff."

She relieved him of his accouterments and stowed them neatly in a closet. Then she quietly left the room, discreetly shutting the door behind her.

Maybe I should fire Antoine, Michael mused, and hire a human female to assist me. It was a thought....

"Have a seat, Michael," Bob said, and as Michael sat in a visitor's chair, Bob returned to his own seat behind the desk.

"You really have things moving around here," Michael said. "I don't think I've seen this much bustle in Heaven since World War II dumped millions of people on us all at once."

"That must have been a strain," Bob said sympathetically. "But you didn't come all the way over here to discuss the past." His eyes narrowed. "We don't have any problems do we?"

"We don't," Michael said, "but I do."

He hesitated. Was he really going to confess his stress to this upstart human? He decided he couldn't. Wouldn't.

"I'm here for a little education on your project," Michael prevaricated.

"We have training sessions and informational videos showing downstairs," Bob said. "And Nanookie can supply you with all the brochures you need."

"All that's hearsay," Michael said. "If we're going to have tourists coming here, I need to find out first-hand what tourism is all about."

252

"You want to take one of our tours?" Bob was surprised. "But you already know all about Heaven."

"That's the point," Michael said. "I can't be a tourist here, especially since I run the place. I'll have to go someplace else."

"You want me to set up a tour for you on Earth?"

"It's about the only choice, isn't it? A trip there will give me a real sense of what being a tourist is all about, and it'll supply you with an opportunity to beta test your organization."

Bob leaned back in his chair, tented his fingers, and stared into space for a moment. Then a big smile pulled back his cheeks.

"Great idea," he said, sitting forward and putting his hands on top of his desk. "What did you have in mind?" Before Michael could speak, wryness twisted Bob's smile into a quirky line. "Let me guess. Mont Saint-Michel."

"Well, yes. For starters. And I want to spend some time—a lot of time, actually—in the French wine country. But aside from that, I really don't know much about Earth anymore. That's why I need you to set up my tour."

"I tell you what, Michael. Nanookie and I will personally plan your excursion. It'll not only be the first vacation you've ever had, it'll be the best."

Bob liked making promises that were easy to keep.

"Wonderful. I can hardly wait."

"When would you like to depart?" Bob asked. "And how long do you want to be gone?"

"As soon as possible. Three weeks, Earth time, should do it."

"Give me a couple of days."

The mention of days reminded Michael of the clocks and watches he'd seen.

"What's with all the clocks?" he asked.

"We're in the business of scheduling tours," Bob replied. "Can't have schedules without time. Can you imagine booking a tour that's going to leave 'sometime' and go places 'whenever'? And how can you offer day trips if you don't have days? Plus, now that we have clocks, we can guarantee our tourists that we can serve meals anytime, all the time. Don't worry. To avoid confusion, all our clocks are set to Eternet time."

"What should I pack?"

"Your wings," Bob said. "They're pretty conspicuous."

"That's no problem," Michael said. "I can disguise myself."

"I hope so. We don't want potential clients wondering why the Captain of the Hosts might want to leave Heaven for Earth."

Michael stood.

"You'll let me know my itinerary?"

"As soon as I have all the details in place," Bob assured him. Michael floated to the door, then paused with his hand on the knob and turned.

"Don't forget to check into the utilities for me."

"Wouldn't think of forgetting," Bob said. "Enjoy the rest of your day. I'll be in touch."

After Michael left, Nanookie came in, question marks in her eyes.

Bob told her what had transpired.

"I only have one question," he said when he finished. "Why did he want to discuss this personally, when a phone call or a text would have been a lot simpler?"

"Maybe he's just nervous about taking a break. He strikes me as something of a control freak."

"He was nervous about something, that's for sure," Bob said thoughtfully. "The only reason to come over here in person would be to avoid having any of the other angels hear about his plans."

"But how would they do that? His office ought to be as private as yours."

"Ought to be," Bob agreed. "You know, Nan, I think we need an IT department. Think you can find somebody to head it up?"

"I can do anything you want, Bob."

This sure is Heaven, he thought, looking at her.

"That's nice to hear, Nan, because as soon as Michael leaves on his vacation, we'll be doing a lot."

"When the shepherd's away," she said, "the sheep can play."

254

❧ 26 ❧

BOB HAD MORE TO DO than he could shake a stick at, and with Michael gone on vacation, he followed Teddy Roosevelt's advice and shook a big one. He had the main elements of his new corporate team in place in the form of his new board of directors—Mary, Jerry, and Larry—and they were all out in the field, doing the early negotiations. But Bob had to finalize many of the negotiations himself, molding agreements heavily tilted in his favor.

Nanookie, who'd already proved her personal worth to Bob, was now showing equal value to Bob's organization. The first person she recruited for the director-level office staff was a scrawny, tousle-headed, bespectacled young man named Minghua to run their IT department.

"He's a brilliant guy," she told Bob. "He was an elite hacker back in life."

"Why does he look like that?" asked Bob. He'd seen absolutely zero other scrawny, tousle-headed, bespectacled young guys in Heaven. Everybody else was buff, coiffed, and clear-eyed.

"I guess that's his personal ideal," Nanookie shrugged. "Nerd Nirvana, or something. Do you want to meet him?"

Bob told her he did, and they went into Ming's office.

255

"I suppose you want to own the Eternet," was the first thing Ming said after Nanookie introduced Bob.

Bob shook his head.

"Too much of a headache. I don't want to fix wires or deal with customer complaints. I just want access. With that, it's easy to create and manipulate desire. We'll also want metrics and that sort of thing."

"Does 'that sort of thing' include hacking?" Ming asked. He sounded hopeful.

"Absolutely." Bob was thinking of the suspicious way Michael had come to his office, acting like somebody might be watching his every move. Something was going on. "I think the angels have set up some sort of surveillance network. What can you find out?"

Ming's fingers flew so fast over the keyboard they were a blur.

"This shouldn't take long," he said. "There isn't much Eternet traffic yet, and even better, the angels are so completely transparent in their activities they haven't even set up any firewalls."

After just a few minutes, he sat back and looked up at Bob.

"Yep. Just like you suspected. Barachiel is running a surveillance network." Ming leaned forward again, squinting at the screen through his glasses. "You'll be interested to learn there's quite a bit of corruption going on at the various utilities." He outlined the schemes being perpetrated by the Dominions in charge of Heaven's infrastructure.

"I know that look," Nanookie said to Bob when Ming finished. "But I have no idea how you're going to leverage this. If we learned it from the Archangels' network, they already know about it."

"But do the guilty Dominions know the Archangels know?" Bob asked. "What they don't know, won't hurt me. If I'm going to set up a pipeline from Earth to Heaven, it could just as easily work the other way. We sent Michael down to Earth, didn't we? I'm going to need some grassroots support among the angel hordes, and there's no better incentive for cooperation than blackmailing managers."

He glanced at the clock on the wall.

"When's the rendezvous with the urchins?"

256

"Tomorrow morning," she said. "Two AM sharp. They'll meet you on the way. The yardmen are at four."

We might be ticking off the seconds, Bob reflected, but time was still an artificial construct. There being no weariness or nighttime in Heaven, there also was no sleep, so one could find oneself doing the oddest thing at the oddest hour.

"Great," he said. "Well, I'm off to make our first acquisitions."

Even though Holy Holidays wasn't yet fully operational, there was no sense in wasting opportunities. He could leverage imagination as easily as he could hard cash. Probably easier. Hard cash required lugging a briefcase, but imagination could be carried on the tip of his silver tongue.

Before Bob left, he gave Ming a set of tasks to work on, then he went down to cloud level and consulted the way-finding sign beside the building's front entrance. When he'd oriented himself, he got in his cart and gunned it toward the Water Treatment and Purification Plant.

Bob hadn't had Nanookie arrange appointments because he wanted to surprise the Dominions in charge of the various utilities. Catch them in the act, so to speak. He had no doubt they'd agree to whatever he demanded. Not only had Michael ordered them to cooperate with Bob and his venture, Bob had the extra leverage of knowing about their schemes.

When he arrived at the plant, he went in only to learn from the Virtue in the front office that Halliwell and his main staff were over in Sector U, inspecting the fountains there.

Yeah, right, Bob thought. He remembered the Dalmore 64 Trinitas he'd drunk from the fountain in Sector P, and his mouth twisted into a sour moue. Payback was at hand for that spoiled drink.

"You have a phone?" he asked.

"Yes."

"Call Halliwell now and have him come back here, pronto. I have business to discuss."

The Virtue, obviously miffed at having to cut his texting short, found Halliwell's number on his screen and tapped it into life. A moment later, he said, "Bob is here to speak with you, sir." Pause. "Yes, that Bob." Pause. "Yes, sir. I'll tell him." The

Virtue looked up at Bob and said, "He says he can't come now. Maybe he can meet with you tomorrow."

"Tell him I know he's going to Sector R next, then Sector I, and tell him I know why. If he doesn't get his ass back here immediately, I'm going to report it to Michael."

The Virtue repeated Bob's words into the phone, then said, "Yes, sir. I'll tell him."

He hung up the phone and said, "He'll be here in half an hour."

"Fine," Bob said. "I'll just wander around the plant until then."

By the time Halliwell arrived, Bob had managed to drive around enough of the plant to get an idea of its operation, and he now stood on the rim of the purification vat. Surely there was some recreational purpose he could put it to.

"Halliwell, I presume," Bob said when the Dominion lit beside him. Bob instantly recognized him as one of the angels who'd been standing around the fountain in Sector P. He was going to enjoy this....

"Bob, I presume," Halliwell shot back. "How did you know about the fountains?"

"It's my business to know," Bob answered. "But I'm not here about just that. I assume Michael filled you in on my endeavor."

"What does our plant have to do with your travel agency?"

"Not a thing, except I want a piece of the pie."

"What pie? And what makes you think I'll give a piece to you? You think you can blackmail me over the fountains? That's not enough. I'll just say we were doing an experiment in quality control."

"Is Angel Eyes quality control, too?" Bob asked, relishing the way the ripple of victory in Halliwell's eyes suddenly shimmered with fear. "And Anti-Zombie Serum? I've been to Hell, Halliwell, and I can tell you the joint is just as bad for the fallen angel jailers as it is for the incarcerated."

"Blackmail." Halliwell hung his head, perhaps in prayer.

"Call it whitemail, instead," Bob said. "I'm offering to remove your guilt by taking over your operations."

"And what do I get out of it?" Halliwell asked.

"Isn't expiation enough?" Bob asked. "Okay, I'll leave you a small percentage of the profits. But I have some ideas to expand

258

your business, so your percentage will be ten times what you get now, with less hassle. And," he said pointedly, "with less risk."

"I'm listening."

Bob gestured to the vat.

"Fly me up there."

Halliwell complied, and in a few moments, they stood on vat's thick rim. Bob pointed toward the middle of the lake of water contained by the titanic vat. He couldn't actually see the tube where the Boss's tears were dripping into the water, but he knew it was out there.

"Frankly, I think the Boss's tears are underutilized. In addition to Angel Eyes and AZS, we can make beauty and health products, food preservatives, and additives for products like paint and plastic. And with all the impotence in the world, marketing them as an effective treatment for that, alone, should make our bottom line. There's no end to what we can use them for, especially since there's an endless supply."

"But we can't just siphon off all of the tears," Halliwell protested. "The fountains...."

"Fountains, schmountains," Bob said. "Most of the people up here have such lousy taste, no one will even notice. Just consider it an expansion of your quality control experiment. And if Michael says anything, tell him I said the Boss's tears are integral to my plans, and I'll deal with him."

Halliwell thought it over for a moment, then nodded cautiously.

"Okay," he said. "But if the bottom line doesn't match your projection, I'm withdrawing my support."

"Fair enough. One more thing I want to take a sample of the tears with me."

"Sure."

A toy remote-controlled motorboat materialized in Halliwell's hands, a shot glass sitting in its seat. Halliwell set the boat in the water, manipulated the controller, and the boat hummed toward the center of the vat. He also produced a pair of binoculars, which he handed to Bob.

Bob used the field glasses to watch the motorboat maneuver beneath a tube magically suspended from a small, stormy-looking cloud hovering a few feet above the surface of the water. After a dozen shimmering drops had plinked into the glass, Halliwell brought the boat back, and by the time it arrived, the shot glass had turned into a glass vial with a black plastic screw cap. Halliwell handed the vial to Bob.

"Thanks," Bob said. "I'll be in touch."

Soon after, Bob was propelling his golf cart toward the Solid Waste and Recycling Center. He hadn't gone more than a few miles, though, when he stopped the cart and peered behind him to make sure the Water Plant was out of sight. He didn't want Halliwell to see what he was about to do. That was when he first noticed the twin dark gray tire tracks trailing behind him instead of a single line.

Making my mark in more ways than one, he thought.

He was far enough from the plant, he decided. He took out the vial, unscrewed its cap, covered its mouth with his finger, and upended it. Turning the vial upright again, he took the finger, now wet with the Boss's tears, and rubbed it over his bald spot.

This should be the true test, he thought as he recapped the vial, slipped it into his vest pocket, and drove on. His scalp felt no different, and he resisted the temptation to run a hand over it to see if anything was happening. If it was going to grow his hair, he didn't want furry palms, too.

In another half an hour, the Solid Waste and Recycling Center came into view, though he'd been seeing the snow-covered peak of a stupendous mountain almost since he'd left the Water Treatment and Purification Plant. The thing his eyes fastened on, however, was what looked like a smudge on the clouds about halfway between him and the mountain. As he got closer, the smudge resolved itself into a crowd of waifish figures clad in white rags.

Bob glanced at his phone's time stamp. Right on schedule.

The urchins crowded around as Bob pulled his cart into their midst. The same boy he'd talked to earlier came forward as their spokesman.

"Some Eskimo lady said we should be here," the boy said. "Say, I remember you."

"And I remember you were complaining that you and your friends don't find the ruins in the Historic District quite as heavenly as they ought to be."

"You got that right," the boy said.

260

"What if I have a way to change that?" Bob asked, and the urchins all pricked up their ears and pressed eagerly toward him.

Bob outlined his plan, and soon he was on his way again, going slow enough for the mob of urchins to keep up. But it wasn't far, and shortly they were massed in front of the recycling center's building while Bob went in to talk to Monte. This conversation was easier than the one he'd had with Halliwell. It seemed the waterworks Dominion had called to warn Monte the jig was up.

They came back out a few minutes later, and Bob drove off, while Monte took charge of the urchins.

Bob's next destination was the Factory, and Festus was as easy a sell as Monte had been.

So far, George at the Farm had escaped the surveillance net, but that didn't mean he wasn't guilty of some malfeasance. He just hadn't been caught yet. So instead of wasting time there, Bob headed toward Eden.

About two miles out, he spotted a dark speck on the clouds moving rapidly on an intercept course with his line of travel. As the speck angled toward him and grew, Bob saw it was a dark-haired, mustachioed man on a riding lawnmower.

Again, right on time. That Nanookie was the best.

The man on the mower arced in, pulled up alongside Bob's cart, and matched speed.

"I'm Jose!" the man yelled over the roar of his engine. "Head of the Yardman Association! The others are on their way! Look!"

He pointed, and Bob saw that two riders were approaching. Then three, then a dozen. As each swung his machine in behind Bob and Jose, the fleet grew until the roar was deafening. Most of the mowers had second riders hanging on, carrying leaf blowers, rakes, shovels, and other tools of the trade. Bob hoped they appreciated their motorized equipment. It had only been a few hours since he'd told Ming to work up the requisitions and make it look like they'd come straight from Michael himself, but apparently, his hacker could work wonders with the system.

In minutes, Bob's fleet pulled up in front of the gate to the Garden of Eden. Dozens of Cherubim rushed from the flanks to guard the gate, while Uriel stepped around the yellow and black striped bar, brandishing his nastily humming light saber. When he saw it was Bob at the head of the pack, he turned off the light saber and stuck the haft into his sash. The Cherubim remained, though, still looking protectively fierce.

"Well, Bob. We meet again. What have we here?"

Uriel waved at the fleet of yardmen.

"The answer to your prayers, Uriel," Bob said. "I've brought them to clean up the Garden."

"You know I can't allow them in," Uriel said, resting his hand meaningfully on the haft of his light saber.

"But angels can go in, right?" Bob pressed. No one ever got anywhere in this life or death by accepting limitations imposed by others. "And saints?" When Uriel nodded, Bob waved to the yardmen and said, "Well, these guys are true angels when it's 100 degrees out and the yard needs mowing. And Michael agrees. He's given them provisional sainthood."

"I'm not sure I should believe you."

"You have a phone, don't you? He was supposed to leave you a text." Bob sincerely hoped Ming had done that, too, or Bob was about to become fried mincemeat.

Uriel checked.

"You're right. All these guys are saints. I guess I can't say no."

Bob's tongue was quicker than Miyamoto Mushashi's sword, and Uriel knew when he was beaten. He also knew when he needed help. If someone didn't do something about the Garden soon, it was going to grow so wild nothing could tame it.

He stepped aside, and the parade of mowers, edgers, rakers, and leaf blowers streamed past. In moments, the Garden was a flurry of activity.

"I don't think you qualify for even provisional sainthood," Uriel said. "So don't expect me to let you in."

Bob's phone chimed.

"I'm busy now, anyway," Bob said, pulling the phone from his pocket. "Gotta run."

262

⚘ 27 ⚘

THE PHONE CALL WAS FROM Jerry, who wanted Bob to meet him at Elysium Field.

"I've got something working here," Jerry said. "I think you'll really like it. I'll be in the press club box."

When Bob arrived, the stadium was a lot more lively than the last time he'd seen it. Instead of the expectant hush of a small bowling audience punctuated by the clatter of balls battering tenpins, the air was filled with whooshing roars and thunderous cheers. Bob found the elevator to the press club box and went up. Jerry hurried over as soon as Bob emerged and led him to the windows overlooking the playing field, where Bob saw the source of the noise.

Or what was usually a playing field. Now, the plastic turf was gone, replaced by a twisty track snaking around the stadium floor. Two dozen or so Ophanim were out there, racing around the track at incredible speeds.

"What do you think, Bob?" Jerry asked, obviously excited. "Look at all the fans." He waved toward the stands, which held tens of thousands of people. It was a lot better than the bowling crowd. "And this is just the speed trials. Wait until the main events. We should draw an audience to rival the Superb Bowl. And we can have every sort of race there is: the Indy 5,000, Le

Mens, the Grand PriXXX. I'm working on a Faster-than-Furious race for the younger crowd, complete with celestial drift."

"What's this about Le Mens and the Grand PriXXX?" Bob asked. "Aren't those a bit risqué for Heaven?"

"Wasn't my idea," Jerry said. "It was theirs." He handed Bob a pair of binoculars and pointed to the track, where the racing Ophanim had finished their heat and were resting in their pit stops. Bob trained the binoculars on the now-still Ophanim and was surprised to see every one of them sporting a mighty set of male genitals hanging in the middle of its—or was it now *his*?—smaller wheel.

"How did they get those?" Bob asked, lowering the binoculars.

"Their racing union boss, Terence, insisted on it as part of their contract. He said racing takes a lot of balls, and since they couldn't grow them themselves, we had to use our Heavenly Desires to give them some. Not me," he held up his hands in protest at Bob's look. "I had some of the women fans do the desiring."

"No wonder they're so well hung," Bob said with amusement. "Well, they got 'em, but not where they'll be of much use. Besides, who would they use them on?"

"They probably love to race so much because that's the only stimulation they can get," Jerry answered.

"This is great work," Bob said. "Come on, let's head over to the country club. Mary and Larry are already there, and I want to show you something."

They left Elysium Field in Bob's golf cart, and Bob steered for the Celestial Country Club. On the way, Jerry told him he also was in the process of promoting concerts by dead rock stars.

"They're not all up here, of course," he said, with a shrug, "but you'd be surprised at how many of them did make it. There's nothing more divine than great music."

When they arrived at the country club, Bob parked in front, and they went inside. Mary and Larry were waiting in the lounge.

"I thought we were going to have a board meeting," Larry said when Bob proposed a game of golf.

"This is a board meeting," Bob said. "I want to show you something out on the links."

They went out to their carts, but instead of driving to the first tee, Bob took them to the eighteenth hole.

264

"We're starting here," he announced, placing his ball on the ground right in front of the cup. After sighting up the fairway, he whacked the ball, and it sailed right toward the tee and disappeared in the distance.

"Let's go," Bob said, and he got on the golf cart with Jerry. Mary and Larry following in their own cart, he sped toward the tee. When they arrived, they all saw Bob's ball sitting squarely on the peg like it was waiting to be hit toward the hole.

"Pretty neat," Larry said.

"Now look at this." Bob held up his automatic scorecard, which registered a -1 in the space by the number 18.

"Negative par!" Mary said. "I think you've just reinvented golf, Bob!"

"Larry said he was bored with regular golf here, and that got me thinking."

"I want to try it," Jerry said, stepping forward with his ball.

"Not now," Bob said. "This is nothing. I thought of something even better."

This time he took them to the first tee, where he set his ball on the pin then squinted left and right down the fairway. The fairway was lined with cloud trees except for a small clearing to the side, which held a small rest pavilion flanked by a fountain and an ambrosia tree.

Angling his body so his drive would head off toward the trees, he swung. The ball sailed toward the trees, bounced off them, then off a cloud rock in the middle of the fairway cloud sand trap, and into one of the pavilion pillars. From there, the ball ricocheted off another clump of trees, the ground, and a sapling trunk. Then it hopped onto the green, rolled briskly toward the hole, and plopped inside.

"You can work with the existing fairway," Bob told them, "and the winner is the one who can devise the craftiest ricochet pattern. Or, you can create your own fairway obstacles and challenge others to work their way through them."

Bob's board members were astounded, and he let them praise him profusely.

"But what about the tourists?" Jerry asked.

"The PGGA will take care of them," Bob said.

"What's that?"

"The Professional Golfer Guide's Association. They'll be the caddies. The tourist can call the shot in a conference with the caddy, who actually is the one who uses Heavenly Desire to make the shot happen."

The praise started up once more as if it had never dimmed, but the chime of Bob's phone cut it off.

"Why don't you guys play a few rounds of Carom Golf," he suggested, as he pulled out his phone. "This is just an idea so far, and we want to iron out any kinks, rebounds, backlashes, kick backs, and recoils."

The phone had a text from Nanookie. For the past few days, Bob had a Principality searching for the prophet, John the Anapest, and the text informed him that John was camped out near an ambrosia tree in Sector Z. The text ended with a code-like string of letters telling Bob that Nanookie was naked and waiting for him to come back to their penthouse, where a bottle of Lafite Rothschild 1787 was chilling in a golden ice bucket. It was, the text code continued, the same bottle that had once been owned by Thomas Jefferson and later sold for a record $156,000.

But first things first, and there were several of them. Before he left the country club, Bob paid a visit to the kitchen, where hundreds of human chefs vied with one another to cook everything for everybody and get the opportunity to bully the Principalities who made up the staff of assistant cooks. He arranged a quick chef cook off, and since all the chefs had done that sort of thing numerous times on Earth and nobody actually had to cook anything, the whole event was over in five minutes. Not only did Bob enjoy an excellent meal of the most divinely prepared ambrosia he'd ever tasted, he had his new executive chef.

Her name was Sydney, and he told her what he had in mind. He had to do something to top Nanookie's bottle of Lafite Rothschild. Sydney assured him a move from the country club to an exclusive restaurant was the next logical step, and he left her to deal with the details.

"I'll be in later. I'd like a nice table with a great view."

"All our views will be great," Sydney assured him. "But yours will be the best."

Bob left the country club and headed to the ambrosia tree where the Principality had traced John the Anapest. He found

266

the prophet living in a cloud yurt, and John perked up when Bob poked his head through the flap door.

"Hey, Bob. Nice to see you around."

"Listen, John. I have a proposition for you. A chance to make a little profit off all the time you spent as a prophet."

"I'm all ears."

"I want to develop some of the vacant space in the Wastelands," Bob explained, "and you know the territory as well as anyone."

"If I do, what's my end?"

"What do you want?"

"A secure place where other monks can foretell and complain and dispute without stop."

"I understand. Like a gated community. You want to protect your friends from outside interference."

"Not at all. To protect us from *them*," John said. "If we start building out in the Wastes, they'll just bug us to death. A bastille would be best."

"I think you just want to eliminate the competition," Bob said. "Have the territory to yourself."

"You're right. And what you want to build in the Wastes is a fake tourist trap to which you can divert lower-class folks who can't pay a lot, so they don't clutter up chic and swank tourist jaunts with loud clothes, low-brow tastes, and low-class bottom line."

"Wow!" Bob exclaimed with admiration. "You really are a prophet, even if you do have clumsy feet. Do we have a deal?"

"It's a deal."

Bob and John shook on it, then Bob hurried off. He wished it was back to Nanookie, but he had one more stop before enjoying her heavenly desires.

This one didn't require a detective, because Bob knew exactly where his target would be. If one lives in total darkness, one doesn't stray far from the nearest ambrosia tree and fountain.

Sure enough, Adriano was near the fountain, drinking from a golden goblet and peering upward through a telescope. An electric lantern sat on the clouds nearby, but even to Bob, it looked turned off.

"Adriano," he said. "How's the evening going?"

"Ah, my friend, Bob," Adriano said, looking up from the telescope eyepiece. "I recognize your voice."

He picked up the lantern and flipped it on. Bob couldn't see any difference, but apparently Adriano could.

"Neat telescope," Bob said. "A Heavenly Desire?"

"No. I got it from a fellow named Tom. He lives in the Celestial. Said he doesn't need it anymore."

"What are you looking at?"

"The planets and stars, my friend. Following Galileo. He had it hard in my time, but all that's past, now."

Don't bet on it, Bob thought.

"You wouldn't believe just how clear the view is from this high above the atmosphere," Adriano went on. "I can just make out all the little blue people living on Arcturus 5." He peered at Bob through his gloom. "What brings you to my dark corner of Heaven?"

"A proposition."

"Wouldn't have anything to do with this tourist thing I hear you're starting up, would it."

"It would, and I want you to be a part by opening a nightclub."

"A nightclub in Heaven?" Adriano waved dismissively. "Who would want to go to one of those?"

"They might not go to a run-of-the-mill nightclub," Bob said. "But yours will be the real deal because you have something to offer that nobody else can: genuine night."

"I'm a Castilian from the sixteenth century," Adriano persisted. "What do I know about running a nightclub?"

"You know about night, and that's the important thing for a night club. The rest will come. Just make it your Heavenly Desire. We can call it Adriano's Night Spot. I can picture it now: candles on every table, casting dim pools of illumination on the faces of your patrons. But you will be the *patron*, no? The *patron* of patrons. Before long, they'll forget the Night Spot part of the name, and it'll be known as Adriano's. How does *that* sound?"

"It *would* bring me companionship in my darkness," Adriano said musingly. Then he looked up at Bob. "I'll do it. Where would you like it?"

"Some out-of-the-way sort of place. Not too spooky or dangerous, but with a hint of menace. On special nights, you

268

could stage muggings, beatings, and knifings in a nearby back alley for the tourists to take photos."

"I get it: discreet, exclusive, and fun, with a hint of wickedness and danger."

"And I have just the act for you," Bob said.

Bob arrived back at Holy Holidays not long afterward. Finally he was learning his way around, and he'd created a lot of direct routes as well as scenic byways for his tourists to travel. He paused on the Marketing Division's floor to inspect the latest travel poster mock-ups, and he made a few suggestions before he boarded his private elevator.

As promised, Nanookie was waiting in the bedroom, the wine on ice next to her, and she was naked. And quite lovely.

Then Bob was naked, but before he could move toward the bed, Nanookie held up her hand and pointed to the wine.

She got up as Bob popped the cork and poured two glasses, then she took one of the glasses and steered him to the plate glass windows. "I've been trying to get the angels to make sure the Boss's crepuscular rays are shining in the sky at all times so the tourists can see them," she said. "That hasn't worked yet, so I came up with this. Watch." Suddenly the head of the Holy Holidays building was haloed in sheets of undulating greenish light. It was pretty spectacular, but Nanookie looked sheepish.

"They were supposed to be more like spotlights," she confessed. "I guess they're just a big shifting glow because it was me who wished for them."

Instead of a crepuscular nimbus, Nanookie's creation was a miniature Aurora Borealis.

"They're perfect and beautiful," Bob said, taking her in his embrace. "Just like you."

He kissed her on the neck, near her ear, where she'd daubed a touch of eau d' seal musk. Bob inhaled. To him, it smelled like violets. It was the only smell he remembered really liking.

She reached behind his head to ruffle his hair then suddenly drew back and turned him around.

"What's the matter?" he asked.

"Your bald spot," she said. "It's gone!"

"I guess Heaven just kinda grows on you," he said, turning back. "I feel like a true Resident already."

❧ 28 ☙

MICHAEL WAS SITTING AT A table in a little street-side café in Nice, sipping espresso and enjoying the warm sunshine and the balmy breeze wafting in off the Mediterranean. He was strongly considering incorporating those elements into Heaven's make-up. They sure would give the place a rosier complexion and less-tepid climate.

The past two weeks had been heavenly: no one bothering him or making demands, no pressing issues that kept him too busy to think, and people waiting on him for a change. The only real problem Michael had was disguising his angelic nature. Despite his best efforts, women tourist from all over the world kept hitting on him. He just couldn't dampen down his aura enough. Or maybe he could but enjoyed the attention too much. He wished he could do something about the women. This might be his last chance to make hay for quite a while. But the thought of more Nephilim made him abandon the images of smooth skin, soft flesh, and mysterious recesses that kept popping up in his mind.

His first vacation stop had been Mont Saint-Michel. The place was interesting, though centuries of additions made it considerably more elaborate than the Gothic monastery he'd ordered Aubert to build. He'd hoped he'd like it better, but he

271

really didn't care for the Romanesque architecture now overlaying the rocky islet. All the crypts beneath the building were neat, though, mostly because the cool atmosphere of their subterranean spaces and dark corners was such a contrast to the pervasive glow of Heaven's open plains.

Since then, he'd explored France, and tomorrow.... Tomorrow! How nice to have real days and nights that followed each other in orderly sequence instead of Heaven's golden eternity. Anyway, tomorrow he was off to Italy, and after that, Greece. His flexible itinerary would allow him to play it by ear. After all, there was a whole world to explore.

He was just reaching for his cup when his phone gave out the subtle beep he'd selected as the ringtone.

With a sigh, he glanced at the screen. Gabriel.

Down here on Earth, he felt he didn't have to answer to anyone, so he almost didn't take the call. But the next sound from the phone wasn't the subtle beep but a loud siren wail. People at the nearby tables stared, so Michael hastily fumbled the unfamiliar phone to life, but not before it blared again, drawing more stares.

"What is it, Gabriel?" Michael snapped. "You know I'm.... What...? When...? How did that happen in so short a time...? Okay, I'm on my way."

Michael nearly slammed the phone down on the table, but several people were still eyeing him suspiciously, so he just slipped it into the pocket of his white linen skirt, which was cleverly designed to resemble slacks. He put enough cash on the table to cover his bill and a generous tip, then he got up and floated off down the street, looking for a convenient place where he could fly off unseen.

Faking walking was the trickiest part of his disguise. He had to envelop himself in a field of visual confusion upon which he projected an image of himself striding along on two legs. It took a lot of concentration to create the illusion and, at the same time, move around without bumping into anything. But it gave him a distracted, aristocratic air, so people usually didn't bother him very much.

At last he found a suitable alley where he dropped his disguise and rocketed skyward. He debouched in front of the

272

Pearly Gates, which irritated him since that left him many, many miles from his office. What we really need, he thought, is an employees' entrance that opens right into the Administration Building lobby.

But that wouldn't have helped him right now since the Administration Building wasn't his immediate destination. With barely a wave to Saint Peter, Michael dove through the Pearly Gates and jetted toward the Solid Waste and Recycling Center. His flight was so furiously blinding it left a thick trail of smoke and, to many on the clouds below, the impression that the Next Coming was at hand.

As Potpourri Peak came into view, Michael noticed it hadn't grown any larger. That was one blessing, at least. Curiously, what looked like black bugs were crawling up and down the white snowcap. But as he neared, it was the face of the mountain where the angels had carved the crescent into its flank and the flat area in front of the domed building that really caught his attention. The little black bug shapes on the white peak were moving in relatively orderly and sparse lines, but the crescent and flat area writhed with what, from Michael's height, looked like a swarming infestation of army ants.

As he descended, he saw with a shock they were children dressed in rags completely blackened with filth. The children were clambering across the face of the crescent, stuffing garbage into big sacks something like those employed by cotton pickers on Earth, and dragging them into the domed building. Their frenzied work raised an odiferous dust cloud.

At that moment, an angel rose from the compound and approached Michael. It was Monte.

"Are those human children playing in the garbage?" Michael demanded when Monte hovered next to him.

"They are," Monte said. "Street urchins from Earth's Third-World countries. We have a tremendous number of them up here. Most of them subsisted off garbage dumps back home, and their lives were so short and brutal that they usually didn't have an opportunity to sin, so they end up here."

"Since when have you conscripted them to work in our garbage dump?"

"It was Bob's idea, sir," Monte said. "As you know, we aren't automated, so we have to rely on manual labor, and we just don't have enough Principalities to handle this." He waved toward towering Potpourri Peak. "We're using the kids in lieu of heavy equipment. It's a great arrangement for everybody. The kids get to play outdoors, we reward them with food and water for things they bring in."

"They would be rewarded without the work," Michael said sternly. "All they have to do is walk around, and everything is free."

"As you told me earlier, sir, Heaven is all about free will. These kids get one look at this—which you have to admit, is the ultimate garbage dump—and they know they're in Heaven and start digging right in. Besides," Monte said with an apologetic look, "we're short-handed. If we didn't have those kids, we'd be neck deep in garbage. Did you notice, sir, that Potpourri Peak has stopped growing?"

"It's still unethical," Michael said, ignoring Monte's feeble justification. But he also remembered all the litter and refuse he'd spotted while flying around Heaven, and he realized something had to be done. And he had to admit the dingy urchins were making more progress in eating away at Potpourri Peak than the Principalities had.

Monte led Michael down to a low observation deck erected next to the work area.

"What's this observation deck for?" Michael asked as he folded his wings.

"Another of Bob's ideas," Monte replied. "He recognized that Potpourri Peak, being the highest pinnacle in Heaven, has a lot of tourism potential. He had a bunch of ideas for it, but so far, we've only implemented two. One is this observation deck, where his tourists can watch 'the poor dear things' as they crawl like ants over the mountain, digging out the trash. The tourists will be encouraged to throw rupees, which are available for a small fee at the concession stand, to the kids as they scamper back and forth. The kids get to keep the rupees, and the tourists get to stroke their own egos with their generosity. Here, sir." An object suddenly appeared in Monte's hand and he passed it to Michael. It was a gold coin. "Care to try it for yourself?"

"I thought rupees were silver."

274

"Not our rupees, sir. Just lean over the railing and toss it out." Michael did, and the result was a scene out of every Victorian Third-World epic ever told. A kid separated from the melee, leapt nimbly upward, and snatched the rupee out of the air. He gave it a quick look and bit it. A big smile creased his face, and he looked up at Michael, teeth gleaming with sparkling highlights in a face artistically spotted with daubs of grime.

"Many thanks, sahib!"

The urchin tucked the rupee into a pouch hanging around his neck then dashed back into the melee. As he did, Michael felt a welling sense of his own self-worth, which he quickly squelched.

"I assume that's a gratuity," he said.

"Not at all, sir," Monte replied. "It's their pay."

"You don't give them a base wage?" Michael was amazed anybody would risk life and limb and health digging by hand through a monstrous mound of garbage to be paid only in hand-outs.

"We let them take what they want from Potpourri Peak," Monte explained. "They use it to build their shanty town over there a couple of miles. Downwind."

Michael sighed.

"And what is all the activity at the top of the mountain?"

"Our second project. Let's go up."

As Michael and Monte rose into Potpourri Peak's alpine zone, the stink from the foothills dropped away—completely frozen, Michael assumed. And now he could see that what had looked like black bugs crawling down the snowy slopes were actually skiers, and the bugs going upward were angels carrying skiers to the top.

"Welcome to Angelcrest Slopes," Monte said. "Instead of a ski lift, Principalities carry the skiers to the top and follow them as they ski down to make sure nothing bad happens."

"All right," Michael said. "I've seen enough. More than enough. And this wasn't even what I came to talk to you about."

"The strike, sir?"

"The strike."

The call from Gabriel had informed Michael that the angels in the Waste Management Union had decided to strike. "What in Heaven's name do they have to strike about?"

275

"Unfortunately, sir," Monte said, peering at Michael, "I think it was something you did."

"Me?"

"It's that soot trail Bob leaves everywhere. You ordered us to clean it up, but no matter what we do, the stain won't vanish. Now my Principalities are complaining that by giving them an impossible task, you're making unreasonable demands, abusing your power, and setting them up to fail."

"But we gave Bob a golf cart so he won't track his soot all over the place."

"The best intentions, and all that," Monte said with a shrug. "It seems Bob's soot infects his golf cart, so the cart has exacerbated the problem by making it easier for Bob to get around. He goes more places faster and thus leaves more soot trails than ever before, though now they resemble tire tracks."

"Listen to me, Monte," Michael said sternly. "I don't care what the Principalities want. They're created to work, not ride on my robetails or the rags of urchins. Order them back to work immediately, or I'm consigning the whole lot of them to the scrap heap." He jabbed a finger toward Potpourri Peak. "Or maybe worse." He glanced meaningfully downward. "Business is booming in Hell, and the Devil has plenty of job openings."

"I already told them that," Monte said. "They just say you have to cave in to their demands or nothing will get done."

"Is that right?" Michael jerked his head toward the mob of children scooping their way into the mountainside. "More and more of these kids are coming here every day, so it looks to me like we'll have an ever-growing army of scabs who'll get the work done with or without your Principalities. They better be at work the next time I visit, or feathers are going to fly, leaving bat wings."

Without waiting for a reply, Michael left Monte hovering over the ski slope and headed toward Eden. No telling what mischief Bob had wrought there. As he approached, he saw Uriel brandishing his sword, and Michael could tell, even from a distance, that it wasn't the light saber but his old flaming blade.

"What happened to the light saber?" he asked.

276

"The batteries died," Uriel said. "Besides, after a while, I couldn't stand the noise that thing made. It just wasn't natural. Isn't this so much better?"

He swung the tongue of flame, which made a throaty, sizzling hiss as it arced through the air.

"Much better," Michael agreed. "It looks more dramatic, too. But what about all the dead brush in the Garden?"

"What dead brush?" Uriel pointed with his sword, and for the first time, Michael noticed how nicely manicured the Garden looked. After ages of neglect, it was again pristine.

"Bob brought a bunch of yardmen over here, and they cleaned the place up in no time."

"You let humans into Eden?"

"You sent me a text saying it was all right because you'd made them provisional saints."

"I did no such thing."

"You did so. Look."

Uriel held out his phone to show a text that had come from Michael's phone. What the hell...?

At least there's no longer any danger of setting Eden aflame, Michael thought. But one good thing coming from Bob's shenanigans didn't excuse the rest of his embellishments.

"Come with me," he ordered Uriel. "I'm convening an emergency board meeting."

Michael turned, took off, and rocketed toward the Administration Building, Uriel trailing in his wake. On the way, he called Antoine and, shouting over the roar of the slipstream, ordered him to assemble the other Archangels in the boardroom.

He was still many miles away when something he spotted ahead made him tremble inside. Out there in the golden mists in the general direction of the Administration Building, lights flickered and shone. They could only be the Boss's crepuscular rays. So he'd finally decided to return, and it couldn't have been at a worse time.

But as Michael got closer, he realized the lights weren't hovering around the Administration Building but around the Holy Holidays tower. And they weren't crepuscular rays, but auroras.

Michael, Uriel wafting behind, circled the Holy Holidays building and tried to dissipate the auroras, but he couldn't.

They must have been Heavenly Desired, and there could only be one culprit.

Anger welled in his breast. Bob. Again Bob. Always Bob.

Turning his back on Holy Holidays, he flew to the Administration Building, and when he and Uriel entered the boardroom, all the other Archangels were there. Michael had never seen them so discombobulated.

"I assume you know about the strike by the Solid Waste and Recycling staff," he began, but that was as far as he got, because all the other Archangels started talking at once. Except for Raphael, who flipped his horn around and started blowing furiously into the bell to demonstrate his displeasure. A constricted squeak emerged from the mouthpiece.

"All right, all right." Michael patted the hubbub down. "Let's not get carried away."

"Easy for you to say," Selaphiel commented dryly, "when you've run off to have fun and leave Bob to run Heaven. So, how was Cannes?"

"It was Nice," Michael said just as dryly. "And how's the new Jack Reacher novel you're reading?"

Selaphiel didn't have much to say to that, but Barachiel spoke up.

"Are you aware that Bob, in collusion with Festus, is cashing in on the trade in 'lost' masterpieces by opening the Gallery of New Art by Famous Dead Artists in New York City? Since the artists don't have to get paid, Bob and Festus are pocketing all the proceeds."

"And that's just a drop in the bucket," Uriel said. "When we established the Eternet, we thought it would aid efficiency, but all it's really done is cause problems. For one, all the cute animal pictures and videos have prompted a huge interest in pets."

"I don't see what's wrong with having a pet," Michael said. "They're often a great comfort."

"Not to us," Uriel said. "Since Heaven doesn't have fences, all the pets run loose, and some of them are downright vicious. Especially the chihuahuas. They're so small, you can't see them in the clouds until they bite your ankles. And you wouldn't believe how many piles of dog crap and puddles of pee are lying around out there. Too much for the conveyor layer to handle.

It's gotten so bad that walking around is more like strolling through a mine field. We've put up displays with pooper scoopers, but the humans just ignore them."

"Can't we convert some of the Principalities to dogs and cats?" Michael asked. "That would eliminate the elimination problem."

"We tried that," Uriel said, "but the owners complained that every time they held one in their lap or petted it, they'd get covered in angel dust and start sneezing."

"There's worse," Raguel said, trying to one-up Uriel. "People have stopped going to Heavenly Choir practice in person. Instead, they stay home, glued to their computers, and Skype in their participation. The resulting music is tinny and muffled."

"Don't they know it's the harmony, not the song, that counts?" Uriel didn't bother saying that the Heavenly Choir wasn't all that harmonious.

"There's more," Uriel went on, not to be upstaged. "Bob has some smart-ass hacker working for him, and he's figured out how to tap into Earth's Internet. Now Bob is letting everybody here order stuff from Earth."

"Why would they do that?" Michael asked, thinking of the fake message from his phone. Bob's hacker? Now Michael would have to get a hacker of his own. "They have everything they want right here."

"I asked Bob that same question, and he told me Earth always has newer products than we have in Heaven. Apparently, we're perpetually behind the curve in terms of development since angels and most people have no initiative or imagination."

"But how do they pay for it all?"

"Bob showed them they can Heavenly Desire open-ended credit cards."

Michael had a sudden sinking feeling.

"On whose account?"

"Whose do you think?"

Crap, Michael thought. Now he was going to have to do a major budget review.

"But how do things get delivered?"

"Bob pulled some Principalities from the Distribution Center and set up a delivery service called Utopia Parcel Service."

"We're losing control," Gabriel groused. "We have to do something."

"What do you suggest?" Michael asked, suspecting that Gabriel was more concerned with his own position than he was with Heaven's operations. "The Boss let Bob in here. We can't make him leave."

"At least we can restrict him to travel along paths he's already taken so he won't keep tracking soot all over the place."

"Good idea. I'll revise his Provisional Resident Visa post facto."

"That's not good enough," Gabriel said. "We all think it's time you went out and got the Boss's explicit permission for all the changes. He might have some suggestions on how to tamp down all the craziness here."

"I'll do it when I have the time...."

"We think you should make the time. Like, now."

All the other Archangels nodded and muttered in agreement.

"You are trying to tell the Captain of the Hosts what to do?"

Michael drew himself up to his full height and amped-up the output of his aura until there wasn't a shadow left in the room. But as soon as he did, Gabriel and Raphael stood up in unison and lifted their trumpets to their lips.

"We can bring the walls crashing down any time," Gabriel muttered around his mouthpiece, and Raphael nodded vigorously in agreement.

"You wouldn't dare," Michael said. "Not without the Boss's say so."

"Like you got his say-so to set up the Eternet and put Bob in charge of everything?"

"Okay, okay. I'll find him. But do you know how long that could take?"

"You won't be back by supper," Gabriel said, lowering his horn. "Unless it's the last supper."

❧ 29 ☙

"WE'VE BOOKED OUR FIRST CLIENT," Nanookie said. "Or should I say, hooked him. Some stick-in-the-mud schmuck from Kansas. Says his daughter, Beatrice, died from a mysterious heart attack, and he knows she was a good girl, even if she was impulsive, so he's sure she's in Heaven. He's determined to find her, which is why he's signed up."

"We ought to have her meet him at the Pearly Gates," Bob said. "Have you managed to locate her?"

"I tried, but I couldn't find her anywhere. I checked with Saint Peter, and he said her name was in the *Register*, but it was crossed out. He didn't know what that meant. What'll we tell the client?"

"His departure date. His expectations aren't our concern. In the meantime, this calls for a celebration," Bob said. "Put on your finest furs, Nan. I'm taking you out on the town."

"But there's no town to take me out on," she said.

"I've been busy," Bob said with a wink.

When she was ready in seconds, Bob reflected that this really was Heaven. And she looked divine in a sleek, short, low-cut, seal-skin sheath dress trimmed with polar bear fur that emphasized her curves and showed off her legs. Her feet were clad in pointy-toed walrus skin flats since high-heels were impossible to walk in over Heaven's carpet.

"Where are we going?" she asked.

"You'll see."

They went down to pick up Bob's golf cart, and he steered toward the distant tower of the Celestial.

"Why are we here?" she asked when they arrived. "Our building is taller than this, and anyway, nothing but snobs live here." She sounded a little hurt that Bob might be suggesting the Holy Holidays headquarters weren't fancy enough.

"Be patient."

He parked in front of the building in a space specially reserved for him then led her into the lobby. Hundreds of people were milling around, waiting for the express elevator to their own versions of the penthouse. Bob and Nanookie got in the elevator with a dozen other people, and the car shot upward. When the doors opened, everybody filed out and vanished into their own penthouses.

Nanookie, though, was surprised to see a pearlescent archway flanked on the left by a tasteful sign on an easel that read, "Upstairs at the Celestial." To the right stood a podium. Behind it was a maître d' Principality, and on top of it lay a reservation list.

"This place has absolutely the finest chef in Heaven," Bob said. "I stole her from the restaurant at the country club. No matter what kind of food you want, she can prepare it to perfection."

He took Nanookie's arm and led her toward the archway. The maître d' Principality came out from behind the podium and stepped obsequiously forward as Bob and Nanookie approached.

"Welcome to Upstairs at the Celestial, Mr. Bob and Miss Nanookie," he said with a bowing incline of his head.

"Your best table, Pierre."

"Of course, sir. It is always reserved for you."

He seated them beside the wide windows on the side facing away from most of Heaven's hoi polloi.

"A bottle of your finest," Bob said.

"Of course, sir."

Pierre swooshed away, leaving them alone with the view and each other.

Out past the windows towered massive cloud mountains, but the Celestial was tall enough that Bob and Nanookie could see beyond them and across the empty, wild, and undeveloped

Wastelands stretching into the distance. The desolate cloudscape out there swirled and whirled and billowed much more fancifully than it did in Heaven proper.

"What a magnificent view," Nanookie said, looking out over the turmoil.

"Yes," Bob replied, looking at her.

Pierre came back with a chilled bottle in a golden ice bucket. He deftly removed the cork and poured a sample sip into Bob's glass.

"Did I order your finest, Pierre?"

"You did, sir."

"Then I suppose I don't have to taste test. Fill 'em up."

After Pierre filled the glasses, he said, "Would you care to hear our specials?"

"Fire away."

"Madam, for you I suggest a raw walrus fillet smothered in a smoke-infused gravy with a side of boiled tubers and roots and a nice tossed kuanniq salad topped with a balsamic vinaigrette made with the finest seal oil."

"Sounds delicious."

"And for you, sir, perhaps you would care to try a rare porterhouse steak accompanied by a loaded baked potato and a Caesar salad."

"Excellent."

When Pierre had gone, Nanookie, who had been looking around the restaurant, said, "This place must be extremely exclusive. We're the only people here."

"They just opened, and we're their first diners. But it'll be hopping once we start bringing tourists here."

He picked up his wine glass and nodded toward hers, and they toasted.

"We're on top of the world, baby," he said, and they sipped.

"I guess I should start calling you Mr. President," she said.

"Only if you'll be my vice president," he said. "With emphasis on the vice."

They engaged in small talk until their meal arrived, and Bob's prediction was right: The ambrosias on their plates were the best they'd ever tasted.

"What now?" Nanookie asked when they finished. "Back to the office? Or should we stop at the penthouse first for a little of that vice?"

"We'll get to that," Bob assured her. "But we have another place to visit first."

They left the restaurant, and when they reached cloud level, Bob called up a way-finding sign.

"Show me the way to the Adriano's," he said. A black line appeared on the map, and Bob drove off, making black tire tracks across the clouds.

"A nightclub?" Nanookie asked when they'd parked on what appeared to be a back street in downtown New Orleans.

"A special nightclub," Bob said, leading her inside.

"It's dark in here," she said in amazement, peering around in the gloom dimly lit by candles on the tables. About half the tables were filled with happy people having a good time.

"It's not just dark," he told her. "It's real, genuine night. The owner is a friend of mine."

"You sure know how to make a girl feel special," Nanookie said, cuddling up to him. "Back home, we had nights that lasted a couple of months, and I've missed those up here."

Almost as soon as they were seated at the best table in the house, Adriano came over. He'd changed his antiquated Spanish outfit for a casual but expensive sports jacket and slacks. His top two shirt buttons were undone, and Bob could see a pair of gold chains hanging around his neck.

"Bob! So nice to see you. And you must be Nanookie." He bowed toward her. "Do you see all my new friends?." He waved at all the occupied tables. "I even have some guests who were astronomers, and they're anxious to join me in the evenings to explore the heavens. Thank you, my friend. You're responsible for bringing light to my darkness."

"I just put the idea into your head," Bob said demurely. "You're the one who's made a success of it."

"You are too modest," Adriano said, and Bob agreed, but he didn't say so. "Make yourselves at home," Adriano went on. "The show will start in about ten minutes." He gestured toward a large stage at the front of the room. "Until then, order anything you like. For you, everything is always on the house."

284

The show began just after their drinks arrived. The candles on the tables suddenly dimmed, and several mini-spots flared on, illuminating the stage. The first act was a cabaret show put on by the Virginians, who did a variety of dances, including a cancan, which sent their gossamer skirts wafting most intriguingly. They were followed by a comedian, a singer, and a jazz combo. There wasn't a magician, probably because everybody could perform magic in Heaven.

At last, they bid Adriano adieu and went out to Bob's golf cart. "What the hell is that?" Bob exclaimed as they neared the cart. The seats were covered by a large brown blob. It looked like some pterodactyl had flown over and dropped a load right into the cart, but as Bob bent closer, his nostrils caught the scent of hotdog chili.

"Where did it come from?" Nanookie asked, peering upward. "I never saw any birds in Heaven, much less one that big."

"No telling," Bob said, though some vague memory was tickling the back of his mind.

"Don't worry about it," Nanookie said, and she used her Heavenly Desire to eliminate the blob. In a few moments, they were on their way back to their penthouse.

After they arrived, Nanookie desired-up a bottle of chilled champagne, and Bob was filling their glasses when his phone rang. He pulled it out, glanced at the screen, then put it back into his pocket without answering it.

"Michael," he explained, handing one of the glasses to her. "Whatever he wants can wait."

Apparently it couldn't, for the phone rang again almost immediately. Bob pulled it out, flipped the mute switch, and put it away.

"To success and us," he said, holding up his glass. She clinked hers against his, and a few minutes later, they were in the process of another hers against his when a loud pounding disrupted their heavenly desires.

"You didn't give anybody a key to the elevator, did you?" Bob asked, staring at the door.

"Nobody. I can't imagine...."

The pounding sounded again, and they realized it wasn't coming from the door but from the other side of the room, which was a wall of windows. They turned to see Michael hovering outside. When he saw them looking at him, he leaned forward and stuck his head through the window, which was disconcerting because the windows weren't open. Instead, his head simply poked through the glass like a ghost passing through a wall.

"Sorry to bother you like this, Bob, but I tried calling and got no answer."

"What's the problem?" Bob asked sitting up in the bed.

"What isn't? Meet me in your office in ten minutes."

Michael pulled his head back and swooped down and out of sight.

"What's that all about?" Nanookie asked.

"You got me, but I'd better go down. I'll get rid of him as soon as I can, and we can get back to business."

Bob dressed and took the elevator down to his office, where Michael was sitting in the visitor chair, waiting for him.

"Okay, Michael. What's so important it can't wait?"

"You," Michael said, with a little less force than he'd intended.

Something about Bob had changed since Michael had last seen him. Then Michael had it. Bob's bald spot was gone, replaced by fresh growth. How had he managed that since he didn't have Heavenly Desire powers?

"Me? What have I done?"

"What haven't you done? How about human trafficking for one. The urchins working at the Solid Waste and Recycling Center," he amplified when Bob looked puzzled.

"You call that human trafficking? I call it utilization of human resources."

"You have them digging out garbage all day for no pay."

"They get paid," Bob protested. "All those gold rupees...."

"Tips, but no base wage."

"They wouldn't know a base wage if it sat up and said, 'Hello,'" Bob said. "Didn't they seem happy to you?"

"They could be just as happy without all the work. The same goes for those yardmen you have working in the Garden...."

"Cleaning up a mess you've neglected."

"You forged my name on the requisitions to give them forbidden motorized equipment."

"You expected them to use scissors? That place was a mess. Look, Michael, you can't complain about me using human labor

286

when you're already exploiting the artists and writers. I don't see what's wrong with exploiting other groups as well, especially when they *want* to be exploited."

"Speaking of the artists," Michael said sternly. "I hear you've cut a side deal with Festus to horn in on his black market in masterpieces by dead artists."

"Oh, that."

"That and your other side deal with Halliwell to purloin the Boss's tears for profane uses."

"Using them to purify water isn't profane?" Bob asked. "Especially when nobody here drinks water, anyway. They just change it into alcohol or soda. Wouldn't chlorine do just as well? Using the Boss's tears on the water supply is a total waste of a valuable resource."

"And what about your hacker? In addition to having him forge requisitions, you had him deceive Uriel and then open a connection between the Eternet and Internet. Now people are ordering stuff from Earth on my dime."

"I thought everything up here was on your dime. Besides, seems to me that ordering things from Earth would help alleviate the stress at the Factory."

"I'm not sure the Boss will see it that way," Michael said. "And he's probably going to be pissed by those phony crepuscular rays you've attached to the top of your building."

"I didn't do that. It was a gift. And I think they look impressive."

"And what's this about you organizing races among the Ophanim?" Michael went on, ignoring Bob's opinion on the auroras. "The Ophanim are our legal system, and now, instead of reaching final conclusions, they're just racing around in circles."

"It gave them some balls, at least," Bob said.

"Balls they didn't need. And what about your plan to build a tourist trap in the Wastelands?"

"More under-utilized resources."

"Are you aware we're having a strike by Solid Waste and Recycling angels?"

"I'm not surprised, I imagine it's a tough job cleaning up all the trash."

"And harder to clean up your soot trail. The other Archangels insist I put an end to your activities."

"You can't do that now," Bob protested. "We've signed up our first tourist."

"For a tour that can't take place without the Boss's say-so."

Bob blanched, which made Michael feel better than he had since his vacation had been so rudely terminated.

"We're actually going to have to go out and look for him? I always thought you'd take care of that."

"You don't think he's going to give you a position without a personal interview, do you? I've spoken with him, and he's instructed me to usher you into his presence."

Boy, are you in for a surprise, Michael thought. He'd never intended for things to go quite this far, but since they had, he knew they had to go all the way to the Edge. Maybe it was inevitable. His only worry was that the Boss would agree that Bob had become such a liability that he'd actually passed the tipping point and become an asset.

"We leave in one hour," he said.

❧ 30 ☙

MICHAEL NEEDED THE HOUR TO figure out how Bob could travel to the Edge. It was much too far to walk, and Bob's golf cart was out, too. Not only did it trail twice the soot his feet did, the clouds in the Wastelands weren't flat enough to drive over.

To Michael's chagrin, the only possible solution was to carry the human, which Michael was reluctant to do, though Bob's weight wasn't a problem. Michael had yet to successfully erase the smudge on his wing tip, and he was afraid Bob's soot would soil his robes permanently if he carried the human in his arms. Anyway, he wasn't sure he wanted to embrace Bob for as long as it would take to reach the Edge. And worst of all might be the damage to Michael's reputation. How would the other angels view him if he appeared to be little more than a chauffeur to the human upstart?

But there was no help for it, and it was Antoine who came up with the solution inspired by Michael's backpack: a specially designed harness from which a chair was suspended by a golden chain. So at the end of the hour, Michael, the harness strapped around his body, set down in front of the Holy Holidays head-quarters, where Bob was waiting beside his golf cart.

"You want me to ride in that?" Bob pointed to the chair. "I might fall out."

289

"It has a seat belt."

"I'm afraid of heights."

"Get in the chair, Bob."

"You aren't going to drop me, are you?"

Bob didn't think an impact with the clouds would injure him, but he was afraid that at terminal velocity, he might punch right through, and then where would he be? Eight miles high without a golden parachute, that's where. Or maybe stuck in the conveyor layer, which would dump him amid all the trash on Potpourri Peak.

"Much as it might please me, no. As I said, we are going to talk to the Boss."

Bob reluctantly sat and fastened the seatbelt, and Michael took off. Bob expected the flight to be rough and windy, but Michael amped up his aura to keep the buffeting breezes at bay. For a time, he was fascinated by the cloudscape unscrolling beneath them, and as Michael rose higher, Bob could see a network of dark gray lines crosshatching the clouds below. Amazingly, he saw numerous people strolling along them like they were pathways.

His paths. His legacy.

At the terminus of several lines sat Elysium Field, which was packed to four overflowing tiers of spectators cheering the blue, green, and beryl streaks of Ophanim racing around the track. Another junction was the Celestial Country Club and Holy-in-One Greens, whose fairways were now littered with obstacles and golfers ricocheting balls. And there was Potpourri Peak, skiers zipping down the upper slopes and urchins digging their lives below. Soon after, they passed over the Water Treatment and Purification Plant, the water in the tremendous vats as luminously blue as Caribbean waters, crossed over Eden, looking from this height like an emerald, and over Sector 1, where Harry had already relocated his Hominid Homes development safely out of sight of the cave-riddled cloud bank, behind which massed stormy cloud mountains.

As Michael rose higher still to clear the mountaintops, Bob could see all of Heaven laid out behind them like an intricate tabletop model completely hemmed in by towering cloud mountain ranges. Ahead of them, beyond the mountains, stretched

290

nothing but empty expanses of tempestuous clouds that seemed to go on forever and ever. Interestingly, the pervasive golden glow of Heaven seemed to be confined to the pan-like area enclosed by the mountain ranges. Outside the mountains, the atmosphere was awash in a pure white light that was a welcome relief to Bob after the golden glow's flickering ambience, though the distances before him boggled his mind.

"How long is this going to take?" he called out. "I have a lot of business matters to take care of."

"Do you expect the Boss to give you carte blanche to profit off his enterprise without consulting him?"

"You sound like you think he won't go for my plans."

"And why should he?"

"Because we have something in common," Bob said.

"You do?" Michael asked skeptically. "Such as?"

"Such as our names, for one thing."

"God and Bob?"

"Sure. Three letters each. Middle letter 'o.' And if you lowercase my name, flip the second 'b' over, then turn the name backward, it spells 'god.'"

Michael gave a derisive snort.

"With enough flipping and turning, you can get 'dog,' 'pop,' 'bop, and 'bog.' Not to mention 'gog.' In olden times, Gog was the leader of a threatening, locust-like army, so maybe you're right about the flipping but wrong about the right flipping. Besides," Michael snorted again. "isn't Bob short for Robert?"

"Well, yeah. So what?"

"God and Robert." Michael shook his head. "Not much similarity there." Then his eyes lit sardonically. "Oh, wait. I get it. Second letter is the same."

"Go ahead and make fun," Bob said. "But isn't the Boss's real name Yahweh or something? And isn't that a pseudonym, too? AKA is the way they put it on police blotters. How are we supposed to believe anything he says if he goes by some alias every time he does something bad to the people on Earth?"

"Ah, now I see what you two have in common," Michael said.

"You still haven't told me where we're going."

"The Edge," Michael said.

"Sounds dangerous."

"Only if you take one step too many."

They were silent for a some time as the empty, squally cloudscape scrolled beneath them. It was about then that Bob started thinking about angel legs—or the potential lack thereof. He managed to restrain himself for a long time, but in the end, he couldn't resist peering up Michael's robes.

Sure enough: kewpie doll legs. No wonder they flew or floated everywhere. Except for the Ophanim, of course.

Despite the constant storminess below, the cloudscape was so monotonously empty that it didn't seem like they were moving at all but simply hovering. But Bob knew they were moving because, when he twisted around in his chair to stare behind them, he no longer saw the cultivated Heaven he'd come to know. Even the golden glow had vanished in the distance.

"I had no idea Heaven was so big," Bob said, breaking the silence.

"If the universe is humongously large, can Heaven be any different?" Michael asked.

"Speaking of the universe," Bob said, "what about aliens? How come I haven't seen any of those around. Don't they qualify?"

"They're in their own Heavens, but those are parsecs away from human Heaven. Some of those people breathe liquid nitrogen or methane. It would be a logistical nightmare if we allowed everyone to interact. It's bad enough with Christians and Muslims thinking each other are illegal aliens. Can you imagine what would happen if we mixed in actual aliens?"

"Maybe we could arrange some sort of spaceship cruise to some of the more exotic alien sectors," Bob suggested. "The weirder the better. Are any of the alien Heavens inhabited by giant slugs or anything like that?"

"You have no idea," Michael said. Even he didn't like to think about some of those aliens. Thank goodness each of their Heavens had its own Michael to oversee operations. Human Heaven was enough of a pain in the ass. Then he pointed to the distances ahead of them. "Look."

Straight ahead, a coruscation of light erupted so brilliantly that Bob had to avert his gaze. It was the Boss's crepuscular rays, closer than Bob had ever seen them. Frightening close. And they were getting nearer with every passing moment. They

292

were so dazzling he couldn't look at them. He didn't want to continually stare up at Michael's kewpie doll legs, so he focused on the turbulent cloudscape below. But the stormier the Wastelands grew, the blanker his mind became until he was paralyzed except for the trembling of his limbs. He felt like a first-year law school student about to submit a term paper to the chief legal officer of a multinational corporation. At last, he just squeezed his eyes tightly shut.

"We're almost there," Michael said, interrupting Bob's febrile apprehension.

Bob was afraid to look ahead, but he risked a peek through one slitted eye. The crepuscular rays had mysteriously vanished. He opened both eyes, and what he did see was a distinct line where the clouds ended, beyond which was nothing. Nothing at all. It was as if the clouds were the shore of an endless sea of roiling, coiling blackness.

"What is this place?" Bob asked, hating the quaver in his voice.

"The Edge of Chaos," Michael replied. "All that out there is unformed void."

In a few minutes, Michael lowered Bob's chair near the Edge. Bob unstrapped and hesitatingly approached the precipice. There was actually a wind out here, and he was afraid of getting blown off into the churning void.

"Are you sure he's out there?"

"Oh, he's out there, all right. Creating more reality. You didn't think his creation is so small he could finish it in six days, did you? It's an eternally on-going process."

"Kind of scary," Bob said. He was having trouble focusing on the churning darkness, which confused his vision mightily, but then his eyes fastened on something not far distant along the shore of the Edge of Chaos. It was a lenticular cloud that had become separated from the rest of the cloud field and was floating out over the void, its rounded sides sculpted smooth by the wind.

"Look," he said, pointing.

Something was fluttering on top of the cloud, and as he peered closer, he saw it was a Principality, looking like a person trapped on an iceberg. The angel seemed to be clinging to the mists at the top of the cloud's center, and he was flapping his

293

wings furiously as if trying to propel the cloud toward shore. He wasn't making much progress.

"Why doesn't he just fly over here?" Bob asked. "It's not far."

"Not allowed," Michael answered. "Sometimes one of us gets caught on a cloud like that, but if he flew off it, he might be seen from below. It happened a few times in the past, so the Boss created the new regulation. Frankly, I think he did it so he could get away from it all if he wants to. People can only walk on clouds, not air, and angels are forbidden to fly over clear skies. The Boss can sit on one of those things for a long time without being disturbed."

"No wonder he's so hard to find."

"I have something to tell you, Bob," Michael said. "But first, tell me what you've seen here in Heaven."

"I see opportunity," Bob said.

"No, no," Michael said. "I mean what do you actually see? Now. With your eyes?"

"Like over there?" Bob pointed to the lenticular cloud, and when Michael nodded, he proceeded to describe it and its frantic passenger, who'd managed to maneuver the cloud within hailing distance and was, apparently, resting from his exertions. After Bob had gone on for several moments, Michael stopped him.

"You describe it well," he said.

"Thanks," Bob said. He'd always been a sharp observer with an ability to scope out any real estate.

"Seems to me that Heaven is a state of indescribable ecstasy and oneness with the Boss," Michael said dryly. "So if you are a discreet unit, can describe all this, and aren't 100 percent pleased with what you see, I guess all this must not be what you thought it was."

"Not it?" A shock ran through Bob as he contemplated Michael's words. "This isn't really Heaven?"

"Do you remember how you got through the turnstile at the Pearly Gates?" Michael asked, watching as Bob's eyes went blank then relit with understanding. Michael smiled. "A token, right? Do you think you can really enter Heaven with a token?"

"I suppose not," Bob admitted after a moment. "When the Devil said he was booting me upstairs, I just assumed I was going to the very top."

294

"Just as there are many shades of gray between black and white, the structure of reality has more than two floors." Michael chuckled. "But true oneness with the Boss doesn't lie in either of the two extremes—or even between them. It's outside of them."

"I don't understand," Bob admitted, slumping.

"Of course you don't." Michael laid a hand on his shoulder. "No one does except those prophets, yogis, and Taoist and Zen masters who come out here to live."

"How come I haven't seen any of them?"

"Because the pretenders all give up and go back to Heaven, and the real ones all end up out there." Michael waved toward the chaotic void before them.

"Heaven is nothing but a scam?"

"Not a scam. Call it a willful distraction. I'm sure you remember that line spoken by one of the Boss's right-hand men some time back: 'On Earth as it is in Heaven.' Equivalence works both ways. The Boss grants humans free will, but the problem is that free will must always contradict Divine Will, if for no other reason than because free will is limited, while Divine Will is not."

When Bob thought about it, he couldn't help but remember that most of the people he'd met in Heaven had barely been aware of things outside of what they already knew. Take Harry the caveman, for instance, hunting saber-tooth tigers and not knowing he could wish for something else because he didn't know what else to wish for.

"So that means he's always out there?" Bob gestured toward the unformed void. "Like the pot of gold at the end of the crepuscular rainbow?"

"It means he can't have a hand in human affairs—and ultimately, that he can't be found by looking where he's not. You ever notice how people can talk about God and the Devil only in relation to each other? The Devil's power and his curse is to be distinctly ubiquitous, while God's power and curse is to be omnipresently absent. You gotta have some sympathy for the Devil. He's under constant scrutiny. No wonder he's pissed off all the time. God has it a lot easier because everybody's always looking for him in the wrong places."

"So what's your role?" Bob asked.

"You said it yourself. I'm Heaven's chief operating officer. I'm the Boss's public face. His stand-in. That's why I'm Captain of the Hosts and why my shield says, *Quis ut Deus?*"

"If this isn't Heaven, then what is it?"

"Purgatory. A lot of people aren't ready for oneness with God, but most of them aren't bad enough for Hell. Here they get another chance, but we still have to force everybody to behave heavenly since most just don't know how to do it on their own."

Bob reflected on that for a few moments.

"This may be Purgatory," Bob said at last, "but almost everybody here seems satisfied to live in an ersatz Earth free from worry and believe it's Heaven."

"Apparently they prefer stagnation and boredom to doing the kind of work necessary to move on."

"So, Heaven is really nothing but a shell company, and all you angels are in on the deception?"

"No. Just me. The rest believe the illusion, too. Even the other Archangels. Loose lips sink ships, and this is the kind of information that can sink our ship, even if it is built on clouds. I'm the only one who knows the reality of the situation."

"You brought me all the way out here to tell me this?"

"I had to show you the Edge to reveal the truth. You wouldn't have believed me otherwise. Also, I don't want this conversation overheard. My office is bugged, and your office, too. We've bugged every place in Heaven except the Wastelands. But of course you know all about that. Your hacker is running surveillance programs on all of our surveillance."

"Why are you telling *me*? Aren't you afraid I'll blab the truth?"

"To what end? Nobody would believe you. They have an image of Heaven, and this is it, and that's that. I'm telling you because it's in my—and your—best interests for you to know the score. There's no profit in revealing the truth, and lots of reasons not to, especially if you want to keep working with me. I hope you'll play along since you're the only one here who gives me hope."

"Me?" Bob was feeling pretty low, and he was willing to grasp at any straw.

"Sure. You have a lot of experience in making empty promises, and if people here get enough of those, maybe some of them will come out here, discover the truth for themselves, and move on. It's the only way we can reduce our population. Besides, I need a chief administrator to help manage the humans, and you've instituted several organizational schemes that seem to work."

"You want me to help you run Heaven?"

"Yes. After all, organization, which is your methodology, is halfway between structured Hell and disorganized Heaven, and we could use a little more organization before we lose our credibility."

Not to mention, Michael, thought, it'll give me a chance to take an even longer vacation. And this time, he was going to do something really exciting and dangerous, like hike the bottom of the Marianas Trench or hit a major winning streak in Las Vegas. He smiled to himself, thinking that Bob was right about leveraging human resources. Bob was Michael's prime human resource, and Michael intended to leverage him to the hilt.

"What about the travel agency?" Bob asked.

"Not going to happen. As you can see," Michael waved out over the boiling blackness, "we're not going to get an audience with the Boss much less permission to bring tourists here. Ever."

"What am I going to do with all those tour guides I've been training?"

"Repurpose them," Michael suggested. "I'm sure you'll think of something to use them for."

"What about my status? Do I get full Residency?"

"I think the Boss will agree to that," Michael said, staring across the Edge toward the angel on the lenticular cloud. "We have to do something to get rid of your soot trail if you're going to stay indefinitely.

"Saint Bob?" Bob asked.

"Don't push it."

"What are you going to tell your board?"

"I'll tell them we had an audience, and while the Boss nixed the idea of tourists, he's all for your promotion."

"And if the Boss doesn't like the arrangement?"

"He'll let me know," Michael said, finally looking back at Bob. Bob mulled that for a moment, then he nodded.

"I can work with that," he said. "Can I wish up a fountain?"

"Sure. You're a Resident, now. Heavenly Desire away."

A fountain suddenly appeared on the edge of the abyss, and Bob stepped over to it. For the first time since he'd entered Heaven, he didn't leave a trail of soot. Holding out both hands, he said, "Two Dalmore 64 Trinitas."

When the golden goblets appeared, he dipped them into the fountain then carried them back to Michael and gave him one.

"Here's to partnership," he said, holding up his goblet, and the angel clinked his own against it.

"Partnership," Michael repeated, and they drank.

"Can we go back now?" Bob asked, tossing his empty goblet over the Edge. "I've got a lot to do, and I want to get busy."

He was thinking of his interrupted tryst with Nanookie.

"You go on," Michael said. "I think I'll stay out here for a while and enjoy the view."

"But how do I get back? It's too far to walk."

"You're a Resident, now, Bob. You can do whatever you like. Heavenly Desire to be back in your penthouse with Nanookie."

"Okay." Bob looked pretty pleased. "I guess I'll see you later." With that, he vanished with a small poofing sound.

Michael drained his cup, dropped it after Bob's, then waved at the angel on the lenticular cloud.

Abruptly, the cloud and its Principality vanished in an explosion of blinding light that shot blazing rays into the void beyond the Edge. This close, they emitted a rounded humming sound that vibrated the air, and where they touched the void, the boiling emptiness coalesced into fantastic shapes.

"What do you think, Boss?" Michael asked, conjuring up a pair of wrap-around sunglasses as the rays moved closer to the Edge.

The rays flickered colorfully.

"Yes, it worked out pretty well," Michael answered. "He's the perfect candidate."

The rays scintillated.

"I agree," Michael said. "He has made things more interesting."

The rays sparked.

"Are you sure he's ready?" Michael asked.

The rays flashed.

"A couple of more things, Boss. Can you please eradicate this soot stain from my wing"

The stain vanished.

"And how about Bob's soot trails."

The crepuscular rays shone brighter for a moment.

"Thanks, Boss. You know where to find me."

Michael turned, lofted into the air, and flapped back toward the Administration Building. His first order of business when he arrived would be to order a case of Dalmore 64 Trinitas.

The crepuscular rays remained for a few moments after Michael dwindled from sight, twinkling and beaming. Then they, too, moved away from the Edge, but their destination was not Heaven, or even the Wastelands. Instead, they soared out into the void, scattering swirls of nebulae and galaxies like pixie dust through the darkness.

The Clay Guthrie Mysteries
from Phosphene Publishing Co.

THE DEAD DETECTIVE

Teetering on the edge of the gutter, ex-cop Clay Guthrie is offered a way out of his bitter isolation. All he has to do is locate a stolen sculpture. The task seems simple enough until Guthrie finds himself enmeshed in a series of surreal events that push him to the breaking point. His disturbingly dangerous employers threaten him with pain and death if he fails, and the mysterious old man who is their antagonist forces Guthrie to act on his behalf, warning that worse horrors will greet his success. The only way Guthrie can survive is to find the sculpture and help the old man destroy the terrible power that lives within it. But first, he must endure a series of trials that test his endurance and drive him into the core of his own corruption.

LANDSCAPE WITH BEAST

"Who better to send into a grave situation to find out what lies buried there than one who has known death? Such as you." With those words, mysterious old Tereba sends Clay Guthrie on the trail of a missing artist. Having to deal with a witch from an ancient lineage and the ultimate hunter seeking the ultimate prey didn't bother him, but the doorway to another world was a different matter. Out there an unknowable predator waited, and it wanted nothing more than to lay waste to everything in its path. But Guthrie couldn't refuse. He knew that anythingTereba directed his way would be as interesting and important as it might be dangerous, and those were lures he couldn't resist. Besides, when he set a trap for his nemesis, the bait wasn't the only thing that disappeared into the unknown along with the artist. Now Guthrie's client had vanished, too.

THE TEXAS TROLL UNLIMITED

When a frightened railroad employee tells Clay Guthrie that a monster in a boxcar ate his co-worker, Guthrie finds himself drawn into a web of corrupt and warped ambition and wanton violence. Traveling to far West Texas in search of the monster, Guthrie and the trainman encounter an organization whose goal is the total destruction of social order and whose weapon is an abomination from the past. Waging a guerrilla war against their enemies beneath the harsh Texas sun, they quickly discover that the nights hold a mortal danger more terrible than their human enemies. With the fate of civilization in the balance, they must eliminate the humans who stand in their way before they can root out and confront a canny and clever inhuman foe.

DARKNESS INSATIABLE

Clay Guthrie is sent by his mysterious employer to track down a missing man, but finding the objet of his search in an unnatural place and in an impossible condition provides no easy answers. Far worse, he encounters a town the grip of an unknown, unseeable, and malevolent force that thrives on turmoil and destruction and has left the utter annihilation of three other towns in its wake. What will it take to learn the cause and remedy it before it's too late? And who —or what—will get in the way?

Phosphene Publishing Company
publishes books and DVDs relating to literature,
history, the paranormal, film, spirituality, and the
martial arts.

For other great titles, visit
phosphenepublishing.com